THE
PERFECT SOLDIER

GRAHAM HURLEY

THE
PERFECT
SOLDIER

MACMILLAN

First published 1996 by Macmillan

an imprint of Macmillan General Books
25 Eccleston Place London SW1W 9NF
and Basingstoke

Associated companies throughout the world

ISBN 0 333 60995 6

Copyright © Graham Hurley 1996

The right of Graham Hurley to be identified as the
author of this work has been asserted by him in accordance
with the Copyright, Designs and Patents Act 1988.

1 3 5 7 9 8 6 4 2

A CIP catalogue record for this book is available from
the British Library

Phototypeset by Intype, London
Printed by Mackays of Chatham PLC, Chatham, Kent

In memory of Joe Brooks,
died 1st September 1994

Without Rae McGrath and Bill Yates, this book would never have been written. Their anger, and their commitment, sustained me through the rougher passages. To them both, my thanks. Thanks, as well, to Ian Bray of Oxfam, Chris Wadlow of Mayfair Dove Aviation, Carolyn Grace, Simon Howell, John Tilling, Tim O'Flynn of Save the Children, and the members of Lloyd's Aviation syndicate 340 who made me so welcome. As did Debbie McGrath and Moira Yates. Simon Spanton, at Macmillan, fuelled the project with his unflagging faith and enthusiasm. And Lin Hurley, as ever, stoked the inner fires.

We call it the perfect soldier.
It's ever-courageous, it never sleeps, and it never misses.

Paul Jefferson, de-mining expert,
Corps of Royal Engineers

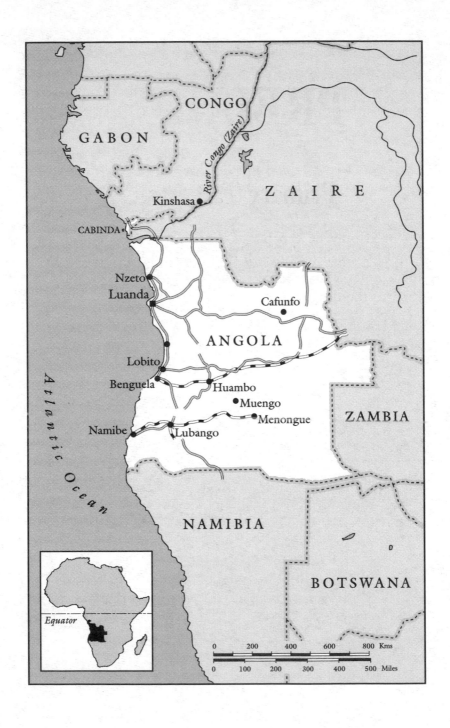

CONGO

GABON

ZAIRE

River Congo (Zaire)

Kinshasa

CABINDA

Nzeto

Luanda

Cafunfo

ANGOLA

Atlantic Ocean

Lobito

Benguela

Huambo

Muengo

Menongue

Namibe

Lubango

ZAMBIA

NAMIBIA

BOTSWANA

Equator

0	200	400	600	800 Kms
0	100	200	300	400	500 Miles

PRELUDE

Primary Targeting

Mines need only be capable of defeating their primary target and whilst a small measure of over-match is desirable to meet positive target enhancements, this precaution should not be pursued to the detriment of an economical design.

Lt.-Col. C. E. E. Sloan
Mine Warfare on Land

Darkness came quickly, stealing everything.

She sat in the front of the Land Rover as the light drained away, peering out through the open window, trying to fix the landscape in her mind. It was flat here, flatter than the bush on the other side of the city. The knee-high grass was a pale green, darkening by the minute, and when the wind eddied across towards the road it rippled like the coat of some animal. Far away, on the horizon, there was a single giant baobab tree. Apart from that, nothing.

Beside her, on the driver's seat, lay the Motorola two-way radio and she wondered again whether she should call for help. James had told her not to. The road was off-limits after dark and he was already in trouble for breaching safety rules. If word got back then there'd be more eyebrows raised, more questions asked, maybe even a report sent back to Luanda. He'd told her he knew what he was doing. He'd said he wouldn't be long. The kid had probably done something silly. Twisted an ankle. Got lost. Whatever.

The football shirt they'd found was still on the dashboard. It was a Manchester United shirt, doubtless passed on by some long-departed field worker, the colour beginning to fade from the sun. James had spotted it first, draped over a cardboard box by the roadside. It belonged to Maria. He knew it did. He'd seen her wearing it only yesterday, like a dress, enveloping her tiny figure, the bottom flapping round her knees as she played on the river bank with all the other kids. The box was a giveaway too, with its distinctive Terra Sancta logo, the upturned hands cradling the earth.

James had pulled the Land Rover off the road, getting out and picking the box up, showing her the faded black stencils on the top. CAUTION went the warning, HYDRAULIC EQUIPMENT. THIS SIDE UP. He'd lodged the box in the back of the Land Rover, ever-tidy, making room amongst the carefully stacked piles of drilling equipment, and then he'd gone back to the edge of the crumbling tarmac, shielding his eyes against the last of the sunset, calling her name. Bet she's gone looking for firewood, he'd said. Bet you anything.

She waited another ten minutes or so, not knowing quite what to do. James had been gone an hour now, far longer than he'd promised, far longer than was safe. There were mines everywhere, the place was littered with them. They called them 'A/P' mines. 'A/P' stood for 'anti-personnel', a neat little phrase that explained the dozens of amputees she encountered every working day. The locals called them '*los mutilados*', the limbless ones. That's why the bush was off-limits, forbidden territory, and that's why – she knew – he'd gone looking for Maria. At her age, he'd muttered, you think you're immortal. Like any kid of ten, you think there are more important things in life than a $3 saucer of high explosive.

She shuddered. Four months' nursing had taught her all she needed to know about high explosives. She'd volunteered for Angola to help in a feeding programme but she'd ended up in what passed for Muengo's hospital, dressing the swollen puckered stumps of recently amputated limbs. Day after day, she'd seen what the mines could do, the way they shredded flesh and blood, the way they left a life in ruins. Looking for Maria, she'd told James, was crazy. They should get on the radio, call for help. To do anything else was madness.

But James wouldn't listen. In this, as in everything else, he had that total certainty that only newcomers to Africa acquire.

He'd said it was simple. All you had to do was read the landscape like a soldier, understanding the way they thought, the way they planned, the military logic behind their decisions. The place was too open, too empty, miles and miles of trackless bush. Even the rebels, even UNITA, didn't have that many mines to waste. She'd watched him disappear into the dusk with his torch and his cheery wave, wanting to believe that he was right, but knowing as well that there were odds you didn't risk. Not if you were sensible. Not if you understood.

She sat in the Land Rover, immobile, listening. Once, she heard the scuffling of something small, away in the darkness, an animal perhaps, but of James there was no sign. After a while, the wind stiffened, bringing with it the dry, dusty scents of the bush. Twice, she flicked on the headlights, twin fingers reaching down the pot-holed tarmac towards Muengo. The gesture gave her a brief moment of comfort but in the back of her mind she knew it was foolish. Whatever James said, there were UNITA soldiers active in the area, moving at night, throttling the cities with yet more mines. Quite what they'd do with a twenty-nine-year-old French nurse she didn't know, but she was in no hurry to find out. All she wanted was James back again, intact, and as the minutes ticked by she realised that she had to get help.

She was about to use the radio, her mind made up, when she heard the footsteps. She froze for a moment in the front of the Land Rover, one hand on the Motorola, then she leaned out of the window, peering back along the road. For a moment or two she could see nothing, just the faintest line where the crust of tarmac dropped away and the bush began. Then she heard the footsteps again, much closer this time, feet scuffling in the dust. She reached for the dashboard, putting on the reversing light, and then pushed open the door. It was James. Had to be. Maybe he'd picked up some injury or other. Or maybe it was another of his little surprises. Here I am. Safe and sound. Sorry to have kept you.

She rounded the end of the Land Rover, flooded with relief.

Instead of James, she found herself looking down at a small, barefoot child with huge eyes and the beginnings of an uncertain smile. For a moment, she could do nothing but stare. Then she understood.

'Maria?'

The child nodded.

'*Si—*'

'*Onde é Senhor James?*'

'*Não sei.*'

Maria frowned, shaking her head, then bent and scratched her knee. At the same time, close by, there was the short, flat bark of an explosion and the sound of debris peppering the metal panels of the Land Rover. For a moment, Christianne had no idea what had happened. Instinctively, she bent to the child, protecting her, then the acrid stench of high explosive came drifting across the road and she was back beside the cab, leaning across the passenger seat, fumbling blindly for the satchel she carried everywhere. Inside, there were tourniquets, bandages, antiseptic. She felt the child behind her again, tugging at her jeans, and she scooped her up, wedging her into the passenger seat, tightening the safety belt across her tiny frame.

'*Restez là,*' she said roughly. '*Bougez pas.*'

The child stared back at her, frightened now, and she repeated the instruction in Portuguese.

'Stay there,' she said. 'Don't move.'

The child nodded, mute, and she reached across and retrieved the Motorola radio. The Terra Sancta people were on Channel Two. They lived in a house near the old Portuguese mission. Across the street, in a converted school, were the mine clearance teams. She held the Motorola to her mouth.

'Tango Sierra,' she said. 'Emergency.'

She repeated the Terra Sancta call sign twice more, her French accent thicker than usual. Two voices replied at once. She recognised one of them, an Angolan called Domingos. Domingos worked with the mine people. She'd shared a beer with him only two days ago. She told him briefly what had happened, giving him directions, trying to keep the panic out of her voice. Domingos repeated the directions, said he'd come at once.

'*Merci.*' She swallowed hard. '*Dépêche-toi.*'

She signed off and clipped the radio to her belt, then stood by the roadside in the warm darkness, listening. She could hear nothing. No calls for help, no cries of pain, nothing. She glanced over her shoulder, back towards the Land Rover. The child's face was pressed to the window. The drive out from Muengo would take half an hour, she thought, maybe longer. Time enough for James to lose a great deal of blood. She stepped across to the Land Rover, shouldering her satchel. She reached inside the cab, turning on the headlights, then locked both doors, aware of Maria's eyes following her every movement. At least one child will be safe, she thought grimly. And the lights will bring Domingos.

Back at the roadside, she hesitated a moment, all too aware of what she was about to do. Then she left the tarmac and began to move slowly towards the source of the blast, the brief blossom of flame like a scorch mark on her mind. The knee-high grass parted before her, the soil firm beneath her tread, the soles of her feet mapping the tiniest pebbles, every nerve stretched tight. The smell of the spent explosive was stronger now, an almost physical presence, a harsh, menacing, bitter-sweet tang that caught in the back of her throat. She wanted to stop. She wanted to turn and run back to the Land Rover. She wanted to be anywhere but here.

She stepped carefully on, trying to concentrate on James, how badly he'd been injured, what she'd have to do once she'd found him. He'd be bleeding, probably heavily, and he'd be in shock. The blood flow she'd staunch with a tourniquet from the satchel and with luck the shock would have numbed him to the worst of the pain. For once, he'd probably have little idea of what had really happened. Coping with that would come later. She paused a moment, glancing back towards the road, fixing the position of the Land Rover, trying to keep a straight path. She was sweating now, the thin cotton shirt clinging damply to her back. Close, she told herself. I must be getting close.

She found him moments later, a dark bundle amongst the flattened grass. She knelt quickly beside him, waving away the cloud of flies, slipping the satchel from her shoulder. He was still alive but his breathing was shallow, the barest sigh, and when she whispered his name there was no response. She tried again, her mouth to his ear.

'James?'

She paused, waiting. She could smell the blood now, the hot, strong, coppery smell of the makeshift hospital operating theatre, and she knew she'd got it wrong. This was worse than a shattered foot or leg. Much worse.

In the darkness, her hands began to explore the rest of his body. Below his chest, his shirt was shredded and where his stomach had once been there was a bottomless soup of blood and ruptured tissue, stirred by the faintest pulse. She rocked back on her heels, swallowing hard, fighting the urge to vomit. She wanted to go no further. Whatever courage had taken her through the minefield had quite gone. No tourniquet, no bandage, could possibly deal with this. What was left of James Jordan belonged on a butcher's slab.

She looked away a moment, forcing the air into her lungs, big, choking gulps, then she turned back, knowing what she must do, knowing the image of James she wanted to take away with her. Not the blood, the spilling intestines, the wreckage of his lower body. But his face. Undamaged.

In the button-down pocket of his shirt, there was a lighter. She'd given it to him just weeks before, a present on his twenty-third birthday. He'd carried it everywhere since. Now she patted his shirt, feeling for the shape, taking the lighter out. As gently as she could, she slipped her other hand beneath his head, easing it carefully upwards. He'd stopped breathing altogether now, and she knew in her heart that he was dead. The lighter flared first time, the yellow light spilling across his face, and she stared down at him, appalled, trying to make sense of what she saw. Then the flame guttered in the night wind and the darkness returned, stealing everything.

BOOK ONE

Counter-Measures

Once a designer has a concept for his mine, he must immediately consider how to include protection against general counter-measures to be used against it. The need to make a mine difficult to see, detect, and counter is a vital element in the design process, having a significant effect on the eventual form which the mine takes.

LT.-COL. C. E. E. SLOAN
Mine Warfare on Land

CHAPTER ONE

Molly Jordan awoke early, slipping out of bed, careful not to disturb her sleeping husband. Frost had crusted the grass in the shadows beyond the kitchen window, and she shivered in the cold dawn light, standing in her track suit by the sink, waiting for the kettle to boil. Friends of hers who also jogged first thing made a point of running on an empty stomach. They had complicated views about lactic acid and energy uptakes but for Molly none of it made any sense. Without a cup of tea, she was useless.

Half an hour later she was a mile down the lane, running easily, her breath clouding in the still morning air. The sky was an icy, cloudless blue, the sun still low over the gleaming wetlands that stretched away towards the North Sea. At the end of the lane there was a wooden picket gate, centuries old, and she slipped through it, the pitted iron of the latch cold to her touch, picking up her rhythm again, following the path around the first of the half-dozen fields she'd skirt before picking up another road and circling back towards the cottage.

She ran every morning now, a series of ever-longer loops around the village. Those same friends who'd so blinded her with science had also warned her about how addictive the running would become, and they'd been right. Already, this was the most precious hour of her day, a space that was exclusively hers, a privacy that was all the more complete because it was fenced in by sheer physical effort. At first, her targets had been modest. A couple of miles with rests whenever she felt like it. But sooner than she'd dreamed possible she was lengthening her step, quickening her pace, drawing on the kind of depthless energy she couldn't remember since childhood.

She'd begun running the day after James left for Africa. Now, just nine weeks later, she was managing six miles a morning. After Christmas, she'd try and ease it up to double figures. And by May, God willing, she'd be joining the others in Greenwich Park, warming up for her first London marathon. Plenty of women her age did it. At forty-seven, you could kid yourself that anything was possible.

She ran through a puddle, scattering shards of ice, thinking of Giles, back in bed. As ever, he'd made it easy for her. Whereas other husbands might have joked about delayed adolescence or wishful thinking, he'd taken a real interest. He never pretended to share her passion, and she wasn't even sure if he understood why she did it, but he was supportive and proud of her and when she got back in the mornings, five minutes either side of eight o'clock, a fresh pot of tea was always brewing.

Lately, she knew, he'd been under more pressure than usual. He'd always worked in the City, an underwriter at Lloyd's, but the last year or so it seemed that the place had been in a state of permanent crisis. The most sensational stuff had been in the papers – terrible problems with certain kinds of insurance, Lloyds Names facing huge losses – but whenever she'd brought the issue up, asking him exactly what had gone wrong, he'd told her not to worry. The issues were complex. Even the guys at the top were bemused. One way or another it would all sort itself out.

Something in his voice warned her not to push it any further and so she hadn't but recently she'd begun to wonder whether she shouldn't insist on sharing just a little of his burden. His job, after all, had brought them everything they had – the cottage, Giles's precious yacht, the surprise trips to Covent Garden and La Scala, the occasional holidays in the Far East –

and she'd become increasingly aware of just how much she'd taken it all for granted. Marriage to Giles had been never less than perfect, the biggest duvet in the world. It had made her feel warm, and secure, and deeply happy. In a world that could be anything but kind, she knew she owed him everything.

When she got back to the cottage, Giles was sitting in his dressing gown at the kitchen table. The Sunday papers lay before him, unopened. He looked up as she came in. When she bent to kiss him, she realised he was crying. She stared at him for a moment, shocked, then put her arms around him. He was a tall, spare, bony man with a weathered, outdoor face and thinning ginger hair. She'd never seen him cry in her life. Her hand closed over his. His skin was icy to the touch.

'What's the matter?' she said quietly. 'What's happened?'

He looked up at her. His eyes were bloodshot.

'On Armistice Day,' he said numbly. 'Can you believe that?'

She shook her head, confused now. The Armistice Day service started in the parish church at 10.45. As chairman of the local Poppy Appeal fund, Giles would be reading the lesson. He'd done it last year, too. Beautifully.

'My love . . .' She held him while he blew his nose. She could feel him shaking through the thin silk of the dressing gown. 'What is it?'

She tried to ease his head round, coax an answer, but he stood up and pushed the chair away from the table, walking across the kitchen, reaching blindly for the kettle. He held it under the tap but it was full already. She watched him for a moment then perched herself on the edge of the table, mopping the sweat from her face with a towel from the back of the chair. Giles was still holding the kettle, staring at the condensation on the window.

'Someone phoned,' he said at last.

'Who?'

'Someone from the aid people.'

For the first time, she began to understand.

'You mean James's people? Terra Sancta?'

'Yes.'

'About James?'

'Yes.'

She was back on her feet now, the towel knotting in her hands.

'And what did they say? Why did they phone?'

He shook his head, unable to answer, and she crossed the kitchen, taking the kettle away from him, turning him round, making him face her.

'Giles, tell me. What did they say? Has he had an accident?' He nodded, head down. 'And has he been hurt?'

'Yes.'

'Is it worse than that? Worse than hurt?'

He lifted his head and stared at her for a long time. Then he began to shake again, the tears pouring down his face, all control gone. She held him tightly, sensing the worst already, thinking unaccountably of the puddle and the skidding shards of ice. The answer to her question, when it came, barely registered.

'He's dead,' he whispered. 'They told me James is dead.'

At Giles's insistence, they still went to the Armistice Day service. St Michael's, Thorpe-le-Soken, lies in the middle of the village, a sturdy brick-and-flint parish church surrounded by ivy-encrusted gravestones.

Molly and Giles were amongst the last to arrive. Inside, the church was full. Two seats were waiting for them in a pew near the front. Molly followed her husband up the blue-carpeted aisle, acknowledging the nods, and smiles, and odd whispered greetings. They knew these people. They'd lived amongst them most of their lives. Yet, in a way she didn't understand, they'd already become strangers, faces from a life to which she felt she no longer belonged.

She knelt quietly beside her husband, aware of him sitting

stiffly on the wooden pew. When she looked up at him, reaching for his hand, he barely acknowledged her. His face had become a mask, taut, emotionless, drained of all colour, and when the time came for him to mount the steps to the lectern and read the lesson, she barely recognised the voice, how thin it had become, and how uncertain.

'*To everything there is a season* . . . ' he read, '*a time to be born, and a time to die; a time to plant, and a time to pluck up that which is planted.*'

She let the phrases roll over her, utterly meaningless, utterly irrelevant. Their little craft had capsized, she knew it, and what mattered now was to cling on to the memories that would keep them both afloat. James as a child, the way he'd totter from one room to the next, always on the move, pushing the little wheeled cart his granny had given him. James paddling in the sea, that first year they'd taken the beach hut at Frinton, Giles in his straw hat and sandals squatting beside him, explaining how to skim stones. And James years later, tall, handsome, noisy, appearing at the door one glorious July morning, his arm around a girl called Charlie. Charlie was extremely pretty. She had green nail varnish and a nose stud. James had announced they were off to Morocco.

' . . . *a time to rend, and a time to sew; a time to keep silence and a time to speak. A time to love, and a time to hate; a time of war, and a time of peace.*'

Giles finished the lesson, paused a moment, then turned towards the altar and bowed his head before returning to the pew. Molly watched him, her vision a blur. The steps to the altar were flanked by the old men from the British Legion with their medals and their berets and their drooping flags. They stood erect, true believers, waiting for the bell to toll eleven o'clock. Giles had arranged for a bugler, a local boy, to sound the Last Post, and when the time came the youth stepped forward and lifted the bugle to his lips, signalling the end of the two minutes' silence. As he did so, Molly felt a movement beside her. Giles fumbled for a handkerchief, doing his best to confect a heavy cold. Then he stepped out of the pew and hurried away towards the door at the back of the church. Molly listened to his footsteps on the flagstones, the hollow clang of the heavy iron latch, and as the last notes died in the big old church she closed her eyes, and bowed her head, utterly certain of what she must do. One of them, at least, must hang together, stay strong. It was the very least they owed their son.

Outside, the service over, Molly picked her way through the departing congregation, moving from group to group, exchanging greetings, kissing cheeks, explaining that Giles had a stomach upset, giving not the slightest indication that anything else might be wrong. Soon enough, she knew, she'd have to share the news about James. Then there'd be people at her door, voices on the phone, letters on the mat, a swamp of consolation. But for now, she didn't want any of that. She wanted time. She wanted privacy. Today, for just a few brief hours, James belonged to no one else but her.

She walked home alone, refusing the offer of a lift. In the lane outside the cottage a car was parked, a battered Ford Escort. Curious, she peered inside. Open on the back seat was a road atlas and a scribbled set of instructions. Strangers, she thought. Up from London.

She let herself into the cottage. A man and a woman were sitting at the kitchen table. They each had a cup of coffee and the woman was reading the back page of the *Sunday Telegraph*. As soon as they saw her, they both stood up.

Molly looked blank.

'Can I help you . . .?' she began.

The man stepped forward. He was young, mid-twenties, with a round, pink face and a tiny pair of thick pebble glasses. Under the Berghaus anorak she could see a hand-knitted sweater and a denim shirt, open at the neck.

'Your husband let us in . . .' the young man was saying. 'He's gone upstairs.'

'Is he all right?'

The couple exchanged glances. The girl was a year or two younger than her companion. She had medium-length blonde hair and a warm smile. She held out her hand.

'My name's Liz,' she said, 'and this is Robbie. He works for Terra Sancta.'

Robbie nodded, offering his own handshake.

'I've come to say how sorry we are. If there's anything—' He broke off, glancing towards the open door that led to the stairs. 'I think your husband's in a bit of a state. Understandably, of course. Maybe you want to . . .'

Molly found herself shaking her head.

'No,' she said, beginning to unbutton her coat, inviting them both to sit down again. They did so, the girl eyeing the pile of discarded running gear beside the Aga.

'Who does the jogging?' she said brightly.

'Me.'

'Really . . .?' She lapsed back into silence, pursuing the thought no further. Robbie cleared his throat, visibly uncomfortable.

'We drove down as soon as we heard,' he said at last. 'Mrs Jordan, it's awful news. I can't . . .' He made a circling gesture with his hands. 'It's just . . .'

Molly was at the Aga now, testing the temperature of the kettle, marvelling at her own composure.

'You know what happened?' she said.

'No, not really, not the details.'

'But you can tell me something, surely . . .' She turned round. 'People don't just die.'

'No, of course not.'

'Then . . .' she paused, concentrating on pouring the hot water over the coffee grounds, 'tell me whatever you know.'

The girl looked at Robbie. Robbie shifted in his seat. Molly joined them at the table.

'Africa's full of mines,' he said at last. 'You probably knew that.'

'Yes,' Molly nodded, 'James mentioned them. In his letters.'

'Yes, well . . .' Robbie frowned, 'it seems he stood on one.'

'And it killed him?'

'Yes, I'm afraid it did.'

Molly lifted the cup to her lips, saying nothing. Somehow she'd assumed that James had died in some kind of road accident. God knows, it might even have been his fault. He'd always driven like a maniac. But this was very different. Getting killed by a mine was an act of someone else's violence. She studied Robbie over the rim of the cup.

'So was he killed outright?'

'I'm sorry?'

'Did it kill him at once? This mine? Bang? Just like that? Or did he . . . did it . . . take longer?'

'I'm . . .' Robbie hesitated. 'Mrs Jordan, in all honesty I can't say.'

'Why not?'

'Because I don't know. Communications with Angola aren't all they could be. So far we've just got the bare bones.' He bit his lip at once, colouring at the phrase. Molly barely noticed.

'This mine . . . where did it come from? Who . . .' she shrugged, 'left it there in the first place?'

'Again, I'm sorry, I don't know.'

'But you will, you will know, someone'll tell you, surely.'

'Yes, oh yes.' Robbie was nodding now, vigorous, positive. 'And as soon as I hear anything, I'll be back, I promise. In the meantime, we just came to say . . . you know . . .'

Molly sipped at the coffee, her eyes not leaving his face.

'Tell me what you do,' she said, 'in this organisation of yours.'

'I'm the press officer. I deal with the media.'

'And Liz?'

'She's my partner. We live together.'

'And does she work for Terra Sancta too?'

'No, but she thought, under the circumstances—' He broke off, uncomfortable again.

'Moral support?'

'Yes.'

Molly looked at Liz. Liz wore the smile of someone who didn't quite know what was coming next. Molly extended a hand, touching her lightly on the arm.

'I'm very grateful,' she said, 'to both of you.' She looked at Robbie again. 'I'll need your help. I'm glad you came.'

'Of course, Mrs Jordan. Anything.'

'Thank you.'

Molly stood up and went to the window. The frost had gone now, and the chickens were patrolling the edge of the lawn, looking for scraps. Beyond the fence, in the field, she could see the four sheep they'd reared from lambs. She thought of her son again, his two years at agricultural college, his impatience to get out into what he called the real world. Desk work had always bored him, too dull, not enough action. She reached for the tap, sluicing her mug.

'Muengo, wasn't it? The place James worked?'

'Yes.'

'You know it at all?'

'Yes. I was out in March.'

'Good,' she glanced round at him, 'then maybe you can tell me how I get there . . .'

The heat bubbled up from the baked red earth and Andy McFaul eased down on his hands and knees, reaching for the thermos of iced water. His left leg was cramping again, up above the knee, same place as before. Nearly time to stop, he thought. Nearly time for Domingos to take over.

He lifted the visor on the big ballistic helmet, sipping the water, then wiped his mouth and glanced back over his shoulder. An avenue of red-tipped stakes marked the extent of his morning's work: ten more metres of this shit-hole cleared of mines, another tiny patch of Angola painstakingly made safe. The mines he'd found and defused lay where he'd dug them out, an irregular row of dark green hockey pucks, no bigger than a man's fist, upended in the dust. Thirteen down, he thought grimly. Twenty million to go.

Up on the road, safely out of blast range, the Angolan reached for a pair of binoculars and McFaul lifted a tired arm, circling one finger in the air, a private signal which meant he was nearly through. Four more minutes, he thought. Then it'll be Domingos's turn.

He sat back for a moment or two on his haunches, rubbing his leg, feeling the cramp beginning to ease. They'd been working this site for five days now, opening another path to the river bank. If the rumours of a big new UNITA offensive were true then the aid organisations would pull everyone out of Muengo, and if that happened then the locals would be on their own again. Little food, no fuel to cook with, and an ever-greater reliance on the loop of sluggish brown water that girdled the city to the north. With luck, the de-mining teams could make it in time. Especially if UNITA held off.

McFaul lowered the visor again and stretched for the bucket by his side, splashing more water to soften the parched earth. Summer had come early this year, a succession of cloudless days that had taken the temperature into the high eighties. With power supplies non-existent, and fuel for the generator scarce, even life after dark had become a series of impossible challenges: how to stay cool, how to stay sane, how to relax and take your mind off the world's worst job.

McFaul shrugged, and began to probe the darkened earth, back on his belly again, reaching forward, sliding the bayonet into the soil, inserting it obliquely, maintaining an angle of between fifteen and thirty degrees. Survival at this game meant sticking to a handful of rules: not hurrying, not cutting corners, learning to trust the simplest of technologies. While the mines got smarter by the year – non-metal construction, clever camou-flage, sophisticated anti-disturbance devices – the guys who were left to clear them up had to rely on eighteen inches of bare metal and their own powers of concentration. To anyone watching, McFaul knew he must look weird, shuffling slowly forward on his hands and knees, testing every inch of soil with the bayonet, in out, in out, time after time. If there was such a thing as Zen gardening, then this was surely it.

McFaul emptied the last of the water from the bucket, eyeing the patch of dampened earth. On top of his overalls, he wore a heavy black waistcoat, specially woven body-armour, and he could feel the sweat running down his chest towards his belly. The waistcoats were compulsory now, standard kit in the mine-fields. Some of the guys called them 'LCV's, a glum, fingers-crossed acronym for 'Last Chance Vests', and after Kuwait, McFaul knew why.

He felt the bayonet snag, the faintest tremor, and he eased the blade out, readjusting his position before inserting it again, the same line. Keeping the bayonet at a shallow angle meant that when you found a mine you were likely to make contact with the side of the thing, away from the sensitive pressure pad on top. The pressure pad was the bit you stood on. Even the weight of a child's foot would be enough to set it off.

McFaul began to work the soil away, using a soft, camel-hair paintbrush, tiny circular movements, gradually exposing the mine. It was the same kind as the others he'd disinterred, a Chinese Type 72A, a tiny thing, no bigger than a tin of shoe polish. Inside, it contained six ounces of high explosive, not the biggest bang in the world but quite enough to take your foot off. Mines like the 72A were perfect for a war like this, and a bargain too if you had three dollars to spare and weren't too fussy about the ethics of maiming women and children.

McFaul scraped away the last of the soil, lifting the mine gently from its bed. Keeping it level, he began to unscrew the top of the body, working the casing anticlockwise. Inside, he removed the tiny metal booster cup, the primary charge which detonated the larger explosive. Putting the booster cup to one side, he screwed the two halves together again, leaving the mine standing sideways on edge, a signal to the clean-up crew that the 72A was disarmed. Later, before the kids got hold of it, the thing would be collected for storage and eventual demolition.

McFaul eased his body backwards and then stood up, his eyes still on the mine. The design was simple but clever. The rubber pad on top rested against a convex carbon-fibre diaphragm which would buckle under the pressure of a passing foot. In Cambodia, the locals called them '*ungkiaps*'. '*Ungkiap*' meant frog, a reference to the distinctive 'crick-crack' of the collapsing diaphragm the instant before it detonated the charge and changed your life for ever.

McFaul stooped to retrieve the bucket and the thermos and then limped back along the safe lane between the stakes. Up on the road, Domingos was standing beside a Land Rover, talking to the driver. The usual crowd of kids had gathered round and some were already climbing onto the back of the vehicle, doubtless looking for goodies, stuff to play with, things to nick. As he got closer, McFaul could hear them chattering to each other, curiosity spiced with shrieks of excitement. He loved their innocence, their appetite for each new day, and their laughter was one of the sounds of Africa that drew him back, time after time, in spite of everything.

Domingos turned round when McFaul reached the Land Rover. He was a small, quick-witted man in his early thirties with a ready smile and a mouth full of broken teeth. He was paler than most Angolans, and McFaul suspected Portuguese blood, a generation or two back. Now he introduced the stranger behind the wheel.

'Senhor Peterson,' he said. 'From Luanda.'

McFaul muttered a greeting, loosening the buckle on the helmet strap and taking it off. He ran a hand through his greying crew cut, aware of Peterson's eyes on his face. McFaul's chin and cheeks were cross-hatched with blue shrapnel scars, a legacy of the accident in Kuwait. They went with the plastic and titanium prosthesis that had replaced the shredded remains of his lower left leg. The prosthesis was state-of-the-art, a real masterpiece, and on a good day McFaul could walk as naturally as any man.

Peterson got out of the Land Rover, extending a hand. He was dressed like a war correspondent. He wore a loose khaki jacket with epaulettes and big button-up pockets, and the logo on the T-shirt underneath read 'Kill The Criminal Justice Bill'. He was a tall man, with a long, narrow face and a shock of iron-grey hair, and he had the pallor of someone newly arrived from Europe. His manner was intimate, as if he were greeting a long-lost friend.

'The famous McFaul,' he was saying, 'bit of a legend, the way I hear it.'

McFaul shrugged. The phrase was familiar. It made little sense.

'You fly in this morning?' he said, wiping his hand on the back of his overalls.

'Yep. Begged a lift on the WFP Beechcraft. I thought they'd be staying over but they've gone on to Cubal.'

McFaul nodded. The big Russian freighters and smaller planes like the Beechcraft were still landing at Muengo but soon he suspected they'd stop. Local rebel units were supposed to have laid hands on American *Stinger* ground-to-air missiles. A *Stinger* could drop an Antonov at three miles. No one liked coming to Muengo any more.

McFaul bent down, his arms held out straight, letting Domingos tug the heavy armoured waistcoat off. Peterson watched the procedure. The smile on his face looked strained.

'I'm with Terra Sancta,' he said at last. 'Acting CR.'

McFaul accepted Domingos's proffered towel, mopping his face. CR meant Country Representative, one of the rungs in Terra Sancta's administrative ladder. The man would have a rented house back on the coast in Luanda and responsibility for maybe thirty aid workers. It was an important job, far from easy, and McFaul began to understand why Peterson's smile seemed so tight.

'You're here about last night? The boy? Jordan?'

'Yes.'

'You want my opinion?'

'Your help.'

'How?'

Peterson glanced at Domingos then took McFaul by the arm, trying to guide him away from the Land Rover. Instinctively, McFaul resisted the pressure, wanting no part of any confidential conversation. For once, Domingos wasn't smiling.

'You'll be writing some kind of report?' Peterson asked.

'Of course.'

'May I see it?'

'Yeah, when it's done.'

'Who else gets a copy?'

McFaul looked at him a moment, at last understanding why he'd bothered to stop by.

'My lot,' he grunted. 'The office in Luanda. The embassy people. The ODA . . .' he shrugged, 'and whoever else my boss thinks may be interested. Up to him really.'

He paused, letting the circulation list sink in. The ODA was shorthand for the Overseas Development Administration, the Whitehall department responsible for funding the mine clearance work. They had close links to all the UK aid outfits. Peterson began to make a point about the importance of proper briefings but McFaul interrupted him.

'Jordan was an arsehole,' McFaul grunted, 'and he'd done it before.'

'So I understand. All I wanted to say was—'

'No.' McFaul shook his head, 'you listen to me. There are rules out here. We don't make them up to keep ourselves amused. They're not for negotiation. They matter. There are things you do and don't do. The boy thought he was immune. He knew it all. He wouldn't be told.'

26

'Of course.'

'You understand that?'

'Yes.'

'Your people understand that?'

'I hope so.'

'So do I. For their sake. And yours.'

McFaul turned away, letting his anger subside. Last night, after the Mayday on Channel Two, he'd driven out with Domingos in the two-tonner. They'd spent the hours of darkness by the roadside, waiting until first light to spade the remains of James Jordan into a body bag. The Médecins Sans Frontières girl, Christianne, had done what she could to help, insisting on staying with them until the body had been recovered, but the price of the boy's stupidity, his recklessness, was plain to see. Everyone knew how much the prat had meant to her. Poor cow.

McFaul stood at the roadside, looking down the line of stakes. Peterson joined him.

'All I came to say,' he murmured, 'was sorry.'

'Sure.'

'It can't make things any easier for you.'

'It doesn't.' McFaul glanced across at him. 'Are you taking the body back? Only there's a space problem.'

'So I understand.'

'There's only one fridge at the hospital and they're short of fuel for the gennie. If the bad guys get their act together, there won't be any fuel at all. Then we'll have to bury him.'

McFaul broke off, watching Peterson working it out for himself. Mercifully, very few aid workers got themselves killed but when it happened, repatriation of the remains became a priority. Africa could claim white lives but white bodies, however mangled, belonged back home.

Peterson was looking at his watch.

'There might be another aid flight this afternoon,' he said uncertainly. 'No one seems to know.'

Peterson eyed the sky, like a man assessing the weather. The

road to Muengo had been off-limits for months, a combination
of land mines and the fear of UNITA ambush. The only way in
or out was by air.

'It's Sunday afternoon,' McFaul grunted, 'no one likes flying
on Sunday afternoons.'

'Tomorrow then. Or the next day. Would that be too late?'

McFaul looked at him for a moment or two, suddenly aware
of how tired he felt.

'You tell me,' he handed his helmet to the waiting Domingos, 'I only work here.'

Robbie Cunningham took the first Winchester exit off the
motorway, peering through the rain to avoid the tangle of
roadworks. He'd dropped Liz at the flat in Chiswick and
doubled back towards the M3, pushing the rusty Escort to the
limit. Westerby, the Director, had called the meeting for half-
past four. With luck he'd just make it.

Terra Sancta was headquartered in a sprawling Victorian
vicarage on the city's western edge. A big new extension to the
rear of the building would treble the office space but the project
was a month and a half behind schedule and what the Director
called 'the worker bees' were still caged in the main building.
Robbie shared an alcove with a fax machine, an unsteady pile
of phone directories and a file of agency press cuttings. The file
was on the thin side, a fact of which he was uncomfortably
aware. In a good mood, the Director would refer to this as
'disappointing', though Robbie had no illusions about what he
really meant. Third World charities survived on press coverage.
Without profile, without your name in the papers, you stayed
poor.

The meeting was to take place in the Director's own
office. The room had once been the largest of the vicarage
bedrooms, and for some reason the Director had hung on to
the hand basin in the corner. He was soaping his face when

Robbie knocked and entered, slipping into one of the two empty chairs at the long deal table. As far as he could judge, the meeting had yet to begin.

The Director returned to the table. He looked older than his fifty-seven years. He was wearing a shapeless grey cardigan and the shirt beneath was open at the neck. There was mud caked on the bottom of his baggy corduroy trousers and his hair looked unusually wild. He settled himself at the head of the table behind an unopened file, murmuring a collective welcome to the half-dozen assembled faces. Robbie looked at the typed sticky label on the file. It said 'James Jordan'.

Before the Director had a chance to begin, the woman beside Robbie took a folded telex from her handbag and slid it down the table. Her name was Valerie. She looked after Africa.

'From Luanda this afternoon,' she said. 'I thought you ought to see it.'

The Director looked at her a moment, a pained expression on his face. He was famous for hating surprises. Aid, in his view, was about development, about the Third World marching to the slow, steady drumbeat of self-improvement. It was folly to rush things, to surrender to mere events. His least favourite words were 'crisis' and 'emergency'.

He unfolded the telex and read it. Then he looked up, sharing its contents with everyone else.

'It's from Peterson,' he said glumly. 'He thinks the press people may be on to us. Already.'

He looked pointedly at Robbie who answered the accusation with a firm shake of his head.

'Not this end,' he said. 'Not yet, anyway.'

The Director gazed helplessly at the telex, then passed it to Robbie. Robbie read it quickly. Before flying to Muengo, Peterson had evidently received a phone call from the Reuters stringer in Luanda. He'd heard rumours about a dead aid worker. It wasn't impossible that he'd been monitoring the radio traffic. Everyone did it. Peterson had naturally stonewalled but soon there'd have to be some sort of announcement. How was he to play it?

'Well,' the Director was sitting back now, polishing his glasses, 'what are we to do?'

Robbie was about to frame an answer when there was a brisk knock at the door. Before the Director could answer, the door opened and a figure stepped in. The white trenchcoat was streaked with rain and the umbrella left a trail of drips across the fitted carpet.

'Came straight down,' the figure said briskly. 'Sorry I'm late.' The Director waved the apology away, visibly brightening.

'This is Todd Llewelyn,' he announced. 'No introductions needed. He's kindly offered to help us out if things get . . . ah . . . sticky.'

The faces around the table offered Llewelyn a collective smile of welcome and Robbie watched him shedding the white trenchcoat, knowing now that the rumours had been true. Llewelyn's was a well-known television face from the eighties. Square-jawed, eloquent, pugnacious, he'd presented series after series of hard-hitting documentaries. Now, somewhere in his mid-fifties, he'd been beached by the broadcasting revolution, his mannered front-of-camera delivery overtaken by a sleeker, glitzier style. Robbie had always wondered where men like Llewelyn ended up. Now he knew.

The Director was beaming at the new arrival, like a child showing off his latest toy, and Robbie leaned back in his chair, trying to decide who'd made the first approach. Llewelyn, probably. Taking initiatives of any kind was something the Director generally tried to resist.

Llewelyn slipped into the empty chair, eyeing Robbie across the table. The look – cold, hard, appraising – was unambiguous, an immediate declaration of war, and Robbie felt himself reaching for his pen, scribbling lines of nonsense on his pad, anything to hide his own fury. Appointing Llewelyn as some kind of media consultant would be typical of the Director, saving himself the embarrassment of confronting Robbie face to face. The Director wanted him out. And this was his way of saying it.

'An update, Todd,' the Director was saying. 'You know about our Mr Jordan. We discussed that on the phone. But there are complications. Valerie?'

With a glance at the others, the woman beside Robbie picked up her cue, addressing Llewelyn directly. For several months, she told him, Terra Sancta had been winding down its efforts in Angola. Plainly, the political situation was out of control. Three decades of civil war had brought the country to its knees and the recent elections had solved nothing. The MPLA, the socialist government in Luanda, had won a narrow victory but UNITA, their right-wing opponents, had refused to accept the result. UNITA's leader, Jonas Savimbi, had renewed the war and fighting had broken out again with pockets of violence flaring wherever government or Savimbi's troops sensed an advantage. The countryside was emptying. The cities were choked. There were thousands of casualties, millions of displaced Angolans fleeing their homes. Under these circumstances, charities like Terra Sancta were helpless. There'd been much agonising, many meetings, but the consensus was plain. Angola was a basket case. Terra Sancta's precious funds would be better spent elsewhere.

Llewelyn listened to the briefing, his eyes never leaving Valerie's face. When she paused for breath, he leaned forward, one finger raised, the pose familiar from a hundred prime-time documentaries.

'So you're pulling out? Is that what you're saying?'

'We . . . ah . . .'

'Yes or no?'

Valerie glanced towards the Director. The Director was looking uneasy.

'We're going through a process of re-evaluation,' he said hurriedly. 'Pulling out sounds a little . . . ah . . . harsh.'

'But that's what you're saying. That's what it means.'

'Essentially . . .' he conceded the point with a nod, 'yes.'

'And you're embarrassed by the decision? Is that it?'

'Not embarrassed, no. But we believe it may be open to . . .'
He paused, frowning.

'Misinterpretation?'

'Yes, exactly.'

The Director smiled gratefully, accepted the proffered lifeline, and Robbie felt the blood rising in his face. He'd spent a
lot of time in Angola. He'd seen the country at its worst and
he loved the place. He'd never been anywhere in Africa that
had so much potential: the oil, and the diamonds, and above
all the people. The last thirty years would have crushed most
nations but here they still were, ever-sunny, ever-cheerful,
making the most of what pitifully little they had. In his view, a
withdrawal of aid was inconceivable. Angola was in big trouble,
no question, but to abandon it now was beyond comprehension.
If Terra Sancta existed for anything, it existed for this.

He raised a hand, rehearsing the old arguments in his head,
but the Director ignored him. They'd had this out before and
the Director had little taste for public dissent.

Llewelyn was musing aloud, his eyes moving slowly from
face to face, his command of the meeting established.

'You're all worried about the downside,' he was saying, 'the
negative publicity. You'll have the media round your neck over
Jordan and you're afraid the rest will come out . . .' His gaze
reached the Director. 'Am I right?'

'Perfectly.'

'So we're into damage limitation. Or perhaps damage
deflection. Yes?'

'Alas, yes.'

Llewelyn nodded, snapping open his briefcase, the visiting
GP. He produced a yellow lawyer's pad. The Director was waiting for his next word. The patient was sick. There was the
possibility of a scandal. What would this enormously experienced
media giant recommend?

Llewelyn was scribbling something on his pad.

'Anyone been in touch with the parents?' he said without looking up. Robbie stirred.

'Yes,' he said quietly, 'I have.'

'And how are they taking it?'

'The father's in a state. The mother . . .' he hesitated, 'I'm not sure.'

Llewelyn glanced up, that same expression in his eyes, open intimidation.

'You're not sure?'

'No.'

'What does that mean?'

Robbie shrugged, refusing to lose his nerve.

'On the face of it she's pretty together, very coherent, very much in control . . .' He paused. 'In fact she wants to go out there.' There was a sharp intake of breath from the end of the table. The Director looked genuinely shocked.

'You're serious?' he said.

'Yes.'

'She wants to go to Angola?'

'That's what she said.'

'Why?'

'To fetch her son. To . . .' he gestured at Jordan's file, 'find out what happened. Say goodbye, I suppose.'

Llewelyn was leaning back in his chair, listening to the exchange, the pose of a man who's heard it all before. For the first time, he smiled.

'It's common enough in these cases . . .' he said. 'Believe me, I've seen it over and over again. The Falklands was a classic example. Every time the casualty lists came in, the M.O.D. was swamped. Mothers mainly, funnily enough . . .'

'I'm sure.' The Director was still looking at Robbie. 'So what did you tell her?'

'I told her it would be extremely difficult.'

'Impossible. It would be impossible.' The Director frowned. 'And what did she say?'

'She didn't say anything.'

There was a brief silence. Llewelyn was making a note on his pad. At length he put his pen carefully to one side, folding his arms.

'Why would it be impossible?' he said softly.

Robbie began to answer but the Director cut in.

'For one thing, it's a war zone . . .' he began, 'just getting in there would be a nightmare. Then there's the situation on the ground. Places like Muengo are in chaos. People are dying. There's a food problem, no drugs, no power, poor water. The situation's appalling, completely out of control.'

'I understand that,' Llewelyn said gently, 'but why would it be impossible?'

The Director was frowning now, confused, watching helplessly as Llewelyn took the conversation back to Robbie.

'This Mrs Jordan . . .' he mused, '. . . what's she like?'

'I just told you.'

'I meant to look at, to be with. Nice woman? Sympathetic? Pretty?'

Robbie shrugged.

'Middle forties, smallish, trim . . .' he paused, remembering the pile of abandoned jogging gear, 'and fit, too, I imagine.'

'Pretty?' he asked again. 'Good-looking?'

'Yes.' Robbie frowned, feeling curiously insulted by the question. 'Yes, definitely. Blonde, slim, nice manner, nice eyes . . .'

'Determined?'

'I'd say so, yes. Difficult to judge, but . . . yes.'

There was another silence and Robbie shifted uncomfortably in the hard wooden chair. For reasons he didn't understand, he'd become involved in some kind of audition. Llewelyn was studying his fingernails.

'And does she trust you?' he asked at length.

'*Trust* me?'

'Yes.'

'I've no idea. I was only there an hour. Maybe less.'

'But what's your feeling? You'd know, surely.'

Robbie gazed at him, at last sensing where this conversation was headed. Llewelyn wanted him to go back there, back to the picturesque little cottage on the northern edge of Essex. He was to carry a proposal of some kind, the opening gambit in a master plan that would doubtless get the Director off the hook. Quite what this proposal might be, Robbie didn't know. But in his own way he was determined to hang in there, whatever the consequences, buffering the poor woman from the likes of Todd Llewelyn.

For the first time, he looked Llewelyn in the eyes, answering his chilly stare.

'Yes,' he said. 'I think she trusted me.'

The third time Molly went up to the bedroom, her husband was awake. She stood in the open doorway a moment, a cup of tea in her hand, looking down at his face on the pillow. His eyes were open, gazing sightlessly at the empty glass on the bedside table. Molly had sniffed at the glass the first time she'd checked him. It smelled of brandy.

Now, she bent quickly to the pillow, leaving the tea beside the empty glass, kissing her husband on the forehead. His flesh was cold to the touch of her lips and she crossed the tiny bedroom to the dormer window, pulling the curtains against the darkness outside. Since the couple from London had gone, she'd been downstairs, curled in front of the Aga, preparing herself for what she knew would be a difficult scene. In twenty-six years of marriage, she'd never once taken the initiative. Not in the important things. Not in a crisis like this.

She sat on the bed, reaching for her husband's hand. It felt lifeless, dead, as cold and empty as the rest of him. She explained about the visit from the Terra Sancta people, the trouble they'd taken, how kind they'd been. She explained about James's accident, what seemed to have happened. For the first time, Giles stirred.

'A mine?' he said.

He made the word sound almost foreign, something from outer space, something that couldn't possibly belong in their lives.

'Yes,' she said, 'apparently they're everywhere.'

'And he trod on one?'

'So they say.'

Giles closed his eyes and groaned, the reaction of a man who wants to hear no more, and Molly squeezed his hand, remembering the church, how full it had been. '*To everything there is a season; a time to be born, and a time to die.*' Giles struggled upright in the bed, trying to get out, but Molly restrained him as gently as she could, plumping the pillows behind his back. He looked at her the way a stranger might, uncomprehending.

'What's the matter?' he said. 'I'm not ill.'

'I know. I just want to talk.'

'But . . .' he began to move again, trying to get his legs out, then gave up. Molly was still stroking his hand.

'We have to go out there,' she said quietly. 'You and me.'

'Where?'

'Angola.'

'Why?'

'Because . . .' she paused, knowing that this question would come, knowing that it had to be answered, 'because it's important. James is dead, Giles. He's gone. But I won't accept it until I've been there.'

She sat back, turning her head away. For the first time, she understood the real depth of her loss, what had been taken from her, what could never be returned. James had indeed gone. No more surprise phone calls from the station. No more midnight bacon sandwiches. No more tussles over the state of his bedroom. She stood up, reaching blindly for the towel on the radiator, mopping her eyes, blowing her nose. Giles hadn't moved, his face chalk-white against the pillows.

'We can't,' he said. 'We can't go out there.'

'Why not?'

He stared at her, pulling the covers to his chin.

'It's impossible,' he said. 'We just can't.'

'But why not?'

He shook his head, refusing to answer, a wild, trapped look in his eyes, and Molly gazed at him, uncomprehending, wondering what had happened to the husband she'd known, the warm, uncomplicated man she'd woken up with. Already, she knew that James's death had taken him away. What was left was someone else.

'I have to go,' she said uncertainly, 'whatever happens.'

'You can't.'

'Why not?'

'You just can't. That's all. What's the point? The boy's dead. Going out there won't get him back.'

'Yes it will. I'll bring him back.'

'What?'

He stared at her, utterly blank, and she hesitated a moment before settling on the bed again. This time, she didn't take his hand.

'I meant the body,' she said quietly. 'I'll bring the body back. And then we'll bury him.'

For a moment she thought he was going to break down again but he managed to stay in control.

'How?' he said at last. 'How will you get there?'

'I don't know.' She shrugged. 'There'll be a way. There are planes and things. I'm sure we've got the money. It's not a problem.'

At the mention of money, he turned his face to the wall. Outside, in the darkness, Molly could hear the cat scratching at the kitchen door. Giles's eyes had closed. A tiny muscle fluttered beneath the ridge of his cheekbone.

'There is no money,' he said at last.

Molly stared at him.

'What?'

Giles opened his eyes, looking at her for a long moment, all emotion spent.

'There is no money,' he said again. 'One of our syndicate's come unstuck. It owes millions. Hundreds of millions. They want our money . . .' he paused, 'everything we've got.'

CHAPTER TWO

The first shells fell after midnight. McFaul had been asleep for more than three hours, sprawled on the camp-bed in a corner of the classroom they'd converted into a makeshift dormitory. He was awake at once fumbling for the MagLite torch he kept on the floor beneath the bed, peering through the filmy gauze of the mosquito net. The beam of the torch settled briefly on the camp-bed across the room.

'Bennie,' McFaul hissed, 'for fuck's sake.'

Bennie grunted and then began to protest, still half-asleep. In three years together, McFaul had never known him master the art of waking up sweet-tempered. McFaul was strapping on his false leg now, then he levered himself upright and limped across the bare wooden floor. Far away he heard a dull crump and he found himself counting the seconds until the explosion. When it came, the blast was uncomfortably close, shaking the old schoolhouse, stirring the blanket they'd hung over one of the windows. Mortars, McFaul thought. Probably 120 mm.

Bennie was on his feet, cursing in the hot darkness. He and McFaul had discussed this situation only three days ago, when the commander of the local government troops had released the latest intelligence. According to captured prisoners, a big UNITA offensive was imminent. As usual, infantry assault would be preceded by some form of bombardment, either mortars or artillery or perhaps both. Courtesy of their friends in South

Africa, the rebels had stockpiled a great deal of ammunition.
The shelling could go on for days.

There was another explosion nearby and then the plaintive
wail of a child. McFaul quickly checked the room, sweeping the
torch from left to right. He had a standing arrangement with
the Red Cross people. They had a secure bunker half a mile
away. In the event of emergencies, he and Bennie had allocated
places. Bennie was getting his kit together, bundling what he'd
need into a holdall and a rucksack. Most of the heavy equipment
they'd agreed to leave behind, locked in the closet they'd turned
into a strongroom. If the schoolhouse suffered a direct hit, the
stuff would probably be destroyed but much of it was too bulky
to take with them. The beam of the torch pooled on the survey
maps pinned to what had once been the blackboard. The maps
were large scale, big blow-ups of the locations where they'd
been working, a painstakingly accurate record of exactly what
they'd achieved. They held all the vital information, which paths
were safe, which fields were still mined, which areas had yet to
be surveyed. Without them, they'd have to start all over again.

McFaul held the torch steady, telling Bennie they'd take the
maps with them. Bennie was crouched in the darkness, rolling
up his sleeping-bag.

'You want me to bring them?'

'Yeah.'

McFaul left the room. Out in the corridor, he peered
through the window at the new rubber dinghy, lashed to its
trailer. They'd only had it a month, airlifted in from the coast,
and already it had proved invaluable on the river. Should he
try and wrestle it indoors? Protect it somehow? He heard the
crump of another mortar and ducked beneath the window,
waiting for the blast. With luck, the dinghy would survive the
bombardment. Tomorrow he'd try and sort something out.

Back in the classroom, McFaul found Bennie unpinning the
maps. He had a torch in his mouth and muttered something
incomprehensible when McFaul told him they'd be moving out

in five minutes. Next to the classroom, through another door, was the storeroom where they kept the generator and the big freezer they'd inherited from an outgoing UN crew. The freezer was powered from the gennie and they normally ran it in bursts, three or four times a day. That was plenty enough to keep the stuff inside decently chilled but now was different. They might be gone for days, quite long enough to lose their precious supply of meat and fish and chilled Sagres beer. McFaul bent to the generator, checking the level of the fuel. On a full tank, it would run for forty-eight hours. Satisfied, he primed the tiny carburettor and pulled the starter cord. The gennie fired first time, settling into a steady thump, and McFaul locked the storeroom door behind him, adjusting the 'DANGER – MINES' sign they used as an extra deterrent against looters.

Bennie was in the corridor now, peering out into the darkness. He'd found a rubber band for the maps and had wedged them under one arm, tightly rolled. McFaul paused by the open door. The place already reeked of exhaust fumes.

'OK?'

'Yeah.'

Bennie slipped out of the building, following McFaul. The agreed route took them down Muengo's pot-holed main street, hugging the shadows, moving from house to house. Many of these buildings were already derelict, carrying the scars of earlier fighting: shattered roofs, fire-blackened walls, whole rooms laid open by weeks of bombardment. What wood they contained – floorboards, doors, the odd cupboard – had long gone, stripped out by the refugees, desperate for cooking fuel. By the big, ghost-like Roman Catholic cathedral, McFaul paused, signalling Bennie to take cover. The UNITA mortars were busy again, five or six of them, firing at what McFaul judged to be maximum range. There seemed to be no pattern to the fall of shell, just the random dispatch of high explosive, the usual bid to bludgeon the city into submission. Already, he knew, the hospital would be under siege, relatives arriving with their dying and their wounded, long queues in the candle-lit darkness, kids sitting cross-legged, their faces upturned, uncomprehending. The surgeons at the hospital were Norwegian. There were just two of them but they only stayed a month at a time and they seemed to have limitless reserves of energy. With the recent drugs resupply, and a great deal of luck, they might just cope.

The mortars fell silent at last and McFaul and Bennie crossed the dusty square outside the cathedral. During daylight hours, this was the heart of the city, the place where the locals spread their mats and traded what few goods they possessed: green bananas, pulped roots, scraps of charity clothing, the odd jam jar half-full of cooking oil, torn paper bags spilling powdered milk, spare ends of the thick, heavy-duty blue polythene scavanged from the aid dumps. The *praça*, the market, supplied the city's life-blood and without it Muengo would have died long ago. The *praça* kept the city going. The *praça* was what you were left with once everything else had fallen apart.

The mortars opened up again and McFaul stumbled into an awkward run, covering the last hundred metres to the Red Cross bunker, oblivious to the pain in his leg where the stump chafed against the shaped plastic socket. Access to the bunker lay through a gaping hole in the wall which surrounded the Red Cross compound. After the last siege of the city, the Swiss had brought in their own engineers to do the construction work, adapting the basement of the existing house, strengthening the beams at ground level and adding a rough concrete scree to the earth floor. The result was a blast-proof underground living space, approximately twenty-feet square, offering reasonable protection against anything but a direct hit from a heavy-calibre shell. The bunker had its own electricity and water supplies and a big dipole aerial on the roof supplied a radio link to Luanda and even – atmospherics permitting – to Europe. The head of the Red Cross mission in Muengo had celebrated the bunker's completion with a party for the local aid community and shortly afterwards drills had been organised in the event of further fighting. The bunker, at a pinch, could hold fifteen.

McFaul found the steps to the bunker's entrance, heavily sandbagged on both sides. Halfway down the steps, a face appeared in the darkness. The tempo of the bombardment had increased again and McFaul was in no mood for conversation.

'*Por favor . . . vamos!*'

He tried to push by but couldn't. The other man muttered an apology in English and it took a second or two for McFaul to recognise the voice. Then he had it. Peterson. The new arrival from Luanda.

'Off somewhere?' McFaul enquired drily. 'Out for a stroll?' Peterson pulled a face in the gloom.

'I've got a billet with the UN people,' he said. 'They've promised to do something about the body.'

'Whose body?'

'Jordan's.'

'Like what?'

Peterson shrugged. His eyes were wide.

'Organise a flight, I hope. Unless there's some other way out.'

McFaul looked at him a moment, then ducked as an incoming mortar shell plunged into the cathedral square, sending shrapnel and fragments of paving stone whining into the surrounding darkness. Back upright, seconds later, he tried to resume the conversation but Peterson had vanished. Bennie was at the head of the steps now, the sweat beading on his shaven head, pushing McFaul down towards the reinforced steel doors at the bottom.

'Who was that?'

'Peterson. The Terra Sancta bloke.'

'What's he after?'

'A flight out.'

At the foot of the steps, both men rapped urgently on the door. Bennie was laughing.

'Dream on,' he said. 'Dumb fucker.'

*

Molly Jordan was late for her appointment with the family solicitor. On the phone they'd arranged to meet in his office at eleven but she'd spent most of the morning dealing with callers from the village. News of James's death had been headlined on the local news bulletins and since nine o'clock the kitchen had never been empty. By ten, she'd run out of vases for the flowers callers had brought and when she finally locked the door and fled, the sink was overflowing with iris and gladioli.

Now she hurried across the road, hoping that Patrick would forgive her. Ever since she could remember, he'd occupied the same suite of offices in a solid thirties building in Frinton's main shopping street. At one end of the street lay the greensward and the sea; at the other, the white level-crossing gates which guarded the town from the outside world. Frinton, she'd always thought, lived in a time warp: old-fashioned, genteel, determined to resist the uglier encroachments of twentieth-century life. No pubs. No buses. Barely even a fish and chip shop. In this strange, walled-off community, Patrick – with his quiet, good manners and passion for golf – was the perfect fit.

He was waiting for her in the little reception area. Unlike most men she knew, he seemed completely at ease with emotional situations. Now, he stepped forward and put his arms around her, hugging her tightly. She could smell the pipe tobacco he smoked in the folds of his battered tweed jacket. Nice man, she thought. Nice, nice man.

They went upstairs to his office. Bright sunshine patterned the carpet. He paused by the drinks cabinet in the corner, waving away her apologies for being late. He offered her a sherry but she settled for tea.

'Alice sends her best,' he said. 'She's there if you need her. You only have to ring.'

Molly nodded. Patrick's wife, Alice, had no children of her own and she'd always taken a lively interest in James. For the first time, it occurred to Molly that the loss to her would be profound.

Patrick talked for several minutes, gentle reminiscences about James, the various scrapes he'd got himself into, his unerring nose for trouble. He used the past tense without any trace of embarrassment or awkwardness and Molly found herself smiling at some of the more outrageous stories, oddly comforted. James had been real. Real blood. Real tears. Real laughter. When the temptation was to sentimentalise, to make the boy out to be some kind of saint, she needed to hang on to that.

After a while, a tray of tea arrived. Molly was nibbling a biscuit, her first food of the day, when Patrick asked about Giles.

'How's he taking it?'

'Badly, he's . . .' Molly tried to find the right word, 'in shock, I suppose. It's hard to recognise him just now. He doesn't seem to want me around. Or anyone else for that matter . . . It's . . .' She shook her head, still nursing the biscuit. Giles hadn't come to bed until two in the morning and even then she knew he hadn't slept. She'd gone running at seven as usual, determined to hang on to this one precious hour of her day, but by the time she got back he'd gone. No note. No explanation. Just another empty tumbler on the draining board, smelling faintly of Scotch.

Patrick sipped his tea.

'He phoned first thing,' he said. 'About half-seven.'

'Giles?'

'Yes.'

'What a coincidence.' She frowned, trying to remember whether she'd told him about her plans to drive over to Frinton. 'Did he know I was coming?'

'No, but he asked me to talk to you anyway. So . . .' he smiled, 'it's all worked out rather well.'

'What about? What did he want you to say?'

Patrick got up and closed the door. When he sat down again the smile had gone.

'You'll know he's in trouble. I gather he told you.'

'He told me we're broke. Is that what you mean?'

'Yes.'

Patrick reached for the teapot, offering a refill, but Molly shook her head. It was a shock to realise that this man probably knew more about their financial affairs than she did. She felt herself colouring slightly, more irritation than embarrassment.

'Patrick . . .' she began, 'it's been a difficult twenty-four hours. What exactly do you want to tell me?'

'That rather depends.'

'On what?'

'On you.' He paused, dropping two sugar lumps into his tea. 'How much do you want to know?'

'About the money? What's gone wrong?'

'Yes.'

'Everything.'

Patrick nodded. Then he sat back behind his desk, the cup and saucer balanced in his lap. Giles, as she doubtless knew, was an active underwriter at Lloyd's. He wrote business on behalf of a syndicate of Names. Names were the folk who put up their capital in return for a share of the profits. In a good year, they could make a great deal of money. In a bad year, there might be losses. In a very bad year, they might be wiped out completely.

Molly nodded, following his explanation. To her shame, she'd never fully understood the way it worked.

'So who makes the decision about the risks?' she asked.

'Giles does.' He paused. 'Did.'

'*Did?*'

'Yes.' He nodded. 'He ceased writing business at the end of last week. I understand the technical term is suspended.'

Molly blinked, taking in the news, beginning to fathom the true depths of Giles's private nightmare. However hard he'd tried to disguise it, she'd always known that he was a fiercely competitive man. It occasionally showed in little things: the parents' race at James's school, his regatta days in the dinghy. Fouling up at work, getting himself suspended, would have crucified him.

'So what happened?' she asked. 'What does "suspended" mean?'

Patrick was sipping his tea again. Her question prompted a frown.

'Giles was investing his own money, your money, as well as relying on the syndicate's Names. Lots of underwriters do it. It's common practice.'

Molly nodded. This much, at least, she knew.

'Eighty-four,' she said. 'That summer we decided to send James away to school. His exam results were so awful at the comprehensive. You probably remember.'

'I do. Vividly.'

'Giles said we'd need a bit extra. Cash, I mean. Lloyd's seemed the obvious place.'

'It was. And he did well, too. In fact for most of the eighties, he did extremely well. Do you want the figures?'

Molly shook her head. The figures were academic. What had mattered infinitely more was what the money had bought. James's school hadn't been cheap. Far from it. She hesitated a moment, remembering how quickly she'd taken this new wealth of theirs for granted. The holidays abroad. The workshop extension on the cottage. The extra couple of acres for the horses, and later, the sheep.

'So what happened?' she asked. 'Where did we go wrong?'

Patrick drained the cup, returning it to the tray. The details, he said, were complex but Giles had written a lot of reinsurance. That meant taking part of someone else's risk in return for a share of their premium. Technically, this practice was known as 'Excess of Loss' insurance, and it had become a Lloyd's speciality. Lots of underwriters had done it during the eighties and the returns could be enormous.

'So what went wrong?' Molly asked again.

'More or less everything. Oil rigs going up in flames. Lockerbie. Hurricanes. Earthquakes. You name it. Huge losses. Huge claims. But the really nasty surprise was pollution, in America especially, and that's where Giles and one or two others came unstuck. He gave me a copy of the cutting. Here . . .'

Patrick opened a drawer and slid out a file, passing a folded newspaper cutting across the desk. The cutting came from *The New York Times*. A grainy photograph showed a sprawl of low factory buildings behind a tall, chain-link fence. A placard wired to the fence read 'DANGER: TOXINS'. Underneath was a two-column story about a New Jersey armaments factory specialising in the production of something called 'A/D Munitions'.

Molly glanced up.

'What does "A/D" mean?'

'Area denial. It's military jargon for keeping the opposition where you want them. Instead of high explosives, these people were contracted to fill artillery shells with various chemicals. The place is closed now. It seems they've been having leaks for years.'

'But what's that got to do with Giles?'

'His syndicate reinsured a slice of the risk.' He paused. 'Quite a big slice, as it happens.'

'And they're claiming?' Molly tapped the cutting. 'These people are claiming?'

'They have no choice. The US government has the power to authorise a clean-up. It's a big site. Hundreds of acres. Physically, the whole thing has to be taken away. The lawyers are still arguing about the bill but the lowest estimate is one billion dollars.'

'One *billion*?' Molly stared at him. The sum was inconceivable. 'And Giles owes all that? That's what he's got to find?'

'No, nothing like. But even a tenth of that is still huge. A hundred million . . .' He shook his head. 'It's a fortune, especially if the syndicate's exposed to other risks.'

'And is it?'

'Yes, I understand that's why Giles has been suspended. I gather the managing agent thinks he's been going for broke. Writing silly business. Double or quits.'

'And is he right?'

'I'm afraid I've no idea. Not that it matters. Lloyd's is a village. Reputation counts for everything.'

Molly nodded, understanding at last why Giles had been so quiet, so unwilling to share his problems. He was a proud man. Even last week, even until the moment when they took away his job, he must have felt there was a chance of rescuing the situation, of piling up fresh business, of honouring his obligations to the other Names in his wretched syndicate. Knowing the man the way that she did, she was absolutely certain that the syndicate's ruin would have weighed more heavily with him than the prospect of their own bankruptcy. The man had always been cursed with a conscience. It was one of the many reasons she'd fallen in love with him.

'So why didn't he tell me all this himself,' she said quietly, 'instead of getting you to do it?'

Patrick looked at her for a long moment.

'We ought to talk about the consequences,' he said at last, 'and then maybe you'll understand.'

Todd Llewelyn pushed his plate to one side, mopping his lips with the napkin. One of the problems of late middle age was weight gain. In his line of work, he told himself that appearance was all-important but the price of staying in shape was the need to stick to an almost permanent diet, a concept that sat uneasily alongside an invitation to 'La Bellissima'.

His host, twenty years younger, helped himself to another plateful of spaghetti Marinara. Martin Pegley had been in his new job exactly a year now, and hauling his old boss to one of Soho's best Italian restaurants seemed a fitting way to celebrate. Not only that, but it might, with luck, put an end to the non-stop stream of phone calls.

Llewelyn reached for his glass of Chianti. His lunch-time limit was two glasses. So far he'd barely touched the first.

'So what do you think?' he said.

Pegley's eyes went to the small lined pad beside his plate. He'd listed the programme ideas one by one, in the order that Llewelyn had pitched them. So far, none had raised even a flicker of interest.

'I quite like the idea of a Hiroshima retrospective,' he said carefully, 'but I have to be candid. It's a bit out of our league.'

'I'd keep the archive to a minimum,' Llewelyn said at once, 'if that's a worry.'

'So what would we be looking at? What would we see? Going out there's not an option. I was in Japan last month. The prices are outrageous.'

'No question.' Llewelyn was nodding vigorously. 'We fly the guys over. On contra deals. Do the interviews here. Use their own stills. Minimum fee. Total buy-out.'

'What guys?'

'The survivors.'

'I thought there weren't any? I thought that was the story?'

Llewelyn looked at him for a moment, uncertain whether he was being taken seriously. Five years ago, when they were both working in what Llewelyn still called 'proper television', Pegley had been his researcher: bright, hard-working, deferential. Now, the younger man headed the programme commissioning arm of the new People's Channel, a consortium of newspaper and financial interests pledged to change the face of UK broadcasting. Pegley's budget, according to the trade press, was in excess of £6 million and in the light of their previous relationship Llewelyn saw no reason why some of it shouldn't come his way. He had the ideas. He had the track record. All Pegley had to do was say yes.

He watched Pegley's eyes straying back to the pad. Beside each of Llewelyn's programme suggestions was a tiny pencil mark. These marks, as far as Llewelyn could judge, were identical. So if Hiroshima wouldn't fly, it was logical to assume that the others were equally doomed. Llewelyn reached for his glass, deciding to try a new tack.

'You're forty-seven years old . . .' he mused, 'you're married, nicely set up, still good-looking in a vulnerable sort of way. You have a son. An only son. He's the apple of your eye. He goes off to Africa. He's working for an aid charity. He's digging wells, piping water, saving lives, all that. This makes you even more proud of him. Then he steps on a land mine. Bang. And suddenly he's dead.'

Llewelyn leaned back, sipping at the Chianti, pleased with himself. Pegley was still winding lengths of spaghetti round his fork. He glanced up. For the first time, he looked genuinely interested.

'Fact or fiction?' He picked a sliver of crab shell from his tongue and laid it carefully on the side of his plate.

'Fact. As of yesterday.'

'Been in the papers? Anyone else know?'

'Not so far.'

'Tell me more.'

Llewelyn took his time, making the most of what little extra he'd managed to prise out of Robbie Cunningham. He'd phoned the young press officer before leaving for the restaurant, telling him they both needed to go back to the dead boy's mother, but Cunningham had refused to play ball. He worked for the Director. Any assignments should come from him. Now, Llewelyn began to mop his plate with a crescent of bread roll.

'Africa's sexy just now . . .' he began. 'Rwanda, Mandela, you name it. But how much do we really know about the place? The way it works? The chaos? The killing? The risks these young guys take?'

Pegley interrupted.

'Which country are we talking about?'

'Angola.'

'Where's that?'

'Exactly.' Llewelyn leaned forward, tapping the table. 'Unknown Angola. The forgotten war. Refugees. Famine. Drought. Disease. A tragedy in the making and no one's even heard of it. Believe me, it's the perfect focus . . .'

'For what?'

'For this film of mine.'

'But what about the woman? Where does she come in?'

'She goes out there. To Angola. To find her son.'

'I thought he was dead.'

'He is. That's the whole point. Another white life. Another sacrifice. For Africa.'

'So she goes out there to bring him back? Is that what you're saying?'

'Yes, but first she has to find him.' Llewelyn had picked up the butter knife now, waving it around, warming to his theme. 'She's blonde. She's pretty. She's middle class. And she's white. But we're with her. Through it all.'

'Who's with her?'

'I am.'

'So you and she go to . . .' Pegley frowned, finding another splinter of crab leg on the end of his finger.

'Angola.'

'Yeah, sure. You and she fly out to find the son?' Llewelyn shook his head.

'The truth,' he said, 'we go out there to find the truth. About what really happened. Then we come home with the body. Film-wise, final cut, we probably start with the funeral, back over here. She lives out in the country, Essex somewhere. There'll be a church, a graveyard, lots of mourners. The mother's obviously there, and the father too.'

'And you?'

'Maybe, maybe not, depends. Could be tacky . . .' Llewelyn paused, his eyes narrowing, trying to visualise the next sequence. 'Flashback might be nice, little dollops of Africa intercut with the funeral, in and out, just a taste, just a glimpse, the filth, the noise, the squalor, the kids, bang, then back to the funeral, bang, close-up coffin, bang, more Africa, bang, coffin into grave, bang, ashes to ashes . . . hey!'

'What?'

'Great title.'

Pegley pushed his plate away, trying to mask his smile. As a researcher, he'd worked for Llewelyn for nearly four years. Despite the bullying and the megalomania, despite the lies and the vanity, he still retained a strange affection for the man. Todd Llewelyn was the all-time survivor. He never took no for an answer. He absolutely refused to lie down. And even now, several years over the hill, he could still come up with a good idea.

'So what would you need,' he said thoughtfully, 'from us?'

'A commission. And a firm go-ahead. We have to move the idea along. Before someone else does.'

Pegley said nothing for a moment. Then he frowned.

'You know it's not absolutely firmed up,' he said, 'this People's thing . . .'

Llewelyn blinked.

'It's not?'

'I don't mean the money. The dosh is there. The backing. We have no problem with any of that. But there's still a tiny glitch on the licensing side. I'm told it's nothing to worry about, but we're still waiting for a go-ahead. Officially, I mean.'

'So where's the problem?'

'You tell me. The engineering boys say it's to do with broadband allocation but that sounds like a cop-out. My own feeling is . . .' He shrugged. 'Take a look at the major backers. We're hardly this government's favourite people.'

Llewelyn nodded. The newspaper group behind the People's Channel was left of centre, a permanent thorn in the Cabinet's side. That's why the concept of People's had raised so much interest in the trade. Serious money chasing the stories no one else would touch. A lone voice in the television wilderness.

Llewelyn eyed the bottle of Chianti. His glass was nearly empty.

'You're telling me you're not commissioning?'

'No, not at all, I'm not telling you that at all. I'm telling you there's a trillionth per cent chance of a problem. And I'm telling you I think it's a great idea. Africa with a human face. Something we can all relate to. Something Joe Soap can get a handle on. What did you have in mind? Length-wise?'

'An hour special.'

'World rights?'

'Absolutely. In return for total funding. Plus I'll throw in a print piece, too. At no extra charge.'

Pegley nodded, agreeing at once, knowing it was a neat idea. Todd Llewelyn and his wandering housewife would sit nicely in a weekend supplement a day or two before transmission. Good promotion. Great profile.

'You'll take a camcorder?' he said. 'Do it yourself?'

Pegley watched the older man thinking about it. Todd Llewelyn came from a world of six-men camera crews and mountains of silver boxes. Using a camera himself was clearly a departure, though already he was visibly warming to the idea. Like most television presenters, Llewelyn had always fantasised about absolute control.

'You want me to shoot it as well?' He nodded. 'Sure, why not?'

News of the fighting around Muengo reached Terra Sancta's Africa desk in Winchester in mid-afternoon. It came not from the charity's Luanda office, which was temporarily unmanned, but from the Geneva headquarters of the International Committee of the Red Cross. Their mission in Muengo was operating from a bunker beneath the house. The city was under intermittent bombardment but so far they'd suffered no casualties. Amongst the aid people they were keeping tabs on was Tom Peterson.

Valerie Askham took the message to the Director personally. He read the telex from Geneva then put it to one side.

'All this fighting . . .' He frowned. 'What about the UN? Are they involved yet?'

Valerie nodded. She'd talked to the UN office in Luanda as soon as the telex had arrived. They had observers on the ground in Muengo and they were trying to arrange a ceasefire to evacuate the aid workers.

'Where on the ground?'

'I'm not sure, exactly. I think they have a bunker of their own.'

'So how are they doing this? How are they going about it?'

'I'm afraid I don't know. Normally they—'

The Director broke in. He hadn't slept well and it showed.

'Do they know about Jordan? The problems Peterson's having? Trying to get the wretched boy out?'

'Yes, I imagine they do.'

'Then why on earth . . .' He shook his head, turning away, petulant, exhausted, and Valerie began to explain the situation afresh. War had swamped Muengo. People were probably dying in their hundreds. The remains of a dead British aid worker would count for precious little.

'I know that, I know, but it makes no difference. We need to tie this thing up. It's messy. And extremely unpleasant.'

Valerie nodded, falling silent. Robbie Cunningham had released the news of James Jordan's death that morning but so far reaction from the media had been muted. A couple of calls from the broadcast organisations. A request for more details from the *Guardian*. Yet in the absence of awkward questions, the Director seemed to be generating fresh tensions of his own. She'd seen him like this before, back in the days when they'd been fellow academics at the Institute for International Affairs. Then, the notion of putting away the books, of founding a new charity and trying to do something practical in the Third World, had seemed beyond reproach. Now, though, she wasn't so sure.

The Director was back at his desk, tugging at an elastic band.

'What did you think of our Mr Llewelyn? Last night?'

Valerie pursed her lips. After the meeting, the three of them had driven into Winchester for a meal. Llewelyn had spent most of the time talking about past triumphs, disappearing abruptly at ten to catch the last train back to London.

'I'm not sure I like him,' she said carefully.

'Is that strictly relevant?'

'Probably not.'

The Director was still plucking at the elastic band. Eventually he returned it to the mug where he kept his pens.

'He's just come up with a proposal.' He gestured at the telephone. 'I find it extremely attractive, given the odd . . .' he smiled for the first time, '. . . tweak.'

It was nearly dusk by the time Molly Jordan got to the marina. The last of the sunshine was spilling over the marshlands to the west and in the windless chill the lines of moored yachts rode easily alongside the sturdy wooden pontoons. According to Patrick, Giles had given work a miss. Rather than face more post-mortems at Lloyd's, he'd decided to take the day off. When Patrick had first told her, she'd stared at him in disbelief. Their son dead. Their lives ruined. And Giles had gone for a sail. Yet the more she thought about it, and the more she listened to Patrick, the more sense it made. Life had backed Giles into a corner. Just now, the yacht was probably his only real escape.

Molly parked the car beside her husband's Rover in the empty members' compound and sat behind the wheel for a moment, still uncertain whether driving across was such a good idea. The yacht had always been Giles's territory, the equivalent – she supposed – to the new-found freedom of her morning run. In the summer, it was true, she occasionally joined him for weekend cruises up the coast towards Aldeburgh and Southwold, and much earlier, when James had still been living at home, they'd all made the crossing to Belgium. But even then there'd been an unspoken understanding that this was Giles's invitation, Giles's space. *Molly Jay*, it was plain, had always been precious to him. God knows how he'd manage to cope without it.

Molly left the car, pulling her coat around her and mounting the steps to the wooden boardwalk that ran the length of the marina. Giles had been one of the earliest owners to sign up, securing himself a berth on the long seaward pontoon. She could see the yacht already, tucked in amongst a line of other craft. It was a Nicholson 35, low, graceful lines, GRP and teak construction, beautifully maintained. It hadn't been cheap, and Giles had agonised for weeks about spending the money, but the late eighties had marked the floodtide of the Thatcher boom and it had been at Molly's insistence that he'd finally taken the plunge. He worked jolly hard. He owed himself a pat on the back, a little present for weekends. He was getting just a touch old for dinghy racing. Why not invest in the real thing?

Closer now, Molly shaded her eyes against the livid sunset, beginning to wonder whether Giles had, after all, been to sea. The mainsail on the yacht was lashed down and the decks were bare of the clutter that normally signalled a recent outing. She paused a moment, looking down at the green skirt of algae on the waterline, struck by another thought. For the first time ever, Giles hadn't bothered about defouling *Molly Jay*'s hull. At the end of every season, without fail, the yacht was always lifted onto dryland and chocked in a wooden cradle. Removing the summer's growth of underwater weed took the best part of a month, Giles disappearing at weekends with his bucket of chemicals and his scrubbing brush. This ritual had become a family joke, Giles obsessed by the state of *Molly*'s bottom, but this year – for whatever reason – the boat was still in the water. Maybe he's just deferred it, Molly thought. Or maybe there's some other reason.

She stepped aboard, feeling the yacht moving beneath her. Clambering down into the well of the cockpit, she called Giles's name. The hatch to the cabin was open and she could see a light on inside. She heard a movement, then Giles's face appeared at the open hatch. To her relief, he was smiling. His hair was everywhere and he was wearing a shapeless old guernsey she'd given him years back. He looked almost normal.

'Darling . . .' he reached up and kissed her, 'just in time for tea.'

Molly climbed down into the cabin. Giles had the little heater on. With the curtains pulled and the kettle singing on the calor gas stove, the boat felt warm and snug. No wonder he'd preferred this, she thought, to another day of humiliation at the office. Molly found a perch on the cluttered banquette behind the table, undoing the buttons on her coat while Giles rummaged through a cupboard, looking for tea-bags.

'Patrick OK?' he said.

'He was fine. He took me to lunch.'

'Anywhere nice?'

Molly named a hotel on Frinton's seafront. Giles whistled.

'Lucky thing.'

He found the tea-bags at last and scalded the battered metal teapot with boiling water. Molly watched him, curious now at this latest transformation. The stranger she'd spent the night with seemed to have become yet a third person: relaxed, benign, even light-hearted. She felt herself losing track again, a sense of bewilderment spiced with a certain irritation.

'We talked about what's happened, the money and everything,' she said quietly. 'I'd no idea it was so bad.'

Giles looked round, the steaming teapot wrapped in a towel. For the first time Molly noticed the oil on his hands.

'It's terrible . . .' he was saying, 'I'm afraid it couldn't be worse.'

'But why didn't you tell me? Am I allowed to ask?'

'Of course.'

Giles put the teapot to one side and then turned towards her again, leaning back against the tiny sink. He was a tall man and the cabin roof made him stoop.

'Well?'

Molly tried to warm the question with a smile. The last thing she wanted was another scene, more tears. Better this Giles than the chilly, thin-lipped wreck she'd run home to only a day ago. Giles was looking at his shoes.

'I couldn't,' he said simply. 'I just couldn't tell you. I tried, believe me. Several times, I almost did it. I used to sit on the train, trying to work out ways of saying it. But somehow . . .' he shrugged, 'it never happened.'

'Until James died.'

'Yes, of course, James . . .' he frowned, 'that really put it in perspective.'

She looked at him a moment, astonished at his tone of voice. It was as if James had been dead a month, a fact of life, just one of those things, already discounted.

'What do you mean?' she asked.

'Well. . . .' he glanced up at her for the first time, 'something like that happens, God almighty, you don't start worrying about the mortgage.'

Molly looked away, pulling her coat around her, anger this time, not simply irritation.

'So it helped, really,' she said at last. 'Got you off the hook.'

'I'm not with you.'

'James dying. Made you realise what really matters.'

They looked at each other for a moment then Giles busied himself with the teapot, decanting UHT milk into tupperware mugs. Without thinking, Molly began to clear a space on the table. The table was covered by a nautical chart. The corners of the chart were weighed down with pots of jam and honey and there was a pile of wooden shavings where Giles had been sharpening a pencil. Molly tidied the shavings into an ashtray, glancing at the chart as she did so. It showed the area around the Cherbourg peninsula, a thin pencilled line dog-legging down towards the Channel Islands. Molly began to roll up the map. As Giles put the mugs on the empty table she noticed that his hands were shaking.

'You'll miss all this,' she said, securing the map with an elastic band.

'Miss all what?'

'The boat.' She looked him in the eye as he settled behind the table. 'Being able to get away at weekends.'

'Yes, I suppose I will.' He nodded matter-of-factly. 'My fault though. No one else's.'

Molly reached for the tea. The mug was scalding hot.

'Patrick says it's curtains. He says we'll have to sell everything. More or less.'

'Except the house.'

'Yes. He mentioned that. Apparently we're allowed to stay. Until we die.'

'Yes.'

'Then it goes to Lloyd's.'

'Yes.'

'Along with everything else.'

'I'm afraid so.'

Molly fell silent for a moment, her hands around the mug. Giles was gazing across at the brass barometer, fixed to the bulkhead. The arrow was pointing to 'Unsettled'.

'Just as well then . . .' she said after a while.

'I'm sorry?'

'Just as well. I was thinking about James. It would have been nice to have left him something, you know, like most parents do. No point now though, eh?'

Molly broke off, not wanting to push the thought any further, ashamed at how easily she'd let the bitterness overcome her. Yesterday, in church, she'd vowed to stay strong, to be the one who held it all together. Yet here she was, barely twenty-four hours later, letting it get the better of her. Maybe the psychologists were right. Women really were the weaker sex. She offered Giles a bright smile.

'I came across to find out how you are,' she said, 'how you're coping. I was worried.'

'Yes, of course . . .' He nodded at once. 'I'm sorry to have been so . . . you know . . . yesterday . . . I'm not sure exactly what happened. To tell you the truth, I can barely remember any of it.'

'You were very upset, my love.' She reached for his hand. 'There's no need to apologise.'

'Yes, but . . .' he ducked his head, shamefaced, 'I wasn't much use, was I?'

'No, but neither of us were very brave.' She smiled at him. 'Patrick's right. We just have to get on with it. There's nothing else we can do.'

He nodded, listening to her, letting the conversation die. Driving across, she'd vowed to try and establish some kind of timetable, what they'd have to do and when, but already she knew it wouldn't be easy. It was as if Giles had shuffled out of the room they called their life. He was as unreachable now as he'd been yesterday, walling himself off behind a series of polite evasions.

'More tea?'

'No thanks.' She covered the mug with her hand. 'I was hoping we might talk. About what happens next. How long do we have? Before they send in the bailiffs?'

'It won't come to that.'

'It won't?'

'No,' he shook his head, 'not if we're sensible.'

'What does that mean?'

'Well . . .' he was frowning now, 'we have to draw up some kind of schedule. Assets. Things we own. They form part of the estate. Once they're realised, the money goes to—'

'Realised?'

'Sold. Then there's another list. Things we're allowed to keep. There are rules about this, procedures. It's pretty straightforward. We're not the first people to go bankrupt. Not by any means.'

'I see.' Molly nodded, looking at the neat row of charts,

carefully stacked away, each of them labelled. Southern North Sea. Eastern Channel. Western Channel. 'So do you think it was worth it?' she asked. 'In the end?'

'What?'

'Lloyd's. Investing. Gambling. Whatever it is we did.'

'I don't know.' Giles shrugged. 'I suppose it served its purpose. James got educated—' He broke off, turning away, and Molly realised after all how frail this recovery of his had been, how a single word could wreck it all. James. Gone. She got up, manoeuvring clumsily around the table. Boats were all the same. Awkward angles everywhere. She put her arms around him, letting him bury his head in the folds of her coat. The soft cashmere muffled his voice but she caught the gist of it.

'I'm sorry . . .' he seemed to be saying, '. . . I'm truly sorry.'

The second night in the bunker was worse than the first.

McFaul lay on the sleeping-bag, trying to keep track of the rise and fall of the bombardment. During the day, the mortars had been largely silent and from time to time there'd come the shattering roar of government MiG-23 fighter-bombers flying ground-attack missions from Catumbela, an air force base on the coast. The jets flew in pairs, silver fish that swooped low over the bush to drop their bombs and then thundered away in near-vertical climbs, the favoured tactic against the rumoured *Stinger* missiles. McFaul had plenty of doubts about the military effectiveness of the MiGs but the noise alone was a comfort, evidence that someone out there cared. After dark, though, the initiative returned to the rebels, and from somewhere they seemed to have laid hands on more kit. As well as the crump of the big 120-mm mortars, McFaul recognised the sharper, flatter bark of smaller pieces, 81 mm and 60 mm. They're getting closer, he thought, shrinking the range, pulling the noose ever tighter around the battered city. Last time anyone tried to count, there'd been upwards of 60,000 *deslocados*, displaced people, in Muengo. Add the original population, at least the same again, and you're looking at a lot of blood.

McFaul got to his feet, easing the stiffness in his limbs. The concrete on the floor had been laid in a hurry and the thin down sleeping-bag did little to mattress the surface ridges. At night, like now, the bunker was full, a dozen or so people, all European. Most of them were trying to sleep, long shapes in the gloom barely penetrated by the single overhead light bulb. Power in the bunker came from a generator upstairs. The Swiss engineers had wisely installed a brand new Honda and they'd evidently left the Red Cross people with a couple of months' supply of fuel. McFaul could hear the generator now, a low purring overhead. Since he'd been in the bunker, it had never faltered.

At the far side of the bunker, beside a flight of wooden steps that disappeared into the house, was the communications set-up: a big HF radio on a steel desk and a couple of Motorolas for local use. All day, one of the Red Cross people had been monitoring conversations between the UN representative in Muengo and the UNITA commander out in the bush. The latter called himself Colonel Katilo. Katilo was Ovimbundu for 'will not run', one of the favoured *noms de guerre*. With Katilo, the UN rep had been trying to broker a ceasefire long enough to organise the safe evacuation of the aid community. In all, according to the Red Cross, there were twenty-eight aid workers in Muengo, most of whom were under orders from their parent organisations to leave. Leaving, though, was difficult. Beyond UNITA lines, mines had made the roads impassable in every direction and without a ceasefire no pilot would dream of taking his aircraft within fifty miles of the city's crumbling airstrip.

McFaul limped between the bodies on the floor and paused beside the radio. The duty Red Cross official was a greying Swiss called François who'd once worked in a Geneva bank. He and McFaul shared the same sense of humour, a wry assumption that making plans in Africa was an act of the purest optimism, and that if anything could go wrong then it surely would. The Swiss glanced up, stifling a yawn. Then he gestured at the HF set, thin far-away voices crackling through the ether, part of someone else's conversation.

'Luanda,' he said simply. 'They wanted an update earlier.'

'What did you tell them?'

'I told them it was like last night. Except worse.'

'And what did they say?'

'Nothing.'

McFaul nodded. The civil war was like a bush fire, smouldering for months on end then suddenly erupting at local flashpoints, stirred by unfathomable political currents. Wherever the rebels or the government troops sensed an advantage, then the fighting would begin again. The slaughter would go on for weeks and weeks until both sides were either bored or exhausted, and the last item on any commander's list was the welfare of the local people. They'd long since ceased to matter, helpless victims of a catastrophe they neither wanted not understood.

A call sign came through on one of the Motorolas and McFaul recognised the rich bass voice of the local UN rep, Fernando, a middle-aged white from Mozambique. Evidently he was still trying to sell a ceasefire to Colonel Katilo, though negotiations appeared to have stalled.

McFaul reached across, dipping a Styrofoam cup into the big 40-gallon drum of tepid water that would supply the bunker until further notice. The water was already rationed, seven cups per day per person, and McFaul knew the ration would be reduced the longer the siege went on. It was hot underground, a stuffy, airless atmosphere that smelled of damp earth and unwashed bodies. From time to time, people would leave to use one of the two lavatories upstairs, but the nearest of these was already blocked and the stench seeped in as soon as the door was opened at the top of the stairs.

François, the Swiss, was still bent to the desk, scribbling on a pad. McFaul watched him, unable to keep up with the stream of Portuguese from the Motorola. Eventually, François leaned back, laying down his pen. McFaul offered him the Styrofoam cup.

'Well?' he said.

The Swiss sipped at the cup, ever thoughtful. Finally, he shrugged.

'Usual problem,' he said. 'Both sides want to handle the evacuation, take the credit.'

'Play the white man?'

'*Tout à fait.*' He glanced up, acknowledging the dig with a tired smile. 'Which means, I guess, another couple of days.'

'Minimum.'

He nodded.

'Exactly.'

'And Geneva? New York?' McFaul gestured at the big HF set. 'You talk to them at all?'

'Only once. To Geneva. They say they're getting everything they need through Luanda.'

'Anything else?'

'Yeah,' he looked up again, a grin this time, 'they told me the weather's awful. Rain. Snow. Big falls in the mountains.'

Another conversation crackled into life on the Motorola and McFaul turned away. He had a small Sony radio of his own and he'd been listening to the BBC World Service, curious to know whether this latest outbreak of insanity in Muengo would feature on the news from Bush House. Inevitably it didn't, though a couple of bulletins had mentioned the death of a young British aid worker. On neither occasion was James Jordan named, though it was plain that it couldn't have been anyone else. McFaul returned to his space by the steps to the garden, musing on the irony. Out in the darkness, hundreds of local people were probably dying yet they didn't rate even a mention. To a world hungry for bigger, starker, simpler tragedies, Angola remained a mystery, an unlanced boil on the face of Africa. The politics were complex. No one seemed to speak English. The world's press had better things to do.

McFaul lay down again, careful not to disturb the sleeping

shape beside him. Off and on, he'd been with Bennie for three years now, and the two of them shared a rapport that had been cemented in the minefields: Kuwait first, and then – after McFaul's convalescence – the six difficult months they'd endured in the madness of Afghanistan. It was there that McFaul had first put it all together – the mines, the money, the victims – and it was there that he'd first truly understood the way the scam worked. The guys in the factories making the stuff and the guys in the suits flogging it like sweets, Dolly Mixtures from the First World, enough cheap high explosive to lasso an entire society and choke it half to death.

McFaul shuddered, all too aware of the ache in his own leg, the price his own flesh had paid. In a curious way, though, none of that had mattered. Not until Afghanistan, not until he'd been up in the high pastures, up beyond Jaji. He'd found the little Afghan goat herd quite by accident, his body curled amongst the rocks. The trail of bloodstains, already brown, led up the mountain to the scorchmarks on the path where he'd lost his foot.

The mine had been Russian, probably one of the little PFM-Is, and the boy had finally died from shock, and exposure, and loss of blood, in sight of his home village in the valley below. Another statistic for the men in the suits. Another tiny triumph for the guys who'd sell you area denial. Later, McFaul had met the family, learned the boy's name, pledged himself to take whatever small revenge he could. The spilling of blood – his own, Mohammed's – carried certain responsibilities. And one day, somehow, he knew he'd repay a little of the pain.

One of the big 120-mm mortars fell nearby, a deafening blast that rocked the building overhead. For a moment or two the generator faltered, dimming the light even more, and McFaul felt a movement beside him. Bennie was sitting upright, staring at the wall opposite. McFaul laid a hand on his arm. Bennie looked at him.

'Boss?'

'It's OK, mate. Fucker missed.'

Bennie nodded, sleep compounding his confusion. Then he rubbed his eyes.

'Meant to tell you,' he mumbled.

'What?'

'That bird from MSF. Christianne. The nurse. She was looking for you earlier. Wanted a word.'

'What about?'

'Dunno.' He yawned, lying down again. 'Some kind of favour, I think.'

CHAPTER THREE

Molly awoke in the middle of the night, uncertain for a moment exactly where she was. She'd been dreaming about James. He was kneeling by some kind of pond or pool. It was very hot. The water was a strange colour, almost green, and he kept dipping his hands in it, cupping the liquid, offering it to her the way he'd sometimes come into the kitchen as a child, carrying trophies from the garden. His expression was childlike, too, the purest delight. I did this, he seemed to be telling her. Mine. My efforts. All my own work.

Molly peered into the darkness, at last recognising the noise at the window. Since they'd gone to bed the wind had got up and now it was raining hard, the kind of rain that drove at the cottage across the bare, flat fields. One of the gutters beneath the big lime tree had become blocked with leaves and she could hear the water spilling over, splashing onto the flagstones below. She thought of James again by his pond, and she eased carefully out of bed, knowing that there was no possibility of getting back to sleep.

Giles began to stir and for a moment she thought she'd woken him up. Then he grunted and rolled over and his breathing resumed the slow, steady rhythm that signalled deep sleep. They'd driven home in convoy from the marina. She'd prepared a simple supper and they'd gone to bed early, closer than they'd been for months. They'd even made love, tender, consolatory, Molly letting him make the running, fitting herself to him, responding gladly to his urgent need to please her. Afterwards, she'd told him how much she loved him, how much he mattered to her, sealing his lips with a single moistened fingertip. No more apologies, she'd whispered. No more tears.

Downstairs, wrapped in Giles's dressing gown, she plugged in the electric fire and made herself a pot of tea. James's letters she kept in the chest of drawers beside the telephone. She pulled them out, a biggish bundle tucked into a Marks & Spencer plastic bag. Since Sunday, she'd wanted to read them again, to rejoin her son, but somehow there'd never been the time nor the space. With the wind howling around the cottage and the rest of the world asleep, now seemed the perfect moment.

She knelt in front of the fire and spread the letters around her. To her astonishment, James had written regularly, more than a dozen letters in all, and although the blue airmail envelopes had been arriving less frequently of late, each one still contained at least six pages of the awkward, backward-sloping scrawl that was unmistakably his. She reached for one of the letters now, a random choice, remembering the night she and Giles had driven him up to the airport. Even in the car, his excitement had been palpable, an almost physical thing. After three diligent years working for the local authority – a junior surveyor's job in the Public Works department – he was at last breaking free and getting his hands on something that mattered. The night-school courses had paid off. He had the skills that Africa wanted. He'd even managed to persuade Terra Sancta to bend the rules about minimum age qualification and let him get out there early.

At Heathrow, she and Giles had waved goodbye beside the queue for International Departures. He'd filed past the man who checked the tickets and he'd paused beside the big smoked-glass doors that led into the security area, glancing briefly back, raising a hand, nonchalant as ever. He'd been wearing jeans and his favourite hooped rugby-style shirt. Over his shoulder, he'd carried the bag Giles had given him as a going-away present.

With his day-old crew cut and his carefree grin, he'd looked about twelve.

Molly blinked. The letter on her lap had dissolved into a blur. She frowned, helping herself to tea, drawing Giles's dressing gown more tightly around her. James and Africa, she told herself, had been made for each other. The fact that the place had also killed him was simply unfortunate. Given the opportunity again – six months in Angola, the chance to run his own programme, make his own decisions – she was sure he'd be back at the airport in a flash, offering them a final wave, turning on his heel and disappearing behind those hideous smoked-glass doors.

She started the letter afresh. It had come from Muengo and it was dated early October. That meant he'd been in the place nearly a month. She turned the page, surprised again at how quickly he'd found his feet, impressed by the life he'd managed to make for himself. James had always hated depending on other people. Wherever he'd gone, he always seemed to have existed in a kind of bubble, insulated from the world outside. Nothing fazed him. Very little upset him. As long as he had his Walkman and his tapes and something half-decent to eat and drink, then he simply got on with the task in hand, not thinking too hard about other people, not thinking too much about anything but the next day's schedule. In one sense it was a blessing, this tunnel vision of his, and in this respect he was a bit like Giles: solid, cheerful, thick-skinned to the point of arrogance. Like father like son, she thought ruefully, turning another page. Whether it was pollution risks in New Jersey or land mines in Angola, there simply wouldn't be a problem.

A phrase caught her eye, making her smile. James's first task in Muengo involved laying on a water supply from the river. To do this he'd had to build something called an infiltration gallery. Molly hadn't a clue what this might be but James had penned a detailed description, complete with diagrams. First he dug a hole near the river. Then he half-filled it with fragments of stone. Then he waited while the river found its way through the soil and into the hole. Once the hole was full, wrote James, it was dead simple to get the stuff away to a storage tank. All you'd need was a pump and a length of pipe and a tank at the other end. She looked at the phrase again, 'dead simple', hearing him saying it, picturing the expression on his face as he did so, impatient, even slightly amused. The world of practical challenges – of nuts and bolts and flanges and grommets – had never held any fears for James. On the contrary, it had made him the person he'd become. Life, he'd recently told her, was a bit like his first motor bike. Stick the bits together in the right order, and it'll probably work.

She reached for another letter, a week or so later, looking for a particular photo. True to form, James's hole by the river had been a triumph. Nearby, on a little mound of spoil, he'd installed a pump and the photo had recorded the moment when the pump had first spluttered into action. She found the photo at last, the kids crowding around the spout of water, their faces twisted up towards the camera, their sleek black bodies already soaking wet. The closest child was a little girl. The bright red shirt she was wearing was at least three sizes too big, hanging comically around her ankles, but the huge grin on her face told Molly everything she needed to know about what her son was doing in Africa. She turned the photo over. On the back, in careful capitals, James had written 'MARIA'S FIRST SHOWER – FRIENDS FOR LIFE!!'

Molly read through the letters, still not bothering to sort them into any kind of order, happy to dip into this new life James had led. There'd been moments of special achievement, duly recorded and passed on. To dig the trench for the water pipes, he'd managed to locate an excavator, a big yellow digger that featured in at least four photos. The digger and the driver had cost Terra Sancta $400 a day but he'd saved weeks of manual labour and got the water to the distribution point in record time. This had won James what he called 'a herogram'

from Terra Sancta's regional office, and in the letter he'd repro-
duced the text in full. 'Terrific news about Stage One. Expect
your pipeline in Luanda soonest. Press on with the good work.'

This pat on the back had obviously pleased James no end but
there'd been bleaker moments, too. James, typically, hadn't made
much of these but there'd clearly been friction in Muengo with
someone on the military side. This person, whoever he was,
seemed to have responsibility for clearing the minefields. One of
his jobs was to brief newcomers on what to look out for, where
not to go, and James had evidently been less than receptive.
'Bloke's got a problem,' he'd written, 'I think he thinks we're all
cretins. Don't do this. Don't do that. Don't do the other. I told
him he ought to try local government. Right up his street!' Molly
pondered the likely exchange. Mines had never meant anything
to her but for the last forty-eight hours she'd thought of little
else. Big mines. Small mines. Green mines. Blue mines. Even
mines with little cartoon faces that rose from the soil and ghosted
through her dreams. In reality, she hadn't a clue what they did,
how they worked, and whenever James had mentioned them he'd
never gone into detail. It seemed they were just there, semi-
permanent, part of the landscape, as inescapable as the weather
or the passage of the seasons. It was obvious now that James
should have listened to the man in Muengo, but it was typical
that he hadn't. James, like his father, always knew best.

Molly looked up, hearing the wind tugging at a loose tile
on the garage roof, wondering how on earth she was going to
get to Angola. Reading his letters again had given her glimpses
of his life out there, scenes from a film she'd only half-seen.
What she needed now was the rest of the story, the whole plot.
To understand exactly what had happened – the friendships he'd
formed, the work he'd done – would be to share with him those
last few weeks of his life. As a mother, it was surely the least she
owed herself.

Her eye returned to the last of the letters. James had been
writing about a girl he'd met, a French nurse called Christianne.

As ever, he'd included a photo. The girl had a soft, oval face dusted with freckles and framed by a mass of auburn curls. Her head was tilted slightly to one side and her smile reminded Molly of moments from her own youth. It spoke of the excitement of a new relationship, of possibilities yet unexplored. It was very James to have found someone so striking and from his letter he sounded more than keen. Christianne, it seemed, spoke perfect English. She worked for an organisation called Médecins Sans Frontières. There were several other girls with her, and where they lived they had crates and crates of incredibly classy white wine. The girls were evidently planning a party. They'd asked James to fix up the music. At the end of the letter, he was musing aloud about getting Christianne to England one day. Then, typically, something else had occurred to him. 'Help,' he'd written, 'post goes in the morning and I haven't sorted out the blokes' rice rations. Eduardo'll go bananas. Got to rush. *Boa noite.*'

Molly folded the letter and reached for the switch on the electric fire. Only last week, she'd gone to a bookshop and looked up the phrase. It was Portuguese. It meant 'good night'.

Robbie Cunningham was still in bed unwrapping his birthday presents when the phone rang. Liz fetched the mobile from the kitchen. The alarm clock on the bedside table read 07.54.

'Hello?'

'Westerby here. Do you have a pen?'

Robbie wedged the mobile to his ear, reaching down for his satchel, wondering why on earth the Director should be phoning so early. At the Terra Sancta headquarters in Winchester, he still kept university hours, turning up at his desk around ten. Now he sounded brisk, even excited.

'Colchester,' he was saying, 'you know the town at all?'

'Yes. We went that way on Sunday. *En route* to the Jordans' place.'

'Good. There's a hotel in the High Street. The Blue Boar. Got that?'

Robbie grunted an affirmative, scribbling down the name. The Director was talking about Llewelyn. Apparently he'd be waiting in the lounge bar at half-past twelve. Robbie was to meet him there.

'Why?'

'I want you to do the introductions.'

'Who with?'

'Mrs Jordan. I phoned her five minutes ago. I said you'd pick her up and take her to lunch. She'll be ready by twelve. Apparently it's only half an hour from her place.'

Robbie frowned. Llewelyn had been on to him twice in the last twenty-four hours, trying to get him to arrange a meet with James Jordan's mother, but both times Robbie had said he was too busy. Now, it seemed he had no choice.

'But why?' he said again. 'Why the meeting?'

'We're taking her to Angola.'

'Who's taking her?'

'You are. With Todd Llewelyn.'

'But I thought we agreed that—'

Robbie broke off, unable to interrupt the Director's flow. Llewelyn, he said, had been talking to some of his media contacts. The new People's Channel were mounting a major series about the Third World. They were looking for good stories at what Llewelyn called 'the sharp end'. They wanted new angles, some fresh way of establishing the realities of the aid business. James Jordan, it seemed, had caught their imagination.

'But he's dead,' Robbie pointed out.

'Exactly. It's a perfect focus. For them and for us.'

'Who says?'

'Todd. He's extremely bullish. We've been discussing our profile and he thinks this could be the breakthrough. He's promising an hour of national television. He understands our reservations, naturally, but he says we're looking a gift horse in the mouth and I must say I agree. Apart from anything else, we can't afford to be left out of this thing. A series without us would be a disaster. We'd disappear without trace.'

'But the boy's dead,' Robbie said again. 'As far as I know, he wandered into a minefield and got himself killed. Is that something we want to be part of? Sending young kids to their graves?'

There was a brief silence. Then the Director was back again. He was beginning to sound irritated.

'You're supposed to understand the importance of all this,' he said. 'It's part of your job description, public relations.'

'This isn't PR,' Robbie said at once. 'PR's something you can control, or at least try to. This could go anywhere. Todd Llewelyn's a journalist. He doesn't work for us.'

'Untrue. He's on a modest retainer.'

'Enough to buy him? Body and soul?' Robbie broke off, knowing that he'd gone too far. Arguing about concepts like PR was one thing. Questioning the Director's personal judgement was quite another. At this rate he'd be celebrating the first day of his twenty-sixth year by looking for a new job. He began to apologise but the Director broke in again.

'No, you're right,' he said. 'Absolutely right.'

'I am?'

'Yes. Of course there are dangers. Of course we have to be careful. That's why I want you there. Llewelyn still has a big following and I have no doubt that he can do us a great deal of good. But we have to keep an eye on him. He can be rather . . . ah . . . tabloid. Do you follow me?'

Robbie nodded, depressed already. Over the years, he'd kept half an eye on Todd Llewelyn's TV career, the kind of line he took, his fascination with trauma and personal tragedy. In Robbie's opinion, the man was an animal, a predator, interested only in the red meat of other people's suffering.

'You want me to mind him? Is that it?'

'Yes, exactly. I have his word that he won't embarrass us. He knows about our wind-down strategy in Angola and he's promised to steer well clear. In any case, I doubt whether you'll be getting much further than Luanda. Muengo's under siege, as you know.'

'So what happens to the boy's body?'

'Peterson came through during the night. He's expecting a ceasefire. He'll fly the body out.' He paused. 'I'm sure Luanda will give Todd everything he needs. I've told him you know the place inside out. He's after a bit of local colour. You know the way these people work.'

Robbie said nothing, thinking about the Angolan capital. In Luanda, local colour was a polite phrase for civic breakdown: pot-holed roads, 1,000 per cent inflation, and mountains of rotting garbage. He thought of Mrs Jordan, the impact the place would make on her. To cope with all that, she'd have to be very strong indeed.

The Director was talking about the small print now, how long the trip should last, whether or not to invite her husband, and Robbie reached for his pad again, jotting down the details. As he did so, Liz appeared from the kitchen with a tiny birthday cake. On top was a single candle. She beamed at him, making space for herself on the edge of the bed, and he blew her a kiss as the Director completed his brief. Llewelyn's passport was already at the Angolan embassy, awaiting a visa stamp. Robbie was to collect Mrs Jordan's and drive it up there after lunch. Three seats had been booked on a Sabena flight out of Brussels late tomorrow night.

'Who's paying for all this?' Robbie asked, still eyeing the cake.

'We are, for the time being. But I understand the television people will be reimbursing us.'

'And Mrs Jordan? Has she said yes?'

The Director made a strange throaty noise on the line. It might have been a chuckle.

'No,' he said. 'I thought the invitation might be best coming from you. You've met her. You've got the relationship. Give me a ring this afternoon. Tell me how it went.'

*

McFaul found Christianne at the house rented by Médecins Sans Frontières. So far, the second morning of the siege had been as peaceful as the first, the rebel mortars silent since day-break, fearful of giving their positions away to the marauding government MiG-23s. McFaul had taken advantage of the lull, walking the mile and a half from the Red Cross bunker to Domingos's house to make sure the little Angolan and his family had survived the night intact. He'd found them gathered round a table in the room they used as a kitchen, sharing a bowl of cassava. No mortar bomb had fallen closer than a couple of hundred metres away but none of the kids had slept at all and Domingos's wife was beginning to fret about water supplies.

Earlier in the year, McFaul had helped Domingos build a collection tank in a recess behind the house, but the rains had yet to arrive and the tank was nearly empty. McFaul had taken a look at the tank himself, and when he left he'd promised to come back with a couple of the big plastic jerrycans they kept at the schoolhouse. Ten extra gallons wouldn't keep the family going for ever, but it would save Domingos and his wife the dangerous trek to the riverbank to replenish supplies.

Already, law and order was breaking down within Muengo. There were rumours of fifth columnists inside the city, UNITA sympathisers in touch with the soldiers in the bush, feeding them information, giving them targets. Indeed, just after day-break, there'd been several outbursts of small-arms fire in the area around the cathedral, evidence of summary executions. Under siege, government troops didn't bother too much about the rules of evidence. Suspicion and hearsay were quite enough to earn you a bullet in the head.

Christianne was in bed when McFaul knocked on the door. MSF occupied a modest one-storey colonial house about a quarter of a mile from the hospital. By Muengo standards, it seemed to have suffered little in the war. The stucco walls and the terracotta roof were still intact, and visible damage was limited to the torn-off branches of the acacia tree in the wilderness of parched brown weeds that had once been the garden.

McFaul stood outside in the sunshine, waiting for the door to open. Already, at ten in the morning, it was hot. At last came the scrape of a key turning in the lock and Christianne was standing in the shadowed hall, her toes curling on the cool tiles. She peered into the bright sunlight, one hand over her eyes.

'I wake you up?'

She recognised McFaul at once and invited him in, checking the street in both directions before shutting the door again. McFaul heard the key turning behind him. At the back of the house was a kitchen, a long, bare room with four chairs set around a table. The table was littered with the remains of a recent meal, a bowl of tinned fish and rice draped in muslin to protect it from the flies. At the far end of the room there was a collapsible camping stove and a couple of Butagaz bottles. Beside the stove was a half-open door, and in the next room McFaul could see a freezer chest similar to the one they had at the schoolhouse.

McFaul sank into a chair while Christianne took a mug from the table. She peered into it, moistening a finger and running it around the inside of the rim. Then she went to the sink. The sink was full of water. She half-filled the mug and offered it to McFaul. McFaul shook his head, his eyes going to a poster on the wall. Pink Floyd were playing the Paris Odeon. Tickets started at 95 francs.

'How are you?' he asked at length. 'Coping OK?'

Christianne shrugged, the mug to her lips. She was a strong-looking girl, broad-shouldered, well-made, with a blaze of auburn curls. She was cheerful and down-to-earth and McFaul had liked her from the start. Now, she was barelegged, wearing some kind of rugby shirt over a pair of knickers. The shirt had red and blue hoops, and the size of the garment told McFaul that it must have belonged to Jordan. She's probably got a whole drawerful, he thought, enough to last her for years. Christianne was telling him about the hospital now. She'd been working there eighteen hours a day. The building had been hit twice during the night, two mortar bombs within the same half-hour, and the second had demolished the corridor where they kept the post-operative patients. She emptied the mug, shaking her head. Eight successful operations, eight patients on the mend, a whole night's work. Gone.

McFaul nodded, toying with the stump of a candle.

'I meant you,' he said. 'How are you coping?'

'At the hospital, you mean?'

'No, inside . . .' He shrugged. 'The other night. Your English friend.'

'Ah . . .' Christianne nodded, understanding the question at last. McFaul's head-to-heads with James Jordan had been the talk of the Muengo aid community and McFaul had never bothered to hide his contempt for the boy. But the night he'd driven out to the minefield, the night James had died, he'd put all that aside. Her friend was dead. Her friend had mattered to her. She therefore deserved a little attention, a little sympathy, a little respect. Twice, since then, McFaul had called round to check how she was, missing her on both occasions, but word of his concern had got back to her and when she'd finally needed help she'd known at once where to turn.

She looked at the empty mug a moment then put it back on the table.

'These bombs at the hospital . . .' she said, 'the other one hit the generator.'

'No power?'

'No. We've got candles but there's no power for the . . . machinery . . . *on comprend*?' She paused, biting her lip, and McFaul sensed at once what was coming.

'You mean the fridges?'

She nodded.

'Fridge. There's only one. A big thing, very old, very noisy.'

'I see. You're telling me . . .'

She nodded again.

'James is there. Still in your bag, the one you brought . . .' She began to wind a curl of hair around her forefinger, letting the sentence expire. Then she sat down opposite McFaul, looking him in the eye. 'I know you and James weren't such great friends but he still matters to me. Very much. He wasn't the person you thought he was. He could be loud, and silly, *bien sûr*, but underneath he was a child. He had a good heart, he was a good man . . .'

'And you . . .?'

'I loved him.' She let the coil of hair go free, her eyes never leaving McFaul's face.

McFaul nodded. He had little taste for scenes like these.

'So where is he now?' he said.

'Still in the hospital. Still in the fridge. But soon . . .' She pulled a face. 'It's like a butcher's shop in there.'

McFaul was looking out of the window now, at the tangle of weeds in the garden.

'So what next?' he said at last. 'You want me to bury him?'

'No.' She shook her head. 'When we were together, before the accident, he made me promise him something. If anything happened, he wanted to go back to England, he wanted his body to be taken there. He gave me the name of a place, he wrote it down for me . . . *moment* . . .'

She got up, heading for the door, but McFaul told her not to bother. Where James Jordan had elected to be buried was immaterial. What mattered was getting him out.

'How cold's the fridge? At the hospital?'

'Nine degrees celsius, three hours ago. Not hot. But not cold.'

'So what's the alternative?'

Christianne indicated the open door at the end of the kitchen. McFaul got up and left the table. The big freezer was a third full, mainly food, but there was plenty of room for what was left of James Jordan. McFaul reached inside, testing a pack of frozen prawns with the back of his hand. The crust of ice was already beginning to melt and there was water pooling beneath it. McFaul pulled the freezer away from the wall, prising off the metal grill and peering at the machinery inside. The power cable snaked away towards the window.

'So what's wrong with it?' he said. 'Why isn't it working?'

Christianne told him to follow her. She went back through the kitchen and into the garden. The cable from the freezer plugged into a junction box. From the junction box, a thicker cable led through the undergrowth to a portable generator of a kind McFaul had never seen before. He knelt beside it. A small green lizard watched him from the foot of the nearby wall. At length, McFaul stood up.

'It's buggered,' he said. 'Someone's nicked the HT lead.'

'*Comment?*'

'The HT lead.' McFaul frowned, making a semi-circular movement with one hand. 'The thing that goes from the top of the spark plug to the ignition coil. The lead that carries the charge. Look.' He showed her the bright scars on the metalwork where someone had gouged away with a screwdriver before removing the lead. Christianne was kneeling beside him. She smelled of antiseptic.

'It stopped working yesterday,' she said. 'Before I got back from the hospital.' She looked at him. 'Can you mend it?'

McFaul shook his head.

'No chance. It's a non-standard connector. Nothing I've got would fit.'

'So what happens?'

He looked at her for a moment.

'We eat the food,' he said at last. 'Bloody quick. Before it goes off. You got any butter? Garlic? I'll bring Bennie round. Hostilities permitting . . .'

McFaul got to his feet and limped back towards the house. She caught up with him by the kitchen door, leading him through to the hall. The bedroom she shared was at the front of the house. The metal shutters were closed over the window and the room was remarkably cool. McFaul stood in the open doorway, peering into the gloom. The framed photograph on the upturned cardboard box beside her bed was unmistakable: the blond crew-cut, the wide-set eyes, the way the boy's smile always suggested he was taking the piss. Christianne was rummaging in a tea chest. Eventually she produced two bottles. She showed them to McFaul.

'We have many,' she said.

McFaul looked at the bottles. The labels said 'Sancerre'. He knew nothing about white wine except the obvious. A crate or two of this stuff would make the prawns taste even sweeter. He frowned a moment, weighing the bottles in his hand.

'Rice?'

'Of course.'

'Beer?'

'*Bien sûr*. Sagres.'

'OK,' he nodded, 'leave it to me.'

He backed out of the room and headed for the front door, knowing that he'd been right about the girl. Nothing had to be spelled out. She understood the way things worked, the barter system, favours offered, favours owed. As well as pretty, she was grown-up. God knows what she'd ever seen in James Jordan.

Back outside in the sunshine, McFaul extended a hand.

'I'll need a trolley,' he said, 'or a barrow of some kind.'

She nodded.

'No problem.' She hesitated, looking at her watch. 'Come to the hospital. Come up the stairs to the second floor. I'll be there in an hour.'

'And the party? My lads? Only the UN bloke's trying to organise a flight out. And the stuff won't keep.'

McFaul smiled for the first time, his hand outstretched. She touched it briefly, returning the smile.

'Tonight,' she said. 'Before dark.'

It was quarter to one before Molly Jordan got to the Blue Boar Hotel. Todd Llewelyn was waiting in the lounge bar, stationed on a chintz sofa in the big bay window. He was wearing light grey trousers and a cream linen jacket and she recognised the Garrick Club tie at once, thinking how well it sat against the pale pink shirt.

He got up at once, nodding at Robbie Cunningham, offering his hand to Molly.

'Todd Llewelyn,' he murmured. 'May I say how sorry I am.'

Molly thanked him for the thought, loosening the scarf at her neck while he summoned a waiter for her coat. Llewelyn looked older than she'd expected, his skin a little slack around the jaw line, his face pouched beneath the eyes. She'd seen him a hundred times on television, mainly because of Giles's interest in current affairs, and she was surprised how tense he seemed to be. She smiled, wanting somehow to put him at ease. If anyone should be nervous, she told herself, it should be me.

They stayed in the bar for twenty minutes or so. Robbie organised the drinks and she joined Llewelyn on the sofa. On the journey over from Thorpe-le-Soken, Robbie had already explained about the Angolan trip, extending the Director's invitation for her to fly out at the charity's expense. Molly, astonished, had reminded him of their conversation only days earlier. Then, Terra Sancta had ruled out any such visit. So what had changed? The question seemed to have embarrassed Robbie. He'd talked vaguely about a film project, and said that Todd Llewelyn would be involved, but it was plain that he hadn't wanted to take the conversation any further. Now – her thoughts a little more collected – she put the question again. This time, to Todd Llewelyn.

'Robbie tells me you're interested in going out to Angola. Some kind of film,' she said carefully. 'What exactly did you have in mind?'

Llewelyn was nursing a gin and tonic. He cleared his throat, leaning forward, using the low, urgent, almost confessional tone that had become his onscreen trademark.

'It's a question of focus,' he said. 'I've been in documentaries all my life. They only work well when you have a story to tell, an important story . . .' He looked down at his drink. 'James died trying to do his bit for Africa. I think that's an important story. And I think you're the person to tell it.'

'Me?' Molly blinked. Robbie hadn't gone this far. Anything like.

'Yes,' Llewelyn nodded, 'you. If anyone on this earth knows a son, it has to be his mother. Who better to tell James's story?'

'But why? Why James? Why me?'

'Because he tried,' Llewelyn said gently. 'Because he did his best. And because, in the end, it cost him his life.'

Molly looked at him, transfixed. For a moment or two he'd become the face on the screen again: the carefully swept-back hair, the steely glint in the eyes, the look of total probity. A sharp prosecution barrister, Giles had called him, with the weekly benefit of a very good brief.

'Robbie tells me you're keen to get out there,' he was saying.

'Yes, I am.'

'Then this might be the best way of achieving that. Angola's at war, as you know. Going by yourself, or even with your husband, wouldn't be easy.'

'My husband can't come,' Molly said at once.

'Oh?'

'No, he's very busy just now. He's got one or two . . .' She shrugged, not wanting to go any further.

Llewelyn was watching her carefully now, newly alert.

'What does your husband do?'

'He works at . . . ah . . . Lloyd's . . .'

'Broker?'

'Underwriter . . .' She paused. 'It's pretty tough at the moment. You probably know more about all that than I do. So . . .' she shrugged again, 'Angola's out of the question. He just couldn't afford the time.'

Llewelyn watched her for a moment, then glanced at his

watch. A waiter appeared with three menus, handing them round. Llewelyn left his unopened. For the first time, Molly noticed the copy of the *Financial Times* lying on the sofa beside him.

'There's a film crew upstairs,' Llewelyn began. 'A cameraman and a sound recordist. They're on stand-by for after lunch but the decision is yours, absolutely yours. No pressure. I promise.'

Molly looked at Robbie, confused now. Robbie was trying to hide his own surprise.

'Here? Upstairs here? In the hotel?' he said.

'Yes.'

'Why?'

Llewelyn was toying with his gin and tonic.

'People's have asked me to do an interview before we leave. That's if Molly decides in favour, of course. They believe it's important that we understand the way she feels now, while it's still so fresh, and actually I think they're right. We have to have a context, a framework. Grief is a strange thing. It changes people. I've seen it time and time again.'

Molly nodded. This much, at least, she knew already.

'But what would happen?' she asked. 'Upstairs?'

'It's very simple. We've put a couple of lights in a bedroom. We'll shoot it in such a way that it'll look like you're at home. The shot will be very close, very tight.' He drew an oblong in the air, framing her face.

'But why not come home? If it's that important?'

Llewelyn smiled, ever-patient.

'Logistics,' he said simply. 'I know it sounds crazy but the crew have to be back in town by six. This way we give ourselves a chance.' He paused. 'But it's your decision and yours only. Please. Let's eat.' He gestured at her menu and picked up his own, skipping the hors-d'œuvres and moving straight to the entrées. Molly looked at Robbie again. This time his expression gave nothing away.

'What do *you* think?' she said.

Robbie had his finger in the menu. He glanced up.

'Todd's right,' he said guardedly, 'it's really up to you. All we . . . Todd . . . can do is explain what's involved.' He paused, looking across at Todd. 'Are the crew upstairs coming to Angola too? Assuming we go?'

'No,' Todd shook his head. 'I'll do it on a camcorder. No hassles. No dramas.' He smiled at Molly. 'Just little me.'

Molly looked between the two men, trying to get her bearings again, while Llewelyn explained a little more about the camcorder, how the system worked, how much time and trouble it would save.

'Just the three of us,' he said finally, 'looking for James.' He leaned across, his hand on Robbie's arm. 'Nice title, don't you think?'

Robbie nodded, nonplussed, and Todd returned to his study of the menu. At length he looked at Molly again.

'Have you decided?' he said.

Molly glanced up. The last thing she felt was hungry.

'An omelette or a salad,' she said. 'Something light.'

'I meant about the film.'

'Oh . . .'

Molly tried to hide her confusion. Given their imminent bankruptcy, Todd Llewelyn represented the only way she'd ever get to Angola. There were limits to what she'd do to earn her passage but she knew how badly she wanted to see the place, to be part of it, to understand exactly how it was that James's life had come to such an awful end.

'Tell me again . . .' she said, 'about this film of yours. Why are you making it? Why go to so much trouble?'

Llewelyn smiled, ever-sympathetic. The project, he said, had already come to mean an enormous amount to him personally. He had kids of his own. He sensed only too well how it must feel to lose someone so close. And so he wanted to get the film right. Desperately. More right than anything else he'd ever done.

He paused, extending a hand across the sofa.

'Your film is simple,' he said quietly. 'It's about sacrifice. And it's about remembrance. If you'll do it at all, you'll do it for James.'

Molly looked away for a moment, turning the words over in her mind. She didn't much like sacrifice. It wasn't a word she'd ever associate with James. But remembrance was different. That mattered. That was important. Remembrance. Yes.

She closed the menu and returned it to the waiter.

'OK,' she said, 'but let's do it now.'

Robbie took Molly Jordan to the interview set. Room 305 was one of the smaller bedrooms and the camera crew had pushed the twin beds together, making a tiny working space between the window and the dressing table. Two chairs occupied this space. The curtains were pulled against the bright sunshine outside and there was a semi-circle of lights on tall metal stands.

Downstairs, before disappearing to make a telephone call, Llewelyn had promised an intimate conversation, just the two of them. She was to forget the camera, the lights, the technicians, and simply concentrate on how she felt. Now, though, she began to wonder whether she could really go through with it. The little room looked so claustrophobic, so intimidating. How could she bare her soul under conditions like these?

She was about to turn to Robbie, asking for help, when Llewelyn appeared at her elbow.

'Molly Jordan...' he murmured, introducing her to the crew.

Molly shook hands with the cameraman and the girl who was doing the sound, forgetting their names at once. They were faces from the darkness the other side of the lights, intruders in this life she'd suddenly decided to make so public. She sat down. The girl clipped a tiny microphone to her lapel, tidying the trailing wire inside her jacket, and she just sat there, passive, letting it happen, marvelling at her own part in this strange act of self-exposure. She felt unreal, detached, as if all this was happening to someone else. Someone else in the pool of light. Someone else on the buttoned velour. Someone else nervously touching a forefinger to an imagined smudge in her lipstick.

She felt a hand on her knee. It was Llewelyn's. He was asking if she was ready, if she was OK. She heard herself saying yes to both questions, simple lies, quite the reverse of what she really felt.

'It'll be fine,' he kept saying, 'believe me.'

She nodded, adrift now, helpless in his hands. He began to phrase the first question, filling in the background, asking her about James, what kind of child he'd been, what kind of son, and she heard herself beginning to talk in a low, hesitant voice, not at all the way she normally spoke. James had been like any other child, she was saying. A real handful. Noisy. Nosy. Naughty. Into absolutely everything. Vaguely, beyond the lights, she was aware of Llewelyn watching her, sympathetic, capping each little story with a nod and a smile. She went on, unprompted. James at school. James learning to ride his first bike. James at the helm of his father's dinghy, his little body lost in the big orange life-jacket. The things she'd remembered. The images she'd filed away.

The interview went on, each question inching her closer to Africa, closer to Sunday, closer to the moment when she'd stepped back into the cottage, her face glowing from the morning run. Giles had been sitting at the kitchen table. She'd known something was wrong though it was a while before he could bring himself to tell her.

Llewelyn broke in.

'What did he say?'

'Say?' She looked suddenly blank. 'What did Giles say?'

'Yes, how did he put it? Can you remember? His exact words?'

She shook her head, suddenly lost, remembering only that

feeling of imminent disaster, a huge wave from nowhere, towering above them both, crashing down on their heads, destroying everything. She felt herself beginning to lose control, her eyes flooding with tears, and she turned her head away a moment, hiding her face, aware of Llewelyn sitting just feet away, totally immobile. Never in her life had she felt so miserable, so alone. She sniffed, swallowed hard, wiped her eyes with the back of her hand. The blur that was Llewelyn's face resolved itself. He was watching her carefully.

'So how did you feel?' he asked her after a while. 'When he told you.'

She opened her mouth. Then closed it again. Then shook her head.

'Terrible,' she said bleakly. 'I felt terrible.'

There was a long silence. Then Llewelyn again.

'He'd gone,' he murmured. 'He was dead.'

'I know.'

'You must have . . .' He paused, leaving the thought unvoiced, her cue, her responsibility.

She closed her eyes. Suddenly, the room was overpoweringly hot. She thought about asking for a glass of water then changed her mind. She began to get up but Llewelyn was leaning forward now, restraining her.

'The microphone . . .' he was saying, '. . . you're still wired up.'

She muttered an apology, sitting back in the chair, feeling foolish, all these tears, all this emotion, all these watching strangers. Then a shadow stepped into the light and she heard a whispered oath.

'For God's sake . . .'

It was Robbie's voice. He was unclipping the microphone, helping her up. In the bathroom, he offered her a flannel soaked in cold water and she found herself clinging to him, grateful, while he dried her face. Her face was still buried in the towel when the door opened. She felt a hand on her shoulder. She looked in the mirror. Llewelyn was standing by the shower curtain. All she could think of to say was sorry. She'd spoiled the party. She'd let him down. He shook his head, smiling at her face in the glass.

'You were great,' he murmured. 'Just perfect.'

Giles was at his desk in the office he occupied at Lloyd's when the telephone call came through. He abandoned the sandwich he'd been eating and picked up the phone. So far the day had been infinitely kinder than he'd expected. No deadline on the closed year settlement. No summons to appear before the Council. Even a cautious word of encouragement from the Managing Agent who'd stirred things up in the first place. Giles knew he was still in deep, deep trouble. Without question, they'd lose most of what they had. But with a little discretion, and a lot of good sense, he might yet salvage a little of his reputation.

The voice on the phone belonged to a woman. She gave a name he didn't recognise. She began to ask him questions about the performance of the syndicate. She'd heard rumours of massive losses. She understood there was an American connection. Certain Names were making a great deal of noise. There was talk of litigation. After each question she paused, asking for a confirmation or a denial, but Giles stonewalled. The information she was after was strictly confidential. She was trespassing in areas where she didn't belong. He had no intention of helping her in any way whatsoever.

Finally, the woman changed tack.

'I understand your son has been involved in some kind of accident,' she said.

Giles stiffened behind the desk. Below the office, the big trading floor was filling up after lunch.

'Who is this?' he asked for the second time. 'Who are you?'

The woman gave her name again. She said she worked for a major Sunday newspaper. She was acting on a tip, what she called 'information received'. The tip was very recent. She trusted the source completely. She paused.

'I take it James Jordan is your son, then,' she said.

Giles nodded, numbed.

'Was,' he muttered, 'was my son.'

'Then maybe we could talk about him, if it's not too painful. My editor wondered whether you might think about giving us an exclusive. We could clear space next Sunday and—'

Giles put the phone down, sitting immobile behind the desk. Minutes later, when his secretary returned with fresh coffee, he'd gone.

The party in Muengo started at six. McFaul and Bennie had spent the afternoon checking and cleaning the de-mining gear at the schoolhouse. Domingos had turned up at the schoolhouse too, eager to help, but McFaul had given him the two plastic jerrycans and the keys to the Land Rover, telling him to ship home as much water as he could. If Domingos and his family were to survive the siege, they'd need every drop they could lay their hands on. Domingos had driven back and forth all afternoon, filling and refilling the jerrycans, and McFaul had accompanied him back home on the last trip, carrying a sackful of tinned food he'd sorted out from their own supplies. If it came to an evacuation, Domingos would inherit everything at the schoolhouse but in the meantime McFaul was determined that he and his family shouldn't go hungry.

Now, past seven o'clock, Christianne met McFaul at the door of the MSF house. Down the hall, McFaul could hear voices in the kitchen and he recognised the tall, greying figure of Tom Peterson. All afternoon there'd been rumours of an impending ceasefire. If anyone knew for sure, it would probably be the Terra Sancta man.

McFaul pushed a paper bag into Christianne's hand. She was wearing another of Jordan's shirts, blue denim this time, a

declaration – McFaul assumed – that she still belonged to someone else. She took the bag, looked inside.

'Is this gin?' she said.

McFaul nodded.

'Gordons.' He grinned. 'And Bennie's brought some
Scotch, too.'

He squeezed her arm and pushed on down the hall. The
kitchen was crowded and McFaul made his way towards the far
corner where François, the Swiss from the Red Cross, was locked
in conversation with one of the Norwegian surgeons. The table
beside them was piled with drink: bottles of Sancerre, tins of
Portuguese and South African beer, and a big glass bowl brimming with some kind of fruit punch. McFaul gazed at it a
moment, full of admiration. Fresh fruit had been unobtainable
for weeks yet Christianne had managed to lay her hands on
oranges, mango, bananas, even slices of fresh pineapple. McFaul
helped himself, aware of Peterson beside him.

'How's it been?' he said, not looking up.

He hadn't seen the Terra Sancta man since the first night in
the Red Cross bunker. According to François, he had a billet
with the UN mission.

'Fine!' Peterson was saying, 'and it looks like Fernando's
cracked it.'

McFaul fished another piece of fruit from the punch bowl.
Fernando was the UN rep, a fat, cheerful Portuguese from
Beira.

'UNITA playing ball?' McFaul laughed.

'Yep.'

'You serious?'

'So Fernando says. Their people in Huambo are promising
a ceasefire and safe passage out. Dusk tonight to dusk tomorrow.
I've been on the telex all day. Luanda are sending a Herc,
subject to confirmation.'

'ETA?'

'Around noon, I hope.' He touched McFaul lightly on the

arm. 'And once they go firm, you'll be the first to know. I promise.'

McFaul nodded, sucking the punch from the wedge of orange. The punch tasted of rum and white wine and God knows what else.

'So you're taking Jordan home?' he grunted. 'Mission accomplished?'

'Fingers crossed. Winchester have booked him onward on the Sabena flight. He should be back by . . .' he frowned, 'the weekend. Ties it all up rather nicely.'

'Yeah,' McFaul looked at him for the first time, 'except he's dead.'

The party went on for four hours. Christianne served prawns and rice, as promised, and there were side dishes of cassava, beans and aid-supplied mashed potato. Around eight o'clock, Fernando appeared and announced that the ceasefire arrangements had been ratified by both sides. The Red Cross people in Luanda had confirmed a Hercules, and the plane would be landing at the local strip around eleven-thirty. There was room on board for every aid worker, and he passed round a photocopied sheet setting out the precise timetable for the evacuation. Wherever possible, transport and other equipment would be left in the hands of the local Angolans. Otherwise, the stuff would simply be abandoned. At the end of this impromptu speech, one of the women from the World Food Programme team raised her glass and proposed a toast, and the kitchen rang with cheers. Most of these people, McFaul thought, have been in Angola long enough to know when to beat a retreat. If the fighting intensified, and UNITA troops entered the city itself, there'd be every prospect of a bloodbath.

A little later, Fernando gone, the dancing began. By now McFaul was sitting on the floor in the hall, his back against the wall, a half-empty bottle of Sancerre between his knees. Couples walked to and fro from the kitchen, joining the sway of tightly packed bodies in one of the darkened front bedrooms. The music they were playing – late sixties, early seventies – stirred memories in McFaul but he preferred the comforts of the '88 Sancerre to Diana Ross and the Supremes. He was singing along to 'Baby Love' for the third time, his head nodding on his chest, when he felt a hand on his arm. He opened one eye. Christianne was bent over him, her face shadowed by the heavy auburn curls. It took him a second or two to realise how drunk she was.

'Why outside?' he protested. 'I'm happy here. It's OK.'

'Please,' she said urgently. 'Please.'

McFaul looked at her a moment, then shrugged and allowed himself to be pulled upright. She led him down the hall and out into the darkness. Someone whistled and clapped their hands in mock-applause before the door shut behind them. McFaul still had the bottle. He offered it to Christianne. She shook her head. They began to cross the road and almost at once Christianne lost her footing amongst a pile of rubble. McFaul leaned down, helping her to her feet.

'You'll miss all this,' he said, 'after tomorrow.'

'I'm not going,' she said at once. 'Not me.'

McFaul glanced across at her face in the darkness. Her head was tilted back, her eyes on the stars.

'Nice punch,' he said drily. 'Nice party.'

'I'm serious. You don't believe me, do you?'

'No.'

'So OK,' she shrugged, 'don't.'

They walked a little further. Now and again, bodies stirred in the shadows. The people who lived here didn't have two-way radios, weren't up with the latest news, didn't know about the promised ceasefire. They relied instead on gossip and their own grim intuitions, and by and large they were right. McFaul kicked at a shredded plastic bag, ghosting softly across the road.

'Why?' he said at last. 'Why stay?'

Christianne caught his arm, a gesture at once clumsy and intimate.

'You were in the hospital today,' she said. 'You saw how it is there.'

'Yeah, but . . .' McFaul shrugged. He'd met her there as they'd arranged. The hospital was a makeshift affair, occupying two floors of a half-derelict apartment block near the river. James Jordan occupied most of the hospital's only fridge, a big Russian model the size of a wardrobe, and carrying the bulky plastic bag over the wounded, broken bodies that covered every available inch of floor hadn't been easy. Christianne had managed to lay hands on a supermarket trolley and wheeling the body bag away from the hospital, towards the waiting Land Rover, McFaul had fought the urge to be physically sick. The place had stunk. Blue polythene over the empty window frames kept the worst of the flies at bay but the result was a heavy, airless fug with an almost liquid quality, a pungent cheesiness that lodged at the back of the throat. The stench had reminded McFaul of similar places in Afghanistan. Then, the problem had been bombing strikes and the sheer numbers of dead. Now, according to Christianne, the dead were lucky.

'We have no drugs,' she said, 'and no rehydrates, either.'

McFaul nodded. Earlier, he'd been talking to the Norwegian surgeon and he'd said exactly the same. McFaul had asked him why he wasn't back at the hospital, saving lives, and he'd shrugged, waving the question away. Once things became this bad, he'd said, surgery made little difference. You might set a bone, or suture a wound, or stop a haemorrhage, but the guy would probably die of a cross-infection anyway. Hopeless, he'd said. Damn, fucking hopeless.

'What about water?' McFaul enquired.

Christianne was singing now, 'Hey Jude', making up the words as she went along. She stopped and pulled a face.

'No good,' she said. 'The water's no good. Yuk. Terrible. . . .'

'So what would . . .' McFaul frowned, 'your boyfriend have done about that? Would he have stayed too? Like you?'

'Yes, for sure. We talked about it. Many times. He loved this place. He thought he could do so much.'

'Yeah, I gathered.'

'And he did do a lot. More than you think.'

'Sure. Just a shame he never listened.'

Christianne staggered again in the darkness, falling heavily, and when McFaul helped her up she was crying.

'You OK?'

'It's nothing. *Merde* . . .' She rubbed her knee.

'What happened?'

She looked at him a moment then shook her head, turning round and beginning to hobble back towards the party, the distant pulse of Tamla Motown in the warm darkness. McFaul caught her up.

'Listen . . .' he said. 'I'm sorry. That was out of order. Comes from getting shitfaced.'

She stopped and looked at him again, her upturned face level with McFaul's chin.

'Tell me it stops hurting,' she said quietly. 'Please tell me that.'

McFaul bent his head, putting his arm round her.

'It does,' he said, 'believe me.'

'You know that? For sure?'

'Yes,' he nodded, 'I do.'

'So after . . .' she touched the scars on his lower face, 'how long did it take?'

McFaul said nothing for a while.

'Getting blown up's nothing,' he said at last. 'Getting blown up's easy. I'd settle for that any day.'

'You would?'

'Yes.' He nodded. 'That's doctors and hospitals. Easy pain. It's the other sort fucks you up.'

'*Comment?*' Christianne's eyes were wide now.

McFaul shrugged. Since he'd left the Falklands he'd done his best to wall it all away. Gill. The marriage. The night he'd nearly killed her. Putting your trust in anyone else could be the worst investment you'd ever make. Yet without it, you were nothing. Explain that, he thought, stroking the girl's hair, thinking about Jordan again, back in the schoolhouse, the big leak-proof body bag safely folded into the freezer chest. He hadn't yet bothered to mention it to Bennie and if they were shipping out tomorrow there'd be no point.

Christianne had her arms round him now, eager for more comfort. He bent his head, his mouth to her ear, telling her what she wanted to hear, that no pain lasted for ever, that the deepest wounds would heal. She nodded, grateful, and they'd started walking again when McFaul saw a flash on the horizon, way out in the darkness. For a moment he thought it was lightning. Then it happened again and again, the boom of the big guns rolling across the city towards them, not mortars this time but artillery, big field pieces, the real thing. For a moment McFaul did nothing, transfixed, then he was running, his arms round the girl, back towards the MSF house as the first shells landed and the ground began to shake beneath their feet.

Todd Llewelyn was at home in Bayswater when he got the call he'd been expecting. The night editor at the *Sunday Mirror* ad been a colleague from way back when both men were subs on the old *London Evening News*. The *Mirror* man, as ever, was in a rush.

'We got a tip today about a Lloyd's bloke,' he said. 'Giles Jordan. Anything to do with you?'

Llewelyn took his time, reaching for the remote control, turning down the volume on the television.

'Who?' he said at last.

'Giles Jordan. He's an underwriter. His syndicate's gone bust and there's word he's lost his nipper, too. Blown up somewhere. That sound about right?'

'Could be.' Llewelyn yawned. 'Why?'

'Because you're supposed to be doing some film for People's. With this bloke's missus. In darkest Africa. True or false?'

Llewelyn's smile widened.

'True,' he said, 'and exclusive, I'm afraid.'

'Yeah, but only on telly. Nothing to stop us taking first dip, is there? Lloyd's man loses all?'

Llewelyn thought about the headline for a moment or two. He'd have preferred something a little less tabloid but he was in no position to quibble.

He glanced at his watch. The weekend was still five days away.

'Is this for Sunday?'

'Probably.'

'Why don't you hold off? Until we get back?'

There was a brief silence on the phone. Then the night editor came back. He sounded suspicious.

'What are you offering?'

Llewelyn shrugged.

'Photos. Quotes from the locals. Nice colour piece.'

'And who writes it?'

'I do.'

'But what about People's?'

Llewelyn reached for the remote control again, switching channels.

'They'll love it.' He smiled again. 'Should get the punters nicely tuned in.'

Molly Jordan didn't find the note until nearly midnight. The interview abandoned, she'd let Robbie Cunningham drive her home. He'd been kindness itself, apologising for the distress they'd caused her, telling her that Llewelyn had been way over the top. In her heart she agreed with him but the decision to do the wretched thing had been hers in the first place and the fault – if there was a fault – was therefore her own. Put yourself in a position like that, she told herself, and you should expect the odd bruise.

At the cottage, she'd insisted on making Robbie tea before he drove back to London and he'd stayed for nearly an hour. The more she got to know him, the more she liked him and when he asked at the end whether she still wanted to go to Africa, she hesitated.

'Will you be coming?' she'd asked at length.

'Yes. For sure.'

'And will he . . . will it be like that again?'

'No,' Robbie had shaken his head, 'definitely not.'

She'd nodded, trusting him, telling him again how important it was for her to get there, and after he'd gone she'd telephoned Alice, Patrick's wife, and driven over to Frinton. With the daylight fading, and no sign of Giles, the last place she wanted to be was the cottage.

She was back by ten, surprised to find the lights off. She knocked a couple of times at the door before fumbling for her keys and letting herself in. She went from room to room, looking for Giles, calling his name. He must have been back. She knew that. There was a dirty teacup in the washing-up bowl and the kettle on the Aga was still warm. She plugged in the electric fire and tried to concentrate on the television news, waiting for his return. Maybe he's gone to the pub, she thought. Maybe, like me, he needs company.

By midnight he still hadn't come back and for the first time it occurred to her to have a proper look in the bedroom. She found the note at once. It was tucked beneath her pillow, sealed in a white envelope, handwritten in blue biro.

'My darling,' it read, 'I've gone away for a little while. Better for both of us, I think. I'll be strong later, I promise. Love me always. Giles.'

She read it twice, numb again. Then she went downstairs, lifting the telephone twice, wanting to call for help, Alice,

Patrick, anyone, but both times she couldn't bring herself to make the call. Only by chance, switching on the television again, did the obvious begin to dawn on her. The weather girl was standing in front of a map of the British Isles. Whirly circles were speeding in from the Atlantic. Heavy weather was forecast for the Channel Approaches. By tomorrow, it would be raining.

The car keys were on the kitchen table. Molly left the hall light on, locking the front door behind her. She drove as fast as she dared, taking the shortcut through the back lanes. The gates to the parking lot at the marina were open. She ran down the steps to the boardwalk, praying that he'd found some other answer, some other escape, but when she finally made it to the seaward end of the pontoon, she knew that she'd been right. Giles's mooring was empty. *Molly Jay* had gone.

CHAPTER FOUR

On the fourth day of the siege of Muengo, the rebel guns fell silent. McFaul was asleep, sprawled on a borrowed airbed in the Red Cross bunker. He'd been dreaming of the Falklands again, the first time he'd been out there, part of the Task Force in 1982. He'd been attached to 45 Commando, yomping west from San Carlos Water, searching ahead of the long line of sodden marines. Then, as now, his business had been mine clearance. And then, as now, his real fear had been enemy shelling. The Argies had shipped in some pretty effective kit: batteries of 105-mm guns and a handful of the big 155-mm pieces which could hurl a shell sixteen miles. Trudging ever closer to Stanley, McFaul had become an expert on the signature of each of these weapons, the distant boom of the field gun, the shriek of the incoming shell, and the terrible moment before impact when the air was sucked away and you clawed at the tussock and covered your head and shut your eyes and lay in the tightest ball imaginable, waiting for oblivion.

McFaul grunted and drew his knees up to his chin, tensing himself for the blast. Nothing happened.

'Andy . . . *viens* . . .'

He opened one eye. François was standing over him in the gloom, gesturing in the direction of the big HF radio. Four days' growth of beard made him look faintly piratical. McFaul blinked. His wrist watch read 06.21. Outside, the shelling appeared to have stopped. He got to his feet, stepping over the long hump of Bennie's body, following François to his table in the corner.

A pair of headphones lay beside a foolscap pad. François told him to put them on. McFaul did so, sitting down, refusing the proffered glass of water. There was a crackle of static on the headphones then a voice he recognised, the distinctive West Country drawl. Ken Middleton was the guy who'd sent him out here in the first place, the guy to whom he'd more or less pledged the rest of his working life.

'Ken,' he said, 'where are you?'

'Devizes. Listen. Guy I've been talking to in Luanda says there's another ceasefire brewing.'

McFaul glanced up at François. Through a second pair of headphones, the Swiss was monitoring the conversation. Now, he qualified the news about the ceasefire with a shrug and the faintest smile. Middleton was talking about evacuation plans. He wanted McFaul's team out as soon as possible. Plus, if possible, the equipment.

'You get that?' he asked briskly, adding the obligatory 'Over'.

McFaul grunted an affirmative, imagining Middleton in the brand-new office he occupied on a windy trading estate in deepest Wiltshire. Global Clearance was Middleton's brainchild, a non-profit-making organisation dedicated to emptying the Third World of mines. A passionate man, with a deep contempt for the big commercial de-mining outfits, he'd even registered Global as a charity. Lives and limbs, he was always saying. Not fucking profits.

Now he was talking about Mozambique. Evidently he'd laid hands on a bucketful of EEC money. How did McFaul feel about transferring to the other side of Africa? McFaul rubbed his eyes. Half of him was still sheltering in a rock sangar beneath the shadow of Two Sisters. He could almost smell the peat where Argie shells had set the stuff on fire.

'There's a lot to do,' he muttered.

'Too right.'

'I meant here.'

'Angola?'

'Muengo.' He paused. 'We could kill a little time in Luanda then get back in. This lot won't last for ever.'

'There's a war on, Andy. The place is under fucking siege. Be realistic, mate. A time and a place. Know what I mean?'

McFaul smiled, warmed as ever by the rough candour of the man. With Middleton, what you saw was what you got. He'd never met anyone so committed, so enthusiastic, so determined, yet so utterly unsentimental. It was one of the qualities that explained the extraordinary reach of Global Clearance. From a standing start, this charity of Ken's was now organising mine clearance programmes in seven countries, all of them staffed by ex-sappers like McFaul. For the last three years, Middleton had asked him to go to some of the worst places on earth. And not once had he dreamed of saying no.

François was on one of the handsets now, talking in French. He reached for the pad and scribbled a note for McFaul. The word 'surrender' was underlined twice. McFaul told Middleton to hang on for a moment, turning to François.

'The government boys have surrendered?'

'Not yet.'

'But that's the bid?'

'That's what Katilo's after.' He nodded. '*Bien sûr.*'

McFaul thought about the news. The radio wasn't the place you discussed the latest political developments. He could hear Middleton repeating himself. He glanced at François, then bent to the set again.

'I want you and Bennie out,' Middleton was saying. 'Thanks for the telex, by the way. James Jordan. The boy sounded a pillock.'

'He was.'

'Shame. Listen, we'll talk again tonight if I can get any action out of Portishead. And say thanks to that nice French guy. Tell him there's a job waiting for him.'

He hooted with laughter, then there was a click on the

line and a sign-off from the British Telecom radio-operator at Portishead. François was back on the Motorola, the speaker pressed to his ear. At length he put the radio down. He'd been up most of the night and he looked exhausted.

'They're going to talk at noon,' he said. 'Should be OK until then.'

Outside, half an hour later, McFaul went on foot to the schoolhouse. A pall of smoke hung over the city. In the still, windless air it smelled of rotting garbage and burning rubber. The place was deserted, no movement of any kind. The wide main street was newly cratered, and a handsome building on the corner opposite the cathedral plaza was still smouldering from a direct hit. McFaul paused on the kerbside for a moment, looking at it. A year ago, according to Domingos, it had been a branch of the Banco Naçional, Muengo's tiny stake in the fantasy world of credit transfers and deposit accounts. Now, it was just another glimpse of the way the country was really going: gaping window frames, fire-blackened walls and piles of fallen masonry in the street beneath. The direct hit had punched a ragged hole where the main entrance had once been, and McFaul could see movement inside, something stirring. At length, a youth appeared, an Angolan, no more than fifteen. He was wearing a pair of yellow shorts and a back-to-front baseball cap and he had a pink lampshade in his mouth. One leg was missing below the knee and he steadied himself on his crutches for a second or two, acknowledging McFaul with a cheerful wave, before tap-tapping off down the street. McFaul watched until he rounded the corner and disappeared. The sound of Angola, he thought. Tap. Tap. Tap.

At the schoolhouse, mercifully, there was no visible damage. The nearest shell seemed to have fallen several hundred yards away and as McFaul circled the little one-storey building he marvelled yet again at the extraordinary lottery that life under shellfire became. Some places you were lucky. Some places you were dead. Simple as that.

At the main entrance, belatedly, McFaul realised that the door had been forced. They'd left it locked. He was sure about it. Now it hung open, boot marks on the lower planking, the wood around the keyhole splintered. He stepped carefully inside, checking first for booby-traps or some kind of ambush. Rebel troops may already have penetrated the city. Getting blown away by some grinning UNITA adolescent was a less than attractive prospect. The corridor that ran the length of the schoolhouse was empty, but the door to the classroom where they'd slept had also been forced. McFaul checked quickly, the obvious things, boxes of spare batteries, the portable Eskie they used in the field, but he found nothing missing. Only when he went through to the storeroom next door did he realise what had happened.

The smell hit him at once, the stench of the hospital, the sweet cheesiness of decaying human flesh. He swallowed hard, stepping across the tiny room. The big chest freezer lay open, the lid propped against the wall. Inside, the food and the beer had gone, and the body bag that he and Christianne had brought over from the hospital now lay at the bottom of the freezer in a shallow puddle of nameless fluids. The bag had been sliced open, presumably to check its contents, and McFaul found himself looking at what remained of James Jordan. His upper body had swollen, like an inflated balloon, one arm sticking out almost vertically through the rent in the heavy plastic. Where the blast of the mine had shredded his belly and groin, the torn loops of viscera were already a treacly black colour, spilling out of the bag, while the surrounding flesh had begun to turn green. Worst of all was the boy's head, the short blond hair plastered against the skull, one eye missing completely, the other hanging down over the wreckage of his nose.

McFaul turned away, revolted, closing the lid on the freezer. Back in the bunker, over the last four days, he'd done the calculations. The gennie would have run for forty-eight hours, keeping the freezer going. With the stuff inside frozen solid, another couple of days should have made little difference. What he hadn't anticipated was this: some passing intruder, taking his chance in the bombardment, forcing his way in, desperate for food. McFaul stooped to the cupboard behind the door, looking for the fuel he'd need to start the generator again. He'd no idea whether refreezing the body would help at all but in truth he didn't much care. What he'd just seen, the grotesque parcel of rotting flesh at the bottom of the freezer, was an affront, an obscenity, and any gesture seemed worthwhile. The boy, after all, had been human. Even James Jordan deserved better than this.

McFaul opened the cupboard and looked inside. Four days ago, there'd been six 20-litre jerrycans, neatly stored side by side. Four had contained diesel, two petrol. Together, the cache represented the sum total of Global's reserves, all they had left for the Land Rover and the gennie. Now, though, the cupboard was empty.

Molly Jordan was still dozing when the pilot of the big Sabena 747 announced the final descent into Luanda. She felt the light touch of Robbie Cunningham's hand on her arm and she opened her eyes, forcing a smile. The young Terra Sancta press officer occupied the middle of the three seats. Beyond him, beside the aisle, she could see Todd Llewelyn finishing the last of his breakfast. For some reason, he'd decided to wear jeans and a denim jacket and it didn't suit him at all. The stuff was off-the-peg, brand new, the fit at least a size too small.

'Coffee?'

Robbie was offering her his own cup. She shook her head, saying she wasn't hungry. The last time they'd eaten was late last night, somewhere over the Sahara. Afterwards, before the stop at Kinshasa, she'd watched some film or other. Both events had left no impression whatsoever, bits of a life that was beginning to seem totally unreal. She'd delayed flying out as long as she could, desperate for word from Giles. Every morning, she'd scanned the papers and listened to the radio news bulletins, dreading news of the *Molly Jay.* Whenever the postman was due, she'd find herself haunting the bedroom with the view of the road, half-expecting a letter or even a postcard, some indication that he'd made a safe landfall. She'd even toyed with contacting the coastguards, asking for clues to his whereabouts. But when nothing happened – no letter, no phone call, no knocks at the door – she'd finally had to accept that he'd meant what he said in the note. He needed a little space, a week or so to sort himself out. By the time she got back from Africa, he'd doubtless have returned.

Now, she pulled up the blind on her window and stared out. The land below was veiled by a thin layer of cloud. She could see a coastline, a thin strip of beach, and what might have been a road. Everything was greyer and somehow flatter than she'd imagined. She felt Robbie beside her, leaning across for the view, and she tucked herself into the corner of her seat, making room for him. The plane began to bank to the left and it was a second or two before she recognised the beginnings of a city. She wiped her own breath from the cold Perspex, peering down at the jigsaw of roads, recognising the line of a railway snaking away inland. The city was built around a lagoon. On the seaward side, a long yellow strip of sand lay parallel to the foreshore, enclosing a natural harbour, and on the mainland there were docks, and tiny toy cranes, and a pair of bathtub freighters tied up alongside. The pilot eased to the left again and from under the wing slid office blocks, traffic jams, the perfect oval outline of a football stadium, all the images you'd associate with any busy city.

She turned to Robbie, trying to put this surprise of hers into words. Somehow, she'd expected something more exotic, more African, not this. He grinned, his eyes never leaving the view below. He'd already told her how much he loved the place, how chaotic it was, how great the people were. There was a rumble as the undercarriage came down and then the pilot made a final adjustment, steadying the big jet for touchdown. Robbie glanced at his watch.

'Quarter past seven,' he said approvingly. 'Early for once.'

Llewelyn got off first, hurrying down the steps, cradling his camcorder. En route, he'd been acquiring a variety of shots and the Belgian stewardesses had warned him about getting more pictures on arrival at Luanda. The country was at war. The airport doubled as a military base. Just the sight of a raised camcorder would expose him to arrest. Llewelyn had listened to the warnings without comment and now Molly stood at the top of the aircraft steps, watching him turn on the apron, the camcorder wedged beneath his arm, the lens pointing back towards the 747. He waved, beckoning her on, and she felt Robbie nudging her down towards the oil-stained tarmac, but she resisted him, looking round, wanting to make the most of this moment. The cloud was beginning to burn off now and it was already hot. Beneath the sharp tang of aviation fuel, she could smell something else, something far earthier, a strange mix of spice, and seaweed, and raw sewage. James, she thought at once. His first scent of Africa.

She began to move again, down towards the apron. There were aircraft everywhere, taxiing out towards the runway, big unmarked freighters, heavy-bellied planes with 'UN' on the tail, and smaller, two-engined aircraft, and she listened to Robbie as he explained what was going on, his mouth to her ear, fighting against the whine of the nearby aircraft. This was the airport's busiest hour, the morning's first aid flights leaving for destinations inland. Each plane would be carrying supplies. They'd be back within hours, he said, reloading, readying for another supply run.

'Why?' she mouthed, watching the queue of aircraft juddering to a temporary halt. 'Why doesn't the stuff go by road?'

Robbie was looking for Llewelyn. He seemed to have disappeared.

'Mines,' he yelled, 'you can't move anywhere without—'

He broke off, realising what he'd said, apologising at once, and Molly turned away, angry with herself for embarrassing him. She squeezed his arm, telling him it didn't matter, then there was an ear-splitting roar of jet engines and Molly followed Robbie's pointing finger, watching a pair of sleek jet fighters thunder down the runway. As they climbed steeply upwards, balls of fire fell from both of them, leaving delicate black smoke trails against what was left of the cloud. Molly glanced at Robbie.

'Decoy flares,' he said briefly.

'Decoy what?'

'Flares. In case anyone tries shooting them down. The missiles are heat-seeking. They think the flares are the aircraft.' He paused, watching the fighters bank steeply to the south and disappear. Then he indicated a line of low concrete shelters on the other side of the airfield. 'That's where the rest live. They normally work in pairs. They're Russian planes, MiGs. Mornings are favourite for ground-attack missions. Set your watch by them.'

Molly nodded, looking again at the queue of departing aircraft, newly thoughtful. Robbie had already briefed her about Muengo. The place was under some kind of siege. The Terra Sancta man who'd gone in for James was living underground. Getting there might be a problem.

Slowly, the Sabena passengers resumed their progress towards the terminal building. Molly and Robbie joined them, Molly looking around for Llewelyn, wondering where next he might appear. They walked beneath the wing of a big freight plane. The ramp at the back was lowered and a truck was waiting on the tarmac. There were injured soldiers inside the plane and in twos and threes they were helping each other off. Those who could walk had injuries to their heads and upper bodies. Some

of the stretcher cases were barely conscious. Molly looked up at
the waiting soldiers, already sitting in the back of the truck.
One had pads over both eyes. Another wore a bloodstained
bandage, wound tightly round his head. There were crutches
propped against the trailer board.

Molly shook her head, sobered again. Lorries were backing
towards the ramp beneath the tail of the big freighter and men
in dirty brown overalls began to manhandle bulky packages into
the belly of the plane. The packages were tightly bound with
cord, and the men piled them onto wooden pallets, securing
each pallet with cargo netting.

'What's happening?' Molly asked. 'What are they up to?'

Robbie shrugged, watching them.

'Resupply, I imagine. Stuff goes in by parachute.'

Inside the terminal building, the place was in chaos: out-
bound Portuguese nursing their passports, languid Angolan
officials taking their time over customs checks, and an endless
queue of recently arrived passengers that seemed to curl round
and round itself to no apparent purpose. Robbie had already
arranged for them to be met by the Country Representative of
a sister charity and the woman was waiting for them beside the
single immigration desk. She was small and intense, wearing her
Oxfam T-shirt like a badge. She carried diplomatic status, signi-
fied by a plastic ID card hung around her neck, and she waved
it with great vigour, carving a path through the customs formalities.

Outside, the terminal building was under seige from
hundreds of kids. Every time the door opened, they fought to
carry a bag to the line of waiting vehicles. Even Llewelyn stood
helpless, swamped by small black hands while Robbie peeled off
a couple of the orange 100,000 kwanza notes and selected the
boys he wanted. Molly watched him, impressed by the way he
handled this wild scene. From the moment they'd landed, he'd
seemed completely at home.

The drive in from the airport seemed interminable, the traffic crawling from intersection to intersection, the Oxfam VW Combi wedged in on every side. Nothing seemed intact. There were cars without windscreens, tyres without tread, even head-lights with neither glass nor bulbs. There were trucks every-where, towering over them, rumbling along in clouds of thick, black exhaust. From the wing mirror of one hung a bundle of dried fish. The door of another sported a ragged line of bullet holes. Yet despite the noise, and the fumes, and the constant jockeying for space, no one seemed the least bit harassed and Molly stared out, astonished at how different this city was at ground level, not at all the place she'd imagined from the air.

Everything seemed to be on the point of collapse: the grey, dowdy apartment blocks with their crumbling concrete and rust-stained air-conditioning units, the traffic lights that didn't work, the cripples begging from car to car, the street kids sifting through the mountains of garbage at the roadside. Once, during a longer hold-up than usual, Robbie pointed out an impromptu restaurant, three men in business suits perched on 40-gallon oil drums, eating skewers of meat from a roaring barbeque. It was an extraordinary sight, framed as it was by three Angolan women walking barefoot into town. One had a baby strapped to her back and the others carried blackened bananas in red plastic bowls on their heads. For some reason, the attention of the nearest woman was drawn to the car and she looked down at Robbie, answering his wave with the widest smile Molly could remember. She had a length of vividly patterned cloth wound around her body and her smile somehow transformed this rav-aged city, giving Molly the first clue to what brought Robbie back here. These people were bigger than their surroundings. They seemed impervious to circumstances or misfortune. And they knew, above all, how to laugh.

Robbie's Oxfam colleague dropped them outside the rented house that was Terra Sancta's Luanda headquarters, a modest two-storey villa with a dusty square of front garden and a limp palm tree that had seen better days. On the drive in from the airport, the woman had been briefing Robbie on the overnight situation in Muengo. Evidently there was again a possibility of some kind of ceasefire though no one was holding their breath. The aid community had gone to ground in a variety of bunkers and to her knowledge, no one had yet been injured. Evacuation would go ahead as soon as both sides stopped fighting but so far the situation was still, in her phrase, 'fluid'.

Robbie paused at the kerbside, stooping to the open window to give her a farewell peck on the cheek.

'Thanks for the lift,' he said. 'Made all the difference.'

The woman looked at him, then at Llewelyn and Molly. Llewelyn was already at work with his camera, filming the exterior of the house. Molly had no idea how much the woman knew about the purpose of their trip but her parting shot seemed clue enough.

'No problem,' she said grimly. 'I wish you luck.'

McFaul was bumping along the road beside the river when he first heard the drone of the big freighter. He'd decided to blow the last of the diesel in the Land Rover's tanks on a circuit of the city. Above all, he wanted to make sure that Domingos and his family had survived the shelling intact.

The freighter was flying in from the north, the pilot keeping the aircraft as low as he dared. It thundered across the city at no more than two hundred feet then climbed a little, dipping a wing and banking sharply at the point where the river dog-legged towards the distant hills of the Plan Alto. As the pilot tightened the turn, McFaul saw the lowered ramp at the back and the line of helmeted dispatchers clinging onto the webbing straps that criss-crossed the interior of the fuselage. The plane was dropping again now, making directly for McFaul, and he brought the Land Rover to a halt, ducking involuntarily as the huge aircraft swept over him, the downwash from the big turbo-props raising the dust on the road.

The dispatchers were on the move now, pushing heavily laden wooden pallets towards the lip of the ramp. The pallets tumbled out, each one piled with bulky looking packages, and as the nearest hit the ground the wooden pallets splintered apart, sending the packages in every direction. McFaul lost count after a dozen pallets, wondering how much of the stuff would survive. The freighter was climbing now, already a mile away, the whine of the turbo-props receding, and as silence returned to the city McFaul heard the rattle of automatic fire from the direction of the cathedral.

He hesitated a moment, identifying the sharp bark of an AK-47. Kalashnikovs, he thought. Government troops. Definitely. He pulled the Land Rover into a tight circle and headed back the way he'd come. From the river, the road curved gently in towards the city's centre. McFaul was driving fast now, swerving left and right to avoid the worst of the pot-holes. If the fighting spilled into the area around the Red Cross bunker, he wanted to be there. What little security remained in Muengo lay in sticking together.

Seconds later, he was braking hard. Ahead, slewed across the rubble-strewn carriageway, was an old burned-out bus. Beyond it was the last of the packages from the freighter. Crouched behind the bus, government troops were taking it in turns to empty a magazine or two in the direction of the cathedral. Answering fire swept down the road towards them. McFaul found reverse gear and sought the protection of a nearby garage, pulling the Land Rover into the shadowed breeze-block recess that had once served as a repair shop. He got out, hugging the inside wall, peering through a slit between the blocks. The makeshift repair bay still smelled of diesel oil and the concrete floor was slippery underfoot.

Out in the sunshine, the firing had become spasmodic, occasional shots, sometimes returned, sometimes not. McFaul began to think about getting out but before he could make a move two of the soldiers behind the bus broke from cover and darted across the road. Almost immediately one of them was hit, sprawling headlong in the dirt, his body jerking with the impact of more bullets. The other soldier faltered a moment, looking round, then he ran on, seizing one of the packages from the air-drop and dragging it backwards with both hands. By some miracle, he survived the forty yards intact, making it back to the shelter of the bus. The other soldiers fell on him, tearing at the cords that bound the package like kids at a Christmas party. Suddenly there was paper everywhere and the sound of laughter and the firing died away and then began again, more distant this time, as government troops and Muengo's police force fought amongst themselves for the lion's share of the goodies from the Antonov.

McFaul waited a couple of minutes longer, making certain that the immediate danger was over. The resupply flights had been coming in for three days now, a lifeline tossed to the Muengo garrison from military headquarters in Luanda. From the Red Cross bunker, with the help of François, McFaul had listened in to the complex radio negotiations between the rebel troops, out in the bush, and Muengo's force of MPLA soldiers. Without an agreement that guaranteed the Antonov safe passage, the resupply drops would never take place, and in the end the commander of the Muengo garrison had been forced to share the incoming supplies with the rebels. This had meant alternate drops – day one over the bush, day two over Muengo – and in broad terms the agreement had worked. Except that the Muengo drops had been further contested by the soldiery and the city's sizeable police force. The latter were heavily armed and saw no reason why they, too, shouldn't have a slice of Luanda's pie. Quite where that left the rest of Muengo's population was anybody's guess, though McFaul had lived here long enough now to suspect that they'd be mere spectators at the feast. Unless you had something to barter – a wife, say, or a daughter – then the incoming food was strictly for uniformed bellies.

McFaul peered through the slit in the breeze-block wall
again. The soldier who'd retrieved the package was standing
behind the bus with a can to his lips. From a distance it looked
like Sagres beer, though McFaul couldn't be sure. The body of
the other soldier was still out in the road. Blood had pooled
darkly round his head and a couple of dogs had turned up,
circling his body, their noses poking at the folds of his combat
smock.

Abruptly, the Motorola clipped to McFaul's belt came to
life and he heard his call sign, Golf Charlie One. He reached
down for the handset, recognising François's voice. He'd asked
the Swiss to keep trying Domingos while he drove across. The
Angolan had a two-way radio of his own, though for some
reason he'd stopped answering calls. Once again, François
reported no response.

'Nothing at all?'

'*Rien.*'

McFaul grunted an acknowledgement and returned to the
Land Rover. The soldiers behind the bus, squatting amongst
the contents of the looted package, barely looked up as he
pulled out of the garage and headed back towards the river,
joining the dusty unsurfaced road that led out of town. There
were people around now, tiny knots of them, women and
children mostly, squatting by the water's edge, filling whatever
containers they owned. For these people, water would come
before everything, though the river itself was heavily polluted.

After a mile or so, beside a gnarled old baobab tree, McFaul
took a left turn, leaving the river and picking his way through
a sprawl of tiny shacks, home to thousands of Muengo's poor.
The shacks were made from broken branches and small lengths
of sawn wood covered in bits of blue plastic sheeting, cardboard,
and ancient pieces of corrugated iron. Shell damage here was
light, the odd crater, the odd direct hit, a dozen or so shacks
flattened by blast. Beside one such pile of wreckage, a woman
was digging what looked like a grave while her children played

nearby with a makeshift toy cart. The wheels of the cart were made of plastic, a light tan in colour, and McFaul smiled grimly, recognising the distinctive shape of the tiny Italian VS-50 anti-personnel mines. One of the problems he'd been trying to tackle was the sheer ingenuity of Muengo's street kids. They seemed to have no fear of high explosives. On the contrary, some of them had been making a living from lifting the mines themselves. They'd learned how they worked – how to defuse them, how to empty the casing of the little tablet of explosive inside – and they subsequently sold them, either intact or in pieces. Intact, you could use them in the river, killing the fish by blast, whilst shaved into tiny slivers, the explosive was good for priming cooking fires.

McFaul drove on. The shacks seemed to extend for miles, an instant slum, but at least here there was still a little room for the notion of ownership. These people still had a stake, however small, in what was left of Muengo, unlike the thousands of others who'd flooded in from the countryside, a tidal wave of displaced people washed up by the war. For these people, even a one-room lean-to beside a shit-filled river was the wildest dream, way beyond their means, and many of them were now camping in what had once been Muengo's cinema, a long, barn-like building with thick breeze-block walls, long since sooted with the smoke of hundreds of cooking fires. The roof of the cinema, huge sheets of rusting red corrugated iron, had fallen victim to an earlier bombardment and so the families inside were now exposed to the elements. Somehow, in spite of everything, they managed to survive and feed their kids and even raise a smile or two at a life that had ceased to offer them anything but abject poverty. They got by on maize porridge and aid hand-outs and an unswerving faith that one day Angola would come to its senses. Quite where they found the evidence for this, McFaul didn't know but living alongside these people had given him a profound respect for their courage, and their fortitude, and like them he'd come to the conclusion that things couldn't get much worse.

Beyond the shacks, McFaul was back on a paved road, heading once again for the centre of the city, and the Romanesque bulk of the cathedral. On this side of town were the Portuguese-built houses where Muengo's tiny middle class lived: native-born Angolans who'd been to college in Huambo or Benguela, picked up a language or two, learned about computers, or refrigeration, or how to run a maize co-operative, and then returned to Muengo to put their new-found skills to work.

Domingos had been one of them, a cheerful thirty-three-year-old with an engineering degree from Huambo University who'd caught McFaul's eye at once. Part of Global's brief was to teach the local people how to deal with mines. Only by doing this, insisted Ken Middleton, could the country ever hope to free itself of mines. And so McFaul had recruited Domingos the first week he'd arrived, impressed by the man's intelligence, and by the speed with which he'd picked up the practical skills. Domingos also spoke good English, rare in rural Angola, and the two men had quickly become friends. Two or three times a week, McFaul would eat with Domingos's family, bringing little presents for Celestina, his wife. After supper, unless McFaul managed to talk his way out of it, he'd be press-ganged into wild games of football in the tiny square of garden, trying to keep the kids from tackling his plastic leg. They viewed this handicap with total indifference, telling him in sign language that friends of theirs played better with no legs at all.

McFaul rounded the corner of the street where Domingos lived. The houses here were all of Portuguese design, with red terracotta roof tiles, pastel stucco walls, and big shuttered windows that opened in the evening to catch the cooling breeze. In the two decades since independence, the area had decayed a little around the edges but McFaul had always liked it. It had space and a certain serenity. Half-close your eyes, he told himself, and you could be in some small Portuguese town, somewhere south of Lisbon.

For the first time since leaving the city centre, McFaul saw serious shell damage. First one house. Then another. 105 mm, he thought, at least. Half a roof gone. A front wall missing. Someone's living room neatly scissored in two. He slowed, easing the Land Rover around a crater in the broken tarmac, thinking again about Domingos's lack of response on the radio. The rebels had been recruiting locally. They'd seized men from Muengo, forced them into uniform. They'd have plans of the city. They'd know best where to target their big guns. Destroy the city's middle class – wreck their homes, kill their children, break their spirit – and you tear out Muengo's heart. McFaul drove on, his right hand already reaching for the Motorola, certain now that something terrible must have happened.

Domingos's house was at the end of the street. At first, fooled by a curtain of drifting smoke from a nearby fire, McFaul thought it had gone completely. Then, dimly, he picked out what remained of the exterior walls. Two shells at least, he thought, and probably some kind of secondary explosion. He braked sharply, leaving the Land Rover in the middle of the street, limping the last fifty yards. The interior of the place was rubble, everything crushed beneath the weight of fallen masonry. McFaul stood in the street, calling Domingos's name, uncertain exactly when the damage had been done. Next door, when he knocked, there was no response. The bungalow opposite, gutted by fire, had been abandoned.

McFaul crossed the road again, clambering over Domingos's shattered front wall, trying not to lose his balance on the loose rubble inside. He began to tear at the wreckage, tossing aside lengths of splintered trusses from the fallen roof, telling himself he had to dig, had to find out, had to know the worst. Then he stopped, sucking at a deep cut in his hand, distracted by something else, something hideously familiar, a garment, yellow and green, crushed beneath a huge chunk of masonry. He stepped across to it, levering the masonry aside, stooping to pick up Domingos's treasured football shirt. Green and yellow were the colours of Brazil's national team. Angolans worshipped Brazilian football, convinced already that their heroes would lift next year's world cup. Across the chest it read: 'BRAZIL – COPA MUNDIAL, '94'.

McFaul shook it out, looking at it. Then he eyed the wreckage for a second or two longer before turning away and limping slowly back towards the Land Rover, the shirt still in his hand.

Molly sat in the gloom of the Café Palmeira, waiting for the rain to stop. She'd never seen rain like it. It seemed to form a solid wall of water, curtaining the café from the street outside. Already the road beyond the pavement had become a foaming brown torrent, carrying rubbish from the pile at the top of the hill, and as she watched she saw the body of a dog wash past, turning over and over, surrounded by a flotilla of rusty tins, discarded bottles and sodden cardboard boxes. In the gutter, the iron grills on the storm drains had begun to lift, forced upwards by the pressure of water beneath. Seconds later, the water was fountaining onto the pavement, forming a long, brown, foam-flecked tongue that began to reach into the café itself.

Molly sipped her coffee, wondering what to do with her feet. The café had a concrete floor, metal chairs and tables. No one seemed to care about the rain. A bulky shape appeared in the street outside. He had a jacket over his head and he was trying to protect a roll of telex paper from the rain. He plunged into the café, splashing through the water inside the door. Molly stood up and pulled out a chair, glad to see him.

'Shit.' Robbie Cunningham beamed at her. 'Can you believe this?'

The rain got heavier. A minute or so later the awning outside began to tear, the cloth bellying downwards under the weight of water. A waiter appeared at Molly's elbow. His sandals were submerged. Robbie looked at the menu and ordered something in Portuguese. Molly said she wasn't hungry but when he insisted she settled for a hot dog.

'*Um cachorro quente,*' he said. '*E dois cervejas.*'

The waiter made his way back to the bar and returned with the beers. Molly watched him pouring hers. She'd had two coffees already and she was dreading having to find a loo. Robbie raised his glass and proposed a toast.

'To drying out,' he said. 'Me, at least.'

He flattened the radio telex against the table-top. The message had come from Muengo within the last hour. It said that there was the possibility of some kind of surrender negotiations and an end to the siege. Molly peered at the name at the end.

'Who's T.P.?'

'Tom Peterson. The bloke I mentioned on the plane. Our man in Luanda. He's new here but he's sound. Good guy.'

'And he's trapped in Muengo?'

'Yeah. Like the rest of them. He went in when we got the word about James. We needed someone on the spot to sort things out and he was our best bet. We weren't expecting a siege then, of course. That wasn't on the menu at all.'

'So what do we do?' Molly gestured helplessly round. 'Just wait?'

Robbie shook his head.

'Llewelyn's working on it,' he said. 'Whatever I tell him about Muengo he just ignores. One way or another, he's determined to get us in. I've told him it's a crazy thing to even try but the guy's on a different planet. I don't think he knows this country's at war yet. I don't think anyone's told him.'

'So will he . . .' Molly shrugged, 'succeed?'

'He might.'

'What would that take?'

Robbie studied her a moment. The run up the hill from the office had pinked his face and he looked even more cherubic than usual.

'Money,' he said uneasily. 'And he seems to have lots.'

*

120

They stayed at the café for an hour, sharing two more beers while they waited for the food. After ten minutes or so, the electricity went off and the waiter came round with candles stuck in empty gazola bottles. It was barely midday but outside it looked like dusk. The rain had stopped now but for some reason there was even more water pouring down the hill, soaking the gaggle of street kids on the pavement.

'So do you trust him?'

Robbie was talking about Llewelyn again. Molly looked glum.

'I have to,' she said, 'I've no choice. I couldn't do it otherwise. Not properly.'

'Do what?'

'Find out about James. Find out what really happened.' She paused. 'And do whatever else he wants.'

'But that's the problem, isn't it?' Robbie gestured helplessly at the telex. 'What's he really after in Muengo?'

Molly thought about the question. It had troubled her since that first interview, the five of them packed into the airless bedroom at the Blue Boar Hotel. She'd tried to raise it a couple of times since, phoning Llewelyn on the London number he'd given her, but whenever she thought she'd pinned him down he managed to avoid giving her a direct answer, sheltering instead behind phrases like 'candid account' and 'ultimate sacrifice'. She'd not seen him face to face again until the evening they'd left for the airport, and by that time he'd become curiously remote, treating her with the kind of lofty concern she'd once encountered in a Harley Street consultant. Thinking about it, the parallels were uncomfortably close. In Llewelyn's eyes, she was plainly one of life's walking wounded. She was suffering. She was under immense stress. And he was there to make her better.

'But that's exactly what he wants,' Robbie said when she tried to explain it. 'That's the way he works. You're the puppet. He pulls the strings.'

'But why?' She frowned. 'Why should he want to pull my strings? What's in all this for him?'

'Fame,' he said at once. 'Glory. Profile. His star's on the wane. His batteries are flat. He needs to recharge. Before he gets too old.'

'You're serious?'

'Completely. These guys run on ego, pure and simple. Without a presence on the screen, they're nothing. It's a kind of sickness, an addiction. Television's full of it. In the UK, it's not such a problem. Out here, it could be difficult.'

'Oh? Why's that?'

Robbie hesitated a moment and Molly realised just how long he'd been working up to this conversation. Relations between the two men, never good, had developed a perceptible chill. The last day and a half, Llewelyn had been treating Robbie like an assistant, someone who'd do his bidding, and the younger man was finding it more and more difficult to hide his irritation.

'These guys are all the same,' Robbie was saying. 'I've met them before. They make up their mind about a story and there's bugger all you can do to open their eyes to anything else. It's a kind of tunnel vision. The facts don't matter. Just me, me, me.'

Molly gazed at him, hearing the contempt in his voice, half-understanding why he should feel so strongly, yet helpless to offer anything constructive of her own. The beer and the candle-light and the puddle of tepid water at her feet had lent her exhaustion a strangely surreal edge. All she wanted to do was get to Muengo. And find her son.

'You're telling me we shouldn't go,' she said wearily. 'Is that it?'

'I'm telling you it could be extremely dangerous.'

'Why?'

Robbie gestured at the telex again.

'I managed to raise Peterson on the HF. The place is wrecked. Four days' shelling. Dodgy water. Not much food. No power. Shooting in the streets.' He paused. 'This is a civil war. I'm not sure Llewelyn understands what that means. This isn't something Angola's staged for his benefit, something he can pop onto video and cart back to London. It's real . . . real blood, real bullets. We could end up dead. All of us. No problem.'

'Then it's simple, surely. If it's that bad then no one will take us, no one will fly, and without a plane it's . . .' she shrugged hopelessly, 'no go.'

There was a long silence. A bus roared by outside, sending a tidal wave of water into the café, producing shrieks of excitement from the street kids. The waiter splashed towards the open door, shaking his fist, cuffing the nearest child. At length, Robbie sat back in his chair. For the first time, Molly realised he was no less exhausted than she was.

'How badly do you want to get there?' he said slowly.

'Badly. That's why I'm here.'

He nodded, toying with his beer.

'And if Llewelyn comes up with some kind of deal? A plane? A pilot? You'll risk it?'

'Of course.'

'After everything I've just said?'

'Yes.' She offered him a wan smile. 'I suppose you might call it tunnel vision. Me, me, me.'

The waiter was singing now, banging a tin tray in time to some Portuguese pop song. Robbie watched him a moment then shrugged, reaching for the telex and rolling it up.

'OK,' he said at length, 'then I guess we'd better get ourselves organised. Fuel. Provisions. Drugs. Stuff they'll be needing. We might as well make it an aid flight. That way they might leave us alone.'

The food arrived. It started to rain again. Molly ate a mouthful or two of her hot dog then knew she had to go to the lavatory. Robbie spoke to the waiter and he produced a key and several sheets of newspaper and a red and white golf umbrella.

The closet was at the back of the restaurant. It didn't have a roof and the tiled floor was under water. Molly found the ceramic footholds on either side of the central hole and squatted as best she could, one hand keeping her skirt up, the other holding the umbrella. By the time she came to use it, the newspaper had turned to pulp, and she squatted there for a minute or two longer, the warm rain pouring off the umbrella, her mind quite blank.

The last few days – Giles's disappearance, the rush for the visa, the vaccinations, the night flight south – had emptied her of everything. Whatever happened next was out of her hands. The only part of her life that remained in focus was James. Finding him. Tending his body. Saying goodbye. She thought about it a moment longer, what Muengo would really be like, whether or not she'd be able to cope, what she could possibly find there that might soften the loss of her son. Then, without warning, the power came back on. The signals bulb began to fizz in its rusty socket over the door and she heard a discreet cough in the yard outside.

'Molly,' Robbie was whispering, 'you OK in there?'

The needle on the fuel gauge had been on 'Empty' for at least three miles when McFaul drove into the ambush. He was returning to the schoolhouse after a fruitless search for Domingos. He'd been to address after address, hunting for friends and relatives, but no one had any news of the little Angolan. The shelling, everyone said, had been terrible. In the chaos of those four days, anything might have happened.

Now, McFaul began to slow the Land Rover, easing down through the gear box, still preoccupied by Domingos's disappearance. Bodies had begun to appear at the roadside, roped in cloth or wrapped in straw mats, waiting for someone to come along and bury them. Ahead was a line of oil drums across the road. Abandoned beneath the stump of a palm tree was a burned-out army truck. Of troops, or police, there was no sign.

McFaul brought the Land Rover to a halt, opening the door to move one of the oil drums aside. He was about to get out when he heard the crack of a semi-automatic rifle. At first he didn't associate it with anything personal. Then there came another shot, and another, followed by a burst of sustained fire. At the same time, the windscreen of the Land Rover shattered, covering him with glass, and he heard the angry whine of bullets ricochetting off a nearby wall. He hesitated a moment, one leg still dangling from the open door, then he saw the line of army troops, six or seven of them, emerging from cover about a hundred yards away. Some of them were laughing. Others were having difficulty standing up. One was raising his carbine again, taking careful aim.

McFaul threw the Land Rover into reverse, pulling into a tight U-turn, cursing himself for offering such an easy target. These guys were drunk. They'd obviously been looting some of the aid houses, stripping them of everything useful, anything they might eat or drink. That's what had happened at the schoolhouse. That's where the fuel and the contents of the freezer had gone.

McFaul was accelerating away now, praying that the diesel held out. He could hear the crackle of small-arms fire behind him and the zip of the bullets past the cab. The guys were having fun, he thought, real turkey shoot. Then there was a sharp metallic clang beside his right ear and he threw himself against the door as the glass in the speedo disintegrated. He looked in the mirror, feeling the engine beginning to falter, seeing nothing but the line of oil drums across the road. He began to weave the Land Rover left and right, try-ing to throw the soldiers off their aim, gathering speed as he did so. Up ahead was an intersection, the right-hand turn blocked by another army truck. There were more soldiers behind it. He could see black faces peering round the driving cab. A hand appeared, then withdrew, and for a split second, seeing the grenade rolling towards him, McFaul knew he was going to die. It was too close. It couldn't fail to kill him.

He stamped on the accelerator, pulling the Land Rover to the left, away from the grenade, pure instinct. The offside of the Land Rover caught the blast. The front tyre shredded and the glass in the door blew inwards and McFaul felt the vehicle lurch on its chassis. For a moment he thought it was going to turn over and he hauled on the wheel, trying to keep it upright, still travelling at speed, knowing now that he had to try and make the last half-mile to the hospital. He could feel something hot and sticky oozing down his right cheek and there was a sharp, burning sensation in his shoulder. Every time he turned the wheel he gasped with pain.

At the end of the road, he wrenched the Land Rover into a right-hand turn. He could hear the remains of the tyre flailing on the road, and a harsh grinding noise as the bare metal rim bit into the tarmac. Up ahead was the abandoned apartment block which housed the hospital. The hospital was on the two upper floors. Over the blue polythene sheeting that hid the windows someone had hung a huge red cross. He concentrated on it, oblivious now to what he'd left behind. The engine was beginning to miss, coughing and jerking, and he took it out of gear for the final few yards, coasting to a halt in the shadow of what had once been the main entrance.

For a moment, he let himself slump behind the wheel. His shoulder had gone numb, no more pain, and when he lifted a hand to his cheek he could feel the fragments of glass embedded amongst four days' growth of beard. His hand found the door release, his fingers slippery with his own blood, and he leaned his weight against the door, opening it. Then, from nowhere, he heard a voice, felt a hand supporting him, and he looked up, infinitely weary, recognising the freckles and the rich auburn curls.

Christianne was out of breath. She stepped aside, letting two Angolans lift McFaul from the driving seat. They carried him into the apartment block, up several flights of stairs, Christianne following behind. He answered her shouted questions as best he could. Yes, he thought he'd been hit. No, it didn't hurt too much.

They got to the second floor, pushing through a dirty sheet hanging from the ceiling. The place was in virtual darkness and there was a strong smell of bleach. The Angolans grunted with the effort of lifting McFaul's body onto a table and then Christianne's face was there again, beside his own, her fingers probing for wounds. She produced a pair of scissors and began to cut away at his T-shirt. He felt the coolness of the scissors against his skin, then her face was at eye level again as she inspected his bare shoulder. She was talking to someone else now, in French, and McFaul heard a man laughing. Seconds later one of the Norwegian surgeons was beaming down at him. A shard from the wing mirror had lodged in his upper arm. It had made a mess of his serpent tattoo but he'd seen worse injuries. He dipped a length of McFaul's scissored T-shirt in disinfectant and began to swab the edges of the wound. The pain made McFaul gasp, a sensation of immense heat, and for a moment he was back in the hospital in Kuwait, semiconscious, trying to make sense of what had happened. It was right what they said about mine victims. It didn't really hurt for several hours. Losing half a leg had been infinitely less painful than this.

Christianne was back beside him, attending to his face with a pair of tweezers. He could hear the slivers of deposited glass tinkling in the kidney bowl as she coaxed each one out. She was smiling now, one hand steadying his head, the other probing for more splinters. At length, satisfied, she stepped back.

'*Un moment,*' she said.

She disappeared and McFaul lay on his side while the Norwegian bound his arm with a length of torn sheet. The wound was beginning to throb now and he winced as the surgeon tightened the final knot. Later, if they could find any Novocain, he'd put some stitches in. McFaul lay back, sweating, his eyes closed. He knew he'd been lucky. At the road-block, sober, the soldiers would have killed him in seconds. The grenade, on any other day, would have torn him apart. The shock finally hit him and he began to shake, pulling his knees up to his chin, pushing his clenched fists deep between his thighs. He felt cold, empty. He felt as if every last ounce of courage had drained out of him.

There was a movement by his head and a stifled cough. He opened one eye. Christianne again, and another face beside hers. The forehead was swathed in bandages, and one eye was purpled with bruising, but there was no mistaking the smile. McFaul struggled to get up but couldn't. He felt his eyes filling with tears and he turned his head away, still trembling. Then a hand closed on his and he heard the familiar chuckle.

'Hey . . .' Domingos was saying, 'good to see you.'

CHAPTER FIVE

Todd Llewelyn was in the lobby of the Presidente Meridien Hotel, wondering whether the South African would show up, when he recognised the face at the reception desk. The woman had just been dropped in the hotel forecourt. She was tall, elegant, expensively dressed. The Angolan in the suit behind the wheel of the big Mercedes was still waiting for a farewell wave. Like most of the newly arrived in Luanda, the woman looked slightly dazed.

Llewelyn picked up his shoulder-bag and approached the desk. A revolving stand offered a selection of foreign magazines, most of them at least a month old. He began to browse through a copy of *Time*, listening as the woman enquired about a pre-booked room. She'd come from London. She'd be staying a week. She put her Dior handbag on the desk, looking for her passport, asking whether there were any messages. The clerk began to check and the woman turned round, at last lifting a tired arm to the driver of the Mercedes. She'd put on a little weight since Llewelyn had last seen her and she'd done something complicated with her hair, but the mannerisms were still there: the heavy mascara, the over-ready smile, the tiny nerve that occasionally fluttered at one corner of her mouth.

At the BBC, as a line producer on a flagship documentary series, Alma Bradley had wedded a skittish femininity to a ruthless talent for mixing it with the roughest competition. She'd kept long hours and taken few prisoners and when the editor's job was boarded there was no one at Kensington House who didn't win money on the inevitable bets. That Alma would end up in charge was never in doubt. The real question was quite where she'd go next.

The clerk behind the desk had found a message. The name of the sender confirmed Llewelyn's worst fears.

'Senhor Tavares,' he said, 'from the Ministry of Information.'

Alma thanked him, reading the message and folding it into her handbag. The Louis Vuitton luggage was already on a trolley, being wheeled across the lobby. She followed the concierge and disappeared into the lift without a backward glance.

Llewelyn returned the magazine to the rack. Alma Bradley was the living proof that there was still money and fame in television documentaries. Her freelance production company, ABTV, had projects placed with all the major outlets. She'd built a team around her who'd managed to generate a flood of irresistible ideas, trademarked by that rare knack of finding the right human face for the really important issues. Molly Jordan was the perfect ABTV vehicle and the note from the Ministry of Information proved it. Antonio Tavares headed the government's Media Liaison Unit. Llewelyn had spent an hour in his office only yesterday. Without his approval, and a hefty fee, nothing got filmed.

'Mr Llewelyn?'

It was a soft male voice, freighted with a heavy South African accent. Llewelyn spun round. A man in his mid-twenties was standing beside the magazine rack. He was much shorter than Llewelyn had somehow expected. He was wearing bleached denims and a cotton leisure shirt. His hair was blond, curling over the collar of his shirt, and under the tan he affected an air of almost permanent amusement. He wore a bracelet of elephant hair on one wrist and a big Seiko watch on the other. In a different life he could have been a minor film star, or the owner of a suddenly fashionable restaurant.

Llewelyn extended a hand. His contact at the airport had described this man as the best pilot in Southern Africa. Not cheap, he'd said, but completely fearless. The kind of guy you pray for when the weather's impossible, and one engine's out, and you've somehow lost the map that matters. The kind of guy you need to get you to Muengo. Real artist.

'Piet Rademeyer?'

'Yeah.'

'Good to meet you.'

At Rademeyer's suggestion, they went through to the hotel's coffee shop. He seemed to know the place well, trading small talk with one of the under-managers on the way. Llewelyn chose a table at the back, beside one of the big panoramic windows. Rademeyer ordered coffee and toast, letting Llewelyn make the running. From time to time he interrupted the older man, his questions direct to the point of aggression.

'Why Muengo?'

Llewelyn hesitated. He was still thinking about Alma Bradley. Somehow she must have picked up the story. Maybe the press report in the *Guardian*. Maybe a pre-publication leak in the *Sunday Mirror*. Either way, it didn't matter. Competition changed everything.

'Business,' Llewelyn muttered. 'It's just important we get in. That's all.'

'What kind of business?'

'My business.'

'You know the place is under siege?'

'Yes, of course.' Llewelyn paused again. 'The people I've been talking to say that might not be a problem. Not for you.'

The young pilot laughed.

'They mean I'd risk it,' he said, 'that's all. It's no guarantee we'd get in there.'

'Of course. But you'd try.'

'Yeah, I would.' He nodded. 'How much are you paying?'

'How much would you want?'

'That wasn't my question. They explain the normal rate?'

'Yes. Five thousand dollars a day. All in.'

'Treble it.'

'For a Twin Otter?'

'No.' Rademeyer was spreading grape jelly on the remains of his toast. 'A Dove.'

'How big's that?'

'Smaller than an Otter. Six up. Or fewer bodies and more cargo. Depending. It's your call. You decide.'

'Is this your aircraft?'

'Yes.'

'You own it?'

'Yes.'

'And it's still fifteen thousand dollars?'

'Afraid so. Like I said, it's your call. Get a better price somewhere else . . .' he shrugged, 'you'll maybe save yourself some money.'

Llewelyn gazed out of the window. A tiny fishing boat was putting out to sea, its wake feathering the flat grey waters of the lagoon. Fifteen thousand dollars was an enormous chunk out of the programme budget, the production equivalent of all their other travel and accommodation expenses.

'Does that price guarantee a landing?' he enquired.

'No.'

'Just getting there?'

'Yep. And taking a look. If they've blocked the field, trucks, tractors, whatever, it could be evil. Depends.'

'On what?'

'On whether they know what they're doing. The Dove's a tough old airplane. There are ways and means.'

Llewelyn nodded, uncertain what lay at the end of this conversation. Until a couple of years back, Piet Rademeyer had been flying for the South African Air Force. Heading north, he'd evidently given himself five years to make his fortune. At prices like these, he'd be rich by Christmas.

'They tell me you flew jets. Back home.'

Rademeyer reached for the last of his coffee.

'Mirages,' he said briefly. 'Plus some of the bigger stuff. They tell you about the payment procedure as well?'

'Half up front, half on completion.'

'Sure, but in dollars.' His hand went to the back pocket of his jeans. Llewelyn took the folded card, flattening it against the table. The card read 'Rademeyer Aviation'. Underneath there was a Luanda box number.

'On the back,' Rademeyer said, nursing his coffee.

Llewelyn turned the card over. There was a handwritten address in Johannesburg and a line of digits underneath.

'Bank of Natal,' Rademeyer explained, 'and the number of the account.'

'You want the money deposited there?'

'Yes.'

'Before we fly?'

'Half of it.' He nodded. 'A banker's draft will do. Dollars, though. Like I said.'

Llewelyn thought about the proposition for a moment. He'd need to organise the banker's draft through Pegley in London. For the time being, he'd pretend that $7,500 was the total fee. That way he'd avoid tiresome arguments about extortion. Not that Pegley wouldn't have a point. He glanced up. Rademeyer was studying the mirror behind Llewelyn's head. Alma Bradley had appeared at the other end of the coffee shop. She'd changed into a mid-length cotton dress, a vivid green patterned in yellow. The long blonde hair, secured by a velvet ribbon when she'd arrived, now hung down her back.

Llewelyn leaned forward over the table.

'It's crazy money,' he said. 'How about five up front, five on completion? Providing we land?'

Rademeyer showed no signs of having heard him. He'd half-turned in his seat now, watching Alma as she sat down and signalled the waitress for a menu. The last thing Llewelyn wanted was Alma knowing he was already here. He put a hand on Rademeyer's arm. The South African didn't take his eyes off the newcomer.

'OK,' Llewelyn said hastily, 'let's talk about the rest, the balance. When does that become payable?'

'Whenever we get back.'

'*Whenever?*'

'Sure.' Rademeyer turned round at last, amused again, lifting his empty cup in a mock toast. 'Welcome to Angola.'

McFaul stood beneath the shower at the back of the school-house, trying to sluice away the smell of the hospital. The smell hung on him like a garment. It was everywhere. In his hair. On his body. Even in the folds of the khaki shorts he'd only just put on. He let the falling water splash over him, determined to rid himself of the heavy animal scent of decaying flesh and blocked latrines.

The shower was Domingos's design, a jerrycan supported on a revolving cradle. A chain device up-ended the jerrycan and three puncture holes spouted a couple of gallons of the clear, cold water he and Bennie hauled daily from the local well. McFaul let the last of the water dribble down his upturned face, returning the soap to its plastic box. The hard-baked earth at his feet had turned to a rich, soupy mud, oozing up between his toes, and he could feel the warmth of the sun on his shoulders. He reached for the towel he'd left on the window sill and began to pat himself dry, taking care to avoid the flap of sutured skin high on his right arm. The stitches had gone in last night. Christianne had brought over some Novocain she'd kept in a stash at the MSF house, and she'd woken one of the Norwegian surgeons with the promise of half a bottle of vodka. By mid-night, his arm bandaged and throbbing, McFaul had been back at the schoolhouse.

Now, his shorts still dripping wet, he stepped round the corner of the building. Christianne had given him a sling, a big square of torn sheet she'd folded into a triangle, and he was still trying to tie the knot one-handed when he saw one of the battered army jeeps bouncing down the track towards them. McFaul gave up with the knot and began to fold the sling. The jeep braked sharply and a young officer got out. He was carrying a zip-up briefcase and his shirt looked newly pressed. He gestured at the bandage on McFaul's arm. The water had penetrated the bandage and it was newly pinked with blood.

'The Brigadier hopes you are well,' he murmured awkwardly. 'We still don't know what happened.'

McFaul looked at him a moment, trying to gauge what lay behind the wary smile. Then he indicated the open door of the schoolhouse. Inside, it was cooler. Bennie had been up for hours, crossing the city to assess the damage to the Land Rover. McFaul pulled two chairs towards the table and poured water from a thermos into the only clean glass. The young officer eyed the water before extending a hand.

'My name is Tomas,' he said. 'I work for the Brigadier.'

McFaul accepted the handshake and gestured for the young officer to sit down. Earlier, he'd been on the radio to Muengo's military HQ. He needed to know what lay behind yesterday's incident. Was it a mistake? A chance encounter? A handful of kid soldiers with too many guns and too much Sagres? Or was it something more sinister? A calculated attempt to blow away an accredited member of the aid community? The latter, in McFaul's view, was unlikely but three minutes' conversation on the radio had left him none the wiser. The Brigadier was busy. There was much work to do. Perhaps someone might be sent to the schoolhouse.

Tomas was nursing the glass. When he put it to his lips, they barely touched the water.

'I nearly got killed,' McFaul pointed out. 'You'll know that.'

Tomas nodded.

'There's an inquiry,' he said at once. 'We need to know exactly what happened.'

'Your soldiers tried to kill me. Once at a road-block. Again with a grenade.' McFaul touched the bandage briefly. 'That's what happened.'

'I understand.'

The young officer began to look uneasy again. He reached for his briefcase and unzipped it. There was nothing inside. He looked nonplussed for a moment, then asked for the Land Rover's maintenance manual.

'Why do you want that?'

'Mr Bennie says we'll need it.'

'You've seen him? This morning?'

'Yes. He's outside the hospital. Our men are helping him.'

'*You're* repairing it?'

'Of course. The Brigadier insists. We have engineers.' He risked a smile. 'Good with their hands.'

McFaul gazed at him for a second or two, recognising the gesture for what it was. There wouldn't be anything as formal as an apology but this was the next best thing. The Land Rover would be seen to. A handful of young soldiers would be taken aside and dealt with. Global Clearance, after all, had its uses.

McFaul reached across the table and took the glass. He swallowed the water and stood up, leaving a damp patch on the wooden seat. His precious supply of beer was in the dormitory next door. When he returned, limping back towards the table, the young officer couldn't take his eyes off McFaul's false leg.

McFaul put both cans on the table, pulling one tab, then the other. He lifted the can of Sagres, inviting Tomas to do the same. The young officer was grinning now.

'Anaesthetic,' McFaul said gruffly. 'Cheers.'

It was late morning before Molly Jordan found the supermarket. She'd left the Terra Sancta house at eleven, armed with a shopping list from Robbie. Todd Llewelyn had evidently been able to sweet-talk a pilot into taking them to Muengo, though it would be at least a day before they'd fly. The guy's plane, said Robbie, was down the coast at Benguela, undergoing an engine change, and he'd be leaving at noon to fetch it back.

Super-Africa lay three blocks from the waterfront, a single-storey concrete warehouse protected by heavy iron grilles over the windows and two armed guards at the door. The shoppers were almost all Europeans, women mainly, and they drifted up and down the aisles, stopping from time to time when they found something worth looking at on the shelves. Most of the stuff on display was either tinned fish from Portugal or South Africa, or roughly packaged bags of basic foodstuffs, staples like rice, maize, sugar and coffee.

The list Molly carried was, in Robbie's phrase, 'pure fantasy', and by the time she'd half-completed her second lap of the store she'd only managed to find three of the requested items. She paused for a moment by the meat counter. The flies were settling on thick slabs of something bloody while one of the Angolans at the back hacked at the carcass of a goat. Molly peered at her list again. She'd ticked sugar, and sorghum flour, and three packets of cereal, and on her own initiative she'd acquired three dozen bottles of mineral water. At the bottom of Robbie's list, in the space beneath the last item, the paper carried the indentations of something he must have written on the page above. With some difficulty, and much to her regret, Molly had managed to decipher the scribbled message. She assumed he'd written it after some kind of conversation with the Terra Sancta man in Muengo. 'Burials imminent,' it read, 'quicklime?'

Molly turned away from the meat counter, revolted by the smell. She was about to head for the check-out when she noticed someone smiling at her. He was dressed like a businessman – lightweight suit, striped tie, polished shoes – but unlike every other shopper in the store he was black. He looked late middle-aged, maybe fifty or more, and he carried a great deal of bulk beneath the light grey chalk stripe, but for a big man he moved

with extraordinary lightness, appearing at the mouth of a neighbouring aisle and gliding across towards Molly's trolley. His
greying Afro lent him an air of slightly wild distinction and
when the smile widened he reminded her of a TV chat-show
host, eager to cement a million new relationships.

'You're Molly,' he said. 'My name's Larry, Larry Giddings.'

He held out a hand, long fingers, two huge rings, perfectly
buffed nails. He spoke in a soft American drawl, a voice that
offered the comforts of instant friendship. Molly smiled back.
She was about to ask how he'd known her name when he
reached out and drew her towards him. Over his arm he was
carrying one of the store's wire baskets. At the bottom of the
basket was a list.

'This place makes you crazy, right? And you know why?
Look at this.' Molly glanced down the list. Giddings' finger
paused at item four. Matches. 'Last week, hundreds of packets
of them. Thousands. Everywhere. And what do I do? I buy
three. Three, ma'am. And you know what? That ship ain't
coming back. Not now. Not ever. So what does that make me?
Apart from stupid? Yes, ma'am. It makes me crazy. Hey—' He
broke off, talking briskly to the Angolan behind the meat counter in Portuguese, then turned back to Molly. 'That son of
yours? Young James?'

Molly blinked.

'Yes?'

'I just wanted to say sorry. That's all. Just that. But I mean
it. I'm real sorry. If I can help in any way, just give me the
word.'

Molly was staring at him now, bewildered.

'How did you know . . .?'

Before she had time to finish the question, Giddings reached
into her trolley and tapped the two-way radio she'd propped
amongst her purchases. Robbie had insisted she take it. She'd
need a lift back from the supermarket. She was to call him at
the Terra Sancta office.

'Everyone heard it, ma'am. Every soul with one of these. It's what we do all day. We tune in and we wise up. May I?' He smiled at her and then turned the radio on, peering at the channel selector. On Robbie's instructions, Molly had left it on Channel Two. Now, she found herself eavesdropping on several conversations at once. English. French. And another language she didn't immediately recognise. Her new friend returned the radio to the trolley. 'One world, ma'am,' he beamed at her, 'and all of us listening.'

They walked on. Larry Giddings worked for an outfit called Aurora. He described it as a Christian fellowship, dedicated to the relief of suffering. The organisation was headquartered in Raleigh, North Carolina, but Larry himself came from Fort Lauderdale. He had a nice apartment one block from the sea. Most times, he missed it real bad but the thing about suffering was to share it. Only that way could you ever truly understand these people.

'Tuning in . . .' he said for the second time, 'and wising up. Your boy's with the Lord. And the Lord cares.'

He talked a little more about James, how his death had shocked the aid community, how people had talked about it on the radio, confiding their own fears to each other. The place was full of mines. Everyone had listened to the briefings, read the specially prepared aid manuals, but that wasn't at all the same as being out there, translating all those tricksy diagrams and horrible photographs into real life. What had happened to James had already shattered dozens of other lives. Everyone knew it. And everyone mourned.

By the time they got to the check-out, Molly had begun to warm to Larry Giddings. His conversation was like a recently opened bottle of something fizzy, a gentle effervescence that raised her spirits and made her feel less alone. He was constantly slipping back and forth, direct one moment, opaque the next, starting one thought, then returning to pick up another before veering off on a third tack, explaining about the rainy season, about the currency rip-offs, about why it was crazy to even think of swimming on the harbour side of the lagoon. He treated her with great gentleness, as a favourite uncle might. He's concerned, she thought. He really cares.

At the check-out, the girl rang Molly's items through twice, then handed her both receipts. Molly looked at them. The difference came to 354,000 kwanzas.

'May I?'

Molly showed Giddings the till receipts and she watched him going through the items in the trolley. Finally, he looked sternly at the girl and said something in Portuguese. The girl nodded and Molly hesitated a moment before handing Giddings her purse. He took out the wad of local currency Robbie had given her, peeling off nine orange notes and then folding a tenth around it. He did this eleven times and then added some more notes.

'How much is that?'

'Eleven million.'

'Eleven *million*?'

'Yeah. Forty-five dollars to you and me.'

He added a handful of other notes and gave it to the girl behind the till, and for the first time, Molly realised exactly what it was that other women in the supermarket were carrying in their carefully guarded plastic bags. Every one was stuffed with kwanza notes.

The other side of the check-out, Molly and Giddings pushed past the security guards. On the street, they were surrounded at once by kids selling identical goods. At the kerbside, there was a big American station-wagon. Taped to the inside of the passenger window was a photocopy of the Aurora logo, a halo circling a cross. Larry unlocked the rear door, shooing the kids away, and then started to load Molly's shopping. When Molly began to explain about the arrangement with Robbie, the lift she was supposed to summon, he put a finger to his lips and guided her gently towards the passenger door.

'Take you home, ma'am,' he explained. 'The least I can do.'

Robbie Cunningham made contact with Muengo again around noon, tuning the big Terra Sancta HF radio to the UN frequency. When the circuit was established, he gave his call sign and asked for Tom Peterson, adding that it was urgent. The girl who handled most of the UN traffic out of Muengo ran to wake Peterson up. Evidently he was down in the basement that served as the UN bunker, taking a nap.

When Peterson finally got to the radio he still sounded half-asleep.

'How is it?' Robbie asked at once.

'Quiet. I think.'

There was a pause at Peterson's end and Robbie could hear him talking to the girl in French. The two men had worked together in the Sudan and Robbie knew that one of his many gifts was a fine ear for languages. To Robbie's knowledge, he spoke at least four. He was back on the circuit now, confirming that the guns were still quiet. The odd fire-fight in town. But nothing really nasty.

'Quiet enough to get a plane in?'

'Why?'

Something in Peterson's voice made Robbie pause. If there was a problem at the airfield, he wouldn't risk mentioning it on air. UNITA might construe it as military information – spying – and if that happened then things could get tricky. Surviving in the aid world meant keeping your distance from both sides. No weapons. No favours. No helpful little updates on the tactical situation. Robbie had his eyes on a note from Todd Llewelyn. The plane he'd chartered had a one-ton payload. Peterson, he was sure, could use every ounce.

'We have an option on an aid flight,' he said carefully. 'What do you need?'

'Antibiotics. Milk powder. Fuel,' Peterson said at once. 'The food situation's grim. Even the dogs have disappeared.'

'And?'

Peterson reeled off a long list of items. Robbie reached for a box of photocopier paper and wrote them all down. When Peterson had finished he looked at the payload again. A ton wouldn't be enough. Anything like. Peterson was talking about the airstrip now, oblivious to listening ears. He'd heard a rumour it was closed. Trucks across the landing strip. Nothing in or out.

'Is this permanent?'

'No idea.'

'How about tomorrow? Any chance if we just turn up?'

'Who? Who just turns up?'

'Me. And a couple of others.' He looked at the list. 'Any chance of a landing?'

'Is this official?' Peterson sounded puzzled now. 'An evacuation flight?'

'No,' Robbie shook his head, 'but we'd bring in the goodies. Or at least some of them.'

He frowned for a moment, thinking suddenly of the Director, back at his desk in Winchester. If the bid was for profile, for plastering Terra Sancta's logo across the nation's television screens, then this was certainly one way of accomplishing just that. A city under siege. A mother determined to recover her son's body. And an airstrip that might – or might not – be open.

'What do you think?' Robbie said. 'You want us to give it a try?'

He bent to the radio, hearing Peterson talking in French again, to a man this time. When he came back he sounded tired.

'Fernando says it's a mess. He sees no way.'

'No way for what?'

'An official flight. Anything he could sanction.'

'So where does that leave us?'

There was a moment's pause. Then a hollow laugh.

'My thoughts entirely,' Peterson was saying. 'Why don't you check again tonight?'

In Muengo, early afternoon, the heavens opened. Clouds had been building over the distant peaks of the Plan Alto all morning, the air slowly thickening, heavy with the promise of rain. Now, it fell from a sky the colour of putty, a relentless downpour, sluicing noisily from damaged guttering, churning the garden of the Red Cross compound into a porridge of mud and rubble.

McFaul and Domingos splashed across to a gap in the wire fence. Bennie had spent all morning wrestling with the Global Land Rover and a couple of army mechanics had honoured the Brigadier's promise of help. Thanks to them, the Land Rover was now back in working order. McFaul was delighted. For a full tank, and a couple of extra jerrycans of fuel, he'd in turn agreed to organise the burial of Muengo's dead.

Bennie was waiting at the wheel of the Land Rover. McFaul and Domingos got in. Like McFaul, Domingos and his family had escaped with flesh wounds. The blast from a near miss had brought down the front wall of his bungalow and they'd fled to a cousin before a direct hit demolished the rest. Domingos's wife, Celestina, had a gashed arm while Domingos's injuries were limited to cuts and bruises.

Now he gave Bennie directions to a construction yard beside the blackened remains of what had once been Muengo's bus station. Bennie drove slowly, wary of submerged shell craters, and McFaul sat beside the passenger door, his right arm back in the sling, his left hand fingering the shrapnel rents where the metal had taken the full force of the exploding grenade. Already, yesterday's incident belonged to another life. After the air-drop, he should have known the way it would be: the soldiers drunk, short of food, trigger-happy, frightened. He'd been handed all the clues. The blame for the ambush lay with no one but himself. Next time, there wouldn't be enough luck in the world to get him through.

He glanced back at Domingos. Domingos had also been talking to Captain Tomas.

'What did you tell him?'

'I said we wanted protection.'

'From his own men?'

'From everyone. Both sides.'

'And what did he say?'

'Nothing. These guys are losing. UNITA are on the airstrip. They could be in town tonight. You know what they did in the north? Round Cafunfo? The diamonds?'

McFaul shook his head, beginning to regret the conversation. When the mood took him, Domingos could be surprisingly stern. He'd noticed it before, when his kids got out of hand with Celestina. Now he was adjusting the bandage round his head, frowning with concentration.

'The people were fleeing. Some of them worked in the diamond mines. They'd collected bagfuls of the dust you get down there. Sometimes you find little tiny diamonds in the dust. Nothing big. Nothing important. But enough to feed a man and his family for a year . . .'

Domingos nodded, gazing out through the mud-smeared windscreen. His voice was low, barely audible over the drumbeat of rain on the cabin roof. McFaul glanced across at Bennie. The Londoner had always been fascinated by Domingos. It was his first job in Africa and the little Angolan wasn't at all what he'd been expecting. Africans, in the books he'd been reading, were either starving or bone-idle, or off the planet on ganja and umpteen wives. For the first time, Bennie's eyes left the road.

'Well,' he said, 'what happened to the diamonds?'

'They swallowed them. Before they ran.'

'And?'

'The soldiers caught them, the UNITA soldiers. They'd beaten another man. They knew what was happening.'

'So what did they do?'

'They cut them open. Alive. Looking for the diamonds.'

'Fuck me. You kidding?' Bennie shook his head in amazement, dropping a gear and hauling on the wheel to avoid a half-submerged electricity pole, and Domingos laughed softly, laying a hand on McFaul's shoulder.

'So you see how it is with the commander here? The man has a lot on his mind. And his soldiers, too.'

The soldiers were waiting outside the construction yard. They were sitting in the back of an ancient Russian truck, immobile, their rifles upright between their knees, water sheeting off the peaks of their forage caps. The rain had soaked through their camouflage fatigues and the thin cotton clung to their bodies, giving them a strangely alien look, mottled and blotched like visitors from another planet. Some of them watched as Bennie pulled the Land Rover to a halt, incurious, listless, beaten. Domingos spotted the officer and got out to talk to him. Inside the compound, he could see the digger Bennie had found earlier. It was yellow, a Japanese model. Apparently one of the aid people had hired it some weeks earlier.

Domingos returned. Already the rain had penetrated his bandage, softening the blackened crust of dried blood.

'The men will help,' he said briskly. 'The officer wants to know where you're going to dig.'

McFaul had already chosen a spot. Bennie had the keys to the digger and Domingos took the wheel of the Land Rover, leading the little convoy back through the city to a hillock beside a grove of mango trees. The run-off from the hillock had turned the surrounding ground into a quagmire and for a moment or two McFaul thought they were going to bog down. The rain had begun to ease now, watery patches of blue appearing between towering stacks of cumulus, the horizon already veiled with rising steam as the sun reached through.

Beneath the trees, already parked, was the Toyota Land-cruiser which belonged to MSF. McFaul limped across, his boots squelching in the mud. Christianne was sitting behind the wheel. She looked pale and drawn, and her fingers kept returning to the thin gold crucifix she wore around her neck. When McFaul's shadow fell across the cab, she wound the window down, her eyes drawn at once to his sling.

'How is it?'

McFaul said it was fine. He was embarrassed by what had happened at the hospital when he'd first arrived. He'd never lost control like that in his life. It was worse, in a way, than the ambush.

'You get him out OK?' he asked, peering into the back of the Landcruiser.

Christianne nodded. She'd just brought James's body from the schoolhouse. She'd disinfected the freezer and done what she could about the smell with a can of borrowed aftershave. With luck, hostilities permitting, the building would be ready for reoccupation by nightfall. She went through it all without a trace of emotion – just another chore, another hour or so of tidying up – but McFaul knew the price she'd really paid. Until the rebels had taken the airstrip, she'd been planning to fly James out. Now, she'd have to bury him.

McFaul reached into the cab, a reassuring hand on her shoulder, and she clung to it a moment before turning her head away. McFaul stepped back from the Landcruiser, hearing the driver of the soldiers' truck gunning the engine as the back wheels slipped on the sodden grass. They were off now to collect bodies from the roadside, four days worth of Muengo's dead. No one knew for sure how many had been killed in the shelling but Bennie had done a quick recce in the Land Rover after the morning's repairs and he was planning to bury at least sixty. He was still at the controls of the digger, eyeing the ground where it began to rise beneath the mango trees. The sun was hot now, crusting the mud on the thickly welted tyres.

McFaul felt a pressure on his arm. Christianne was standing beside him, watching Bennie at work. Bennie was getting the feel of the controls, moving the arm of the digger up and down, scoring a deep line in the earth with the scoop. The soil here was a dark, rich brown, tinged with ochre, the colour of drying blood.

'Has he done this before?' Christianne said.

'Years ago. On a building site.'

'*Alors.* It's good you use the machine. I thought . . . you know . . .' she made a digging motion, 'it would take all day.'

'Nothing like.' McFaul shook his head. 'Bennie says an hour or so.'

'Good.' Christianne was still watching Bennie. 'James used this too. You know that? This same machine? Those pipes he laid from the river?'

McFaul nodded, not taking the conversation any further. Finally, Bennie began to dig, the scoop taking huge bites from the newly softened earth, piling it up beside the deepening trench. After a while, McFaul heard the whine of the returning truck. He glanced round. The soldiers were standing up in the back. Some of them had wrung out their shirts and tied them around their face, covering their nose and mouth. Another man had appeared. He was young. He wore slacks and a pale blue shirt. Christianne said he was a priest.

'I never asked you . . .' McFaul began.

'*Pardon?*'

'. . . whether you wanted a separate grave.' He nodded back towards the Landcruiser.

Christianne shook her head, watching the soldiers jumping off the truck. Bodies were stacked on the floor like cords of timber.

'No,' she said at last. 'In Africa, he would have wanted this. To be buried together. One grave.'

'You're sure? Only—'

'No.' She shook her head emphatically. 'One grave.'

The soldiers began to file past, staggering under the weight of the shrouded bodies. Christianne watched them approaching the yawning trench trying not to lose their footing in the mud.

'Children died too,' she said. 'Several at the hospital. One of them was Maria.'

'Maria?'

'The little girl James tried to save.' She made a vague, hopeless gesture before her hand again found the crucifix around her neck.

Molly Jordan was due at the British embassy at three o'clock. She'd phoned earlier for an appointment, surprised that the ambassador's secretary was already aware of her presence in Luanda. The ambassador himself had been trying to make contact. There were certain issues on which he'd welcome a discussion. Perhaps she'd be kind enough to pop over.

Larry Giddings, her new American friend, insisted on giving her a lift, reappearing outside the Terra Sancta office in his battered estate car while Robbie scoured Luanda for a ton of assorted supplies. Todd Llewelyn had by now confirmed a flight for tomorrow morning. They were to meet Piet Rademeyer at the international airport at 8 a.m. At the very least, the South African would be able to gauge whether a landing at Muengo was possible.

Now, Larry Giddings sat behind the wheel of the Buick, inching across the city. The traffic stretched ahead down the Avenida Comandante Valodia towards the distant bulk of the São Miguel fortress, a soft brown shimmer in the heat. The air-conditioning in the Buick had broken and Giddings had the window down, one arm draped over the rusty sill, the other nursing a can of something warm and fizzy he'd just bought from a kerbside trader. Molly sat beside him, one eye on the dashboard clock. Conversation with the big American was easy. You just listened.

Giddings had been explaining about slavery. Angola had

148

evidently been a prime source of slaves for the sugar plantations in Brazil. The English and the Portuguese had shipped them across the Atlantic in their hundreds of thousands, hauling them to the coast from the interior, shackling them to trees at night. In Giddings's view, this had set a pattern from which the locals had never fully escaped. Once a slave, he seemed to be saying, always a slave.

Molly frowned, half-following the logic. They had barely twenty minutes to make it to the embassy and the traffic showed no signs of moving.

'You mean they're still slaves? Even now?'

'Technically, ma'am, no. Ain't nobody are slaves now. But think about it. Nineteen seventy-five. You know what happened then?' Molly shook her head. 'The Portuguese left. Little trouble back home. Army coup. And you know what? They took every last damn thing with them. They'd had the country trussed up like a chicken, real tight. The white guys ran the mines, the fishing, the railways, you name it. Out in the bush, same story. Anything that moved, anything that needed growing, or harvesting, or repairing, or selling, there you'd find some fat Portuguese bossman. The blacks, the *mestiços*, knew squat about squat. Famous for it. So no prizes for what happened when the white guys left. Independence? Nationhood? Are you serious? Come '75, we're talking the biggest orphanage in Africa, millions and millions just waiting to be told what to do, what to think, and believe me . . .' he waved a languid hand towards the sea, 'the bad guys couldn't wait.'

Molly nodded. The traffic, at last, was beginning to move.

'Bad guys?'

'Soviets, ma'am. Operation Carlotta. Ever hear about that?'

'No.'

'Well, now . . .' he pulled into the next lane of traffic, brooding, 'the Soviets were clever. They used the Cubans. Nice play. Same colour. Same, I guess, temperament. Believe me, you couldn't move round here for guys from Havana. They just rolled in, thousands of them. Course, to begin with, we were there too, us and the South Africans. That was cool. Line in the sand. Hey, guys, so far and no further. Know what I mean? Sure you do, but then the college kids in Washington all woke up from that horrible Vietnam nightmare and started hollerin' about covert activities, and secret stuff, and spooky-spooky, and violations of sovereignty, and all that bullshit, and you know what? We left them to it.'

'Left who to it?'

'The Soviets, ma'am. I been telling you. Operation Carlotta. Milk and rusks and a damn fine happy Christmas from Ol' Mother Russia. What's good for us is good for them. Know what we call that? Down where I come from?'

'No.'

'Communism.'

Giddings shook his head, more sorrow than anger, and Molly found herself wondering exactly how old he was, and what he'd been up to in the mid-seventies. Her knowledge of the Cold War was minimal and certainly didn't extend to whatever had happened in this tormented city.

Giddings had turned left now, the old Buick wallowing through a series of side-streets. Soon, they were bumping over cobblestones. The houses here looked centuries old, the narrow windows shuttered against the harsh afternoon sun. Giddings coasted past a mountain of rubbish, tossing the empty can out of the car window. Then he licked his fingertips, one after the other, grimacing at the taste.

'You think I talk too much? Just say—'

'No,' Molly shook her head, 'not at all. It's fascinating.'

'—only I know some folks don't like it. Me? I'm fascinated by the place. Was then. Am now. And, hey . . .' he touched her lightly on the arm, 'good luck with your Mr Ambassador.'

They swung left again and came to a halt. A uniformed Gurkha stood beside a security gate. A tall white wall stretched away down the street. Behind it was a pale blue building wreathed in pink and purple flowers. Giddings was already out of the car, opening Molly's door. He was beaming again, exactly the expression Molly had first seen beside the meat counter in the supermarket. Molly began to thank him for the lift but he waved her courtesies away.

'You want me to wait? Sure. I'll be here. Take care now. And say hi for me.'

Todd Llewelyn sat in the downstairs office at the Terra Sancta house, waiting for the phone to ring. He'd been here for nearly an hour now, sprawled in the broken armchair, trying to resist the temptation to fall asleep. He'd tried for most of the morning to get a message through to London, and at lunch-time he'd finally succeeded in making contact. It was vital, he'd told the girl on the People's Channel switchboard, that he talk to Martin Pegley. He needed to organise the banker's draft for the Muengo flight. And he needed People's to know about Alma Bradley. Someone should have a word with ABTV and tell them not to waste their time.

Pegley, though, was out of the office and not expected back until two. Irritated, Llewelyn had left the Terra Sancta's Luanda phone number, plus the six-digit country code for Angola. He repeated it twice, making sure that the girl had got it right. Pegley was to phone back the moment he returned. Llewelyn would be waiting for the call.

Now, past three o'clock, he was still waiting. The house was empty, Cunningham out somewhere, and every now and then Llewelyn got to his feet and prowled from room to room, trying to rid himself of an overpowering sense of fatigue. Since his meeting with the young South African pilot, he'd felt physically exhausted. At first he'd blamed it on jet lag and the novel pressures of having to shoot his own pictures. The hour he'd spent on the streets with the little Sony camcorder had given him some marvellous shots – crippled kids, one-legged veterans, pitiful human debris washed up by the war that had taken James Jordan – but the sheer business of pointing a camera, of being white and rich in one of the world's poorest cities, had taken its toll. But even this kind of pressure – the kids in his face all the time, the demands for money – couldn't explain the sheer depth of his exhaustion. Llewelyn normally thrived in situations like these. Indeed, within the industry he'd become a byword for stamina and a certain dogged persistence. Maybe he'd picked up some infection or other. Maybe a siesta might not be such a bad idea.

Llewelyn circled the office. The room was cool and spacious. There were straw mats on the polished wooden floor and a view of the garden through the tall, half-curtained windows. Both desks were piled high with paperwork and on one of them, beside the computer, stood a plastic canister about the size of a biscuit tin. Inset into the top was a dome-shaped object with a series of metal probes sticking out. The probes were a couple of inches in length and Llewelyn picked the canister up, weighing it in his hand, knowing it must have been disarmed.

He sank into the chair again, holding the canister at arm's length against the glare of the sunshine through the window. The shape was unmistakable, a Valmara 69, one of the family of Italian anti-personnel mines he'd read about only a couple of days ago. The simplest mines you simply stood on. The weight of your body triggered the explosion and you lost a foot or a leg. This, though, was a bit more sophisticated. Llewelyn ran his finger along one of the prongs, finding the little eyelet with its length of attached wire. According to the sales literature he'd acquired from a contact at the Ministry of Defence, you tied the other end of the wire to something nearby, preferably at ankle height. Anyone snagging the wire would fire a charge in the canister. This, in turn, would blow the centre of the mine upwards. At the base of the mine was another wire, tethered to the canister. Stretched tight, this wire would trigger a bigger charge, blasting hundreds of razor-sharp fragments into anything within fifty metres. The secondary charge was the one that killed you and the length of the wire determined exactly the height it went off.

Llewelyn unscrewed the dome at the top, putting the diagrams he'd seen in London to the test. The centre of the mine came free in his hand and he stationed the canister between his feet, tugging the centre of the mine upwards until the wire was taut. The sales literature had been right. Not until the mine reached belly height would the thing go off.

Llewelyn went through the movements again, wondering about a piece to camera. He'd read the manual for the little camcorder twice and he'd already practised what they called 'self-video' in the privacy of his bedroom. The best way to do it was in front of a mirror. First you lined up the shot, marking the place you had to stand to frame your head properly, making sure you weren't shooting into the light. Then you steadied the camera on something solid and hit the button marked 'X'. That gave you ten seconds to get yourself organised, plenty of time if you'd been in the game a while and you knew exactly what you wanted to say.

Llewelyn picked the mine up again, reseating the dome in the canister. Terra Sancta obviously used this for demo purposes. That in itself was worth a line or two, graphic evidence that these things were threatening Western lives. Llewelyn sat back, closing his eyes, putting together a paragraph or two, say thirty seconds, nice and punchy, good strong visual background, the bush probably, outside Muengo, some location they could dress with a couple of those death's-head warning signs, DANGER – MINES. He'd talk about the hours before James had died, what he'd been up to, why he'd strayed into a live minefield, and he'd make room at the end for the phrase he'd circled in the sales literature. They called it 'The Killing Zone'. Anywhere closer than fifty metres, and you were hamburger. Llewelyn tried a version or two, imagining the impact on a mid-evening audience. The thought brought a grim smile to his lips, and he was reaching for a pen and a sheet of paper from the nearby desk when he heard a buzzing sound and then the chatter of the Terra Sancta telex machine.

The telex was in the corner beside the big HF radio. Llewelyn got up, pleased and impressed that Pegley had managed to find the Terra Sancta number. He must have contacted the people in Winchester, he thought. He must have been trying the international phone lines since two, and given up. Llewelyn bent to the machine, reading the message as it came through, aware at once that it wasn't for him.

'ATTENTION: ROB CUNNINGHAM,' it read, 'MOST URGENT, TANKER EX-ROTTERDAM REPORTS FINDING SURVIVAL DINGHY SOUTHERN NORTH SEA. ITEMS RECOVERED FROM DINGHY INDI-CATE MISSING YACHT *MOLLY JAY* REGISTERED GILES JORDAN. BELGIAN/UK AIR/SEA RESCUE SEARCH LAUNCHED SURROUND-ING AREA. NO INDICATION OF SURVIVORS OR YACHT TO DATE. SUGGEST YOU RETURN WITH MRS JORDAN AT ONCE. PLEASE ADVISE SOONEST. OPERATIONAL DIRECTORATE, WINCHESTER.'

Llewelyn read the telex for a second time, then looked at the machine. If Molly read this, there'd be no flight to Muengo, no trips to the minefields, no moody pieces to camera. On the contrary, she and Cunningham would be on the next plane home, leaving the People's Channel with ten minutes of street scenes and absolutely no prospect of progressing the story a single inch further. And that, as Llewelyn knew only too well, would be curtains. Even Pegley wouldn't risk it a second time round.

In the kitchen next door there was a glass cafetière beside the sink. The coffee grounds had settled at the bottom and there was an inch or so of thick, viscous liquid on top. Llewelyn fetched the cafetière and returned to the office. A fold-over sheet of clear plastic protected the machine from dust and debris. He hinged it back then poured the coffee into the machine. There was a sizzling noise, and the softest pop, and the acrid smell of something burning. The green light on the control panel flick-ered and went out.

Llewelyn bent down and pulled out the wall plug then reconnected the current a couple of times, making sure. When nothing happened – no green light, no 'stand-by' signal – he left the plug on and stood up again. The roll of telex paper included two carbon sheets. He tore off all three, readjusting the paper roll as if the message had never arrived. Then he folded the news about Molly Jordan's husband into his jacket pocket, wiped the telex keyboard with a handful of tissues, and returned the cafetière to the kitchen. Minutes later, in his assigned bedroom upstairs, he was sound asleep.

For the second time Molly Jordan asked to see the field report. The ambassador sat behind his desk, visibly embarrassed. She'd liked him at once, a small, sandy-haired man with a youthful grin and a warm handshake. He'd come through personally to the reception area where she'd given her name and by the time they got to his office there was a tray of tea and biscuits waiting on the table beside her chair.

'Please . . .' she said again, extending a hand.

The ambassador sighed, still reluctant to pass over the single sheet of paper.

'This is tricky,' he began, 'strictly speaking . . .'

'It's my son we're talking about. The least—'

'I know, I know. It's just . . .' He sighed again, then leaned forward, still uncomfortable, sliding the report across the desk. Molly picked it up and read it quickly. In three terse paragraphs it spelled out exactly what had happened to James. He'd been out of the city in the Terra Sancta Land Rover. He'd returned at dusk. He'd stopped by the roadside to investigate an abandoned piece of clothing. This had led him into the bush. His companion, a French nurse called Christianne Beaucarne, had stayed in the Land Rover. The child he'd gone after had turned up. Shortly afterwards, James had stepped on a mine. The girlfriend had come through on the radio. On recovery, the boy had been dead.

Molly looked up. The ambassador was studying her over the rim of his teacup.

'I'm sorry, Mrs Jordan,' he said quietly. 'It doesn't make for pleasant reading.'

Molly nodded, saying nothing, her eyes returning to the report. Somehow she'd never expected it to be like this. This mundane. This ordinary. Six days living with the fact of James's death had invested it with something altogether more significant. He'd been in the Third World. He'd been helping the poor and the disadvantaged and in the end it had cost him his life. That she could cope with. Just. But this was like the traffic accident she'd first imagined, simple cause and effect, one wrong decision, a moment's recklessness, savagely punished. Could even James have been this foolish? This headstrong? Could he?

She read the final paragraph again, hearing the sound of someone's voice behind the brutal prose. There was incomprehension here, and anger too. Her son had been briefed. He'd been made aware of the dangers. He'd been shown slides, told about previous incidents, warned off in the only language that mattered, the language of torn flesh and spilled blood. Yet there he was, blundering through the bush, risking other people's lives, ending his own. Crime and punishment, Molly thought. Break the rules. Take the consequences. Ugh.

She sat bolt upright in the chair, the piece of paper limp between her fingers. There was nothing to say, absolutely nothing, except to acknowledge her own need to go there, to get to Muengo, to meet this person and to explain that perhaps her son's life merited just a line or two extra. Who'd made these mines, for God's sake? What were they doing there in the first place? Who'd sold them? Who'd laid them? Who'd forgotten about them afterwards? In short, who'd killed James Jordan?

The ambassador was on his feet now. Molly refused the offer of more tea. He sat down again.

'I understand you have plans to ... ah ... visit the scene ...?'

Molly understood the question at once, hearing the inflection in his voice. Robbie Cunningham had already warned her
that the trip to Muengo would never win official approval. On
the contrary, the people at the embassy would probably do
everything in their power to stand in her way.

'No,' she said, 'I've come to be here when they fly him in.
I understand that's the procedure. Before he goes home.'

The ambassador studied her for a moment or two.

'So you're not trying to get to Muengo?'

'No.'

'Because you know, of course, that the place is under siege?'

'Yes.'

'And you know what that means? Civil war? Untold casualties? No water? No power?' He paused. 'You realise the . . .
ah . . . folly of exposing yourself to a situation like that? What
you'd jeopardise? The difficulties you'd cause for yourself
and . . . ah . . . very possibly for us?'

Molly ducked her head, permitting herself a smile. They
were playing a game now. She knew it. Lines to be spoken. A
position to be taken. A warning to be issued. Just in case it ever
came to an inquiry of some kind. For a moment she wondered
whether he was taping the conversation, then she decided he
wasn't. The man was too nice, too ordinary, too human.

She looked up. His hand was extended. She leaned forward,
shaking it awkwardly. The ambassador blushed.

'The report, please,' he said. 'I'm afraid I can't let you hang
on to it.'

Molly passed the report over the desk with a word. The
ambassador opened a drawer and took out a file. Molly recognised her own name, neatly typed on a white sticky label on the
front. The ambassador carefully folded the report in two,
glanced at his watch, and made a note on the inside leaf of the
file.

'Who wrote that report?' Molly asked.

The ambassador glanced up.

'A man called McFaul,' he said. 'He's in charge of the mine clearance operation out there. I gather he has a personal interest in . . . ah . . . James's accident.'

'Have you met him?'

'Yes, as it happens.'

'What's he like?'

The ambassador gave the question some thought.

'Able,' he said at last. 'Committed. Passionate, even.' He paused, frowning. 'I believe he was blown up himself, in Kuwait.'

'Is that why he's got this . . .' Molly shrugged, 'personal interest?'

'No.' The ambassador closed the file. 'He was the one who brought your son out. He and the French girl he mentions in the report. They could have been killed, too. I'd call that pretty personal . . .' he slid the file back into the drawer, avoiding her eyes, 'wouldn't you?'

It was dusk by the time the last bodies were lowered carefully into the mass grave. A small crowd had formed beneath the mango trees and the setting sun cast long shadows as the Africans swayed and keened, mourning their dead.

McFaul stood beside the digger, watching Christianne, waiting for her to get to her feet. She was kneeling at the head of the long trench, her lips moving, her head bowed in prayer.

'*Requiem aeternam dona eis Domine, et lux perpetua luceat eis . . .*'

She crossed herself before getting to her feet. Then she returned to the Landcruiser, getting in and closing the door without a backward glance.

McFaul lifted a hand to Bennie, perched in the cab of the yellow digger, and there was a puff or two of blue smoke before the engine caught. Then the long arm reached forward, and the cab revolved, and the first scoop of moist red earth settled on the line of waiting bodies.

Hours later, the grave filled in, McFaul was still sitting beneath one of the mango trees, listening to the soft African lament, watching for the first stars. He stayed there all evening, motionless beneath the canopy of leaves. Finally, past midnight, he stirred, getting up. For a moment or two he stared down at the long dark scar at the foot of the hillock. Then he turned and limped away for the long walk back to the city.

BOOK TWO

Lethality

Whilst steel balls have the ideal shape for range, they have a poor shape for wounding because the worst wounds are caused by an unstable fragment tumbling inside the body. Such a shape is provided by the fragmentation of a prenotched case, chopped bar, or scored wire body. Of course, the effectiveness of shrapnel-type mines depends not simply on the individual particles expelled, but the collective damage induced by a large number of such fragments attacking the target simultaneously.

LT.-COL. C. E. E. SLOAN
Mine Warfare on Land

CHAPTER SIX

It was still dark when Molly Jordan finally got up. She'd spent most of the night flitting in and out of consciousness, lying under the mosquito net, trying to fathom the noises outside the window. For a while it had been raining again. Past midnight, she'd heard the rattle of distant small-arms fire. And once, in the small hours, there'd come a long groan, barely human, from the room next door.

Dressed now, she ventured into the corridor. There was a strip of light beneath the adjoining door. She knocked twice, very softly. According to her watch, it was barely 5 a.m. She knocked again. When nothing happened, she opened the door, recognising the smell at once. Todd Llewelyn lay across the bed, naked except for a towel wrapped around his waist. A bowl on the floor was half-full of vomit.

Molly hesitated a moment, then stepped across to the bed. Llewelyn's eyes were closed and his breathing seemed normal. She reached for the single sheet, one corner balled in his right hand. The sheet was wet to her touch. She returned to her own room and fetched the thin cellular blanket under which she'd slept. As she draped it over Llewelyn, his eyes opened.

'You're ill,' Molly whispered at once, 'sick.'

Llewelyn gazed up at her. The normal flush had drained from his face, leaving tiny spots of colour high on each cheek. He swallowed a couple of times then licked his lips. His tongue was furred with a chalky-white deposit. He reached out for the glass of water, discarded on the floor.

163

'05.09?' he queried.

'Yes. Still early.'

'Can you see a bag? Under the bed? An old sports bag?'

Molly looked at him for a second or two then got down on her hands and knees. The bag had the word 'Santos' emblazoned across it.

'It's there,' she said, getting up again.

'Thank Christ for that.'

He got up on one elbow, rubbing his face. His chin was grey with overnight stubble. Molly was looking at the bowl again.

'How do you feel?' she said.

'OK. Now.'

'What happened?'

'I'm not sure. I remember being cold when I went to bed. Freezing cold. Shivering cold. Then hot. Sweating like a pig. Then . . .' he shrugged, 'you came in.'

'And you're really OK?'

'Yes,' he nodded, 'I think so.' He took a deep breath, letting his head sink back onto the pillow.

Molly bent to the bowl and carried it along the corridor to the closet at the end. She emptied it down the lavatory and sluiced it in the bathroom next door. When she got back to Llewelyn's bedroom he was already half-dressed, pulling on a short-sleeved white shirt, brisk, over-purposeful movements, like a drunk determined to prove his sobriety. Molly watched him unconvinced.

'Are you sure you're OK?'

'Fine,' he said curtly. 'Thank you.'

'What do you think it was?'

'No idea. Something I ate. Something I drank.' He looked her in the eye for the first time. 'Who can tell in this bloody place?'

They left for the airport at half-past six. Robbie had borrowed a big American flat-bed from a sister charity and by the time he appeared in the street outside, he'd already been up for three hours, bumping down to the docks for the supplies he'd pur- chased the day before. Most of it was food – sacks of maize and rice, army surplus boxes of high-protein biscuits, catering-size tins of milk powder – but also visible beneath the tarpaulin was a big 40-gallon drum of diesel fuel.

Molly stared at it all before getting into the four-seat cab at the front.

'Why the docks?' she asked Robbie. 'Why so early?'

Robbie was adjusting one of the ropes that secured the tarpaulin. His hands were black with grease.

'Had to,' he said. 'Stuff gets nicked otherwise.'

The road to the airport was already clogged with traffic, most of it grinding towards the city. There were long queues for fuel at the handful of Sonangol petrol stations and twice they had to stop for police road-blocks. On the second occasion, the police were reinforced by a line of armed soldiers and after an exchange of words Robbie was obliged to roll back the tarpaulin whilst a couple of the policemen clambered up and rummaged amongst the carefully stacked cardboard boxes.

Molly was sitting in the back of the cab beside Llewelyn. After a while, she realised that he was using the camcorder, holding it up to the window and shielding it with his jacket. Finally, the policemen climbed down to the roadside. One of them was carrying a box stamped 'WITH CARE – EC AID'. Robbie got back behind the wheel and slammed the door, winding down the window and saying something terse in Portu- guese as the older of the policemen waved him on. Pulling out onto the pot-holed carriageway, he caught sight of Llewelyn's camera in the rear-view mirror.

'Put that bloody thing away,' he said, 'before we get arrested.'

Molly blinked. It was the first time she'd seen Robbie lose his temper. Llewelyn was peering at the footage counter on the side of the camcorder. In the grey morning light, he looked drawn and pale, and for a moment Molly wondered if he'd even heard what the young Terra Sancta man had said. Then he looked up, catching Robbie's eye in the mirror.

'Quite a challenge,' he murmured.

'What?'

'Trying to make your film without shooting any pictures.'

'My film?' Robbie didn't bother hiding his contempt. 'Are you joking?'

There were more soldiers at the airport. They ringed the terminal building, standing in twos and threes, eyeing every vehicle that turned in from the approach road. Robbie ignored them, driving past the glass doors of the main entrance and taking an access road through a pair of open gates. Beyond the gates stood the line of aid planes that Molly had seen the morning they'd arrived. At the end of the line, a little apart from the rest, was another aircraft, much older. The cockpit was set high in a faired Perspex bubble in the nose and there was a line of four windows down the side of the fuselage. The aircraft was painted sky blue and carried the outline of a bird in white on the tail.

Llewelyn was leaning forward now, the camera to his eye again, muttering directions to Robbie. Molly saw someone jump out of the rear door of the aircraft and lift a hand. He looked young. He was short and stocky. He wore trainers and jeans and a light suede jacket. When the flat-bed stopped, he went straight to the back, lifting the tarpaulin and inspecting the goods underneath.

They all got out, Llewelyn still shooting with the camera. He circled the aircraft, walking slowly backwards, then disappeared inside. A helicopter gunship had appeared from nowhere, swooping low over the airport terminal then settling beside a big TAP passenger jet. Molly watched as the helicopter's door slid open and half a dozen soldiers jumped out. They were laughing amongst themselves, easing the straps on their helmets as an unseen hand tossed out a steady stream of rucksacks. One by one, they bent to the oily tarmac, cradling their weapons, shouldering the heavy packs, then trudged away towards a waiting truck.

Molly felt a touch on her arm. The voice was soft.

'Piet Rademeyer. Pleasure to meet you. I'm the pilot.'

Molly shook the outstretched hand and followed the pilot across to the plane. Inside, the tiny cabin smelled of hot oil and old leather. There was room for a line of four single seats on either side of a narrow aisle, though most of the seats had been taken out to make room for cargo. Llewelyn was already prowling up and down, peering out of windows, a look of intense concentration on his face.

'What do you think?' he said to Rademeyer. 'Where's best?'

'Best for what?'

'Pictures.' Llewelyn made an impatient gesture with the camcorder.

'Movies?' The height of the cabin made even Rademeyer stoop. 'Are you some kind of media guy? Is that it? Are you a cameraman? Out here on your ace?'

Llewelyn ignored the question, settling into the front right-hand seat, putting his nose to the window.

'How about here? Can I get the take-off from here? The landing? Or would I be better off with you?' He nodded at the open door that led through to the cockpit. 'Up front?'

'Up front's OK. You can take the co-pilot's seat but once you're in you're in. Back here you can get up, walk round, do whatever. Plus you can shoot up ahead if you want.' He indicated the step that led up to the cockpit. 'Just stand there. No problem.'

'For take-off? And landing, too?'

Rademeyer shrugged.

'Whatever. You're paying.'

They took off forty minutes later. Robbie had organised a couple of Angolans to help out with the cargo and the food and fuel were carefully stacked at the back of the aircraft, secured beneath a thick rope netting. At Robbie's insistence, Molly had taken the co-pilot's seat, strapping herself in and accepting a pair of headphones from Rademeyer. Already, she'd had a chance to talk to him while they waited for the last of the cargo to be loaded. He had homes in Cape Town and Florida but he worked most of the year in what he called 'the front-line states', shuttling people and cargo into places no one else would touch. The airplane was his own and perfect for the job, an old De Havilland Dove he'd managed to pick up from a broker in Miami. To his knowledge it was the only one left south of Cairo, and when he'd got tired of risking his life in southern Africa he planned a luxury conversion, flying millionaires and their mistresses to some of the continent's better-kept secrets, beauty spots remote and inaccessible enough to have survived the ravages of the package tour.

In the ten minutes' conversation they'd shared before take-off, Molly had warmed to the young pilot. She liked his confidence and his enthusiasm. It reminded her just a little of James – the same tilted chin, the same bluff dismissal of difficulties or the possibility of failure – and she'd been amused when he'd rummaged under his seat and produced a handful of blue T-shirts, each with a white dove printed on the chest. Apparently the shirts were a souvenir from the recent national elections. The UN had distributed hundreds of them, a peace token, more oil for the wheels of democracy. According to Rademeyer, the elections had been a farce, civil war resumed within days, but in the aftermath he'd been able to lay hands on a couple of dozen T-shirts and had subsequently painted the plane to match.

'Colour's important around here,' he said. 'You may have noticed.'

'You mean black and white?'

'Blue.' He grinned. 'They think I'm UN. Saves getting shot down.'

Now they taxied slowly out across the tarmac towards the strip of rubber-scorched concrete that marked the start of the runway. Molly had never flown in the cockpit of a plane before and even the presence of Llewelyn behind her, standing in the gap between the seats, failed to puncture the bubble in which she sat. On the left a hundred metres ahead, she could see the charred remains of some earlier incident, a blackened stencil, aircraft-shaped, against the pale cropped grass, and further away on the other side of the airfield was a line of brutal-looking combat jets, heavily camouflaged. As she watched, ground crew were attaching bombs to the pylons beneath the wings of one of the jets, tiny figures in dark green overalls wrestling with the sleek silver containers. According to Rademeyer, bombs like these had flattened whole areas of Huambo, a once-beautiful city to the south and the home of UNITA's high command. Molly shook her head, taking in the implications. Days ago, all of this would have been hopelessly remote, pictures on some news report, but already she felt at home here, no longer surprised or even alarmed by it.

Llewelyn spotted the wrecked aircraft, leaning forward across Rademeyer, and as the pneumatic brakes hissed beneath their feet Molly remembered the supper she'd shared with Larry Giddings the previous evening. They'd been talking about exactly this, a society torn apart by war. Giddings, it turned out, had been living in Angola for the best part of fifteen years, nursing Aurora through crisis after crisis as the country drifted towards disintegration. Abandon the stuff we all take for granted, he'd said, and the results are all too predictable. Take away freedom, and opportunity, and a government you can vote out of office, and you end up with chaos, and violence, the country bleeding like a wounded animal. But Angola was worse than that, he'd said. Angola was a homicide case, robbed blind, and the fingerprints of communism were all over the corpse. Molly had written the phrase down when she got back to the privacy of her own room. Her father had said something similar, years ago, when the Russians had blocked off East Berlin and turned their backs on the twentieth century, and she'd thought of him at once, watching Giddings in the restaurant, musing on the follies of mankind. Her father had been right. The finger-prints of communism. Everywhere.

Llewelyn tapped her on the arm. They were at the end of the runway now, Rademeyer lining up the aircraft for take-off. She lifted the headphones, listening while Llewelyn tried to explain where he wanted her to look for the next shot, but the roar of the engines was getting louder all the time and in the end she simply gave him a nod and a smile, none the wiser about what he was really after.

Rademeyer glanced across, his thumb raised, and she nodded, grinning back, forgetting about Llewelyn and his camerawork. There was another hiss as the brakes released then the little plane began to move, bumping down the runway, Rademeyer's right hand easing the throttles up to maximum. They were moving fast now, the white lines beginning to blur down the middle of the runway, then Rademeyer hauled back on the control yoke and the nose of the plane lifted and the bumping suddenly stopped.

Before take-off, he'd shown Molly how to use the intercom. Now she pressed the little button on the window sill beside her elbow.

'Two hours twenty,' he was saying.

'To what?'

'Muengo.'

Tom Peterson got news of the flight twenty minutes later. He was sitting in a government army truck, trying to explain Muengo's water situation to the garrison's second-in-command. Before the siege began, Terra Sancta had been planning to sink a series of new wells to augment the city's supply. One of the new wells was a day or two off completion and shell damage to the riverside pump-house made this extra source all the more important. Many townspeople were now drawing their supplies untreated from the river. They had no fuel to boil the muddy broth that passed for water and it would only be a matter of days before disease became epidemic. Dysentery was already widespread. Cholera would be a nightmare.

Peterson urged the officer to get out of the truck and take a look at the new well. According to the paperwork at the Terra Sancta bungalow, it had been dug by local labour under the supervision of the luckless James Jordan. He'd located an aquifer, using data from an earlier Oxfam survey, and had sunk an exploratory borehole. The aquifer was relatively shallow, no more than fifteen feet below ground level, and a week's digging had opened a well deep enough to produce fresh water. The well was lined with precast concrete rings to within a metre of the surface, and a couple more days' labour would see it through to completion.

The officer finally agreed to inspect the well. He was a young man, no more than twenty-five, and he came from Sombe, a city on the coast. Peterson sensed that he had no enthusiasm for either the countryside or the war, and the events of the last four days had plainly shaken him. Now he stood beside the well, peering in. A rusty iron pulley hung from the wooden tripod erected over the mouth of the well and Peterson could smell the water below, a damp earthiness that reminded him of early summer mornings in his native Somerset.

The officer tossed a pebble into the well, listening for the plop. They were talking in Portuguese.

'How many men do you need?'

'Six. No more.'

'For how long?'

'Three days. Four days. Less if it doesn't rain.'

The officer nodded. The ceasefire had held now for nearly sixty hours while arrangements were finalised for the evacuation of Muengo's aid community. Colonel Katilo's UNITA troops had thrown a noose around the city, and nowhere was the truce line further than six kilometres from the cathedral. Once the evacuation was over, the fighting – it seemed – would resume.

Peterson stepped back from the well. The road to the airport was only a couple of hundred metres away across the rough scrub and in the distance he could see the line of oil drums the rebels were using as a barrier. There were rebel soldiers on the other side of the barrier, motionless figures in full combat dress, and one of them had a pair of binoculars trained on the well.

'The water situation's serious,' Peterson pointed out. 'We could have the well working by the weekend. If we're still here.'

'One well?' The officer looked at him. 'Sixty thousand people?' He shrugged, turning away, no longer seeing any point in the conversation, but Peterson followed him, determined to press the point. He'd met this kind of attitude before, a listless surrender to overwhelming odds. This man spoke the language of the battlefield and he understood the implications of the nearby road-block only too well. In a couple of days he'd probably be dead. Why should he bother about someone else's hole in the ground?

Peterson began to argue afresh, pointing out that the soldiers too would need clean water, but the officer had stopped again, his attention attracted by the blue UN Landcruiser bumping towards them. The vehicle came to a halt in a cloud of dust. Peterson hadn't seen Fernando since late last night when the UN rep had returned, exhausted, from yet another session with the UNITA high command. Now, if anything, he looked even more harassed.

'You know anything about this?' he said at once.

'What? About what?'

'This aid flight? Coming in this morning?' Peterson shook his head, opening the door of the Landcruiser, letting Fernando get out. The ashtray in the dashboard was brimming with cigarettes. Fernando produced a dirty handkerchief and mopped his face. 'Luanda came through ten minutes ago. The people at the airport cleared a flight this morning. It left at eight-thirty. One of your guys on board.'

'But the airstrip's blocked.'

'I know. I just checked.'

Fernando's hand had gone to the breast pocket of his rumpled shirt. Peterson declined the offered Gitane, glancing at his watch, doing the calculations in his head. Flight time from Luanda, unless you were a MiG, was two hours or so. Already it was nearly 9.15.

'So what happens now?' he said.

'You tell me. I raised Katilo on the way down here. Told him what had happened.'

'And what did he say?'

Fernando grimaced at the question, turning his shoulder to the wind and lighting his cigarette. Peterson watched the smoke drifting away, waiting for an answer. Fernando picked a shred of tobacco from his lower lip.

'Just laughed,' he said at last. 'The way he always does.'

The Dove droned on, the needle on the airspeed indicator nudging 130 knots, the landscape unrolling slowly below. They'd been airborne now for more than an hour and a half and Molly was beginning to feel drowsy, the sun hot through the unscreened Perspex above her head. From time to time, Rademeyer would lean over and attract her attention, indicating some feature beneath them, a range of hills, the loop of a river, and – only minutes ago – the thin black line of the Benguela railway. Once, Rademeyer mused, you could buy a ticket all the way through to Beira, riding the train from one side of Africa to the other. Now, though, the war had restricted services to thirty miles of track between Benguela and Lobito, a port city further up the coast. Inland, UNITA troops had blown up bridges and mined the track, determined to first isolate rural communities, then destroy them. Molly, still gazing down, had picked up the thought. There were clouds beneath them now, big white puffballs against the greens and browns of the bush.

'Doesn't all this upset you?' she asked.

'All what?'

'The killing? The war? The waste?'

She looked across at Rademeyer. Behind the aviation sun-glasses she could see he was trying to mask a smile.

'Why should it upset me? It's the way the place is. They've been at war now for thirty years. The war's older than me.'

Molly nodded, thinking of Larry Giddings.

'Communism solves nothing,' she said lightly. 'It didn't then and it doesn't now.'

Rademeyer was looking across at her. The smile was wider.

'Communism? Are you kidding?'

'No.' Molly frowned. 'The government's communist, isn't it? That's what the war's about. That's why people are in such a mess.'

'Who told you that?'

Molly looked away, beginning to regret the conversation. Maybe Larry Giddings wasn't such an authority after all. Maybe there were other points of view.

'A friend,' she heard herself saying, 'in Luanda.'

'And what did he say? This friend of yours?'

'He said that nothing works. It's true, too. You only have to look.'

'And is that because of communism?'

'Yes.' Molly nodded. 'Yes. It has to be.'

'Why?'

'Because the government should be in charge. They should be the ones sorting everything out.'

Rademeyer was laughing now, his head back against the seat.

'Our MPLA friends? The government? You think they're *communist*? Are you kidding?'

Molly felt herself blushing. She was sure she had it right. The MPLA were the government. The government were com-munist. The opposition was UNITA.

'We back UNITA,' she said uncertainly. 'The West, your

country, South Africa . . .' she glanced across at the young pilot, 'that makes the government communist, doesn't it?'

Rademeyer's smile had gone. He was peering at something ahead, leaning forward in the seat.

'Used to be that way,' he muttered at last, 'back in the eighties. Now it's about power, pure and simple. Two gangs, two lots of gangsters, one on either side, the big guys wanting it all. Most days you can't tell the difference between them.'

Molly thought about the proposition for a moment or two, hearing Giddings's voice again, the soft American drawl, the incessant talk of communism.

'So why,' Molly gestured down at the landscape below, 'is the place such a mess?'

'Because they're off the planet, all of them, both sides. The place is rich, potentially. You're talking a lot of oil here, up in Cabinda. That's serious wealth. But all they ever do with it is buy weapons. Billions of dollars' worth. And that's just the government.'

'What about UNITA?' Molly frowned, remembering the name of the opposition leader. 'Savimbi?'

'He's just as bad. Instead of oil, it's diamonds. The diamonds pay for his end of the war.' Rademeyer shook his head. 'A thousand people a day dying of starvation and all these guys can buy are guns. You ever tried eating a gun? Pathetic . . . shit!'

Molly looked up in time to see a dark green blur streak past. Instinctively, she reached for the dashboard as the Dove shuddered and bucked in the disturbed air but the safety straps held her back in the seat, her arms flailing around in front of her. In the far distance, miles ahead, she saw an outline she recognised, arrow-shaped, climbing almost vertically, rolling over, then growing rapidly bigger. Rademeyer saw it too and he pulled the Dove into a tight wingover, banking to the left, diving for cover in the clouds beneath. The fighter flashed past, another blur, and suddenly they were in cloud, the sun gone, beads of moisture streaking the Perspex.

Molly's hand went to her mouth. She hadn't had time to be frightened but now she was beginning to shake. Rademeyer pulled out of the dive and she felt her stomach yawn, a terrible emptiness inside her, then one wing was vertical again and they were making another turn, to the right this time, the aircraft plunging out of the cloud, the ground beneath suddenly much closer. Behind her, in the cabin, she heard a thump that shook the whole aircraft as something heavy landed in the aisle.

Molly was terrified now, knowing in her heart that she was going to die. Rademeyer had tightened the turn even more, pivoting the plane on one wingtip, and she felt her whole face being tugged sideways, as if a giant hand was pulling at her flesh. Through the side window, she could see a forest, individual trees, water tumbling into a gorge. Then, abruptly, the land folded up towards them, the mouth of a deeply shadowed valley, the long, bare, treeless flank of a big mountain. Molly braced herself for the impact, wondering whether there'd be any prospect of survival, then she felt the plane lift beneath her, the engines screaming as Rademeyer fought for height again, threading his way between the surrounding peaks, his eyes flicking left and right, still hunting for the fighters.

'See?' he muttered after a while.

'See what?'

'Bastards can't even shoot straight.'

McFaul stood on the river bank, downstream from Muengo's only bridge, watching the kids and the women knee-deep in the water. It had been raining all night and the river had risen at least a foot, giving McFaul the opportunity to use the dinghy to scout for stray mines. Garrison troops in Muengo had seeded the approaches to the bridge on both sides of the river. They'd used hundreds of Romanian anti-personnel mines, the thick Bakelite MAI-75s, and floodwater sometimes disinterred them, washing them onto the margins of the shallow pool where the women washed their clothes and the kids played submarines.

McFaul half-turned, signalling to Domingos to back the dinghy trailer down to the water line. Global's first task in Muengo had been to sweep this area clear of mines and periodically – like now – McFaul made a point of returning. The people had learned to trust him. A single rogue mine, a single accident, could change all that.

Domingos inched the trailer slowly into the river and water began to lap around the bottom of the dinghy. The kids were already climbing aboard, yelping and laughing when McFaul tried to shoo them off. They called him 'O Mutilado Inglês', the English cripple, and McFaul had at first been stung by the phrase until he'd seen the grins on their faces. To be crippled in this country was far too commonplace to warrant even a moment's pity.

McFaul signalled to Domingos to stop and bent to unhitch the trailer. When he stood up again he found himself looking at Peterson. The tall Terra Sancta man had followed the safe lane down from the road. Now he was gazing across the river at the rapids where the older kids were testing each other against the current.

McFaul edged his body around, blocking the view. He'd heard the rumours about an aid flight only minutes ago. There were passengers, too, down from Luanda. Peterson evidently knew the details.

'How many on board?'

'Three. Robbie Cunningham I know. He's our press officer back in the UK. Nice bloke.'

'And the others?'

'One's some kind of journalist. The other's apparently the boy's mother.'

'Boy?'

'James Jordan.'

Domingos was gunning the Land Rover's engine. McFaul waved away the exhaust smoke.

'Jordan's mother?' he said blankly. 'What's she doing here?'

'I don't know. Not that it matters. They can't land anyway. The strip's closed. Our friend's decision.'

McFaul grunted, watching the Land Rover's wheels trenching in the wet sand. Like Fernando, the UN rep, he'd been trying to negotiate with Colonel Katilo. An evacuation was clearly imminent and before his team pulled out, McFaul wanted to clear a handful of vital paths around the city, making sure the local people at least had safe access to other parts of the river and to the handful of old wells still producing clean water. Most of the paths were now within small-arms range of Katilo's men, and before he started work he wanted a cast-iron guarantee that no UNITA marksman would play the hero. So far, McFaul had conducted negotiations on the radio, speaking to Katilo in French through Christianne. Katilo had been interested enough to arrange a face-to-face chat for tomorrow morning behind rebel lines but whether or not his interest extended beyond meeting Christianne, McFaul couldn't be sure.

'So what does Katilo do,' he wondered aloud, 'when this plane shows up?'

'Nothing, I imagine. If the pilot's got any sense he'll be taking a look from way up. Ten, fifteen thousand feet. Apparently the strip's got trucks all over it. There's no way he can land. He'll just have to go back to Luanda, or divert.' He paused, glancing skywards. 'Assuming he's got the range.'

The Dove was still low, hugging the foothills of the Plan Alto, when Rademeyer spotted the distant smudge of Muengo. He banked away at once, heading back towards the high ground, handing Molly a map without once taking his eyes off the approaching crestline.

'There's a frequency at the top,' he said over the intercom. 'My handwriting.'

Molly peered at the map as the plane began to climb. The city of Huambo was circled in red.

'What's a frequency?'

'Four digits. Four numbers. Just read them out.'

There was a new note in his voice. Since the incident with the MiGs, he'd said virtually nothing. Now he was cool, businesslike. Molly found what he wanted, four pencilled numbers on the top of the map. She tried to keep the map steady in her hands, reading them out, watching him making adjustments to something on the dashboard. When the line of digits matched the numbers on the map, he pressed the button on the control yoke again and began to transmit his call sign. At length, a voice answered in Portuguese and a brief conversation took place. Evidently satisfied, Rademeyer signed off, plunging the Dove into a steep left-hand turn.

When Molly opened her eyes again, they were flying over dense forest, very low. Gradually, mile by mile, the woodland began to thin until the trees gave way to a pale green blur of savannah, wind-rippled and sleek like the coat of a sleeping animal. They flashed over a river, then they were flying beside a road. On the road there were armoured cars, and trucks, and soldiers sitting on benches in the back, looking up at the Dove, waving. Without thinking, Molly began to wave back, suddenly aware of Llewelyn standing at her shoulder. She looked round at him. He was steadying himself with one hand and in the other he had the camera. He leaned forward, an inch from Molly's face, trying to frame the road in the window of the cockpit. There was a deep gash in his forehead and the blood had caked down the side of his face. Some had reached as far as the collar of his safari jacket, blackening the soiled cotton. The scabs of blood against the pale grey flesh reminded Molly of vagrants she'd encountered on trips to London – unkempt, distraught – and when he finally lowered the camcorder she could see a kind of madness in his eyes, a wild gleam that hadn't been there before. She was about to ask him how he was, how he'd gashed himself so badly, but by the time she put it into words he'd gone.

Rademeyer again. His voice in her headphones.

'Ahead,' he said. 'Look.'

Molly turned back, settling into the co-pilot's seat, tightening the harness, telling herself that the worst was over. The ground was rising now and she suddenly spotted a stretch of cleared scrub tufted with yellowing grass. Wheel tracks down the middle of the scrub told her that this must be the airstrip but there were vehicles dotted everywhere, trucks mostly, and the way they'd been parked made a landing impossible. Seconds later, as they roared over the far end of the airstrip and began to bank to the left, Molly saw men running across the scrub, getting into the trucks. One or two of them started to move, bumping away towards a rough dirt road, and by the time the aircraft had completed a full circuit of the field, the centre strip was empty.

Rademeyer banked sharply, his right hand reaching for the throttle controls. The engine note rose, and the nose dipped, and Molly heard a rumble beneath them as the undercarriage came down. They were still side-slipping in, Rademeyer enjoying himself now, shedding height as quickly as he could, the wing flaps fully down, slowing the aircraft still more. At fifty feet, he kicked the plane level, perfectly aligned for the landing, the aircraft dancing through the bubbles of hot air rising from the ground beneath. The nose was still down, the first line of wheel ruts coming up to meet them, and at the last moment Rademeyer throttled back, lifting the nose, letting the main undercarriage settle on the baked earth. He began to apply the brake with his thumb and Molly heard a hissing noise as the nose came down and the aircraft juddered to a halt.

Llewelyn was back beside her, the camera raised, shooting through the windscreen. One of the trucks was racing out to meet them, three soldiers hanging on in the back. They looked like kids at Christmas. They could barely contain themselves.

Rademeyer reached for the throttle controls again, putting the engines into idle. Llewelyn was still busy with the camera, following the truck.

'Who are these guys?' he asked.

Rademeyer released his harness and stretched in the seat.

'Mine hosts,' he said, 'or yours, anyway.'

'Are you turning the engines off?'

'No. You owe me seven and a half grand.'

'It's in the back. Bag marked "Santos". I'll get it.'

Llewelyn retreated to the cabin. Molly heard the door open, the growl of the exhaust and the propellers suddenly magnified. She found the release for her own harness and lifted a hand to her face. Only in the last ten minutes or so, with the shock of the MiGs behind her, had she begun to absorb the real signifi-cance of the journey she'd made. This was where James had come, and this was probably the way he'd arrived, emerging from some clapped-out aircraft, ready for the time of his life.

Molly reached for the sun visor over the windscreen. On the back was a mirror. She studied her face for a moment, determined to look her best. Somehow, over the last couple of days, she'd acquired the faintest tan and it gave the lie to the way she really felt, setting off the blonde curls that fringed the wary smile. She'd lost weight, too, and it suited her, hollow-ing the planes of her face. She looked at herself a moment longer, feeling the plane rocking beneath her as someone jumped out. Then there were voices outside, and Rademeyer's, much closer.

'You getting off or what?'

Molly nodded, apologetic, wriggling out of the seat. She paused at the cockpit door, thanking the young South African for the flight. He grinned back at her, exactly the way James used to, immensely pleased with himself.

'Pleasure,' he said. 'Here. Little souvenir.'

He gave her the T-shirt he'd shown her at Luanda airport and she looked at it a moment, then began to thank him again as he plunged a hand into the back pocket of his jeans and produced a small card.

'Here,' he said again.

'What's that?'

Rademeyer didn't seem to hear her. He was peering back through the cabin, a frown on his face. He shouted something in Portuguese to one of the soldiers, then slipped out of his seat, gesturing for Molly to go ahead.

'Address and phone number,' he muttered, 'in case you need me again.'

Outside, the soldiers were unloading the cargo, rolling the heavy fuel drum across the grass and then manhandling it onto the back of the truck. Llewelyn appeared round the tail of the aircraft and began to use the camcorder, walking slowly towards the truck. Molly watched from the aircraft door as Robbie moved to intercept him but one of the soldiers got there first. He was a big man, older than the rest. He held a hand up, the huge spread of his palm cupping the end of the lens. Llewelyn looked annoyed, the expression of a man troubled by a passing insect. He lowered the camcorder, moved to one side, then began to shoot again. The soldier gazed at him and muttered something under his breath. Then he stepped across to Llewelyn and hit him hard beneath the ribcage. Llewelyn folded up with a tiny gasp, curling himself on the ground, protecting the camcorder. The soldier studied him a moment, insulted. Then he kicked him in the small of his back and wandered away, shrugging.

Molly jumped down from the aircraft and ran to Llewelyn. His eyes were closed. He was breathing hard, the way people do when they get excited, and his lips were moving, some wordless curse. Molly bent low, cradling Llewelyn's head in her arms. The sun was fierce on the back of her neck and when she looked up she could see the soldiers watching her curiously from the truck. Llewelyn's hand found hers.

'Nothing's easy,' he muttered, 'believe me.'

They left the airfield on the back of the truck. As they bounced along the red dirt road Molly had seen from the air, she heard the Dove beginning to move. She looked back, both hands on the grab rail, watching the plane taxiing to the end of the strip. It made a final turn then gathered speed, a little blue toy against the greens and browns of the surrounding scrub. Four hundred metres later, it was airborne, climbing steadily away as the trucks resumed their positions on the airfield, Muengo's door firmly closed against further arrivals. Seconds later, their own truck lurched to a halt. Molly heard voices again, turning to see a line of oil drums in the road. There were more soldiers here, heavily armed teenagers, their skinny frames crisscrossed with bandoliers of ammunition. Someone in the cab was arguing with one of the soldiers. Looking down, Molly could see a black hand gesticulating angrily. Beyond the oil drums was a Land Rover with the Terra Sancta logo on the door. Beside her, Robbie was waving at it.

The soldier in the cab got out and told Robbie to join him on the road. The stuff from the Dove would have to be transferred to the Land Rover. Robbie helped Molly and Llewelyn off the back of the truck. Llewelyn was still bent double, walking with difficulty. Robbie began to help with the oil drum but the soldiers waved him away. Half of the food and the fuel was carried to the Land Rover. The rest stayed in the truck. When Robbie began to protest it was Llewelyn who pulled him aside.

'Not worth it,' he mumbled, 'believe me.'

The truck drove away, disappearing in a cloud of dust towards the airfield, and the soldiers at the road-block abruptly lost interest. The man in the Land Rover finished securing what was left of the cargo and approached Molly.

'Tom Peterson,' he held out his hand, 'I'm amazed you made it.'

McFaul and Domingos knelt in the dinghy at the foot of the embankment watching the little blue Dove circling the city. At length it levelled out and began to climb away to the north.

Without question, it had landed and McFaul wanted to know why.

Domingos shrugged. Nothing in this war could any longer surprise him. He'd spent an hour or so at first light picking through the ruins of his bungalow and the games UNITA played had ceased to interest him. The pile of dented cooking pots, torn clothing, and salvaged tins of fish and corned beef were all that remained of sixteen years of family life but even this was a blessing compared to the wilderness in which most of Muengo was now living. Only the previous evening, he'd visited the town's derelict cinema, looking for a neighbour who'd also lost his house. Camped inside were hundreds of families, exposed to the rain, living in conditions that left Domingos shamed and speechless. Now, he flicked through his working notes. Anything he could do, any gesture he could make in the face of such primitive chaos, would be a fingerhold on the life he'd left behind.

He glanced towards the bank, looking at the stretch of pockmarked earth that served as a path to the river. The river here was upstream of the pool beside the bridge where people washed and the water was less polluted. The rebels had been aware of this and during earlier hostilities they'd seeded the path with mines, mainly the little Chinese Type 72s, no bigger than a tin of shoe polish. They'd worked under cover of darkness, scattering the mines at random, digging some in, leaving others on the surface, giving McFaul's teams no choice but to search every square inch of the hard-baked soil, probing with the bayonet, opening a corridor down towards the river. Because of the shelling, they hadn't been back to this site for four days and the rains had come on the second night, softening the earth.

Domingos looked round. Unlike the other sites he'd listed for priority clearance, this one was close to the encircling front line. Through binoculars, it was possible to pick out the dark smudge of newly dug UNITA trenches, about a kilometre away, but Domingos had his doubts about their marksmanship from such a range.

'We could do it this afternoon,' he said. 'Me and Bennie.'

McFaul shook his head, throttling back the outboard, keeping the dinghy steady against the tug of the current.

'No,' he said firmly.

'Why not?'

'Too dodgy. Give me a day to sort it out with Katilo. Then we can do it properly.' He balanced himself in the dinghy and then reached across and tapped Domingos's notes. 'How far did we get? It seems like a year ago.'

Domingos consulted his notes. As usual, he'd marked the furthest extent of the de-mined area on the site itself but the rains had carried the line of wooden pegs away.

'Eighty metres,' he said, squinting into the sunshine. 'About seven metres to go. Half a day?'

McFaul followed his pointing finger, then shook his head.

'Double it,' he grunted.

Tom Peterson was driving Molly Jordan to the MSF house where Christianne lived. He'd already dropped Robbie Cunningham and the TV man at the UN compound where he knew Fernando would offer them floor space. Their safe arrival must have been the result of some special leverage with the UNITA people, and Fernando would doubtless want to know about the small print of this mysterious relationship. Like it or not, Robbie Cunningham and his party appeared to have lifted the siege single-handed.

Peterson slowed the Land Rover to a crawl, trying to avoid a woman in the middle of the road. She was pushing a wooden barrow. On the barrow was a very small coffin. As they passed, Molly turned in her seat to see the woman's face. She'd said nothing since they'd dropped the others at the UN compound, staring out at the rubble and the shell damage and the abandoned, burned-out vehicles. Even Peterson's murmured consolations for the death of her son she'd barely acknowledged. At first, he'd put this reserve of hers down to exhaustion. Now, he was beginning to wonder.

'Bit of a shock, I imagine,' he said lightly.

'I'm sorry?'

'All this. After London.' He paused. 'Is it London you live in? Or out in the sticks?'

'Thorpe,' Molly said, 'in Essex.'

She was twisted round in her seat now, still looking at the woman with the coffin. There were soldiers up ahead, guarding a truck. There were a dozen or so sacks in the back of the truck, barely visible from street level, but the crowd around the truck was growing by the minute. Peterson slowed again, still thinking about Thorpe. He'd been there once, years ago, for a wedding.

'Nice church,' he said. 'Good pub, too. King's Head? King's Arms?'

'Maid's Head.'

Molly had seen the crowd now. One of the soldiers was clubbing a youth who'd tried to clamber onto the back of the truck. He had both hands up, protecting his head, so the soldier started beating his legs instead.

'Why's he doing that?' Molly said. 'What's going on?'

Peterson bumped the Land Rover over the broken kerbstone, avoiding the milling crowd. The women at the back of the crowd turned and peered in, their faces barely an inch from Molly's. Hunger and the shelling had given them a gaunt, rawboned look and when one of them tried to wrench open the passenger door, Peterson accelerated away, curtaining the scene behind a cloud of dust.

'The army still has food,' Peterson was saying. 'Maize, mostly. The local folk are desperate, poor buggers. We do our best but . . .' he shook his head, 'in the end it's down to them.'

'Down to who?'

'The army,' he corrected himself, 'armies. When they decide to stop fighting, the people eat. Until then, too bad.' He glanced across at her. 'If you're young and black in this country, it's a tough choice. Stay out of uniform, and you risk starvation. Join the army, and you'll probably end up dead anyway.'

'What sort of choice is that?'

'None. But at least the soldier dies on a full stomach.'

Molly shut her eyes, leaning back against the seat. She was beginning to sweat in the heat, dark patches of perspiration blotching her shirt.

'I'd no idea,' she said quietly. 'I thought Luanda ...' She shrugged, unable to finish the sentence.

'Luanda what?'

'I don't know. I just thought ... the poverty, the rubbish everywhere, the kids in the street, the beggars ... but this ...' she shook her head, 'it's medieval.'

They were at the MSF house now. Peterson pulled the Land Rover to a halt at the kerbside and helped Molly out, locking both doors behind him. Christianne appeared under the porch. Peterson had already alerted her over the radio about Molly's arrival and she'd volunteered her own bed at once. Now she stepped into the sunshine, her hand extended. Molly stopped on the path, confused for a moment, looking at her. Then she opened her arms, recognising the soft, oval face, the auburn curls, the look of quiet determination beneath the girlish smile, and Peterson turned on his heel, heading back towards the Land Rover as the two women embraced.

McFaul's first reaction was to laugh.

'You're doing what?'

'A film.'

'Here? You've come here? To make a film?'

'Yes.'

The visitor had walked into the schoolhouse uninvited, a

tall man, slightly stooped, with bloodstains on his collar and one side of his face purpled with recent bruising. Already, from his shoulder-bag, he'd produced a small camcorder, leaving it on the table, much as one might proffer a calling card. McFaul studied the camera. Global had something similar. They'd bought it to pick up field footage for training sessions. McFaul had used one in Afghanistan and had been impressed with the results. He looked up again.

'You came in the Dove? This morning?'

'Yes. For my sins.'

'So you're the journalist?'

'Correct. Todd Llewelyn, People's Channel.' He began to sway a little on his feet, reaching automatically for the table for support. 'Bloody hot,' he muttered at once, 'and a flight you wouldn't believe.'

'How come you got to land?'

'Money.'

'How much money?'

'A lot.'

Llewelyn was looking at the survey maps now, newly pinned to the classroom blackboard. Beneath the maps, neatly stacked against the wall, was some of the equipment McFaul and Bennie wouldn't be needing over the next few days. Bundles of wooden stakes. Rolls of red and white tape. Spare sets of protective clothing. A box or two of battery chargers. Llewelyn stepped across the room and picked up one of the old Schiebel mine detectors. McFaul kept them for back-up in case of problems with the new Ebingers.

'Impressive,' Llewelyn was saying, 'I'd no idea you carried so much kit.'

'That's only part of it. The rest's still operational. This lot'll be crated up this afternoon. Ready for the off.'

'You're leaving?' Llewelyn looked up sharply.

'Yeah.'

'When?'

'No one knows. Couple of days maybe?' He paused, watching Llewelyn picking through the rest of the equipment, then examining the survey maps. The man's curiosity was boundless.

'This film . . .' McFaul began, 'what's it about?'

'You . . .' Llewelyn's finger was on one of the maps now, tracking the line of the river, 'and this operation of yours. The risks you run. The little miracles you work.' He paused, glancing round. 'That's Ken Middleton's phrase, not mine.'

McFaul blinked. Last time he'd made contact with the boss, Middleton had been insisting on evacuation, and the merits of a transfer to Mozambique. Not once had he mentioned a film.

'You've talked to him?'

'Of course.'

'You go down there? To Devizes?'

'No, we met in London. Nice chap. Dedicated, too.'

'And he said it was OK?' McFaul frowned. 'Doing this film of yours?'

'He was delighted, providing we hammered the training angle. I gather that's where the miracle comes in. Getting the locals to sort themselves out.'

McFaul nodded. 'Working miracles' wasn't a phrase he'd ever associate with Ken Middleton but the sentiment was true enough. The man was obsessed by spreading the word. Always had been. Llewelyn had returned to the table, perching his long frame on one corner.

'But why me?' McFaul began. 'Why here?'

Llewelyn studied him for a moment or two.

'Films like these need a focus. A lure. Something to get people on the hook.' He paused, glancing at his watch. 'I understand you lost an aid worker recently. Kid called James Jordan . . .'

It was mid-afternoon before Christianne took Molly to the grave. They went on foot, walking slowly through the hot dusty streets, Molly at last oblivious to the wreckage all around her. The girl's relationship with James had been much closer than she'd imagined, much closer – in truth – than she'd ever thought her son could possibly merit. The James she'd known – energetic, reckless, single-minded to the point of arrogance – wasn't at all the person Christianne described. The James whose adolescence had seemed never-ending had, on a different continent, become a man.

'He used to cook for you?'

'Often.'

'And was it . . .' Molly shrugged, 'OK?'

'*Oui*. It was simple, of course, but here you have no choice. He liked rice very much. With chillis. Spicy food.'

Molly nodded, remembering James's passion for Indian curries. One of the excuses he gave for not staying longer whenever he came home was Thorpe's lack of a good takeaway.

'And other things? Apart from cooking? He helped you with those as well?'

'With lots of things. He helped all the time. He was . . .' she frowned, hunting for the right expression, 'very practical. And fun, too. He made me laugh. Silly things. Little jokes.' She nodded. '*Oui*.'

They were on the outskirts of Muengo now, the shell damage less visible, the wattle-and-daub dwellings largely intact. Ahead, shimmering in the heat, was the place Christianne had described earlier. The hillock was crowned with a clump of mango trees and at the foot of the rising ground lay the grave. Only this morning, Christianne had discovered that the hillock had a name. The Africans called it '*O Alto dos Mil Espiritos*'. The hill of the thousand spirits.

'You'd been here before? You and James? Was it a special place?'

'No.'

'Shame.'

Molly had her arm linked to Christianne's. She liked the feel of the girl, her warmth, her sturdiness. She had a rare candour, too, a talent for asking direct questions without risking the slightest offence.

'You came to take him away,' she was saying. 'Were we wrong to bury him here?'

'No, not at all.'

'You're sure?'

'Yes.' Molly squeezed her arm. 'I feel close to him now, just talking to you.' She glanced across. 'You understand what I'm saying?'

Christianne shook her head.

'No,' she said.

Molly paused, stopping in the road, trying to frame the thought anew. The girl's question had opened doors inside her own head and what lay beyond them seemed suddenly important.

'I think James must have changed,' she began. 'I think something must have happened to him. Maybe he grew up. I don't know. But you were here. You must have seen it.' She paused. 'Does that make sense?'

'Yes. *Absolument.*'

'So what happened? What made the difference?'

Christianne eyed the nearby hillock. Crude wooden crosses had appeared at the head of the long grave. Some were draped with strings of beads. At the foot of one was a Coke can full of flowers.

'I don't know,' she said at length, 'except I miss him.'

McFaul got out of the Land Rover and stood beside the road for a full minute. The bush stretched away to the horizon, scrub and grass newly greened after the recent rains. Down the blacktop, away from the city, he could see yet another UNITA road-block, the torn-off bough of an acacia tree supported on two oil drums. Soldiers were watching them through binoculars, ever-curious.

'It's the closest I can get,' McFaul said at last.

'No chance of going to where it happened?'

'None. Unless you fancy talking to our friends there. And that could take several days.'

Llewelyn shrugged and told him not to bother. He'd already erected the tripod and fixed the camcorder to the metal plate on top. Now he was squinting through the viewfinder, lining up the shot. Satisfied, he opened the back of the Land Rover and took out the red placard he'd borrowed from McFaul's storeroom back at the schoolhouse. The placard was already fixed to a stake. Under a white skull and crossbones, it read 'DANGER – MINES'. He stepped off the road, the stake in one hand, a mallet in the other. McFaul was watching him.

'Where are you going?'

'Over there.' Llewelyn indicated a patch of bare earth ten metres in from the road. 'To put this in.'

He began to move again, the knee-high grass parting in front of him. Then he felt a hand on his shoulder, pulling him back. McFaul was laughing now, derisive.

'What's the matter?' Llewelyn said, visibly irritated.

'What's the *matter*? What do you fucking think's the matter? You come all this way, thousands of miles. You give me all this righteous shit about the Third World and what we've done to it, fucking mines everywhere, ninety per cent of the country off-limits. You spend all afternoon filming me at it, giving you chapter and verse, where you find the fuckers, what a pain they are to lift, what happens if you get it wrong. You look at all the pictures, all those horror shots we use, kids bleeding to death, kids with no legs, kids mangled beyond belief, and you're asking me what's the matter? You serious?' He nodded at Llewelyn's feet. 'Or is this just research? Seeing if they really work? Seeing what it feels like, losing a leg?'

Llewelyn looked uncertain for a moment.

'You're saying this is dangerous?'

'Yeah. I'm saying you're a step away from the full Angolan experience. Only give me a moment or two before you try one out.'

'You mean this bit might be mined?'

'Sure. That's why the guys up the road have got the binos out. It's like us and fireworks. Everyone likes a good bang.'

'Shit.'

Llewelyn stepped carefully back towards the road, tiptoeing like a child in very cold water. Then he stopped, planting the stake firmly in the loose soil beside the road.

'What are you doing now?'

'Putting this in. Here has to be safe.' Llewelyn frowned. 'Doesn't it?'

Ten minutes later, Llewelyn was ready for the take. He'd moved the tripod back to the middle of the road, tightening the shot to exclude the tarmac. Over his left shoulder, the death's-head placard was clearly visible. McFaul had already pointed out that there'd been no such warning at the spot where James Jordan had met his death but Llewelyn had ignored him. Reality, he said, occasionally needed a helping hand. Sticking to the facts one hundred per cent could sometimes get in the way of the story. Viewers had to have a reason for staying with the film, an assurance that something dreadful was about to happen. Otherwise their attention might stray.

Now, McFaul stood behind the camera. Llewelyn had given him a pair of miniature headphones to monitor the sound. In the viewfinder, he could see Llewelyn's upper body turned towards the camera, one shoulder slightly lowered, a pose that evidently gave the delivery more punch.

'Ready?'

McFaul nodded, fingering the Record button. A red light began to wink in the viewfinder and he watched, fascinated, as Llewelyn lifted his head and began to talk about James Jordan. On camera, the man was transformed. He became authoritative, grave, concerned. He talked about the Terra Sancta boy as if he'd known him most of his life. Here was someone young, white, idealistic. Someone who cared. Someone who wanted to make a difference. He'd lived and worked amongst the native Angolans. He'd sunk wells for them, piped clean water from the river. He'd eaten with them, sung with them, danced with them. Then, one hot summer's night, he'd taken one step too far.

At this point, Llewelyn gestured back towards the bush.

'That sound OK?'

McFaul looked up. The camera was still running.

'He didn't live with them,' he pointed out, 'no one lives with them. And he didn't eat with them either. Most Europeans hate mealies.'

'I meant the delivery.'

'The what?'

'The delivery, the performance.' Llewelyn was frowning. 'Did it sound all right? Look OK?'

'Fine . . .' McFaul shrugged, putting the camera on Pause, 'I suppose.'

'Good.'

Llewelyn told him to tighten the shot still further. Llewelyn's head was to fill the frame. The second piece to camera was to butt straight onto the first. Cut together, it would add to the effect.

McFaul was beginning to lose his temper.

'Effect?'

'Just tighten the shot.'

'I have done.'

'Good.'

Llewelyn looked away again, over his shoulder, the way he'd done before. On a cue, McFaul pressed the Record button and Llewelyn's head turned into camera, picking up the story. James Jordan had gone looking for a child from the town. Darkness was falling. Everyone had known there were mines but a child's life, in the eyes of the young aid worker, was more important.

James Jordan had always been a gambler. But in the hot Angolan darkness, his luck had finally run out.

Llewelyn paused. Then his voice took on a new gravity.

'He died instantly,' he intoned, 'his body ripped to pieces by just half a pound of high explosive.'

There was a long silence. Then McFaul stood up behind the camera. Llewelyn was looking at him, waiting for a reaction.

'Well?'

'Luck didn't come into it. The boy died because he didn't listen.'

'That's what you said this afternoon. We've got that, lots of it. It's important, too, all that stuff about manuals for aid workers. Makes the point.'

'I know. So why all this shit about luck? This was an incident, not an accident. You should be talking about blame, not fate, or luck, or whatever fucking excuse you want to use.'

Llewelyn crossed the road and began to rewind the video-tape, one eye to the viewfinder, ignoring McFaul's outburst. When he got to the start of the first take, he played it back. McFaul watched the smile spread across his face.

'Good,' he was muttering, 'excellent.'

One hand had come up to his face, fingering the bruise. At length he got to the end of the take, lifting his head from the viewfinder and looking for McFaul. McFaul was already behind the wheel of the Land Rover. Llewelyn removed the camcorder and collapsed the tripod. Beside the driver's door, he paused.

'I was worried about the bruising,' he said, 'but actually it looks quite good. Even adds a little something.'

McFaul studied him a moment, then started the engine and engaged gear. Over the chatter of the diesel he leaned out of the window and jerked a thumb towards a distant curl of smoke.

'City's back that way,' he said. 'Shouldn't take you long.'

*

Molly spent the evening with Christianne at the MSF house. Robbie had dropped off a handful of the tins spared by the UNITA troops at the airstrip and Molly cooked a risotto of tuna, rice and a sprinkling of black olives while Christianne hunted for a spare battery for her two-way radio. The old rechargeable had run down and without a handset she was, in her own phrase, 'stuffed'.

Molly had laughed, recognising one of James's favourite epithets. After supper, they sat in candle-light while Christianne mused aloud about where life might have taken them both. They'd had plans to travel. They'd made a list. Berlin, for some reason, was at the top. Followed by Dublin, Bali and California. In this, as in so many other ways, they'd thought alike. Food had been the same. And music, too. And the simple, physical things. Swimming. Playing volleyball with the kids. Going for long hikes in the mountains.

'The mountains are miles away,' Molly pointed out, 'and travelling's supposed to be dangerous.'

'Doesn't matter. We'd have got there somehow, I know we would. You know what he used to say? If you're hungry, you eat. If you want to do something badly enough, you'll do it. Anything's possible. As long as you're serious. Mountains?' She looked wistful. '*Pas de problème.*'

Past ten o'clock, Christianne finally gave up on the spare rechargeable. Molly watched her circling the room, restoring things to their proper places, making ready for bed. Tomorrow, with luck, there'd be news of an evacuation flight.

Molly got up, stretching, one last question still unvoiced.

'Did you see him at all?' she began. 'James? After he died?'

Christianne was chasing a mosquito with a slim paperback. She shook her head.

'It was very dark.'

'But afterwards. When you'd brought him back here. Did you see him then?'

'No.'

'At the hospital at all?'

'No. His body was inside a sack, a bag, you know...'
Christianne had the mosquito trapped in a corner. She flattened
the book against the wall and then stepped back.

'And after that you buried him?'

'As soon as we could, yes.'

'And he was...' Molly stared hard at the smudge of blood
on the wall, 'pretty much in one piece?'

'Yes, oh yes. Excuse me.'

There was a second knock at the front door. Christianne left
the room. Molly heard voices in the hall. Then a shadow
appeared, someone tall, stooping into the room. Molly turned
round. She'd been examining a photograph propped on the
mantelpiece, James standing knee-deep in a river, grinning at
the camera, kids all over him. The photograph was still in her
hand.

'This is Andy McFaul,' Christianne was saying, 'he knew
James, too.'

Molly stared up at the face above her. The hair was greying,
cropped brutally short against the skull, and the candle-light
played across the hollows of his face. The bottom half of his
face was latticed with deep blue scars, giving the smile a curious
deadness. McFaul, she thought. The name at the end of the
report she'd read at the embassy. The man who'd wasted so few
words on her dead son.

Molly glanced across at Christianne, offering her the photo
of James. McFaul withdrew his hand.

'There's a message from Luanda.' He nodded at Christianne's radio, lying on the bed. 'We've been trying to raise you.'

'Oh?'

'Yeah. The ambassador. He wants you to get in touch.' He
paused. 'I get the impression it's urgent.'

CHAPTER SEVEN

Next morning, McFaul was still half-asleep when Bennie told him about Katilo. A message had come in via Fernando at the UN compound. The UNITA commander had scrubbed their morning meet. McFaul and Christianne were now to present themselves at a road-block on the northern edge of the city at two o'clock. Arrangements would be made to take them on to Katilo's headquarters from there.

Now, getting dressed, McFaul was still furious. Deferring the meet by half a day meant losing precious time in the mine-fields. If the rumours about the evacuation were true then Muengo might yet be denied access to fresh water. The existing safe paths led straight to the most polluted stretches of the river. A couple of days' work could transform the situation.

Outside, McFaul heard the chatter of a diesel. The engine died, a door slammed, and there were voices. One of them was Christianne's. The other belonged to the woman he'd met last night, the dead boy's mother, Molly Jordan. McFaul cursed, hopping across the room on his good leg and fumbling beneath a pile of dirty laundry for his last clean shirt. He was still pulling it on, snagging the stitches on his upper arm, when the door opened behind him. McFaul manoeuvred himself round. His plastic leg with its straps and its Velcro lay on the camp-bed. He felt utterly naked.

Molly Jordan was first into the room. McFaul could see Bennie behind her, trying to explain to Christianne that the boss had been a bit late getting up. Molly was staring at McFaul's left leg. The amputation had been an inch or two below the knee. The skin was gathered and tucked into the stump, the flesh above scarred and pitted where the surgeons had removed fragments of shrapnel.

McFaul stood on one leg, motionless. Under the circumstances there was little else he could do. Molly was already backing through the door. She was wearing a blue T-shirt with some kind of bird on the front.

'I'm so sorry,' she was saying, 'I'd no idea.' McFaul shrugged.

'Heavy night,' he muttered. 'Slept in a bit.'

'No, I meant . . .' Molly shook her head, making way for Bennie. 'We'll come back later.'

She turned and hurried out through the schoolroom. McFaul heard a door slamming, footsteps outside, then the growl of the diesel as the Landcruiser restarted. Too late, he remembered the change of plan.

'Tell her Katilo's off until this afternoon,' he shouted to Bennie. 'Tell her it's back here for one-thirty.'

The two women returned an hour later. McFaul gave them the last of the instant coffee he'd been saving. They were sitting round the table in the schoolroom while Bennie and Domingos readied the piles of spare equipment for crating. Word had finally arrived from the UN in Luanda. Negotiations with UNITA's national leadership were going well and an evacuation flight had been scheduled for three days hence. The World Food Programme people had volunteered one of their big Hercules freighters and with Katilo's acquiescence, they'd all be out of Muengo by the weekend.

Now, McFaul emptied the coffee-pot into Christianne's cup. Bennie had organised some biscuits from somewhere, Peek Frean dry crackers, and McFaul nudged the plate towards Molly

Jordan, apologising gruffly for the absence of cheese. Last night, at the MSF house, he'd met her only briefly but a couple of minutes' awkward conversation had been enough to sense her bewilderment and her vulnerability. Under the tight smile, this woman was plainly lost.

McFaul glanced across at Christianne. She'd already checked into the UN compound, hearing first hand from Fernando about the postponed meeting with Katilo.

'Did Fernando let you use the HF,' he asked, 'to talk to the embassy people?'

Christianne looked at Molly, then shook her head.

'We didn't ask.'

'Why not?'

'I'm . . .' she shrugged, 'not sure.'

There was a silence. Then the sound of hammering from the road outside. Molly couldn't take her eyes off the stretchers. There were four of them, lightweight aluminium, neatly propped against the wall.

'My fault,' she said at last, colouring slightly.

McFaul reached for a biscuit, breaking it between his fingers. Food was beginning to be a problem and he hadn't eaten properly for days.

'You didn't try?'

'No.'

'Why not?'

'It's . . .' Molly exchanged glances with Christianne, 'a bit awkward. Before I came out here I met the ambassador. Nice man, extremely helpful, but . . .' she looked at McFaul at last, 'he didn't really approve.'

'Of what?'

'Of me coming here. He was very fair. He didn't stand in my way. He just made it plain that I shouldn't be going . . . shouldn't have come.'

'He's right.'

'Yes, I'm sure. So you'll understand why . . .' She offered

McFaul a wan smile. 'I expect I'll see him when I get back to Luanda. He can get it off his chest then. Whatever it is he wants to say.'

She fell silent as the hammering started again and McFaul wondered just when they'd get round to talking about James Jordan. In his own mind the boy's death had already become a classic, the kind of textbook case history he'd quote when he next talked to incoming aid workers. The way McFaul read it, this woman's son had taken his own life. Explaining just how wasn't going to be easy but it had to be done.

McFaul got up and limped across to the window. Bennie was hammering as well now and the noise was getting on his nerves. McFaul pulled the window shut. The glass had long gone and the replacement plywood plunged the room into semi-darkness. The hammering abruptly stopped. McFaul glanced down at Molly.

'That OK for you?'

'I'd prefer it open. If you don't mind.'

'I just thought . . .' McFaul shrugged, opening the window again then resuming his seat at the table. Looking at Molly, he'd settled on the word that best summed up what her son had really done. Suicide. The boy had committed suicide. By not listening. By thinking himself somehow invulnerable. McFaul stirred, aware of voices outside the window. The newcomer was Llewelyn. He must have walked over from his billet in the UN compound. He was talking to Bennie, running through some kind of check-list he'd evidently compiled, sequences he'd need for his precious film before the Hercules descended and brought the shoot to an end. There was stuff he wanted to do around the schoolhouse, a classroom situation to mock up. It might feature Bennie, he said, going through the basics with the locals. Then there were the survey maps Llewelyn had already seen, close-up material, a hand adding fresh details, somebody working at the computer keyboard, inputting new data, someone else on the radio, conducting a pretend conversation, material to establish just how hi-tech the de-mining business had become. The list went on and on, punctuated by grunts from Bennie, and McFaul was on the point of going out there and telling Bennie to get on with the crating when Llewelyn mentioned Molly's son.

'This boy Jordan,' Llewelyn was saying. 'Your boss tells me you had him in the fridge for a while. At your place.'

'Yeah. Too fucking right.'

'Because the power was off at the hospital?'

'Apparently.'

'So your boss brought him here?'

'That's right.'

'For how long?'

'Dunno. Couple of days at the most. Long enough to knacker everything else in the freezer.' McFaul was on his feet now, returning to the window. He could hear Bennie laughing but he was too late to bring the conversation to an end. 'Gennie failed,' Bennie was saying. 'Ran out of fuel. You could smell him half a mile away, the state he was in. Believe me, I've seen a lot of stiffs in my time but nothing like this. You ever watch *Alien*? That sequence when the guy's flat on the table and this thing comes bursting out of his—'

McFaul shut the window with a bang. The room went dark again. Molly sat at the table, motionless. When Christianne tried to comfort her, she shook her head, crossing and uncrossing her arms, taking a deep breath.

'You should have told me,' she said quietly. 'However bad it was you should have told me.'

'I couldn't.'

'No?'

'*Non.*'

Molly looked at her for a long moment, her face quite impassive.

'So how bad was he?' she said at last. 'When you buried him?'

Christianne looked at McFaul, out of her depth now. McFaul sat down at the table. Molly's hands were ice-cold to his touch.

'He was a mess, Mrs Jordan,' he muttered. 'He was a mess when we found him. And a mess when we buried him. There was nothing we could do.'

'Molly. My name's Molly.'

'Yes, I'm sorry.'

'That's OK, just tell me. That's why I'm here. That's why I've come.'

McFaul hesitated a moment, remembering the night he'd driven out with Domingos to recover the boy's body, the long hours they'd spent with Christianne at the roadside. By the time they'd swept a path to the site of the explosion, Jordan's remains were black with flies. One or two had somehow survived the transfer into the body bag, the buzzing audible for days afterwards.

Molly was still watching him, still waiting for an answer.

'What do you want to know?' McFaul said at last.

'Everything.'

'There's nothing else I can tell you. He stepped on a mine. Probably a bounding mine.'

'What's that?'

'It's a mine that . . .' McFaul shrugged, 'jumps up.'

'And explodes where? At what height?'

'Metre. Metre and a half.'

Molly raised her hand, palm down. When it reached belly-height, McFaul nodded. Molly's hand shook for a moment.

'So who makes these mines?'

'Everyone. The Americans. The Russians. The Italians. They've been around for years. Soldiers hate them. As you might imagine.'

'And do they sell them? To these people?' Molly gestured vaguely towards the window.

'Yes. Or to middlemen. That's the likeliest. That's the way it normally works.'

'And they . . . these middlemen . . .?'

'Sell the mines on. To whoever wants them.'

'Buys them?'

'Of course.'

'For a profit? They're sold for a profit?'

'Yes. First to the middlemen. And then ...' McFaul shrugged again, 'to the customers. We call them end-users. In the business.'

'Business?'

There was a long silence. Christianne leaned forward, her second coffee still untouched.

'I told Molly about Maria ...' she said. 'The little girl, you know, that night.'

McFaul nodded. Unlike James Jordan, Maria had survived the minefield, only to be killed a week or so later during the second night of shelling. Christianne knew the mother, a woman called Chipenda, and Molly had said she wanted to meet her.

McFaul nodded, glad that the conversation had changed tack.

'You know where she is?'

'Yes. She's in the cinema. Camping out.' Christianne paused. 'I was wondering about Domingos. We need someone to translate. She only speaks Ovimbundu. I thought ...' she glanced at Molly, 'if Domingos's not too busy.'

McFaul was already on his feet. He limped out of the schoolroom. Llewelyn was crouched in the sunshine, the camcorder cradled in one hand, explaining a sequence to Bennie. They were pretending the equipment had just arrived. On a cue from Llewelyn, Bennie was to start unpacking it. McFaul watched for a moment, then intervened.

'Molly Jordan's here,' he said to Domingos, 'she needs a bit of help.'

At the mention of Molly's name, Llewelyn looked up.

'Now?' he said. 'She's here now?'

'Yeah.'

'What's she doing?'

'Having coffee,' McFaul glanced at Bennie, 'and listening to you, fuck-face.'

Bennie looked nonplussed for a moment, then closed his eyes and groaned.

'Shit,' he said quietly, 'I'm sorry, Boss.'

'Yeah. And so you fucking should be.'

Llewelyn was on his feet now, the unpacking sequence forgotten.

'What's she doing next?' he asked. 'Why Domingos?'

'She wants to meet a woman in the city.'

'Who?'

'Just someone.'

'Yes, but who?'

McFaul took a step towards Llewelyn, tired of arguing with this clown who'd appeared with his camera and his tripod and his fantasies about James Jordan. He was about to settle the debate when Molly appeared at the schoolhouse door. McFaul lowered his fist and turned away, taking Domingos by the arm. The Global Land Rover was parked nearby. Beside it, McFaul explained about Molly, still shaking with anger. Mrs Jordan wanted to talk to Maria's mother. He and Domingos would go with her. Domingos would translate. Under the circumstances, it was the least they could do. Domingos nodded, watching the Englishwoman walking towards them, deep in conversation with Llewelyn. Beside the Land Rover, they stopped. Llewelyn was looking at McFaul.

'I need to get this on tape,' he said at once, 'it's important.'

'Get what?'

'This meeting you've set up. Mrs Jordan and the girl's mother. It makes all kinds of points. In fact, it's vital, absolutely vital.'

McFaul stared at him a moment, another surge of anger darkening his face. He should have hit him earlier, he knew it. He should have established the rules, brought this sick media game to an end. Llewelyn was already opening the passenger door of the Land Rover. McFaul looked at Molly.

'You want him along? You want it all filmed? Taped? What-ever he does?'

Molly was watching Llewelyn as he made himself comfort-able in the back of the Land Rover.

'No,' she said quietly, 'I don't.'

Molly stepped towards the Land Rover. Llewelyn moved across the bench seat, making room for her. She looked him in the eye, shaking her head.

'I'm sorry,' she said, 'I don't want this on camera.'

Llewelyn stared at her.

'What?'

'I said I don't want you here. This is private. Myself and Domingos and Mr McFaul.'

'Andy,' McFaul muttered.

'Andy.' Molly glanced up at McFaul, correcting herself. 'Just the three of us.'

Llewelyn shook his head, disbelieving.

'We're here to make a film,' he said thickly. 'It might help if you remembered that.'

'You're here to make a film. I'm here for lots of reasons. Please . . .' she held the door open, gesturing with her hand, 'if you don't mind.'

Llewelyn began to argue about contracts. Molly interrupted.

'I haven't got a contract,' she pointed out.

'You have. You signed one. That first afternoon, that first session in the hotel. In Colchester.'

Molly frowned remembering a sheet of paper on a clip-board, thrust under her nose minutes before the interview had begun.

'You said that was a formality. I remember. You called it a blood-chit. Not a contract.'

Llewelyn shrugged.

'Same thing,' he said. 'It binds you into the project. We've brought you out here. We've paid the expenses. If it wasn't for us, you'd still be in Essex.'

Molly hesitated, all too aware that she needed advice. Robbie Cunningham had disappeared first thing with Tom Peterson. She glanced at McFaul. He didn't look like the kind of man who'd bother much about contracts. He bent towards her.

'What do you want to do?'

'I want to go and see this lady. The little girl's mother.'

'Alone?'

'With you and Domingos.'

'And our friend here?'

'No,' she shook her head, 'thank you.'

McFaul nodded. Llewelyn was examining the camera now, holding it up to his eye and making adjustments to the focus ring. McFaul limped round to the other side of the Land Rover. He opened the rear door and pulled Llewelyn out into the sunshine. Under the creased linen jacket, he was surprised how thin the journalist felt. Close to, he looked pale and drawn, his face more grey than white. McFaul escorted him towards the schoolhouse. When Llewelyn had stopped protesting about his lost footage, he released his grip.

'You know the call sign you lot use for Terra Sancta?'

Llewelyn nodded, rubbing his arm.

'Tango Sierra.'

'Exactly. And you know what that means? In the real world?'

Llewelyn shook his head, watching the smile spread across McFaul's face. For a moment, the two men looked at each other. Then McFaul patted Llewelyn roughly on the shoulder.

'It means tough shit,' he said, turning away.

They drove into the centre of the city. The streets were coming alive again, hunger and thirst forcing the people out of the shelter of their homes. In the square beside the cathedral there was even the beginnings of a market, women squatting behind squares of grubby matting, trading what little they still possessed for a handful of maize or a corked half-bottle of cloudy paraffin.

The cinema lay beyond the cathedral. Once, it had been the hub of Muengo's social life, a long barn-like building, white-washed cinder-block walls with a decorative façade at one end. Two wide steps led up from the street and there was still the remains of a poster beside the yawning hole where once the doors had been. The poster was rain-splashed and torn but Molly recognised the bleached outline of two faces, nose to nose in a passionate embrace. Ali McGraw. Ryan O'Neal. *Love Story.*

Molly smiled, feeling the touch of Domingos's hand on her elbow. They stepped into the gloom of the vestibule. Only the steel frame of the booking office remained, the timber stripped away. Molly stopped a moment, catching her breath. She could smell smoke. The place was on fire. She was sure of it. Domingos had disappeared through another opening, a jagged hole in an inner wall. Molly followed him, McFaul behind her. Molly could see daylight now, a curious ash-greyness that washed in through the hole punched in the masonry. Beyond lay the body of the cinema, the auditorium, and she was about to step through when she stopped again, her breath gone completely, on the edge of a world no film she'd seen had ever pictured.

The cinema was a sea of bodies, women and children and old men huddled in groups, the walls towering above them, blackened and sooted, the roof gone, the whole scene veiled by the drifting smoke of a hundred cooking fires. Domingos began to pick his way between the squatting families and Molly ventured after him. Two Angolan nuns stepped aside, acknowledging Domingos's whispered greeting. One of them was nursing a tiny infant, naked except for a scrap of thin sacking, and Molly paused a moment, looking down at it, wondering whether it was still alive. Outside, through a ragged shell hole in the wall, she could see piles of rubbish – rusty tins, rain-soaked cardboard, torn shreds of the thick blue polythene favoured by the aid charities – and there were kids in amongst it, turning the stuff over, sifting through it, desperate to retrieve anything edible.

There were women out there too, and some of them had covered the lower half of their faces against the smell. Molly did the same, one hand to her nose, trying to mask the stench of sweat and smoke.

Domingos had stopped now. He was squatting beside a woman who'd made a home for herself beside the wall. Above her head, in the space between two cinder-blocks, a pair of bare wires dangled from a broken socket. A child lay on her lap. To Molly it looked no more than a couple of months old, a tiny thing, swaddled in a threadbare cloth. Its eyes were closed, one cheek pressed to the woman's bare breast, its wrists no thicker than an adult's thumb. An older child stood beside it, naked except for a pair of ragged shorts. It had a chronic eye infection, yellow pus oozing down one cheek.

Domingos was talking to the woman. He gestured up towards Molly and the woman followed his pointing finger. She nodded. Domingos stood up.

'Her name is Chipenda,' he said. 'Maria was her eldest child. The child your son tried to save.'

'Maria,' the woman nodded, recognising the name, 'Maria.'

Molly knelt quickly beside Chipenda. The child on her breast stirred, opening one eye as Molly extended a hand. The woman looked at Molly's hand, the rings, the perfect nails, openly curious.

'I've come to say I'm sorry . . .' Molly glanced up at Domingos pausing to let him translate, 'about your daughter . . . the shelling . . .' she hesitated, 'all this . . .'

The woman, Chipenda, nodded at once, muttering something in Ovimbundu.

'It's terrible.' Domingos was playing with the older child. 'She says it's terrible.'

'I'm sure it is. She's right. It's dreadful . . .' Molly hesitated again, not knowing quite what to say next. McFaul had joined them now, pale, grim-faced, gazing down at the wreckage of three lives.

'Ask about her husband,' he suggested. 'Ask her where he's got to.'

Molly nodded. Domingos obliged with a translation. The woman began to talk very fast, leaning towards Domingos as if she was sharing some family secret. Domingos listened without comment. Finally he nodded, getting to his feet. He looked tired and dispirited, as if he'd heard the same story a thousand times before.

'She says she hasn't seen her husband for nearly a year. They used to live in a village about three days away. The soldiers came and set fire to the village. Many people died in their huts, burned to death. She and her husband tried to go back afterwards and start again but the soldiers had put mines in the fields so everyone was frightened of going there. Then one night the soldiers returned and took her husband for the war.'

Molly was looking at the woman.

'Which soldiers?'

Domingos translated. The woman shrugged. She was drawing patterns in the dirt to keep the child amused.

'Just soldiers,' Domingos said. 'She doesn't know which side.'

'So . . .' Molly frowned, 'when will she see her husband again?'

Domingos glanced at the woman but didn't bother to translate this time.

'She wouldn't know,' he said. 'He may be dead already. He may come back one day. She can't tell.'

'And there's nothing . . .' Molly shrugged, 'she can do? No one she can see? Ask? She just accepts it?'

'Of course.' Domingos gestured around. 'What choice does she have?'

Molly nodded, trying to fathom the kind of life this woman must lead. Never knowing. Never being sure. An eternity of loss.

'Tell her I'm sorry,' she said helplessly.

210

'I just did.'

'Tell her again.' She paused. 'Did she know my son? James? Did she ever meet him?'

Domingos bent to Chipenda, putting the question, and she looked up at Molly, smiling for the first time. She had the mouth of an old woman, several teeth broken, others missing completely. She was nodding now, talking to Domingos. Domingos smiled.

'What is it?' Molly asked. 'What's she saying?'

'She says that your son was crazy.'

'Why?'

'Coming out here at all. She says he should have stayed at home. And had lots of sons.'

'I agree.' Molly was looking at Chipenda now. 'Tell her I agree.'

The woman laughed at Molly's vigorous nod and finally extended a hand. Molly gave it a squeeze and leaned quickly forward. The baby at her breast shivered under the kiss, then both eyes closed again and the huge head lolled forward.

Molly got up. Domingos was talking to McFaul, pointing towards the far end of the cinema. McFaul nodded and then bent to Molly's ear.

'Domingos wants you to meet someone else. Guy called Guringo. He's the chief, the elder, the head man. They call him the *Soba*. Domingos thinks he may be able to help you.'

'How?'

McFaul hesitated a moment. Domingos was already making his way through the watching families.

'Domingos thinks he knows the man who laid the mines. Where James got killed.'

Molly stared at him.

'Here? Someone here?'

'Possibly. Domingos isn't sure. But since we've got this far . . .' McFaul shrugged, 'why not find out?'

The chief was camped beneath the expanse of end wall that

had once served as the cinema's screen. The white paint was barely visible beneath a grey film of rain-streaked soot and at the foot of the wall there was a tidy pile of firewood, newly scavenged from the wreckage of shelled houses. The chief himself was a man of uncertain age, bald, very thin, with a straggly grey beard and yellowing eyes. He sat cross-legged, surrounded by a circle of carefully husbanded possessions: a tin cup, an empty sack, a hoe blade, a handful of twisted iron nails, six melon seeds, two blackened billycans and a tiny bunch of wilting greens. Molly studied the tableau from a respectful distance, determined to take this mental snapshot back home with her. However bad things got, however desperate she might feel, no life could be as bare as this.

Domingos was crouched beside the chief, explaining why they'd come. At length the old man got to his feet, standing erect, inclining his head gravely towards Molly. When he'd finished speaking, Domingos translated.

'He says he's sorry to hear about your son.'

'Didn't he know before?'

'Apparently not. Many have died in the minefields. He says he's lost count.'

Molly nodded, looking at the old man again, feeling unaccountably guilty. Why should her loss be anything special? Why should James's death be of any conceivable interest to these people?

McFaul was asking about the man who might have laid the mines. While Domingos put the question to the *Soba*, Molly watched a nearby woman coaxing a colourless mush into a child's mouth. She used two fingers to feed the child, licking them after each mouthful. McFaul was watching too. Molly touched him on the arm.

'What's that?'

'Pulped maize. It grows everywhere. It's called *funje*.'

'And what will she eat?' Molly was still looking at the mother. 'Afterwards?'

McFaul shrugged, indicating the inch of *funje* in the bottom of the earthenware pot.

'Whatever's left,' he said. 'There's nothing else.'

'So what's it like?'

'Completely tasteless.'

Molly nodded, her eyes returning to the chief. For the first time, she realised exactly what his T-shirt said. 'The Grateful Dead' went the faded logo across the chest, 'Ventura Stadium, '85'. James, she thought. One of his favourite groups. She glanced at McFaul again.

'Where did he get the T-shirt?'

'It's charity stuff. Cast-offs. Flown in.'

The chief was reaching for the bundle of greens. He extracted one and offered it to Molly. Molly was about to refuse but McFaul told her to take it. The *Soba* would be offended, he said. She must eat with him. Molly did what she was told, tearing off the leafy part of the plant. She put it in her mouth and began to chew. At first it tasted bitter, then it made her mouth burn, a strange, prickly sensation. For a moment, she thought she was going to throw up. She heard McFaul beside her, oddly comforting.

'Just a couple of little chews,' he was saying, 'no big deal.'

Domingos was on his feet again.

'The chief's talking about a fella called Zezito. The rebels took him several months ago but he's back in the city now.'

'Where?'

'In the hospital. He was dumped at one of the road-blocks a couple of nights ago. It often happens.'

Molly frowned, not understanding, and McFaul explained the discipline in UNITA ranks was harsh. Anyone who stepped out of line was instantly punished and some of the punishments were barbaric. Afterwards, as a warning to anyone else who might one day be pressed into service with UNITA, the half-dead soldier would be returned to his home city.

'So what happened? To this one?'

'They cut his ears off. And one or two other bits.'

'And he's still alive?'

'Yes. Apparently he's been talking about the minefields. Because he knew the area so well, they made him lay them. He was supposed to stick to certain areas, places where the people plant crops and draw water. It drives them off the land. Destroys communities. Our friend in the hospital evidently had other ideas. Silly man.'

'Meaning?'

'Meaning he wasted all their precious mines on useless bits of scrub.'

'Including the bit James . . .?'

'Quite possibly. If we're talking the same minefield.'

McFaul looked at Domingos. The Angolan nodded, confirming McFaul's account, and Molly turned away. An hour ago, sitting in the schoolroom listening to Bennie outside the window, she'd been engulfed in a kind of primitive rage. She'd wanted revenge. She'd wanted a name. Now she had one. Except that nothing was quite as simple as it seemed.

'So Zezito . . .'

McFaul shrugged.

'. . . thought he was doing the right thing.'

'So does that mean the rest of the place is . . . safe?'

'Shit, no.' He looked at her a moment, a flicker of life in his strange dead eyes. 'You know how many mines there are in this country?'

Molly shook her head.

'No.'

'Twenty million. That's two for every Angolan.' He smiled. 'Or one for each leg.'

Todd Llewelyn stepped back from the tripod, inviting Bennie to help himself to the camcorder and take a look at the sequence they'd just taped. They'd rearranged the furniture in the schoolroom, putting two rows of seats between the desk and the window. In front of the display of survey maps, Bennie had erected the easel they used for training sessions and on the blackboard he'd chalked the outline of a minefield. Llewelyn had asked him to talk for at least a couple of minutes, and when the camera had finally rolled, Bennie had found himself expounding on the theory and practice of minefield clearance.

Mines, he explained, were normally laid in distinctive patterns. The 'A' pattern, for instance, had a big anti-tank mine protected by a triangle of three anti-personnel mines. Once you'd sussed a pattern like this, driving a number of exploratory breaches or 'safe lanes' across the minefield, you went for something called 'roll-up', clearing the rest of the mined land. This was a lovely theory and worked a treat on a proper battlefield. In the Third World, though, 'roll-up' was a non-starter because the mines were usually scattered at random, obeying no comprehensible pattern. In this case, you had no choice but to clear the site an inch at a time, leaving nothing to chance. This was known as '100 per cent clearance'. Another phrase, said Bennie, was 'pain in the arse'.

Bennie stepped back from the viewfinder, impressed with his own performance.

'Great,' he said. 'Where does this go out?'

'People's Channel.'

'What's that?'

'It's a new satellite operation but I'm sure it'll get sold elsewhere. These things usually do.'

'ITV? BBC?'

'Maybe.' Llewelyn shrugged. 'Who knows?'

Bennie eyed the camera. As well as the training sequence they'd also done a lot of stuff with the survey maps, Llewelyn building up a library of shots he'd need to compile his final report. Bennie looked round at the line of empty chairs.

'What about an audience? Won't it look a bit daft? Me talking to no one?'

'We'll get some people in later. It's a simple reverse shot. I can pick it up any time.' Llewelyn began to detach the camcorder from the tripod. 'What I really need is something in the minefields. You guys actually doing it.'

'I know. You said already.'

'This afternoon then?'

Bennie shrugged.

'Love to. Love to. You know I would. Depends on the boss, though. He says he's got to talk to the UNITA boys. In case they get funny.'

'Is that likely?'

'No.'

'Then what's the problem?'

Bennie laughed.

'There's isn't a fucking problem. Not if you want it that bad.'

McFaul and Christianne were several minutes late at the UNITA road-block. They'd left Molly at the MSF house, already exhausted by her first real taste of life under siege. McFaul parked the MSF Landcruiser in the shade of an acacia tree and walked across to the line of watching soldiers. Most of them were young, still teenagers, and their eyes never left Christianne.

Christianne approached the nearest soldier. He was wearing a rumpled forage cap and the side of his face was seamed with a long, thin scar. She began to explain in French about the rendezvous with Katilo but he indicated with a shrug that he didn't understand. When she started again in Portuguese, he turned his back on her and walked away.

Ten minutes later, a big Toyota appeared in the distance, travelling at speed. It ground to a halt, broadside on to the road-block. A small, neat man got out. He wore dark glasses, camouflage trousers and a newly pressed US Marine Corps shirt. He had a revolver strapped to his waist and the tall, lace-up boots looked freshly polished. He studied McFaul a moment then signalled to the Toyota without looking round. Another man appeared. He was much bigger, dressed in black fatigues. He carried two lengths of material, evidently the remains of someone's T-shirt. McFaul eyed them without comment. Blind-folds, he thought. One each.

Christianne was explaining about Katilo again. The man in the dark glasses ignored her. McFaul submitted to a body search, the man's hands pausing at the bottom of his left leg, feeling the smooth plastic beneath his jeans. Afterwards, the man stepped back.

'OK?'

McFaul shrugged, bowing his head, letting the soldier in the black fatigues tighten the blindfold around his eyes. Beside him he could hear Christianne protesting.

'No sweat,' he called, 'it's just a precaution.'

They were led through the road-block and helped into the back of the Toyota. McFaul heard the doors shut and the engine start. Then they were accelerating away, the big springs soaking up the ruts and the pot-holes on the baked-earth road. McFaul could feel Christianne's body beside him. He reached for her hand and squeezed it. Somebody was smoking in the front now. He could smell the tobacco, the harsh, acrid tang of the stuff they shipped up from South Africa, and he took a deep breath, glad of the chance to mask the stale, sour smell of the blindfold.

The journey went on, the driver punishing the gears, the Toyota swaying and bouncing from one corner to the next. Twice McFaul tipped his head back, trying to see out beneath the blindfold, but both times he got no further than a thin strip of light, the tops of the front seats, and the wide, blue African sky diffused through the tinted windscreen.

At last, they began to slow. In the silence after they'd stopped, McFaul heard voices, someone laughing. Then the door beside him opened and he felt an arm tugging him out. He'd abandoned his sling now and he tried to protect the line of stitches with his left hand. Upright, he waited for Christianne to join him.

'Ask them to take these things off,' he told her, 'for Christ's sake.'

He heard her putting the request, first in French, then in Portuguese. There was more laughter. Then they were walking again, uneven ground, tripping and stumbling. Suddenly it was much cooler. McFaul could feel pebbles beneath his feet and a damp, weedy smell, like the breath of some creature from the swamp. Somebody was talking, definitely French, and he heard Christianne's reply. She sounded wary, even a little frightened. For the first time, he began to wonder whether the rendezvous with Katilo was such a great idea.

'What's going on?' he murmured.

Christianne didn't answer. The other voice was closer now and McFaul could smell aftershave, Calvin Klein, the stuff Bennie used. Without warning, the knot on his blindfold was loosened, then untied. At the same time, McFaul felt a chair nudge the backs of his legs. By the time the blindfold was off, he was sitting down, rubbing his eyes, peering into the gloom of what looked like a cave.

Katilo sat opposite, sprawled in a collapsible director's chair. The only photo McFaul had ever seen of the man didn't do him justice. He was wearing combat trousers, belted at the waist, and a simple olive green T-shirt. He had a broad chest, and well-muscled arms, and when he smiled his whole face seemed to radiate energy, like an athlete in peak condition. He was speaking in French to Christianne but his eyes flicked back and forth between them, ever playful. According to the big Seiko watch on his wrist, it was five past two.

'He says he's sorry about the blindfolds,' Christianne touched her face, 'but he hopes you'll understand.'

McFaul grunted, non-committal. Five past two meant they'd been travelling for little more than twenty minutes. Ten miles, say. Maybe less.

'Tell him about the minefields,' he said, 'tell him what we want to do.'

'He's asking whether you'd like a drink. He's offering beer or whiskey.'

'Lager,' McFaul said briefly, offering Katilo a thin smile. The last thing he wanted to do was waste time but he knew that meetings like this got nowhere without the ritual courtesies.

Katilo clapped his hands and McFaul heard a movement behind him. He looked round. Naked light bulbs hung from loops of black cable and the fissured rock above their heads was glistening with moisture. Behind him, the cables disappeared behind a hanging blanket and somewhere close by McFaul could hear the chatter of a generator. Katilo was talking again, a deep bass rumble. Whatever the joke was, it made Christianne laugh. McFaul turned back in time to see Katilo leaning forward, his arm outstretched, one hand on Christianne's knee. He wore an enormous silver ring on the forefinger of one hand.

Christianne glanced at McFaul. She was plainly terrified.

'What does he want?'

'He says he's got some videos.'

'*Videos?*'

'Yes. We can have *Terminator 2* or *Baywatch*. I don't think he's joking.'

The makeshift curtain parted behind McFaul and the cave was briefly flooded with daylight. A soldier in full combat dress offered McFaul a can of lager. Katilo was watching him, a smile still curling the wide, fleshy lips. McFaul accepted the can, waving away the proffered cup.

'South African?' he murmured.

'Of course.' Katilo nodded. 'Castle. The best.'

'You speak English?'

'Yes. Doesn't your girlfriend want anything?'

McFaul shook his head.

'She's not in the mood,' he said briefly. 'And she's not my girlfriend.'

McFaul took a deep pull from the can. UNITA logistics evidently extended to proper refrigeration.

'We're here to talk about the minefields,' he said at last, 'around Muengo.'

'You want to clear them?'

'Yes. Like I said on the radio. Just a handful, two or three, before we leave.'

Katilo considered the proposal, his elbows propped on the arms of the chair, his fingers steepled together. Finally, he shrugged.

'Why not?' he said. 'We have plenty more mines.'

'But I need to be sure.'

'Of what?'

'My men. Their safety.' McFaul lifted two fingers, aiming into the darkness at the back of the cave. 'No accidents. No silly mistakes. None of your soldiers getting the wrong idea.'

Katilo was studying Christianne again. He had the indolence of someone with limitless time and limitless patience. McFaul swallowed another mouthful of the lager. For Christianne read Muengo, he thought. When I want you, I'll take you.

'We're flying out in three days,' McFaul began, 'you'll know that.'

'Of course.'

'Three days isn't a long time. Not in our trade.'

'*Comment?*' Katilo was frowning at Christianne.

'*Trois jours n'est pas longtemps,*' she said at once, '*pour trouver les mines.*'

'*Ah, bon. Je comprends. Exact.*' He grinned at her. 'Your Mr McFaul here, your friend . . . why does he do this work? Why does he bother? When we,' he clicked his fingers, 'just start all over again?'

Llewelyn rode out to the minefield in the Global Land Rover with Bennie and Domingos. Back in the schoolroom, the three men had spent nearly an hour arguing about the sequence Llewelyn insisted was vital to the film's success: where it should take place, what it should include.

Domingos wanted to wait for McFaul's return, not because he was nervous of the rebel troops but because he respected McFaul's judgement. He'd worked for the Boss for nearly five months now and he couldn't remember a single occasion when he'd got it wrong. He was methodical, he was cautious, and he was more or less intact, three reasons for postponing the shoot until they were sure it had his approval. Bennie, listening to Domingos, had shaken his head. Time was short. This programme of Llewelyn's was all-important. Saving lives meant spreading the word and just now Bennie couldn't think of a better way of doing exactly that. Working in a real minefield could wait until tomorrow. Doing what Llewelyn called 'the tight shots' in a safe area, a place they both knew had been cleared, would be the best possible use of time.

Now, the Global Land Rover came to a halt on the embankment overlooking the path to the river. In all likelihood they'd be back here in the morning, protected by Katilo's blessing. According to Domingos's records, there were just seven metres left to clear. Between the road and the live remnant of the minefield there were nearly eighty metres of secured terrain, ample scope for the TV man and his menu of shots.

Bennie got out and went to the back of the Land Rover. At Llewelyn's suggestion, he'd brought a boxful of demo mines, plastic casings emptied of explosives and used in the schoolhouse for training. Reburied, these would serve as real mines, targets for Global's repertoire of tricks.

First, Llewelyn wanted an electronic search, the team working together, one forward, one back, both men fully kitted up in the protective gear, using the new Ebingers to sweep the ground before them. The soundtrack, put together back in the UK, would signal the likelihood of a mine, the distinctive yowl as the electronic sensors picked up the tiny particles of metal in the firing mechanism without which the mine wouldn't explode. Once located, Llewelyn wanted Domingos and Bennie to go through the whole procedure, laying down the Ebinger, getting to work with the bayonet and the camel-hair brush, establishing the exact position of the mine, scraping away the soil around it, exposing the thing to the naked eye. There was real drama here, big fat close-ups, sweaty faces, steady hands, flesh and blood pitted against the terrible chemistry of high explosive.

Bennie hauled the box of demo mines from the back of the Land Rover, wondering what the film would look like once everything had been cut together. He didn't much like Llewelyn – too pushy, too pleased with himself – but he'd recognised the face the moment he'd met him, and just listening to the man you knew he'd do the biz. Where the film might lead was anyone's guess but just now Bennie would do anything to get himself out of the front line. In this trade you were wise to follow your instincts. A thousand quid a week was good corn but Bennie's instincts were beginning to tell him it was time to look for something a little safer.

He scrambled down the embankment and left the box of dud mines at the start of the path. Domingos was standing beside the Land Rover, his binoculars trained on the rebel positions he'd spotted the previous day. When Bennie rejoined him, he was frowning.

'What's the matter?'

Domingos didn't lower the glasses.

'They're all looking at us,' he said quietly, 'and I don't know why.'

Katilo had started on the whiskey. They'd been in the cave nearly an hour. Behind him, deep in the shadows, two soldiers were glued to an episode of *Baywatch*. Evidently, on Katilo's insistence, cassettes were shipped in weekly from South Africa. It was, he said, invaluable for morale.

McFaul stirred. A third can of lager had given his anger a hard, brittle edge. If Katilo had invited them here for some kind of game, so be it. The man had touched a nerve. What he sanctioned, the means he used to wage his war, deserved a little attention.

'What was the matter with the fella Zezito?' he said. 'The one you dumped at the road-block? No use any more? Damaged goods?'

Katilo had moved his chair. Side-on now, he could keep an eye on *Baywatch* while looking round from time to time to raise an eyebrow in Christianne's direction. At the mention of Zezito's name, he shrugged.

'There was an argument,' he said. 'Some of the men wanted to kill him.'

'Maybe they should have done. Might have been kinder.'

'You think so?' His eyes were back on the TV screen. A lifeguard called Stephanie was splashing through the shallows on some Californian beach. The film dissolved into slow motion, her breasts rising up and down inside the tight orange one-piece bathing suit. Katilo muttered something to one of the watching Angolans. The soldier reached forward, respooling the video, then playing it again. McFaul glanced across at Christianne. Her face was a mask, her gaze fixed on the empty cans by her feet. McFaul took another pull at the bottle of Black Label.

'Zezito piss you off?' he enquired. 'Laying mines where they wouldn't do any good?'

Katilo ignored the question. The soldier with the remote control was laughing now, putting the video into fast-forward then stopping it again. Stephanie emerged from the lifeguard's look-out, stooping to pick up a towel. The camera angle left little to the imagination. The sequence juddered to a halt, Katilo admiring the still frame. He peered round at McFaul.

'You know something, Mr McFaul? My men prefer this to pornography. We have lots of pornography. We get it from our friends in South Africa. White women. Yellow women. Black women. Animals. Anything you want. But this . . .' he waved his glass towards the screen, 'is really hot. My men love it. Ask them. Please. Be my guest.'

McFaul declined the invitation, wondering again where Katilo had learned his English. He spoke with an American accent and the drunker he got, the more authentic he sounded. He wore a gemstone, too, through the lobe of his right ear. It looked like a diamond, catching the light when he turned his head.

'You took a knife to Zezito,' McFaul said. 'Just tell me why.'

'Is he a friend of yours?'

'No.'

'You've met him?'

'No.'

'Then why do you care what happens to this man?'

Katilo had abandoned *Baywatch* now, swinging his body round in the canvas chair, and McFaul recognised the quickening note in his voice. The questions were getting under his skin. The man was angry.

He leaned forward, the huge head lowered, thick slabs of muscle visible beneath the tight T-shirt.

'What's the matter, Mr McFaul,' he was saying, 'don't you like the way we make war?'

'No,' McFaul shook his head, 'I don't.'

'Because of Zezito?'

'Because of lots of things.'

'Like what?'

'Like mines.'

'Is that any of your business? These mines?'

'Yeah,' McFaul smiled, 'as it happens, they are. And you want to know why? Because you think it's all so fucking simple. You ship them in by the thousand. You chuck them around. And hey, they do your bidding. Man steps on one, it goes off. Kid goes for a walk, he's hamburger. Woman looks for firewood, she loses both legs and her face maybe too.

224

Nice war, Colonel. Must take a lot of courage, laying those mines.'

McFaul paused, aware of the soldiers staring at him. Katilo's head was up now, the eyes bloodshot. He held the whiskey bottle loosely by the neck, his arm dangling beside the chair.

'It's our war, Mr McFaul. You know what that means? It means our people, our land. Ours. Not yours. Ours.'

'Your blood?'

'Yes, Mr McFaul, our blood. Exactly. Ours to spill, ours to waste. If you were part of this country, if you were born here, you'd understand that. War is war. The only important thing is winning. The people suffer, sure. But the people win, too. In the end.'

McFaul looked away, not bothering to hide his contempt. He'd heard this shit before. War was a noble calling. The people, the *povo*, could take it.

'Tell me something,' he mused. 'How many mines does a hundred dollars buy you? How many arms and legs? How many months of lying around in hospital? How many years of learning to walk again? Ever do the sums? Add it all up?'

'Mines work,' Katilo murmured, 'and they cost us nothing.'

'You're right.' McFaul nodded. 'Especially if you're buying knock-offs.'

Katilo lifted the bottle to his lips, his eyes never leaving McFaul's face. 'Knock-offs' were cut-price copies of the classic mine designs. More and more were pouring out of factories in Pakistan and China, fuelling the Third World's hunger for war on the cheap. For the price of a Western saloon car, a man like Katilo could drive thousands of people off the land. The armchair warriors called it 'area denial'. Another word was starvation.

Katilo extended a leg towards Christianne. He was wearing rubber flip-flops, and he began to rub one toe up and down her ankle.

'You think we buy knock-offs?'

'I don't know. I'm asking.'

225

'You can't tell? When you find them?'

'Sometimes.' McFaul nodded. 'Sometimes not.'

Katilo brooded, withdrawing his foot. Then he half-turned and said something to one of the watching soldiers. The man got up at once and blundered past McFaul. Light spilled into the cave as he pushed through the blanket. Then he was gone.

Katilo was offering the bottle to Christianne. He looked thoughtful. His interest in *Baywatch* seemed to have disappeared.

'Every man needs to work, Mr McFaul. To live. To eat. You agree with that?' McFaul nodded, his hand on Christianne's arm, reassuring her. 'So maybe you should consider yourself lucky, no?'

'Why's that?'

'Because you'll never be out of a job. Wherever you go, here, Asia, Afghanistan, everywhere there are mines. And you know why? Because mines make the best soldiers.' He smacked a fist into an open palm. 'Bang. Always there. Always watching. Never tired. Never lazy. Never drunk.'

'Never disloyal? Never one of your guys on the receiving end?'

'Yes, often. Of course my men are injured. It happens all the time. But that's because we're poor, Mr McFaul. We can't afford your kind of war. Expensive missiles. Radar. Stealth fighters. In Africa, everything is cheap.'

'Including blood?'

'Yes,' he nodded, 'including blood. You understand that?'

McFaul leaned forward, engaged now.

'Sure,' he said, 'but what I don't understand is this. You're fighting a civil war. You're using mines to try and win it. But by the time that happens, there'll be no country left to win. The whole lot will be off-limits, a desert. Mines work. Of course they work. But you know how long it's going to take to clean up Afghanistan? Assuming it can be done at all? Maybe a century. A hundred years. Think about it. A whole fucking country laid waste. Taken out. As good as nuked. That's what it means. Your kind of war.'

Katilo was watching the blanket now, waiting for the soldier to return.

'You remember our elections?' he said at length. 'In ninety-two?'

'I read about them.'

'OK. I was in Luanda. You know what happened in Luanda? We were massacred. The government wanted to kill us all. Thousands died. But you know what happened to me? I got away. With my men. Everywhere there were government troops, MPLA soldiers. We were running, running. Sometimes we had to stop, to sleep. So each night we put out mines, a little present for anyone who might try to kill us.' He paused. 'The mines looked after us, Mr McFaul. I owe those mines my life. When things were really bad, when the mines had nearly gone, we used to wear them round our necks. Not active. Not live. But ready.' He nodded. 'Sure, round our necks, believe me . . .'

McFaul stared at him and then began to laugh. The metaphor was perfect. A whole country, an entire nation, putting its trust in six ounces of high explosive strung around its neck. The latest mines were 98 per cent plastic. That made them virtually indestructible, sensitive to the merest footfall for decades, maybe centuries to come. Just like Afghanistan.

McFaul felt a sudden draught round his shoulders. Two soldiers came in. Between them they were carrying a heavy wooden box. Katilo told them to put it down. He leaned forward, unsheathing a long bowie knife. He slipped it beneath a length of wood and levered upwards. The wood splintered and then lifted. Inside the box, neatly cocooned in straw, McFaul could see dozens of small, palm-sized anti-personnel mines. Their surface was subtly textured. They looked like stones from the riverbed.

'You know what these are?'

Katilo took one out and tossed it across to McFaul. The soldiers exchanged looks. McFaul turned the mine over.

'Difesa,' he heard himself saying, 'SB-33.'

He checked the firing mechanism and then fingered the rubber diaphragm on top. The diaphragm was mottled and it had a gentle resistance to the touch, like a computer keyboard. His hand closed around the mine and he shut his eyes a moment feeling the blood pumping in his head. He was word-perfect on exactly what this mine could do. He knew it could be air-dropped. He knew it could function upside down. He knew you could coat it with a special finish, making it resistant to infrared detection. Jesus, you could even stipulate a choice of colour, depending on where you wanted to use the thing. The one McFaul had triggered in Kuwait had been 'desert sand'. He knew that because he still had the fragments the surgeons had dug out of his thighs and buttocks, once they'd amputated his lower left leg, and he'd compared them to the colour chart in the sales brochure nearly a year later. Desert sand, he'd thought at the time. Nice enough phrase until you knew different.

McFaul slumped in the chair, the mine in his lap now. A box of SB-33s was the last thing he'd expected Katilo to produce.

'They call it the Gucci,' he said drily. 'You ever hear that?'

Katilo nodded, grinning, pleased with the word.

'And you think that's a copy? A knock-off? You really think we can't afford the real thing?'

'You said you were poor. That was your word, not mine.'

'Of course. But poverty is relative, Mr McFaul. Even these are cheap. Compared to your kind of weapons.'

McFaul nodded, weighing the little mine in his hand. Katilo was right. The SB-33 was made by an Italian company, a subsidiary of Fiat, and they continuously battled to guard their design against Third World rip-offs. McFaul looked at the open box at his feet, wondering what else Katilo had outside. The stuff they'd been lifting around Muengo had been mainly Chinese,

Romanian and Russian, lethal enough but not as sophisticated as the latest offerings from Western designers.

'You've got US mines? M-14s?'

'Yes, and M-16s as well. You want to see them?'

McFaul shook his head, thinking suddenly of the boy, James Jordan. Until now, he'd assumed that he'd trodden on one of the Soviet OZM-3s. His injuries had clearly been caused by a bounding mine, and Angola was littered with thousands of the Russian version. Now, though, it occurred to him that Jordan might have fallen to a piece of Western technology. Not that it mattered.

Katilo signalled to the soldiers and they bent to the rope handles on the box. McFaul leaned forward, about to replace the SB-33, but a hand closed over his. Looking up again, McFaul found Katilo's face inches from his own. For the first time, he realised that the man was offended as well as drunk.

'You really know about these? How much they cost?'

'Sure.'

'So you know what a fool like Zezito can expect? Wasting stuff like this? SB-33s?' Katilo paused. 'UNITA buy the best. Everyone knows that. The best for the best.' He nodded, bunching his huge fist, driving it once again into the palm of his left hand. 'You know Kinshasa, Mr McFaul? You know the friends we have there? How well they look after us?'

McFaul said nothing, easing back in his chair, aware what a dangerous turn this conversation had suddenly taken. Katilo was tired of offering rationales, of defending himself against McFaul's flabby Western disapproval. In his war, there was no room for qualms about civilians, worries about starvation, second thoughts about kids blown apart. None of that was remotely relevant. He'd said it himself. What mattered was winning. And winning came down to a very simple calculation. How much violence your money could buy. And where you went shopping to get it.

Katilo was talking about Kinshasa again. Kinshasa was the capital of Zaire, the neighbouring state to Angola's north where

UNITA had always been able to count on support. McFaul had spent a little time there once, a troubled week and a half waiting to bribe the right customs official for access to a Global shipment of spare parts. He'd hated the place, its viciousness, its corruption, and he'd sworn never to return. Luanda, by contrast, was Disneyland.

'You bought this stuff in Kinshasa?'

'Buy, Mr McFaul. We buy this stuff in Kinshasa.'

'You get a good deal?'

'You mean money?' Katilo roared with laughter. 'You think we pay money? In *Kinshasa?*' He began to rock in the chair, backwards and forwards, hugging his knees like some enormous child. Then, abruptly, he barked an order. Before McFaul could react, he felt his arms pinioned to his sides. Then everything went black and he smelled the sour, sweaty taint of the blindfold. The knot tightened at the base of his skull and he heard a tiny gasp beside him from Christianne. McFaul tore his arms free, reaching for her, trying to get up. There was a scream, Christianne again, and hands around his throat. McFaul could smell the whiskey on Katilo's breath, feel the press of his body. Then the pressure on his windpipe eased and someone was slipping a length of cord around his wrists, lashing them together behind his back.

Katilo's voice, very quiet.

'Sure you can clear your paths, Mr McFaul. I'm grateful. We'll need the water, too.'

McFaul stumbled backwards, nearly falling. Then there were hands pulling him round and the rough kiss of the blanket on his face as he left the cave. He tried to stop, calling for Christianne, thinking the worst, imagining her back with Katilo, unprotected, but she cannoned into him, cursing in French as she did so. McFaul heard laughter, Katilo again, very close. The ground was rising beneath his feet and he recognised the sound of water from somewhere below.

He came to a halt, disorientated. There was wind here. He could feel it on his face. It carried the hot, dry smells of the bush. He moved his head, left and right, up and down, trying to find a chink of daylight, his arms still pinioned. Then, abruptly, he was free. For a second or two he did nothing, just stood there. No one stirred. No one said anything. His wrists were still bound but he could move in any direction.

'Christianne?'

Nothing. The squawk of a nearby bird. The flapping of wings. Then silence again.

'Christianne?'

McFaul began to turn, his instinct telling him to get off the rising ground. As he did so he felt a hand in the small of his back, and a peal of laughter, and Katilo's voice, inches from his ear.

'Hot day, Mr McFaul. We hope you can swim.'

Too late, McFaul lunged backwards, gasping as the huge arms closed around his body, crushing his sutured wound. Then his feet left the ground and suddenly he was in mid-air, falling, disorientated again, knowing only that something infinitely terrible awaited him below. An instant later he hit the river bed, feet-first, the water up to his waist, the stump of his left leg absorbing the shock of the landing. He folded onto his backside, hearing himself bellow, more surprise than pain, then there was another splash beside him, a second body in the water, and fingers tearing at the knot on his blindfold. His hands went to his face, covering his eyes. Through his fingers he could see Christianne's face, close to his, her shirt soaking wet, clinging to her body. Soldiers lined the bank of the river, a row of heavy boots no more than six feet above McFaul's head. McFaul looked up, wiping the water from his face. Then Katilo appeared, the whiskey bottle in one hand, the SB-33 in the other, rocking with laughter. He raised the mine in a derisive salute as Christianne pulled McFaul towards the waiting Toyota.

'*Viva UNITA!*' his men were shouting. '*Viva!*'

*

By mid-afternoon, Llewelyn had finished the trickiest bits of the demining sequence. Twenty years on location had given him an encyclopaedic knowledge of camerawork – what looked good, what wouldn't cut – but until now he hadn't realised how demanding it could be. Master shots, reverses, POVs, close-ups, Domingos's actions repeated again and again until Llewelyn was certain that he'd covered every angle.

In this game, he told himself, the real drama was in the detail. The first scary bleep from the electronic detector. The yowl as the fix was confirmed. The delicate dance steps as Domingos manoeuvred around the hidden mine, unsheathing his bayonet, settling himself on his belly, covering his face with the visor, the thick shield of toughened Perspex that would help protect him if he got it wrong. They'd been using the little Chinese Type 72As as dummies, and for Llewelyn the key moment of all had been the first appearance of the mine, the disk of dark green plastic emerging from the loose soil. He'd shot this sequence from three angles, re-covering and re-exposing the mine each time, and he knew that with the right music and the right sound effects it would work a treat.

Now, pleased with himself, Llewelyn walked back to the Land Rover. He'd already explained the final shot to Domingos. On a cue from the camera position on top of the embankment, he was to repeat exactly what he'd done before. Once the mine had been lifted and laid to one side, he was to shoulder the Ebinger and walk forward perhaps ten metres. The latter part of this shot would serve as an introduction to the whole sequence, Domingos on his way to work, tooled up and ready to go.

Llewelyn settled the camcorder on the tripod and tightened the nut beneath the baseplate. Bennie was sitting beside him, rolling a cigarette. Once Llewelyn had finished with Domingos, it would be his turn on camera. Amongst the promised sequences was an interview on the tensions of fieldwork.

Llewelyn zoomed the camera on Domingos and checked the footage on the video-cassette. He was using one-hour tapes and there was nearly thirty-five minutes in hand. His eye returned to the viewfinder and tweaked the focus for a moment or two, then adjusted the framing until the little Angolan was kneeling in the centre of picture. Space, his favourite cameraman had always told him, always leave space around the subject.

Llewelyn called to Domingos and then waved, the agreed cue. Domingos began to sweep left and right with the Ebinger. After a while he stopped. Then he sank to his knees and spread himself full-length on his belly, getting to work with the bayonet and the brush, carefully sweeping the soil away. Finally, with great caution, he lifted the mine and went through the motions of disarming it.

Bennie was watching him, impressed.

'Fucking natural,' he said. 'Sign the bugger up.'

Llewelyn frowned, putting a finger to his lips, still shooting. Domingos got to his feet and reached for the Ebinger. He put it over his shoulder, raising the visor on his helmet, then he glanced up towards the embankment, a quizzical grin on his face. Llewelyn waved him on, impatient to get this last sequence on tape, and Domingos turned away, walking down the cleared strip of earth towards the river bank. The agreed limit of the safe area was eighty metres. Domingos had plenty in hand.

Llewelyn watched through his viewfinder, tightening the shot a little as Domingos walked away. Same size, they always said, keep the walking shots the same size. Domingos's step faltered a second then picked up again. Llewelyn lifted his eye from the viewfinder, checking how far he'd got. At least sixty metres in hand, he thought. Maybe more.

The explosion was flat, a short, vicious bark, not especially loud, Domingos's body disappearing behind a swirl of smoke and dust. When the smoke cleared, a full minute later, all Llewelyn could see was the hump of Domingos's fallen body, motionless, and then Bennie bent over him, cradling his head, looking back towards Llewelyn, screaming.

CHAPTER EIGHT

Molly Jordan was taking a photograph when she heard the explosion. She'd been inside the cathedral for the best part of an hour, perched on a cool stone ledge beside the door, looking down the aisle towards the altar. Beyond the altar, in the arched recess where the window had once been, the crumbling plaster-work framed the intense, clear blue of the African sky, castled with clouds. The clouds were building all the time, hot air condensing as it rose from the bush below, and Molly had been transfixed by the effect, infinitely more uplifting than any stained glass she'd ever seen. In Europe, she thought, we need to put something between us and God's heaven. Here, thanks no doubt to UNITA shellfire, glass simply didn't exist. Not that it mattered. Because nothing could possibly better the real thing.

She lowered the camera, wondering where the bang had come from, what it meant. It hadn't been loud, no more than a distant backfire, but she could hear women's voices raised in the square outside and the flap of wings in the gloom above her head. There were birds everywhere, flying in and out through the yawning hole in the east wall, and the noise had disturbed them. One swooped low in front of her face, bat-like, and she slipped the camera into the string bag she'd borrowed from Christianne, turning to beat a retreat.

Outside, the women in the market were looking at the sky and as she crossed the square she recognised one or two faces from the cinema. They stared at her as she hurried past and she wondered what they made of her nervous smile and her hand half-raised in a hesitant greeting. She'd like to know more about these people – where they came from, how they coped – but her Portuguese was virtually non-existent and the conversation with Chipenda had taught her that the gulf between their two worlds was infinitely wider than she'd ever imagined. Nothing had prepared her for lives stripped so bare. No clean water. Precious little food. And absolutely no prospect of any improvement. The odds these people faced were beyond comprehension and she swore again that she'd take the lesson back home with her. No matter how bad things seem, she thought, they can always get a whole lot worse.

Molly paused on the other side of the square, looking back at the cathedral. The building itself and its setting reminded her of similar scenes in Portugal. With its bleached walls, and lilac trim, and stand of closely spaced shade trees, it could easily belong in any of the little towns that dotted the foothills of the Algarve. She and Giles had been down there three summers running when James had been very young, and she thought of him now, sitting in her lap in the hire car, his cheek turned to the cooling breeze through the open window, his blond hair blowing in her face. After a couple of days by the sea, his skin took on a special smell, a delicious saltiness gilded by sunshine, and she caught her breath, reaching for the camera again, remembering it.

Bennie found the ampoule of morphine Velcroed to the bottom of the trauma pack. He broke open the seal on the disposable syringe, plunging it into the plastic ampoule. He knew there were problems with using painkillers. Too much of the stuff could delay surgery. There were horror stories of guys arriving at hospital, stoned out of their heads, dying in the queue for the operating theatre. Bennie eased the plunger back, watching the clear liquid fill the syringe, wondering whether or not he should use it.

Domingos was still in shock. He lay on his back, his body half-twisted, his eyes closed. His right leg was shredded beneath the knee, the foot unrecognisable, the exposed calf muscle hanging by a single tendon, the surrounding flesh charred and blackened by the searing heat of the explosion. The knee itself was torn open, the shattered end of the thigh bone clearly visible. Domingos stirred, getting up on his elbows, his eyes open but unfocused. As the pain hit him he began to groan, collapsing back, one hand grabbing down, trying to loosen the tourniquet Bennie had wound around the top of his right thigh. Without the tourniquet to stop blood loss, Domingos would already be dead.

'Hey . . . fella . . .'

Bennie reached for Domingos's hand. The Kevlar waistcoat had protected his chest and belly from the worst of the blast but there was a big entry wound in his other thigh, and his chin and neck, unprotected by the visor, was a mass of lacerations.

Bennie looked up, shouting to Llewelyn again. He'd let him no further than a couple of metres into the cleared minefield, telling him to raise help on the radio. Llewelyn was cupping his ear. Bennie tried again.

'What happened?' he yelled.

Llewelyn was still carrying the camcorder. He put it to his eye then lowered it again. His voice was thin, almost inaudible.

'He's coming.'

'Who is?'

'Peterson.'

'When?'

'Now.'

Bennie turned back to Domingos, wondering how best to move him. The little man wouldn't be heavy. He didn't have the build for it. He glanced at his watch, trying to work out how long the tourniquet had been on. Already the explosion seemed light years away. Bennie frowned, eyeing the shattered leg. The book said the knot had to be eased every fifteen

236

minutes, otherwise the healthy flesh would begin to die for lack of blood. He reached forward, waving away the cloud of flies, loosening the tourniquet. As he did so, the wound began to glisten with fresh blood and he let the knee drip for a full minute, controlling the flow with the tourniquet before tightening the knot again. Domingos was fully conscious now, shaking his head as if to dislodge some terrible memory. He thinks it's a nightmare, Bennie thought, and he's fucking right.

He looked up, hearing the clatter of a diesel engine. One of the army trucks came to a halt behind the Land Rover. Government soldiers jumped out of the back, looking nervously towards the rebel positions to the west. Behind them, Bennie recognised Peterson's tall, spare frame.

'Tell them to turn the truck round,' he shouted to Llewelyn.

Llewelyn made his way back to the truck. Bennie could see him talking to Peterson. The truck began to reverse into a clumsy three-point turn. Bennie reached for the syringe, capping it and slipping it into the breast pocket of his shirt. Domingos was a tough little bugger. If he'd get through at all, it would be without morphine. He squatted beside the Angolan, his mouth beside Domingos's ear.

'Can you hear me, fella?'

Domingos nodded, his tongue moistening his lower lip.

'I'm going to lift you up,' Bennie said, 'get you out of here.'

Domingos nodded again, making a limp movement with his right hand. For the first time, Bennie saw the raw flesh on his lower arm where he'd been carrying the Ebinger.

'Help me,' Domingos whispered. 'You can help me.'

'Walk?'

'Yes.' Domingos tried to get up. Bennie restrained him.

'I'm carrying you.' He paused. 'You trod on a mine, old son. You remember any of that?'

Domingos looked vague, his eyes fighting to keep focus. Then he sighed and his head fell back and Bennie realised just how little time he had. He slipped his hands beneath Domin-

gos's body and then stood upright, lifting him in a single movement, fighting for a moment to keep his balance. The little man
weighed more than he'd thought. He was heavy, and it was
awkward trying to scoop the remains of his leg into some kind
of manageable parcel.

Bennie turned, frowning, trying to remember the path
Domingos had taken, stepping stones across the sixty metres of
pockmarked earth that lay between him and the embankment.
This was the one situation you never wanted to face, extracting
a good friend from a live minefield. All the training manuals
told you to wait for a proper breach, a swept path, but by the
time that happened Bennie knew Domingos would be dead.
Saving his life meant taking the odd risk. Now.

Bennie began to move, one step at a time, scanning the
ground in front of him. Perhaps twenty metres ahead, little
piles of scooped earth indicated the area where Domingos and
Llewelyn had been taping earlier. They'd walked all over it.
They'd been working with the Ebinger. Had anything been
there, they'd surely have found it. He walked on, closing the
gap, Domingos's body sagging in his arms. Some guys dealt
with this through prayer. Others said it was a lottery, simple
odds, thumbs up or curtains. Either way, it didn't really matter.
What you did was keep walking. What you didn't do was dwell
too much on what might happen if you got it wrong.

Bennie was a step away now from the first of the upturned
duds, the area where Domingos had been working earlier. The
Angolan was groaning again, his head lolling back, the blood
crusted beneath his chin.

'Fella . . .' Bennie urged. 'Fella . . .'

He stumbled a moment, caught his breath, and then began
to run, a clumsy shuffle, oblivious now of the chances of triggering another mine. Ahead, he could see Peterson coming towards
him. He was wearing a white shirt. His arms were outstretched.

'Here,' he said, 'let me.'

Bennie came to a halt, exhausted, letting Peterson take
Domingos's weight. He saw the expression on the other man's

face the moment he realised the extent of Domingos's injuries. Already, there was blood all over Peterson's shirt. Bennie stumbled towards the embankment, trying to keep up.

'Ten minutes,' he gasped, 'then loosen it again.'

'What? Loosen what?'

'The fucking tourniquet.'

Peterson nodded, his eyes never leaving Domingos's face. Then he was at the foot of the embankment, looking up at the row of waiting soldiers, gesturing helplessly at Domingos's broken body.

'Someone help me,' he was shouting, 'for Christ's sake.'

Two of the soldiers scrambled down the embankment, taking over, carrying Domingos between them, and Bennie watched as they lifted him onto the back of the truck, Peterson behind them, shouting in Portuguese. Moments later, he was climbing into the cab, telling the driver to move, and the dust was still settling when Bennie became aware of Llewelyn, standing beside the Land Rover, the camera to his eye, taping everything.

Bennie stared at him a moment, then his hand went to the pocket of his shirt, feeling the outline of the syringe. He was about to yell to Llewelyn for the keys to the Land Rover when the TV man lowered the camcorder and ducked into the driver's seat. The engine caught first time, the wheels spinning as he set off in pursuit of the distant truck.

Christianne dropped McFaul at the schoolhouse. The journey back from Katilo's headquarters in the Toyota had taken less than half an hour and he was still soaking wet. He limped towards the door, surprised to find it locked. He felt for his keys, cursing when he remembered he'd left them in the MSF Landcruiser. At the back of the schoolhouse, beneath a broken air-brick, they kept a spare. He fetched it now, letting himself into the classroom.

Two rows of chairs faced an easel. Chalked on the blackboard was a crude diagram of a minefield. McFaul peered at it a moment, recognising Bennie's scrawl, then he went through to the adjoining room they used as a dormitory. He found a towel and began to strip off. Then he stopped and returned to the classroom. They stored the radios and rechargers beneath a desk in the corner. Bennie's had gone. McFaul unclipped his own from the belt around his waist. Bennie's call sign was Golf Charlie Two. He answered within seconds and McFaul knew at once that something was wrong. Bennie got to the end of the story. He was close to tears.

'Pick me up,' McFaul said curtly. 'En route to the hospital.'

'I can't, boss.'

'Why not?'

'The telly bloke's gone off with the Rover. I'm just clearing up.'

Llewelyn abandoned the Global Land Rover beside the army truck. The soldiers in the back of the truck watched curiously as he stumbled across the rubble-strewn wasteland that surrounded the remains of the apartment block. The hospital was up on the third floor, the red and white Red Cross flag still hanging limply from the roof, the windows still screened by lengths of dirty blue polythene. Llewelyn entered the building, picking his way up four flights of stairs. The place was in semi-darkness and stank of urine. On the second floor, a sleeping dog lay sprawled beside a gaping shell hole in the outside wall. Llewelyn went up two more flights of stairs. There was fresh blood on the concrete, big dark splashes of it, and he paused, retracing his steps and then raising the camera and climbing again. POV, he thought. Millions of viewers sharing this journey of his.

Up on the third floor, a hanging sheet screened the rooms that had been converted into a makeshift hospital. Llewelyn pushed through, the camcorder still to his eye. A symbol in the viewfinder signalled Low Light. He ignored it, coming to a halt, panning slowly around. The sunshine outside, filtered through the polythene, cast strange blue shadows across the room. The floor was littered with bodies, jigsawed together, head to toe. Most of them lay on the bare concrete, or on thin straw mats. The mats were stained with blood and nameless other effusions. Llewelyn tightened the zoom, watching the faces grow bigger in the viewfinder. One of the kids was newly bandaged, his head swathed in white. Inches away, a soldier in camouflage trousers and an ill-fitting singlet had lost an eye and both ears. Llewelyn lingered on the wreckage of his face, wondering how well the detail would show, the flies patrolling the depthless void beside his nose.

Wind stirred the polythene sheets. In another room, some-one was screaming. Llewelyn stepped over the bodies, taping the scene from the other angle, a simple wide shot. This, he knew, was the very heart of the film, the closest he'd ever get to what had happened to James Jordan. Back in London, he'd find experts who'd defend the use of mines. They'd come from one of the military think-tanks, the Institute for Strategic Studies maybe, or even the Ministry of Defence. They'd talk about the pressures of the modern battlefield and the need to maintain a full inventory of weapons. They'd doubtless point out that mines could be used responsibly, in accordance with some UN protocol or other. They'd be articulate and immensely grave, but none of their careful rationales could possibly stand up to footage like this.

Llewelyn paused, picking out a woman by the window. Her head was turned towards the wall and as the polythene stopped moving in the wind Llewelyn could hear her moaning softly, one hand outstretched, the fingers tightening with pain. In truth, he'd no idea whether these people were all mine casualties but in the context of what had just happened to Domingos, it wouldn't matter. The story was so strong, the images were so powerful, that no one would bother asking. This was the reality, they'd think. This was where kids like James Jordan could so easily end up.

Llewelyn lowered the camcorder and went through to the next room. The screaming had started again and there were more bodies on the floor. Crouched beside them was a young nurse. She had a baby's bottle in her hand and she was trying to tease the teat into an old man's mouth. The old man had no visible injuries but Llewelyn had never seen anyone thinner.

'Domingos?'

The girl looked up and indicated the door. Llewelyn nodded. At the end of a corridor, Llewelyn found another room. The door was ajar. He could hear the murmur of voices, a foreign language he didn't immediately recognise, something Scandinavian. He stepped inside. Domingos lay on a wooden table, naked. By his head stood a middle-aged Angolan woman. The sleeve of her dress had been rolled up and from her right arm a tube carried blood to an empty one-litre Coke bottle on the floor. With her other arm, she was cradling Domingos's head, singing to him very softly, her lips barely moving, the words of the song scarcely audible.

Llewelyn stared at her for a moment, the camera forgotten. Then a white face looked round at him, one of the two men working on Domingos's wounds. He had a saw in one hand and the remains of the Angolan's right leg in the other. Seeing Llewelyn raise the camera, he hesitated a moment and then returned to work with a shrug. Llewelyn heard the rasp of the saw against bone, and Domingos began to yell again, a raw animal howl of pain. Llewelyn tried to steady the camcorder. A corner of the polythene at the window had been lifted to let in light and there were flies everywhere. Llewelyn tightened the shot a little more until it was almost abstract, scarlet muscle, yellowish streaks of fat, and the startling white of exposed bone.

One of the surgeons was talking now and it was a second or two before Llewelyn realised that the question was addressed to him.

'My friend, what are you doing?'

The accent was heavy. One of the Oslo mob, Llewelyn thought. One of the young doctors Peterson had mentioned from Norwegian People's Aid. The question came again and Llewelyn explained he was making a film for English television.

'About what?'

'Mines,' Llewelyn said at once, 'and all this.'

'*Ja?*'

The surgeon looked up again. He was wearing a blue checked shirt and jeans. His only concession to surgical procedure was a pair of blood-wet rubber gloves.

'You want me to talk? For this film of yours?'

Llewelyn nodded, easing back on the zoom. The gloves appeared. Then the hacksaw.

'OK, what we do now is pretty simple. We take off the leg, so, as high as possible.' He indicated the cut he was making, a line across Domingos's thigh at least three inches above the knee. 'Otherwise we have to come back and do it again. So. There you have it.'

The saw bit into the bone. The other surgeon was having trouble keeping Domingos still.

'You've given him painkillers?'

'Vodka.'

'No painkillers?'

'Vodka.'

The saw was almost through now. Domingos was moaning.

'And what happens afterwards?'

'We do the other leg.'

'Take it off?'

'No, reset the bone.'

'And the rest of him? His face? His arm?'

'Not a problem. Minor injuries. Superficial.'

The sawing stopped and the surgeon separated the two ends of the bone. Then he began to sever the remaining tendrils of muscle and tendon, pausing now and again to pincer out tiny fragments of jagged dark green plastic. He held one up, giving Llewelyn time to focus.

'Even with X-rays we wouldn't find these.' He let the shrapnel fall into a bowl at his elbow and then he lowered his eye to the exposed stump of Domingos's thigh, probing in the pulp for more debris. Mines, he explained, were designed to blast stuff upwards, deep into the legs. It might be anything: soil, grass, sand, bits of shoe leather, fragments of denim from a pair of jeans. Once, he'd even found a complete buckle from someone's sandal. Unfortunately, all this took time. Which is why, he mused, they'd probably invented mines in the first place. One man injured. Two or three to carry him away. And a complete surgical team, occupied for hours, trying to clean him up.

'Clever,' he murmured, 'don't you think?'

He glanced at his colleague and a bottle of mineral water appeared. The other doctor opened it and the surgeon began to pour it over Domingos's stump, wondering aloud about the Angolan's chances of resisting infection. If they were very lucky, the wound might heal. If it didn't, they'd have to return time and again until all the dying flesh had been excised away.

'We call it salami,' he said, raising the bottle to his lips and swallowing the last of the water, 'because we take a slice at a time.'

He glanced round, wiping his mouth with his arm, offering the camera a tired smile. Under the heavy growth of beard he looked exhausted. Finally he called for a bucket and Llewelyn followed his left hand with the camcorder as he picked up the lower half of Domingos's leg and then wrapped it in newspaper. The bundle of moist newsprint disappeared into the bucket and Llewelyn had a sudden image of the dog, one floor down, still asleep beside the gaping hole in the wall.

The surgeon was talking to the woman now, switching to Portuguese. Llewelyn panned slowly along the line of Domingos's body until he found her face.

'Who is she?' he asked, interrupting the conversation.

The surgeon looked round again. He was in the process of extracting the drip from her arm and sealing the puncture wound with a square of Sellotape.

'She's this man's wife,' he said. 'Her name is Celestina.'

McFaul got to the hospital forty minutes later. He'd tried to raise Christianne on the radio but in the end he'd given up, crossing the city on foot. Outside the hospital, he spotted the Global Land Rover. Llewelyn was sitting behind the wheel, his head back against the seat, his eyes closed. McFaul pulled the door open, shaking him roughly by the arm.

'What happened?'

Llewelyn opened one eye. His face looked grey and his body was hunched, like a man trying to keep warm. He looked at McFaul, uncomprehending.

'Accident,' he said at last. 'He had an accident.'

'Yeah, but how? Why?'

Llewelyn looked at him, puzzled, then shook his head.

'Third floor,' he said, 'room at the end.'

'Is he bad?'

'Very.'

'Shit.'

McFaul slammed the door, telling Llewelyn to wait, then limped across towards the apartment block. As he began to mount the stairs he heard the cackle of the Land Rover's engine and the clunk as Llewelyn engaged gear. He hesitated a moment, wondering whether to go back, then decided against it.

Domingos was up on the third floor, unconscious now, still in the hands of the surgeons. A single glance told McFaul everything he wanted to know. The heavy Kevlar waistcoat had shielded his upper body from serious damage, and most of his face looked OK, but below the waist he was a mess. The stump of his right thigh was heavily bandaged and the two Norwegians were bent over his other leg.

Above the knee, a gaping entry wound had been cleaned

with swabs and packed with dressings and now the surgeons were trying to drill a fixing rod through muscle and bone. They were using an old hand-drill, rusty and squeaking, and the rod kept slipping as it made contact with the bone. After a while, the sharp end of the rod began to grind through the bone and McFaul watched as the rod finally emerged through the flesh on the other side of Domingos's thigh. He'd seen similar operations in Cambodia. With the rod through the bone, the surgeons would be able to apply traction, using weights to realign the splintered ends of bone either side of the fracture. The procedure would take weeks but with luck Domingos might be able to regain the use of at least one leg.

McFaul edged carefully past the surgeons, exchanging nods. He knew these men well. He'd drunk with them often, sharing their appetite for good vodka and an hour or two of oblivion. Beside Domingos's head, he paused. The injuries to his neck and chin weren't as bad as they looked and his breathing seemed regular enough. McFaul touched the Angolan's cheek with the back of his hand, wondering how long it would be before he regained consciousness. The pain would be indescribable, and with it would come the realisation that his life had changed for ever.

McFaul brushed away the flies, remembering the early days of his own convalescence. At first he'd been numbed, refusing to accept the reality of what had happened. Then he'd been plunged into weeks of the blackest despair, resigned to spending the rest of his life in a wheelchair. Only later, fuelled by a deep anger, had he resolved to put his life back into some kind of working order. McFaul bent to Domingos again, his mouth to the little man's ear, wishing him luck. The job would still be there. He'd make sure of that. But the wild evenings of backyard football were probably over.

The surgeons were cleaning up now. One of them indicated a small, jagged triangle of plastic, lying in a chipped saucer beside a pile of bloodied swabs. McFaul ignored it.

'How is he?'

The bigger of the two men shrugged, pouring mineral water over his rubber gloves and then putting them carefully aside for the next operation.

'OK. Normally he'd make it, no problem, but . . .' he gestured round, 'this isn't normal.'

'We'll take him out. On the evacuation flight.'

'Sure. He should be OK till then. Not comfortable. But alive.' He produced a pair of forceps and lifted the shrapnel from the saucer. 'That's the biggest bit we found.'

McFaul studied it a moment. It was smaller than the corner of a postage stamp, part of the mine's plastic casing, designed to blast apart into a thousand tiny fragments. It was a dark mottled green and the edges were razor-sharp to the touch.

The surgeon was cleaning his glasses on a corner of his shirt.

'What do you think?'

'Could be anything. Anti-personnel, certainly, but what kind?' McFaul shrugged, returning the shrapnel. 'Impossible to tell.'

He paused, looking down at Domingos, struck by a sudden thought.

'You need blood?' he said.

The surgeon shook his head.

'His wife gave a litre. Same group. Should be enough.'

'Celestina? Here?'

'Next door,' the surgeon nodded, 'helping us out.'

McFaul found Celestina sitting on the floor of what had once been the apartment's tiny kitchen. She was knotting lengths of torn sheet, her back against the wall. On a nearby chair was a pillowcase and a pile of small rocks. McFaul knelt beside her and put his arm round her shoulders. Like Domingos, she spoke good English.

'He'll be OK,' he said at once. 'It's not as bad as it looks.'

Celestina eyed him, unconvinced. She was a big, handsome, ample woman, a head taller than Domingos, and so far she'd weathered the siege with stoic good humour. She'd lost her home, and most of her possessions, but she was camping with relatives, determined to keep her family together. Domingos had been at the very heart of all that – energetic, cheerful, tireless – and McFaul knew how much the little man had meant to her. She'd always called him '*cabritito*', my baby kid goat, and the phrase had exactly captured Domingos's spirit, his playfulness, his boundless appetite for whatever each new day might bring. Working with the man had been a joy. Marriage, thought McFaul, would have been no different.

'We'll fly you out,' he said. 'There'll be room for you all.'

'Where to?'

'Luanda.' He nodded, trying to coax a smile. 'Benguela. Wherever.'

'We belong here.'

'You'll be back, I promise.'

Celestina looked at him, not believing a word, and McFaul squeezed her hand, knowing only too well what she feared. Amputees were bad karma. You saw them everywhere in the cities, begging in the street, lurching through the morning traffic jams, insensible with drink. To lose a leg was to risk joining these derelicts, scraping a life from the very edges of a society already on the point of disintegration. The UN, as ever, had a phrase for it, a neat little acronym. Amputees were EVIs. EVI stood for Extremely Vulnerable Individual. Just now, in Angola, they numbered 15,000.

McFaul rocked back on his heels. Celestina had finished with the sheets and now she was filling the pillowcase with rocks.

'What are you doing?'

'This is for the doctors. For Domingos. They've put something through his leg. They say they need weights.' She gestured at the sagging pillowcase. 'I make this for them.'

McFaul nodded. Tie one end of the knotted sheets to the rod through Domingos's thigh, tie the other to the pillowcase and suspend the rocks over some kind of frame, and the shattered bone should realign.

'I'll get him back here,' he said again. 'He's too valuable to lose. He's learned too much. The war will end one day. The war will be over.'

Celestina shook her head. Next door, the surgeons were manhandling Domingos off the table, cursing in Norwegian as something fell to the floor.

'He's very bad,' she said. 'Very bad.'

'He'll get better.'

'You think so?'

'I know it.'

The surgeons appeared in the corridor. They were carrying Domingos between them, shuffling past. The bandage on his amputated stump was already dark with blood. Celestina couldn't take her eyes off it. The corridor empty again, she put her head between her knees and began to sob. McFaul tried to comfort her but he could feel at once how cold she'd become, and how remote. Reassurance was useless. It was far too late for that. At length she turned her head sideways, simple accusation.

'You always said you'd look after him,' she whispered. 'You always said he'd come home safe.'

By the time McFaul got back to the schoolhouse, Bennie had returned. He was lying on his camp-bed in the half-darkness, his eyes open, staring up at the sagging plasterboard. On the partition beside the wall, McFaul could just make out the solemn faces of his kids, three passport photos Blue-Tacked beneath a colour poster of the '92–'93 West Ham football team.

McFaul slumped against the wall across the room, his left leg stretched out, trying to ease the pain in his stump. Walking back from the hospital, he'd been trying yet again to work out how the accident had happened. Must have been a mistake on Domingos's part. Must have been.

Bennie was looking at him now, his face turned on the pillow.

'How is he?'

McFaul described Domingos's injuries. With luck, they might save one leg. Then he fell silent again. Celestina, he thought. And her little sack of rocks.

'You should have fucking checked him,' he said at last.

'I did.'

'Double-checked him.'

'I did. I told you, boss, on the radio. He had the notes. He showed them to me. Shit, you were only there a couple of days back. Four? Five days?'

'Sunday,' McFaul said briefly. 'Nearly a week.'

'Yeah, but what's a week? You don't forget these things. You don't. He knew exactly how much he'd done. It was down there on paper. He'd entered it into the laptop, too. Black and white. Check, if you want.'

McFaul nodded, falling silent, picturing the minefield. He'd need a print-out from the laptop for the inquiry. Middleton would insist.

'So how far had he gone?'

'Fifty metres. Sixty. Absolute max.'

'I don't believe it.'

'Fucking don't then. Only it's true.' Bennie sounded aggrieved, turning his face to the wall. Seconds later, he rolled over again. 'What about a stray? A rogue? One you missed last week?'

McFaul didn't answer. The same thought had been haunting him since the first conversation with Bennie on the radio. If it wasn't a fault on Domingos's part, if he was still within the safe area, then maybe he'd stumbled on a mine they hadn't found before. He closed his eyes, examining the possibility afresh, trying to take himself back to the afternoon they'd last worked on the path to the river. It had been hot, hotter than usual. Peterson had arrived on a flight from Luanda. They'd had a brief discussion about the boy Jordan. Peterson had wanted a sight of the field report he was putting in. They'd been talking on the embankment while Domingos took the final turn. McFaul shook his head, swamped by a sudden wave of remorse, remembering the little figure out on the bare, red earth, diligent as ever, sweeping left and right, interlocking arcs, textbook stuff, nothing left to chance. No, if they were talking human error then the fault was more likely his own.

He looked across at Bennie again, changing the subject.

'So whose idea was all this,' he asked, 'in the first place?'

Bennie got up on one elbow, affecting surprise, and McFaul knew at once that he'd been expecting the question.

'Being there, you mean? Doing it?'

'Yeah, last time we talked it was all down to stuff in the classroom. Training sequences. What happened to all that?'

'We did it,' Bennie said at once. 'Next door. Me at the blackboard.'

'But why go to the river? Afterwards? When you knew I had to see Katilo first?'

'I . . .' Bennie shrugged. 'It just seemed obvious, the best use of time. The place had been swept. Matey was banging on and on about how important it was, all the stuff we had to do, all those shots. Takes for ever, he said. Plus we might be out of here by tomorrow, who fucking knows?'

'So you did it? Went right ahead?'

'Yeah, he's got a mouth on him, that bloke. You've heard the way he goes on. Plus . . .' He rolled over again, punching the pillow. 'I dunno, I just got the idea you were up for it, that's all.'

'Up for what?'

'You know, all this training shit. Teaching the locals how to do it, spreading the word, all that. Domingos's a natural. Right fucking colour for a start. Poor little bastard . . .' He shook his head. 'I never want to see anything like that again. Ever. I'm fucking out of it, me. Nice little newsagent's place. Corner shop somewhere. Pub. Seaside B and B. Anything but this . . .'

Bennie fell silent, rolling himself a cigarette, and McFaul reached for a towel, flicking at a mosquito, halfway up the wall. The corner of the towel left a smudge of blood on the chipped plaster. He closed his eyes again, trying not to think about Domingos. Bennie was stirring. He heard his footsteps padding across the room, then the rasp of a match and a long sigh as he exhaled.

'If you don't believe me about Domingos,' he muttered, 'you can always see it for yourself.'

'How?' McFaul asked drily.

'Matey's video.'

'What video?'

'The one he was shooting. At the time.'

'He was shooting when Domingos . . .?'

'Yeah.'

'It's all on *tape*?'

'Yeah. And quite a bit afterwards, too.'

McFaul found the Global Land Rover at the UN compound. It was parked untidily on the street outside and McFaul limped past it, ringing the bell on the open gate and then taking the path up towards the reinforced front door. It was dark now and he could see chinks of light through the makeshift blast-proof curtains. Generator, he thought. Fernando must have laid hands on some of the diesel that had come in with Molly Jordan on the flight from Luanda.

McFaul knocked twice and waited. Eventually the door opened. Peterson stood in the hall. There were dark splashes of blood on his white shirt and he looked harassed. As soon as he saw McFaul he extended a sympathetic hand.

'I'm very sorry,' he said. 'How is he?'

McFaul explained again about the operations. Domingos and his family should go on the evacuation list. He needed a hospital bed in an acute ward in Luanda and a couple of months afterwards at the rehabilitation centre at Bomba Alta.

'That may not be easy.'

'Why not?'

'Question of precedent. If they get on the flight, how many others will want the same treatment? Think about it. They'd have a point.'

They were in the kitchen now. A single candle stood in an empty sardine can. McFaul sank into the only chair. He suddenly felt very tired.

'He's badly hurt. He may die.'

'Lots of them are badly hurt. This is an aid flight. Not a mass exodus.'

'OK.' McFaul shrugged. 'I'll stay. He can have my place. Simple.'

'You're priority listed. Orders from Global UK. I was talking to Ken Middleton this morning. He wants you back.'

'He wants the team back. Domingos's part of the team.'

'Flat on his back? Without a leg?'

McFaul looked at Peterson a moment, knowing at last what it was that pissed him off about the man. He was as compassionate, and committed, and as keen as the next man to help in Angola but he had the mentality of a civil servant. Talk to Peterson, and you were back in the world of meetings, and sub-committees, and long turgid memoranda about the importance of toeing the party line. Policy had to be consistent. Everything had to be subject to endless analysis. Africa, alas, wasn't like that. In Africa, you did what seemed best at the time. And hoped to fuck it worked.

'Who's drawing up the passenger list?'

'Fernando. It's done. You've had a copy,' he smiled, 'for two days now.'

'Put Domingos's name on it.'

'I'll . . .' Peterson made a helpless gesture, 'do my best.'
'Where's Llewelyn?'
'That's another problem.'
'Why?'
'He's got malaria.'

Todd Llewelyn lay in bed at the MSF house, covered only by a single sheet. Molly Jordan sat beside him, a sponge and a bucket in her lap. Llewelyn was delirious now, his head moving constantly on the pillow, left to right, his eyes wide, saliva bubbling from the corners of his mouth. His skin was hot to the touch, his face flushed a deep pink.

'*Quarto vinte e três,*' he kept shouting. '*Quarto vinte e três.*'

Molly squeezed excess water from the sponge, mopping Llewelyn's forehead. He seemed completely oblivious, unaware of her presence. Molly glanced at Christianne, standing in the shadows behind her. MSF had invested in three solar-powered lighting units and the only one not to be stolen had developed a battery fault, shedding a dim, yellow light that barely reached beyond the bed.

'He's talking about room twenty-three,' Christianne murmured. 'Whatever that means.'

Molly shrugged, returning the sponge to the bucket. It was her mention of the previous attack, back in Luanda, that had led Christianne to diagnose malaria. Before dark, they'd had a call from Peterson at the UN compound. Llewelyn was in bed with a fever. Earlier, he'd complained of extreme cold. Now, his temperature was way up. What should Peterson do?

Molly and Christianne had driven over, returning with Llewelyn. In the Landcruiser he'd sat at the back, completely motionless, oblivious to the offer of a blanket, his hands clamped around the camcorder. Now, it stood on the bedside table, beyond his reach.

'You started taking the tablets?' Christianne asked. 'Before you came?'

Molly nodded.

'But only for a couple of days. That's all the warning we had.'

'And him?'

'The same, I imagine.'

'He's taking them now? Maloprim? Something similar?'

'I've no idea.'

Christianne nodded, her eyes returning to Llewelyn. He'd quietened a little, his head briefly motionless on the wet pillow, but she'd nursed enough malaria to recognise the pattern. His temperature was already nudging 104°. Within hours it might rise to 105°, even 106°. After that, the fever would break, his whole body running with sweat, the headache and the pains beginning to ease. By morning, with luck, he'd be through it, wrung out, exhausted, but almost normal again. Then, a day or two later, the whole cycle would begin afresh.

There was a knock at the front door. Christianne stepped to the window, peering out, recognising McFaul's long frame. She let him in. Llewelyn had started shouting again, someone's name this time, and McFaul paused in the darkened hall, listening.

'Who?' He frowned.

Christianne shrugged. McFaul had brought Llewelyn's bag and the light safari jacket he'd worn on the flight down from Luanda. Leaving the UN compound, he'd had the firm impression that both Peterson and Fernando were glad to see the back of Llewelyn. Expecting an evening or two of amusing anecdotes, stories from the glitzy world of television, they'd found themselves living with an obsessive. The film. Always the film. What it would look like. What it would say. The impact it would make. The heads it would turn.

McFaul stepped into the bedroom. Molly was on her feet now, physically holding Llewelyn down. He was trying to sit upright in the bed, the single sheet in a wild knot by his feet. Apart from a pair of Paisley briefs, he was naked. McFaul limped across the room, forcing Llewelyn down onto his back. The eyes stared up at him without a flicker of recognition. His neck was corded with veins and his shoulders and chest were mottled scarlet. For a second or two he fought against McFaul then he gave up, sinking back with a low sigh before his whole body began to convulse. Molly turned to Christianne. For the first time, she looked alarmed.

'What is it?' Molly was saying. 'What's happening?'

'I don't know. Sometimes . . .' Christianne nodded at the bucket. 'Try more water.'

Molly tried to sponge Llewelyn's face but whenever she did so, he twisted away, thrashing wildly with his arms and legs, then lying rigid for a second as some spasm seemed to pass through him. McFaul, watching, caught Christianne's eye.

'Cerebral?'

Christianne nodded.

'Maybe.'

'You got any drugs? Quinine? Pyrimethamine?'

'Not here. At the hospital perhaps. I don't know. We tried to pool all the drugs. Last week.'

McFaul looked at Molly, the question unvoiced. She shook her head.

'The best I can do is Nurofen,' she said, 'or some antibiotics.' She paused. 'What's cerebral?'

McFaul and Christianne exchanged glances. Then McFaul looked at Llewelyn again.

'Cerebral malaria. Your temperature just goes up and up, way off the scale. I saw it in a squaddie once, in Belize. It's not nice.'

'Is it fatal?'

'Very.'

McFaul bent low across the bed, seeing the camcorder for the first time. Llewelyn lay rigid in the bed, his lips moving, some wordless message. McFaul put his ear to Llewelyn's chest, hearing the hesitant rasp of his breath. The man was seriously ill. No question about it. McFaul reached for the camcorder and stepped away from the bed.

'Nothing we can do for now,' he murmured, settling himself against the wall. 'See how he goes.'

He held the camcorder up to the light and peered at the footage counter. The video-cassette was nearly at its end. His fingers found the rewind controls and he began to spool back through the tape, wondering how much life was left in the battery. The camcorder they'd used in Afghanistan had worked on rechargeables, giving you three or four cassettes a whack. If anything, this one looked even more professional.

He got to the head of the tape and lifted the camcorder to his eye. Pressing the review button replayed the recorded pictures back through the viewfinder. McFaul smiled. Bennie was standing awkwardly in front of a blackboard, expounding on the theory of minefield clearance. He was trying very hard to play the tough guy, understating everything, Mr Cool. Every now and then he'd run his fingers slowly through his crew cut, always the right hand, and the third time he did it McFaul realised why. The tattoo, he thought, the big striking cobra that wound around his forearm. Yet more evidence that Bennie was committed to the business of living dangerously.

The sequence came to an end. There were more pictures – maps, Bennie's stubby fingers tapping at the laptop computer, an exterior shot of the schoolhouse – then they were suddenly in the back of the Land Rover, bumping away towards the road that led out to the river. McFaul recognised Bennie and Domingos in the front. Bennie began to tell a joke about a walrus and a donkey but a word from Llewelyn shut him up. The Land Rover came to a halt. Then it was Domingos in close-up. Llewelyn was holding the camera low, catching Domingos's eyes scanning left and right behind the visor, the big white clouds piling up behind his head. Other shots followed – the loop at the business end of the Ebinger, Domingos's hands, the blade of his bayonet, and then the first glimpse of one of the little Chinese mines emerging from the ochre soil. The sequence went on and on, endless repetitions, Llewelyn's voice on the soundtrack occasionally prompting some fresh reaction. Then, abruptly, the camera was back on top of the embankment and Domingos was a dot in the distance, growing rapidly bigger as Llewelyn worked the zoom. Full-length in the viewfinder, he turned and smiled. Then a little wave, and the sunshine briefly dancing on the visor as he lowered it again, heading away towards the river bank, the Ebinger over his shoulder.

McFaul's finger hovered over the stop button, knowing they must be close. Domingos was halfway to the edge of the cleared strip. Very soon now, according to Bennie's account, it would happen. McFaul looked up. Llewelyn was convulsing again, his body lifting on the mattress, twisting and turning, then slamming down, as if possessed. Both women were bent over him, Molly beside his head, trying to calm him down.

'Easy,' she kept saying, 'take it easy.'

McFaul watched for a moment longer then returned to the viewfinder. There was smoke and debris everywhere. As it cleared, the shot began to yo-yo in and out, Llewelyn not knowing what to do. With the shot at its widest, McFaul stopped the action, trying to orientate himself, trying to work out exactly where the explosion had taken place. Beyond the smoke, he could see the river bank, at least fifty metres away. Bennie had been right. No question about it. The mine had been triggered in the cleared strip.

McFaul pressed the play button again and the sequence rolled on, the shape of Domingos's fallen body emerging from the smoke. As the smoke drifted away, the remains of his right leg were clearly visible, the blood glistening in the fierce sunshine. McFaul watched, horrified. He'd seen accidents like this before, men blown apart by foolishness or simple bad luck, but in real life it was somehow different. Terrifying, yes, but fragmentary as well, so many things happening at once, the brain fighting to keep up with the flood of images. This, though, was grotesque. The shot just went on and on, Domingos lying there, trying to get up then collapsing back again, helpless, not understanding what had happened.

McFaul glanced up again, aware that Llewelyn had calmed a little, wondering what kind of man could point a camera and carry on shooting when someone else was bleeding to death. What did it take? Guts? Professional dedication? A missing fuse or two? He returned to the viewfinder. Bennie had joined Domingos. He was kneeling beside him, gesturing desperately towards Llewelyn. Help me, Bennie seemed to be saying. For fuck's sake help me do something. The shot went on, perfect focus, perfect framing, and McFaul shook his head again, his finger finding the fast-forward button, knowing that his appetite for this kind of material was strictly limited. Guts and professional dedication were nothing but alibis. This was pornography, pure and simple. To do this for a living, you had to be sick.

He checked the footage, wondering what else could possibly be on the tape, his eyes returning to the viewfinder. For a moment or two, he was lost. Everything looked murky. Then faces appeared, and bandages, and wounds, hugely magnified by the zoom lens. The images wound past, each one compounding the effect of the last, then there were two men standing beside a table, the blur of teeth in a hacksaw blade, a ribbon of muscle shredding under a scalpel. The camera panned up and for a moment or two, recognising the face behind the screams, McFaul was too shocked to know quite what he felt. This man had tracked Domingos. He'd followed him to the hospital. He'd walked right in there, hungry for grief, and he'd put the full menu on tape. A la carte. Blood, and tissue, and sawn bone, and the agony of a man who, just now, McFaul would have gladly traded his life for.

McFaul stopped the video, sickened. Christianne was standing over him.

'Where's the jacket?' she was saying.

'What jacket?'

'Llewelyn's.' She nodded towards the bed. 'We've been through his bag. There's nothing there. He may have tablets in his jacket.'

McFaul looked up at her, the camera in his lap, wondering

whether trying to save Llewelyn's life was really worth the effort. Then he shrugged and struggled to his feet. The jacket was outside, draped over a chair. He picked it up and returned to the bedroom. Llewelyn was moaning now, a new sound, quieter, weaker. McFaul began to go through the pockets. In one he found some money and a book of matches. In another, a ball of Kleenex tissue. He looked in the inside pocket, pulling out a folded wad of paper. A line of text across the top sheet caught his eye. He flicked through the rest of the sheets, realising that they were copies. A telex message, he thought, with a complete set of carbons. He peered at the addressee.

'Who's Cunningham?' he said aloud.

Molly turned round. She was sitting beside Llewelyn, holding his hand. His eyes were closed and he appeared to be deeply unconscious.

'Robbie,' she said, 'from Terra Sancta.'

McFaul barely heard her. He was reading the telex. When he'd finished it, he looked at her, remembering the message that had come in from Luanda. The ambassador wanted to talk to Molly Jordan. Urgently.

McFaul folded the sheets of telex paper. Molly was bent over Llewelyn. At the mention of Giles's name, she looked up.

'He's my husband,' she said. 'Why?'

Domingos died at 04.37 next morning. Christianne brought the news to McFaul in the schoolhouse. She'd been contacted by radio from the hospital and she thought it best to deliver it in person. McFaul thanked her, returning to the chair beneath the porch where he'd spent the night.

Dawn broke an hour later. McFaul woke Bennie and told him they were returning to the minefield beside the river. They needed the Ebinger, the protective gear, and a single bayonet. Nothing else. Bennie began to argue but McFaul walked away.

By half-past six, the sun up, they were parked on the

embankment overlooking the minefield. McFaul sat behind the wheel and smoked one of Bennie's roll-ups. When Bennie tried asking him what they were doing there he told him to mind his own business. When he tried conversation, he ignored him.

McFaul finished the roll-up and got out of the Land Rover. He put on the protective gear and told Bennie to back the Rover sixty metres and turn it round. If anything happened, he was to take him straight to the hospital. Bennie did what he was told, parking the Rover and getting out.

McFaul began to scramble down the embankment, then stopped, his weight balanced on his left leg. He stood motionless for at least a minute, staring down, then he lowered himself very slowly, hugging the bank. The grass on the bank was tufty, growing in clumps, loose soil in between. McFaul unsheathed the bayonet and began to probe an area to his right. Bennie watched him working, bewildered now. They'd been up and down the embankment all yesterday afternoon. It was clean. He knew it was.

McFaul had found something. The bayonet was back in the sheath. He looked round, signalling to Bennie, retracing his steps to the road. When the two men met, McFaul showed him the mine. It was no bigger than a hockey puck, a mottled dark green. Bennie peered at it.

'What's that?'

McFaul's head was up now. He was looking down the road, towards the rebel trenches.

'Difesa,' he said, 'SB-33.'

It was mid-morning before McFaul found Tomas, the young officer he'd dealt with after the grenade incident. He was sitting behind a makeshift desk in a corner of the big bus garage the army had commandeered for its Muengo headquarters. When McFaul asked him to step outside, away from the stares of the other men, he got up without a word. Outside, two soldiers were kicking a football against the wall of the garage. Tomas dismissed them with a wave, turning to ask McFaul about his wound. McFaul ignored the question.

'I need a weapon,' he said, nodding at the retreating soldiers. 'Something like that.'

One of the soldiers had picked up his gun. It was an Armalite, a light carbine, standard American issue. The young officer looked surprised.

'Why?'

'Doesn't matter.' McFaul paused. 'A couple of spare magazines, too.'

'I can't—'

'Please.' McFaul had stepped very close. 'An M16 and a couple of mags. Then we'll call it quits.'

'Quits?'

McFaul touched his upper arm. The wound was still bandaged. Tomas nodded, understanding.

'How long?' he said. 'How long do you want the gun for?'

McFaul shrugged.

'Couple of days.'

'You'll bring it back?'

'Of course.'

Tomas looked round, visibly uncomfortable. Aid workers never carried weapons. Staying unarmed was their best guarantee of protection. Why did this man want to risk all that? Why did he suddenly want to become a part of the war? He voiced the question, then repeated it, but McFaul just stared at him, a strange dead look on his face, a man for whom conversation – questions and answers – had ceased to have any significance.

'Your men nearly killed me,' he said at last.

'Is that why you want the gun?'

'No, but that's why you should give it to me.' McFaul paused again. 'You know Domingos?'

'Of course.'

'You know he works in the minefields?'

'Yes.'

'And you know how dangerous that is?'

'Yes.'

'Well, he's dead,' McFaul said softly. 'Domingos is dead.' Tomas stared at him, his eyes wide.

'A mine? You mean he got killed by a mine?'

McFaul looked away a moment. The soldiers had reached the corner of the building and one of them had stopped, openly curious.

'Good question,' McFaul said at last, taking Tomas by the elbow and steering him back towards the garage.

CHAPTER NINE

McFaul left Muengo at dusk the following day. When Bennie asked him where he was going he said it didn't much matter, and when Bennie looked pointedly at the Armalite carbine cradled in his left arm, McFaul simply shrugged and stepped out of the schoolhouse, carefully closing the door behind him. Deep down, he knew that Bennie was relieved not to be part of whatever his boss was planning. Domingos's death had robbed him of the last of his courage. All that mattered now was safe passage back to the UK.

Outside the schoolhouse, McFaul checked the lashings on the rubber dinghy and then stooped in the gathering darkness, hitching the trailer to the back of the Land Rover. With the Armalite beside him, he drove slowly out of the city, watching the trailer in the rear-view mirror, trying to minimise the bounces. Beside the river, a dirt track ran south towards the encircling UNITA lines. He'd swept the track himself, one of his first assignments, and it had been used every day since by people from Muengo. A kilometre short of UNITA territory, a low bluff beside the river offered cover and he pulled the Land Rover into a tight turn, using the last of the daylight to back into a narrow re-entrant, hidden from view.

McFaul stood for a moment beside the Land Rover, flexing his injured arm, running through the calculations in his head. Katilo's camp was about five kilometres downstream. Getting there on foot was out of the question. There were mines everywhere. But drifting downriver on the current, he should make it comfortably before daybreak. He'd lie up somewhere close, waiting for dawn. And when Katilo appeared, taking the bait he'd so carefully prepared, he'd spring the trap and kill him.

McFaul limped towards the river bank. The simplicity of the plan warmed him. Unlike so much of the life that he'd led, it was untainted by compromise or ambiguity. Killing Katilo might well lead to his own death but that was no longer of any consequence. Until yesterday, he'd thought that his years in the minefields had blunted his feelings. He'd thought he'd become immune to feelings of any kind. But he'd been wrong. Domingos's death was one too many. The little man deserved revenge.

Beside the river, below the Land Rover, was an abandoned plastic jerrycan, riddled with bullet holes. McFaul up-ended it, sitting in the semi-darkness, cupping his hands to hide the flare of the match. He hadn't smoked regularly since Afghanistan but somehow it felt suddenly right, a comfort, an adieu. Christianne had given him the cigarettes. They must have belonged to the boy Jordan, a South African brand, untipped.

McFaul drew the smoke deep into his lungs, removing a shred of tobacco from his tongue. His hands still carried the sweet, marzipan smell of C4, the explosive he'd been using to blow up the cache of defused mines. He'd spent most of the afternoon preparing the charges, checking off each mine from the master log he kept at the schoolhouse. In all, there'd been 374 mines, the harvest from seventeen weeks' hard labour in the fields around Muengo. The mines came in all shapes and sizes, and looking down at them before he'd wired the detonators, McFaul had felt like an archaeologist reviewing his trophies after a successful dig.

He tipped back his head, expelling a thin blue plume of smoke, thinking of Katilo again and the brutal simplicity of the war he'd chosen to fight. To control the countryside, you needed to drive the peasants off the land and into the cities. Mines did that for you, limb by limb, village by village, at a price most armies would consider derisory. No wonder the man was obsessed by the things. No wonder he'd insisted on showing off his latest box of goodies.

McFaul's hand strayed to the breast pocket of his shirt. He still had Llewelyn's precious cassette, an hour's worth of pictures that would tell any audience in the world why Katilo deserved an ugly end. Using mines at all was indefensible. Seeding them the way Katilo had done, luring a brave man to his death, was the sickest of jokes.

McFaul got to his feet, flicking the remains of his cigarette into the river. Blowing up the afternoon's pile of defused mines was the last thing he'd done before leaving. The roar of the explosion had rolled across the shattered city, sending clouds of birds into the sky, drawing yelps of excitement from the knots of watching kids. Within seconds came anxious voices on the radio net. Had the ceasefire ended? Was this the start of some new bombardment? McFaul had listened for a moment, wondering whether he owed the world some explanation, then he'd turned on his heel, telling Bennie to check the smouldering crater for duds, no longer caring about the small print of this squalid little war.

Now, back on his feet beside the Land Rover, he knew he'd been right. The time for talking was over. These guys would be killing each other for years to come. You could see it in their faces, the government troops inside the city, the UNITA guys out in the bush. There was a madness about them, a limitless potential for rage and brutality. That's what the salesmen fed on. That's what kept the mines coming, thousands and thousands of them, not just here in Angola but all over the Third World. Fighting the tide made fuck all difference. At its heart, the thing was evil. And evil, once recognised, compelled a choice.

McFaul began to rummage in the holdall he'd packed earlier. Beside the plastic flasks of chlorinated water, he could feel the shape of the bomb he'd lashed together, the sharp-edged contours of the nails and shards of broken glass he'd taped around the slab of C4 he'd saved from the afternoon's demolition job. Two pounds of the stuff was way over the top. It would cut Katilo in half. The thought brought a smile to McFaul's face and he zipped up the holdall again, pocketing the spare magazines for the Armalite Tomas had reluctantly given to him. He'd said nothing about his intentions to the young officer. If this thing worked the way he'd planned it, he'd know soon enough.

Molly Jordan spent the evening in the Red Cross bunker, wedged between a 56-pound sack of rice and the table where François bent to the big HF radio. She'd been trying all day to get through to the British embassy in Luanda but whenever contact was established there was always more important business to transact. No one had yet bothered to brief her, partly she suspected because no one knew for certain what was happening, but the conversations she'd overheard and the messages she'd seen scribbled on the corners of notepads suggested that an evacuation was once again imminent. Something had happened way up the chain of command. Some kind of deadline had been imposed, hours rather than days, and the people in charge were talking of getting everyone out by noon. After that, as far as she could gather, Muengo was in danger of renewed bombardment.

François, the tireless Swiss who manned the Red Cross radio, leaned back from the set. His fingers were blue from the crudely inked carbons he used to circulate incoming messages by hand. He gestured towards the radio.

'They're calling us now.'

'Who?'

'Your embassy. In Luanda.'

François muttered an acknowledgement into the lip mike then took off his earphones and passed them to Molly. By the time she'd put them on he was halfway up the wooden steps that led to the bunker's only working closet.

Molly fingered the tiny microphone. She could hear a thin voice, heavily accented, calling her name.

'Hello?' she said, feeling slightly foolish. 'Over . . .'

The voice faded, then returned. She was to wait. There was someone to talk to her. Molly was still asking for a name when another voice came on, stronger this time. Through the crackle of static she recognised the ambassador she'd met in Luanda. She began to colour at once, feeling the blood flooding her face. She wasn't supposed to be here. She was supposed to be back on the coast, killing time, waiting for the body of her dead son.

The ambassador was asking her how things were.

'Chaotic,' she heard herself saying, 'everyone rushing around. I'm afraid I'm not much use.'

She heard the ambassador chuckling, a gentle admonition, and she pictured him behind the desk in the office where they'd met. Behind him on the wall was a framed photograph of the Queen with one of her dogs and she'd been surprised by its informality.

'I'm afraid there's no news,' the ambassador was saying. 'I wish I had something definite to tell you.'

Molly cursed herself. The telex still lay on the corner of the desk. She'd read it so many times it had ceased to have any meaning. Giles's beloved yacht reported missing. *Molly Jay* gone. No sign of a body.

'Any wreckage?' she said numbly.

'Not that I know of.'

'Are they still looking?'

'I assume so.'

'He had a radio beacon, a little tiny thing.'

'So I gather. That's how they found the life-raft, according to the reports I've . . .'

The ambassador's voice battled briefly with a burst of static and lost. A few seconds later, contact re-established, he was talking about flights to Europe. Molly was booked through to

London via Lisbon. He'd taken the liberty of talking to TAP, the Portuguese airline with the next available departure, and they'd agreed to accept the return half of her Sabena ticket. His advice was to leave Luanda as soon as she could.

Molly nodded, her mind quite blank. She'd been anticipating this conversation all day, the news it might bring, the difference it might make. In the event, she'd learned nothing. People were dying in Angola in their thousands. Her own spot of bother – a son dead and buried, a husband lost at sea – simply turned her into a logistical footnote, the umpteenth item on some list or other.

The ambassador was promising transport from the airport once she got to Luanda. With Terra Sancta under pressure, he might even be able to manage temporary accommodation at the embassy. Molly managed a smile at last, pushing the telex away. This time he's leaving nothing to chance, she thought. Tucked up inside the embassy, her travelling days would be over.

'It's kind of you to take the trouble,' she said, 'but I expect I'll find somewhere.'

The ambassador signed off with another chuckle, wishing her luck, and Molly was still debating what to do about the electronic howling in her ears when someone clattered down the wooden steps beside her. She glanced up, recognising the face. McFaul's friend, she thought. The one who'd been so graphic about James.

Bennie was swaying slightly, the T-shirt beneath his jacket blotched with sweat.

'Lost the boss,' he said simply. 'Can't find him anywhere.'

McFaul drifted slowly down the river, flat on his back in the bottom of the dinghy. He could sense the water beneath him, and when he turned his head and lay his cheek flat against the thick rubber floor, it felt cool and alive. Now and again, he peered over the sides of the dinghy, trying to judge the speed of the current, but downstream from Muengo the stream was wide, nearly a hundred metres in places, and it was impossible to make out where the water ended and the river bank began. Low cloud veiled the moon and in the warm darkness he felt caged in a world of his own. Soon, he knew he'd have to start edging towards the further bank. There was a wooden paddle clipped to the transom and in any case the water was shallow enough for him to slip overboard and tow the dinghy inshore. He needed time for a decent recce, time to dig himself in. Then, at last, he could settle Domingos's debt.

McFaul lay back again, thinking of Celestina. He'd left a wad of dollars for her. The money was doubtless more than anyone in Muengo had ever seen but just now it was probably useless. What could money buy when the man you loved was dead? How could you comfort your children when their father would never be home again? McFaul closed his eyes, smelling the damp, swampy breath of the river, knowing again that this journey was long overdue. The time for excuses, for telling himself that nothing could be done, was over. He felt for his watch, peering at the luminous dial. 02.20. This time of year, the sky began to lighten around five. By four, at the latest, he should be in position.

Bennie sat on his camp-bed, his head in his hands. He'd been describing the pictures Llewelyn had shot. McFaul had made him watch them and he hadn't spared Molly any of the details. The way the surgeons had dealt with Domingos's leg. The noise the hand-drill made, grinding through the bone.

Molly was sitting cross-legged on the floor, her back against the wooden partition. The last of Global's beer had left her feeling slightly light-headed, and she was only half-listening to Bennie. I gave him the radio beacon for Christmas, she kept thinking. I wrapped it up and put it in a stocking at the foot of the bed and even then it hadn't saved his life. Was it a kind death? Drowning? Or was it violent? Would he survive long? In November seas? Or was it so cold you just slipped into unconsciousness? She chased the questions around her head, trying hard not to imagine his body, washed up on some foreign beach, making the news for a day or two, just like his son. She'd read somewhere that bodies bloated in the water and she remembered footage from a D-Day film she'd seen, dead soldiers parcelled in khaki, bumping around in the Normandy shallows. The waste of it all. The telegrams. The funerals. The endless grief. She shuddered, thinking suddenly of the cottage back in Thorpe-le-Soken. The place would be cold and empty. The threat of bankruptcy would be as real as ever and she'd have to sit down and sort out her life. Sell up. Move away. Whatever. She'd hate it. She knew she would. Anything would be better than that.

She shut her eyes, forcing herself to listen to Bennie. He was mumbling about McFaul again, how strange he'd been all day. Detached. Out of touch. Off the planet. Bennie's trailing fingers found the empty bottle of vodka beside the bed. He picked it up and looked at it then let it fall again, cursing softly.

'My fault,' he said at length.

'What is?'

'Him disappearing like that.' He paused. 'Domingos. The TV geezer. Every fucking thing. I should have waited. Muggins gets it wrong. Again.' He shook his head, choked with self-pity, trying to focus on the stump of candle in the saucer between them. 'You got kids at all? Only it would be nice to see them again. Know what I mean? This place? Jesus . . .' He gestured vaguely towards the line of family snaps Blu-Tacked to the wall above the bed and Molly fought the urge to compete, comparing the wreckage of her own life to Bennie's maudlin ramblings. Nice to have kids at all, she thought. Nice to have someone to go home to.

'Tell me about McFaul,' she said instead.

'Andy?' Bennie was frowning now. 'Funny bugger, fucking head case sometimes. Does things you wouldn't believe.'

'Like what? What kind of things?'

Bennie stared at her for a moment, as if he hadn't heard the question. Then his fingers circled the empty vodka bottle again and he picked it up, nursing it in his lap, telling her about Kuwait. He and McFaul had met there. They were both refugees from the army, out on their own after thirteen years of service, and they'd both signed up with the same commercial outfit, tackling the mess in the minefields after Desert Storm. Compared to McFaul, Bennie was a novice. He'd served in the Paras for most of his army career. Only towards the end had he managed to con a nine-month attachment to the EOD course run by the Royal Engineers.

Molly rubbed her eyes. She wanted to go to sleep.

'EOD?'

'Explosive Ordnance Disposal. Blowing stuff up.' Bennie gestured vaguely towards the window. 'What we did today.'

'That huge bang?'

'Yeah.'

Molly nodded. She'd been in the cathedral when she'd heard the explosion and she remembered the flap-flap of the birds disturbed by the blast of the explosion.

Bennie was talking about Kuwait again. He and McFaul had shared an air-conditioned hotel room in a tourist development south of Kuwait City. Every morning, the company four-wheel would turn up in the plaza outside and ferry them out to the minefields. The contract was worth a fortune but the deadlines were tight and the company was starting to cut corners. From time to time men went sick, or got themselves blown up, and the call would go back to London for reinforcements. Skilled de-miners were thin on the ground. Bullshit artists with zero experience started turning up, guys who'd talked good clearance at the interview and covered their tracks with phoney paperwork.

Molly was listening now, aware of a new tone in Bennie's

voice. He was concentrating very hard, the bottle discarded, his eyes fixed on the puddle of wax at the foot of the candle.

'So what happened?' she asked quietly.

'Andy had an oppo, bloke called Tosh. He got arseholed one night and had a run-in with the thought police. The ragheads slung him in the nick and threatened to cut his hands off. After that, he didn't want to know. When they let him out, he took the next plane home.' Bennie looked up, brooding. 'Bloke they replaced him with was hopeless, real dickhead. Turned out to be a thicko ex-squaddie from Luton. Knew fuck all about mines.'

'And he was working with . . .' Molly touched the empty camp-bed by her shoulder, 'McFaul?'

'Yeah.' He nodded. 'Andy knew right off, of course. He had the bloke sussed from the start. But this geezer was clever. He told Andy some story about his marriage cracking up, and having to find money for his kids, and Andy believed him, took pity on the poor bastard, said he'd teach him just enough . . . you know . . . to get by. Turned out the bloke was a liability. Just couldn't pick it up. Completely brain-dead. No bottle, either.'

Bennie broke off and Molly remembered the deep-blue scars that latticed the lower half of McFaul's face. It was the first thing she'd noticed, the night he'd stepped into Christianne's bedroom with the message from Luanda. That, and those pale, dead eyes.

'Wasn't that a bit silly? Risking his life like that?'

'Yeah, but . . .' Bennie shrugged, 'Andy had been through it, too. He thought the bloke was kosher.'

'Been through what?'

'Marriage. Responsibility. All that stuff. His first wife went off with a male nurse when he was down south. And his second marriage was a disaster. Lasted under a year. Left him gutted.'

Molly nodded, thinking of the eyes again, wary, defensive.

'So this man you're talking about. The one he helped—'

'Blew himself up. Andy, too.'

'How?'

Bennie hesitated a moment then fumbled under his pillow and produced a tin of tobacco. He began to roll a cigarette.

'They were working as a team, Andy and this other bloke. We had a foreman, an American guy, real bastard, but Andy never said a word to him about the other bloke. We had quotas, targets we had to hit every day. Either mines lifted or territory cleared, one or the other. Andy was having to do the work of two guys, just to keep up. Plus he was trying to teach this clown how to survive—' Bennie broke off, moistening the edge of the Rizla with his tongue.

'It must have been hot.'

'Baking. You're wearing this heavy Kevlar kit and the sweat just rolls off you. One hundred and ten, one hundred and twenty degrees. Half an hour of that and your concentration's shit, believe me. Even Andy was knackered.'

'But he was covering for this other man.'

'Exactly.'

'So what happened?'

'He was teaching this bloke how to pull a mine. That's lifting it out, the dodgiest bit. It's tricky but it has to be done. That's what they're paying you for.'

'And this other man was there?'

'He was doing it. You expose the mine first, then you make sure there's nothing fancy alongside, no booby-traps, then you lift the fucker out. That's what this guy was doing, lifting it out. Andy was beside him, down on one knee, talking him through it. He'd seen the burrow, of course. He knew it was there, a couple of feet to one side of the mine. But it was no drama. No big deal.'

Molly looked blank.

'Burrow?'

'Yeah, you get these big lizard things. So long . . .' He measured the space in the air. 'Maybe eight inches, maybe a bit more. They call them kangaroo rats. Ugly bastards. Anyway, this thing comes barrelling out. The noise, I suppose. All the disruption.'

'And the mine?'

'He dropped it.' Bennie nodded. 'Dropped the fucker. Right there, right between them. Bang. End of story. Matey down, Andy down, and the lizard doing the funky chicken. Unbelievable.'

'You were there? You saw it happen?'

Bennie shook his head. The flare of the match briefly lit the planes of his face.

'I was miles away, over towards the coast, different minefield. The hospital was back in Kuwait City. I saw him that night. He was choked. No leg. Face a mess. And angry, really angry.'

'What about the other man?'

'Died. That's when the company wised up about his qualifications. We all carried insurance, had to, but it turned out this bloke never bothered. Andy tried to get a settlement off the company but they refused. Said it was his own fault. Should have reported the guy, not covered up for him. That fucked up Andy's own insurance, too.'

'So what did he do?'

Bennie up-ended the top of the tobacco tin, using it as an ashtray. He was smiling now, his face softer.

'They kept him in hospital nearly a month. Before they flew him back to the UK we went back to the minefields, just him and me. I had the keys to one of the four-wheels. We knew where everyone lived. We were after the foreman, the American guy. Andy blamed him for part of the accident. Said the targets were unrealistic. He'd tried to have it out with the guy but the bastard wouldn't listen.' Bennie sucked at the roll-up, grinning. 'We got him out of bed, roped him up, dumped him in the desert. Andy told him he was in the middle of a live minefield. Said we'd pushed a single breach across and we were off back home now and he was welcome to try and follow us. Guy was blindfolded. Couldn't tell the fuck where he was. Apparently he didn't move an inch until they found him.'

'When was that?'

'Next day. Late afternoon. Bastard was cooked. Not a stitch on him.'

Molly was frowning now, trying to visualise the kidnapping.

'Your friend did this? McFaul? Straight out of hospital?'

'He watched mainly, helped where he could. It was his idea but he needed me to do the legwork.' Bennie laughed. 'We were out of there that night. Company was shit, anyway. I went to Global after that. And Andy joined, too, when he got better.'

He broke off, then began to talk about Global Clearance. Working for the commercial de-mining companies might earn you a fortune, he said, but losing a leg to keep the shareholders happy was a lousy proposition. Better, in Bennie's opinion, to sign up with guys you believed in, blokes who had more in mind than a quick buck. Working in the Third World, you got to see what really mattered. The last thing you worried about was money.

'And that's what McFaul thinks?'

'Word for word. More than me, really. You can take so much of this game then . . .' he shrugged, peering round, 'it just gets to you.'

It took McFaul several seconds to recognise the music. He'd been crouched in the bottom of the dinghy for nearly half an hour, alert for the slightest movement, the dimmest light, knowing that Katilo's camp must be close, but the darkness was as impenetrable as ever, cutting him off from everything but the nudge of the current and the heavy promise of impending rain. The music was Dvořák, the New World symphony, a favourite of McFaul's. It seemed to be coming from somewhere up ahead, and McFaul levered himself over the side of the dinghy, rolling softly into the water, his feet finding the river bed at once. The water was barely waist-deep and he reached for one of the rope pulls on the side of the dinghy, hauling it backwards against the current, making his way towards the further bank. Katilo had an audio set-up in his cave. McFaul had seen the speakers when he and Christianne had come to negotiate. It was impossible to make a judgement in the darkness but the music sounded uncomfortably close.

McFaul waded onwards, his body bent against the current, trying hard not to think about crocodiles. After a couple of minutes, he felt himself beginning to tire. The stump of his left leg was chafing against the socket of the prosthesis and he paused in the water, trying to keep his balance, taking the weight off his leg for a moment or two. Ahead, he could see the low swell of the further bank. The music was a little fainter now, and he could hear the sound of laughter, fainter still. Miles away, off to the left, a flicker of lightning crazed the night sky and he heard the first fat drops of rain dimpling the water around him. Rain was good. Rain kept soldiers under cover. Not that anyone appeared to be watching.

McFaul tightened his grasp on the rope and began to haul the dinghy onwards. The water was shallower now, knee-deep, and a stretch of gravel bottom made the going easier. He trudged upstream, his head down, the rain heavier, soaking quickly through the thin denim of his shirt. He wondered about Llewelyn's cassette, whether or not it was waterproof, and he thought about transferring it to the holdall. On reflection, though, he decided against it. Putting the cassette in the holdall might risk losing control of the dinghy. And if the dinghy floated off downstream, this journey of his would have been pointless.

He glanced over his shoulder, trying to guess at the geography on Katilo's side of the river. What he needed was somewhere to get his head down, a little pocket of cover where he could hide the dinghy and rest up until daybreak. He started wading again, edging closer and closer to the further bank. He could see the water's edge now, and the shallow rise of baked mud that lay between the river and the bush. There were birds on the mud. He could hear them twittering softly as they strutted to and fro. Good sign, he thought. No crocodiles.

He struggled on, the dinghy getting heavier by the minute. Up ahead, a spur of land reached into the river. As he got closer he could see the pale stands of grass and the stump of an old tree. There were rocks at the water's edge and he stood amongst them, wondering whether to risk leaving the safety of the river. In the tall grass he could rest. He could haul the dinghy up across the mud and after daybreak he'd be invisible. There'd be time for a decent recce, time to use the binos, time to make a sensible plan. He thought about the proposition a little longer, listening to the dry rattle of the cicadas, then he shook his head, turning away and plodding onwards, splashing through the shallows, following the finger of land as it reached upstream into the river. Features like these were exactly where you'd put your mines. Even Katilo would know that.

Minutes later, he knew he'd made the right decision. The little promontory became a sand-bar which curled back on itself, enfolding a wide pool of slack water, protected from the main current. McFaul explored it yard by yard, tugging the dinghy behind him, getting a feel for the shape of the place. Between the pool and Katilo's camp lay the sand-bar. The closer it got to the river bank, the denser became the vegetation. Yards from the shoreline, though still in the water, McFaul was sure he'd be hidden from view.

He smiled to himself in the darkness, securing the dinghy's painter to an overhanging branch. He tested the knot twice, then tumbled aboard. There was half an inch or so of rain inside the dinghy and he sat in it, reaching for the Armalite, wiping the weapon down. In the holdall was a towel. He mopped the rain from his face, smelling Bennie's aftershave. Then his hand was back inside the holdall, feeling for the Motorola two-way radio he'd doctored back at the schoolhouse. Using the Motorola was a trick he'd picked up in Northern Ireland. To trigger the C4, he needed a radio detonator, a hand-held device tailor-made for a job like this, but Ken Middleton distrusted them. The frequency they used was often shared with other traffic and early on he'd lost a good man in Kurdistan to a chance radio emission that had set off an explosion. Since then, he'd banned radio detonators from the Global field inventory, and so McFaul had been obliged to rig up a device of his own, wiring a detonator into the circuit of one of the spare Motorolas, and then testing it to make sure the current was sufficient to trigger the charge. The voltage was ample and the crack of the little detonator had been enough to bring Bennie running into the schoolhouse.

Now, McFaul checked his watch and dug in the holdall again. Setting the bomb off would be simple. All it needed was a call from his own radio, another Motorola. Both of the handsets were multi-channel and he'd chosen one of the least-used frequencies for the few minutes or so when the bomb would be live. He fingered the handset in the darkness. Channel six, he thought grimly. Endgame.

The rain had stopped now and he tipped his head back, looking up, wondering what difference the clouds would make to the coming of daylight. It was already gone four-thirty. This time last week, he'd been watching the sun rise at five. He frowned, peering across the river again, trying to guess the distance to Katilo's camp. After he'd first heard the music, he must have retreated a couple of hundred metres. At least. Double that, and you were probably looking at the kind of range he'd have to work with tomorrow morning. In combat terms, he knew it was nothing. Aimed fire at 400 metres was supposed to be 90 per cent accurate. He reached down, touching the Armalite, wondering whether a bullet or two might be simpler. Then he put the idea out of his mind, knowing that his first plan, the one that had come to him so instinctively, was favourite. Katilo deserved a taste of the real thing. With luck, he might even survive long enough to feel what Domingos had felt. A bullet would be too clean, too swift, too kind.

McFaul swallowed a yawn. Tomorrow, after Katilo, he'd

have to make his way back upriver, back towards Muengo. Whether he'd make it or not was anyone's guess but travelling overland was out of the question. Too many soldiers. Too many mines. He tried to imagine the journey. If everything went according to plan, there'd be no search. The soldiers would put Katilo's death down to an accident, fate, black magic. There'd be no evidence of an enemy at work. There'd be no gunshot. No footprints. Nothing human. Just a shredded dinghy and the smoking remains of their beloved commander. Using the transmitter, triggering the bomb by radio, was the nearest McFaul could get to the kind of death Katilo had inflicted on so many of his countrymen. It also, in theory, gave McFaul a chance of getting away.

He looked across the water again, sensing the darkness beginning to thin. There was the pipe of birdsong now, rising above the steady chatter of the surrounding bush, and down-river, towards Katilo's camp, the Dvořák had come to an abrupt end. For a moment, nothing happened. Then came the bellow of an animal, something big, something goaded beyond endurance. It sounded, McFaul thought, like a cow. The bellowing went on for a full minute. Then it stopped and McFaul heard the soldiers again, laughing and clapping, and the swirl of a different kind of music, something infinitely more modern than Dvořák, drums and maracas and guitars, hot Brazilian rhythms rolling across the inky water.

McFaul listened, slapping at the first of the day's mosquitoes, thinking again about Domingos. Alive, he'd disapprove of this. Violence, he'd argue, was never justified. McFaul smiled, hearing his voice, picturing the way he'd put it, remembering the expression on his face when he fought to make a point. Then he reached for the holdall, unzipping it, wondering whether there was enough light to check the bomb.

*

When Molly awoke, it was daylight. She blinked, getting up on one elbow, looking across the shadowed room. Bennie was sprawled on the other bed, his mouth wide open, still fully dressed. He was snoring noisily, his chest rising and falling, one hand dangling limply over the side of the bed. Molly watched him for a moment or two, wondering how she'd come to spend the night at the schoolhouse. She remembered the drone of Bennie's voice, more stories about the minefields, and she remembered abandoning the floor for the comfort of McFaul's bed. After that though, there was nothing. Just an air of faint surprise that she should have shared this room with a stranger and woken up feeling totally shameless.

She slipped off the bed as quietly as she could and went to the window. Something had disturbed her and she didn't know quite what. Outside, the road was empty. Molly crossed the room, glancing at her watch. 05.47. Still early. She opened the door to the schoolroom, remembering the water Bennie kept in the row of chipped old fire-buckets. He'd shown them to her the previous evening as she'd helped him back from the Red Cross bunker. She'd suggested then that he drank a glass or two but he'd shaken his head, preferring to finish the bottle of Smirnoff he carried in the pocket of his threadbare combat jacket.

Now, Molly bent to the nearest of the buckets, cupping the tepid water in her hands and sluicing her face. Only when she stood up again did she see the youths sitting behind the schoolroom's wooden desks. There were three of them. The one with the Santos football shirt stood up and offered her a shy smile. In broken English, he explained that he was a friend of Domingos's family. Domingos was dead. The Englishmen would need another Domingos. He and the others had come to volunteer.

Molly stared at him, listening to the little speech, water still dripping from her face. When the youth began to ask her what

281

they could do, when they could start, she held up her hands, stepping back into the dormitory and shutting the door behind her. It took a full minute to shake Bennie awake. She tried to explain about the boys next door. Bennie frowned, not under-standing. Then he swung his legs off the bed and blundered through to the schoolroom. Molly could hear him snarling at the youths. There was the scraping of desks on the wooden floor, and then footsteps as they left. Bennie was back in the open doorway. Molly was at the window. The youths had disap-peared.

'Were they serious?' she asked. 'Did they really want Domingos's job?'

Bennie looked nonplussed. He was staring at a Jiffybag on the table at the foot of his bed.

'Yeah,' he said at last, 'anything to get them on that fucking plane.'

He picked up the envelope, feeling it. Then he handed it to Molly without a word. Molly took it. It was thicker than it looked. It had Christianne's name scribbled on the front. Molly weighed it in her hand.

'Whose writing is that?'

Bennie was back in the schoolroom. Molly could hear him scooping handfuls of water into his mouth.

'Andy,' he muttered through the open door, 'must have left it last night.'

Gunfire awoke McFaul. For a second or two, his head pillowed on his folded arms, he remained completely motionless. The gunfire was coming in sporadic bursts. It sounded like small-arms. McFaul opened one eye. The sun was still low, gilding the mist that hung above the river. He eased his head up, his body still sprawled across the dinghy. The Armalite lay across his lap. His hand crabbed along the stock, releasing the safety catch. The gunfire had stopped now and he could hear men's voices, the bark of orders, then the cough of an engine stirring into life. McFaul looked across the river. The further bank was eighty metres away, the bush dotted with trees. Of soldiers, there was no sign.

Downriver, his view was blocked by a dense screen of thorn bush and elephant grass. McFaul reached for the holdall and pulled out a pair of binoculars. Then he slipped into the water, staying close to the sand-bar. Underfoot, the bottom of the pool was matted with rotting vegetation. McFaul could feel twigs breaking beneath his boots. There was a bad smell here, too, the smell of human shit, and the closer he got to the sand-bar, the worse the stench became. He frowned. Normally, you'd shit downstream. Not here.

McFaul paused in the water. Through the thinning stands of grass, he could now see down the river. Katilo's camp was further than he'd expected, more than five hundred metres away. He put the binoculars to his eyes, adjusting the focus ring. A line of trucks was drawn up beside the water, their outlines blurred by camouflage netting. There were soldiers everywhere, some standing in groups, others squatting round a handful of cooking fires. Curls of thin blue smoke hung in the windless air and as McFaul watched, one of the soldiers got to his feet and disappeared behind a truck. Seconds later he was back again, driving a cow before him, pushing and kicking at it. The other soldiers were laughing. Through the binoculars, McFaul watched one of them fashioning a lasso from a length of rope.

McFaul got a little closer to the sand-bar, widening his view. Inland from the river, on a bald patch of scrub, he found a battery of big field guns. There were more soldiers here, stripped to the waist, piling shells in five-layer pyramids. The barrels of the field guns were elevated towards Muengo and beneath the camouflage netting McFaul thought he recognised the brutal outlines of the South African G5. A G5 could hurl a shell fifteen miles. Muengo's agony was clearly far from over.

McFaul traversed the binoculars back to the river bank, trying to match the shape of the landscape to the images stencilled on his memory from his last visit. The blindfold walk from the cave to the river had been no more than thirty metres. The four-wheel had been parked nearby. He looked at the line of trucks. Beyond them stood a spindly acacia tree and to the left of it there was a tumulus of some kind where the land shouldered upwards before flattening again. At the foot of the tumulus, clearly visible, were two soldiers standing several metres apart. Unlike the men around the fire, they were obviously on duty, their bodies criss-crossed with heavy bandoliers of ammunition, their carbines cradled in their arms. McFaul was about to put the glasses down when a third figure appeared, emerging between them. The build and the body language were unmistakable. The way he paused to flick an insect from his face. The passing word he shared with one of the sentries. The slow, languid, early morning stretch, hands behind his neck, hands raised in the air, hands finally propped on his hips as he looked across at the men around the camp-fires. Katilo. Very definitely.

McFaul felt the first stirrings of fear. If he got this wrong, if the plan misfired, Katilo would tear him apart. Literally. In front of an audience. Was this what he really wanted? Would Domingos have thought any the less of him if he jacked it in and called it a day? McFaul hesitated a moment, then dismissed the thought. Domingos wouldn't be asking any questions. Ever. Domingos was dead. And this man had killed him.

McFaul returned to the dinghy. He went through the hold-all, item by item, making sure he kept everything he needed. The water containers he clipped to his belt. A third spare magazine for the Armalite went into the waistband of his jeans. The last of his precious Kendal mint cake, he ate. Finally he unwrapped the taped slab of C4 and inserted the tiny, pencil-thin detonator in the gap he'd left at one end. The detonator was wired to the Motorola, and he bound the whole parcel together with more tape, making sure that the power switch on the radio was off. Beneath his fingers he could feel the shapes of the nails and the broken glass he'd lashed around the explosive. In the bow of the dinghy was a triangle of sturdy rubberised material that acted as a spray cover. Using more tape, he fixed the bomb beneath the cover. To anyone looking in, the bomb would be invisible.

McFaul slung the Armalite over his shoulder. Then he untied the dinghy and began to tow it out towards the river. Still hidden behind the sand-bar he paused, eyeing the eddies that curled in from the main current. He reached into the dinghy, pulling out the holdall. Inside the holdall was the other Motorola. He pushed it inside the waistband of his jeans, then filled the holdall with water and let it sink. Finally he reached under the spray cover, his fingers finding the power switch on the Motorola. The receiving radio was now on. A call on his own Motorola would trigger the bomb.

McFaul lifted the binoculars, gazing downriver. The water was deeper here, nearly up to his waist. Through the binoculars, he could see the soldiers loading the trucks. The camouflage netting had gone. Of Katilo, there was no sign. McFaul glanced back at the dinghy, measuring the distance between himself and the tell-tale ripple that indicated the middle of the current out in the river. Then he turned the dinghy round until the bow was pointing downstream and gave it a hefty push. The dinghy nosed out across the river, slowing and slowing until it snagged on the current and half-turned and then began to drift sideways downstream.

McFaul was already back behind the thickest vegetation, metres from the river bank, the binoculars to his eyes, tracking the dinghy through the blur of grass and thorn bush. The dinghy was still revolving, turning and turning, already fifty metres downstream. McFaul followed the river down towards the camp. Some of the soldiers were still working amongst the trucks. Others were stamping out the fires. No one seemed to have noticed the dinghy. Minutes went by. To the naked eye, the dinghy was slowly becoming a dot. Then there was a shout. McFaul raised the binoculars again. One of the soldiers had seen the dinghy. He was standing on the river bank. He was pointing. He was very close to Katilo's cave.

McFaul traversed the binos. One of the sentries outside the cave had disappeared. The other one was shading his eyes with his hand, staring upriver. McFaul found the dinghy. It was still two hundred metres from the camp. Back outside the cave, Katilo had appeared. He was pulling on a white T-shirt, tucking the bottom into his fatigues. He was following the sentries towards the river bank. McFaul lowered the binoculars a moment, one hand finding the Motorola tucked into the waistband of his jeans. He pulled the radio out and switched it on. All he had to do now was transmit. The transmission button was yellow. Yellow, for Katilo, was the colour of death.

McFaul took another look through the binoculars. There were soldiers in the water now, a little semi-circle, ready for the dinghy. McFaul counted four of them. They were chatting amongst themselves. Katilo was on the river bank, watching them. The soldiers would capture the dinghy. They would bring it to Katilo. They'd manhandle it out of the water and present it to him, their tribute, their offering, and he'd bend to inspect it. The colour yellow. Channel Six. A tiny blossom of flame. A puff or two of smoke. And a mist of bone and blood where Katilo had just been standing.

For the first time, McFaul heard the voices. They were men's voices. It sounded like they were walking towards him, on his side of the river, up from the direction of the camp. Instinctively, McFaul edged forward, ducking low, seeking the cover of the sand-bar. The soldiers were clearly visible. There were three of them. They were looking back towards the camp, watching the capture of the dinghy. They were laughing. Only one of them was armed. They paused for a moment, barely fifty metres away, one of them undoing the buttons on his fatigues, and McFaul suddenly realised why they'd come. Shit, he thought. The stench of human shit. These men, for some reason, had chosen this place to defecate.

McFaul peered down towards the camp. The dinghy was only metres away from the crescent of waiting troops. They were reaching out for it. Katilo was still watching them, his arms folded across his chest. McFaul began to edge onto the sand-bar. If the men came here to shit, the place was mine-free. Had to be. If only he could find enough cover, if only he could hang on long enough to see the job through, then the chaos after the explosion would save him. The men would run back to the camp. No one would think of looking upriver. If only. If only.

McFaul waded out of the shallows, slipping the Armalite off his shoulder, keeping his body low. He went to ground almost at once, prone behind a thick clump of thorn bush, the Armalite beside him. The smell of shit was overpowering. The soldiers were still watching the men in the river. As they seized the dinghy, he heard them cheering and clapping. Then they were heading towards him again, moving faster this time. One of them turned onto the sand-bar, his trousers already halfway down his legs. The others followed, still laughing. The taller of the two joined the first man, already squatting in the grass. The other, the shy one, ran past, heading straight for McFaul. McFaul was watching the men in the river. They were manhand-ling the dinghy towards Katilo. McFaul could see him with the naked eye, a solitary white T-shirt, awaiting his prize.

The young soldier was very close now. Both hands were at his trousers. Then he saw McFaul. He froze for a moment, not quite believing it, watching – transfixed – as McFaul threw the Motorola aside and reached for the Armalite. The first shot took the soldier in the thigh. He screamed and collapsed, holding his leg as the blood fountained up through the torn fabric. McFaul struggled to his feet. The other men were shouting and the one with the rifle came bursting through the tall grass. For a second, bending over his injured comrade, he didn't see McFaul.

Then he followed the pointing finger, looking up as McFaul reached desperately for the transmitter, and McFaul saw him fighting with the heavy Kalashnikov, trying to bring it to bear, loosing off a burst of unaimed fire, wildly inaccurate. The flat bark of the automatic echoed down the river and McFaul saw the men at the camp drop the dinghy and start running along the strip of baked mud beneath the overhanging bank.

The third soldier had appeared now. He'd drawn a machete and he lunged at McFaul, his arm raised, the blade slicing down. McFaul parried the blow with the Armalite, closing with the soldier, smashing the barrel of the carbine into his face. He heard the crack of splintering bone but the soldier was immensely strong. Abandoning the machete, his hands found McFaul's throat and he began to squeeze, grunting with the effort. McFaul dropped the Armalite and the two men fell to the ground, McFaul gasping for air. He tried to wriggle free but the soldier's body-weight was pressing down on him, forcing his head back, exposing his throat. McFaul stared up at him, his eyes half-closed, his vision beginning to grey. He no longer cared whether he lived or died. Everything smelled of shit. The whole fucking world smelled of shit. End of story.

Across the river, someone was shouting. The soldier hesitated, relaxing his grip. His front teeth were broken and a thin trickle of blood was dripping from his lower lip. McFaul watched it, wholly detached now, a mere spectator, curious to know what might happen next. The soldier was frowning. He muttered something to one of the others and McFaul felt his body-weight shifting. Then there were hands behind him, pulling him upright, and the soldier with the broken teeth was suddenly very close. The whites of his eyes were bloodshot and yellowed and McFaul could smell liquorice on his breath. The soldier began to grin, reaching forward, running a finger down the side of McFaul's head. Then he lifted it to his nose, sniffing it, grunting something to himself, reaching forward again, motioning for McFaul to open his mouth. McFaul was staring at the finger. The finger was smeared with shit. It's all over me, he thought. All over the back of my head, matted in my hair, caked in my ears. I must have fallen in it. Head back. Splat.

The soldier still wanted McFaul to open his mouth. McFaul shook his head. His arms were pinioned now, the other soldier standing behind him. McFaul tried to look round, wondering about the injured man, why the screaming had stopped, but the soldier with the broken teeth reached out, pinching McFaul's nostrils, the way you might deal with a child refusing medicine. McFaul fought the urge to open his mouth. The finger was waiting, slightly bent, coated with shit. McFaul shook his head again, humiliated already. Anything, he thought. Anything but this.

Abruptly, he heard the sound of splashing from the river. Then voices nearby. The grip on his arms loosened for a moment and he wrenched his face away, half-turning in time to see Katilo stepping over the inert body of the fallen soldier. He recognised McFaul at once, barking an order to the soldier with the broken teeth. A length of cord appeared. McFaul's elbows were bound behind his back. Then he was stumbling through the grass, back down the sand-bar, onto the river bank. The sunlight was fierce on the water. McFaul lowered his head, shielding his eyes, letting the babble of voices swirl around him. When he finally looked up, Katilo was standing beside him, shouting orders at the men in the elephant grass. They finally appeared with the injured soldier, carrying his body between them. Blood was still pumping from an ugly hole in his thigh.

The soldiers laid him at Katilo's feet. Water lapped at the torn flesh. Katilo studied the soldier for a moment or two, stirring his body with his foot. He was wearing calf-high, lace-up paratrooper's boots and he stooped to wipe them clean before turning to McFaul.

'You did this?'

McFaul nodded, not bothering to explain. The last of the soldiers had emerged from the elephant grass. He was carrying the Motorola. He gave it to Katilo. Katilo turned it over, examining it. Finally, he looked at McFaul.

'Yours?'

McFaul didn't say anything for a moment. Downriver, three soldiers had returned to the dinghy. It lay abandoned at the water's edge and they were bent over it, pointing. McFaul looked at Katilo. He glanced up, telling one of the soldiers to untie McFaul's elbows. Then he held out the radio.

'Call your people,' he said.

McFaul shook his head.

'No.'

'Call them. Tell them you've shot one of my men.'

McFaul looked at the wounded soldier lying in the water. He could feel the shit drying on his face. Katilo was still offering him the radio. With his other hand he was loosening the flap on the holster strapped to his thigh. Inside the holster, McFaul could see the butt of a big automatic. Katilo was watching him carefully. McFaul took the Motorola. The watching soldiers began to edge backwards, sensing danger.

'Call them,' he said. 'Now.'

McFaul shook his head.

'No.' He glanced downstream. A fourth soldier had joined the group around the dinghy. He looked back at Katilo. The automatic was in his hand, pointing steadily at McFaul's head. He stepped very close.

'Call them,' he said softly.

'No.'

McFaul closed his eyes and took a tiny breath, knowing this was the end. Then he felt a pressure on the yellow button, Katilo's hand, and a long, hollow explosion came rolling up the river. McFaul opened his eyes. There were birds everywhere, flapping away across the bush. On the foreshore, by the camp, a curtain of brown smoke blew lazily across the river. Behind it, on the baked mud, small parcels of flesh lay beside the shredded remains of the dinghy.

McFaul looked at Katilo. He was gazing downriver. He

seemed impressed. He reached for the Motorola, taking it from McFaul. His finger found the button. He pressed it again. The soldiers around him exchanged glances. Nothing happened. Katilo looked at McFaul a moment, then returned the transmitter. One of the men was carrying McFaul's Armalite. Katilo gestured at it, impatient now.

'Yours?' he asked McFaul.

'Yeah.'

Katilo examined the carbine then fired twice into the soft mud at McFaul's feet. The soldier with the broken teeth was knee-deep in the water, washing his hands, watching Katilo. Katilo looked at McFaul a little longer, curiosity as well as amusement. Then he stepped towards the injured soldier lying in the shallows and put the muzzle of the Armalite in his open mouth. He emptied the magazine in a long burst before tossing the Armalite aside. McFaul watched, sickened, as the soldiers manhandled the corpse into midstream, releasing it to float slowly away on the current.

Katilo was looking at his watch. He nodded towards McFaul and said something brisk in Ovimbundu. Then he turned to ford the river, a tuneless whistle on his lips. The soldiers closed around McFaul, roping his elbows behind his back again, and began to push him after Katilo. They were nearly halfway across before McFaul recognised the tune. Dvořák, he thought. The New World symphony.

Christianne opened McFaul's Jiffybag as soon as Molly arrived back at the MSF house. The French girl had been up all night nursing Llewelyn. His temperature had climbed again at dusk and now he lay in Christianne's bed, semiconscious, his eyes still bright with fever. Molly looked down at him while Christianne scissored the sticky tape that secured the Jiffybag. In three days, Llewelyn had aged ten years. Thin, gaunt, helpless, he'd become an old man.

Christianne was emptying the Jiffybag. Twenty-dollar bills

cascaded onto the bed. She began to count them, bewildered. There were seventy.

'Fourteen hundred dollars,' Molly murmured, 'and this.'

She handed Christianne a single sheet of graph paper, a grid of tiny blue squares. There was writing on one side. Christianne read it quickly.

'The money's for Celestina,' she said. 'He says it belonged to Domingos. Here.'

She passed the note to Molly. Llewelyn was peering at the pile of dollar bills, uncomprehending. Molly folded the note and returned it. McFaul had careful, backward-sloping writing, like a child.

'He wants you to get her on the plane,' Molly pointed out. 'Her and the kids. Maybe he thinks the money might help.'

'It won't. They'll never allow it. I know the way these things go. You take one African, you take them all. That's what they'll say.'

'But why don't you try?'

Christianne looked at the note again. She was frowning.

'How much did you say?'

'Fourteen hundred dollars. About a thousand pounds in sterling.'

'And this is supposed to be Domingos's money?'

'His wages, I imagine.'

'Impossible.' Christianne shook her head. 'I know how much they paid him. Fifteen dollars a day, maybe. Good money in Angola but not this.' She picked up the wad of dollar bills, weighing it in her hand.

Molly was watching her carefully. So far, Christianne had packed no bags and time was running out. On the doorstep, just now, Molly had found a handwritten note from Peterson establishing a schedule for the evacuation. The plane was due mid-morning, a big Hercules from Luanda. Everyone was to report to the UN bunker at 09.30. Vehicles would leave for the airstrip fifteen minutes later in convoy, personal belongings only, no additional equipment. The list of instructions had gone on and on, detailed, precise, businesslike, an elaborate master plan covering every eventuality. Luanda were sending a second aircraft, one of the little Twin Otters. The Otter would remain airborne, circling the grass strip. If the rebels seized the Hercules, cutting off communications, the Otter would provide radio back-up, sending word to the coast. What might happen after that was unspecified but a final line from Peterson left Muengo's aid community in no doubt about their individual responsibilities. 'My job is to get you all out intact,' he'd written. 'One mistake, one miscalculation, could hazard the entire operation.'

Molly nodded at the money.

'Aren't you even going to try? With Peterson?'

Christianne shook her head.

'No.'

'Why not?'

Christianne stooped to retrieve Llewelyn's bowl. He'd been throwing up most of the night and the smell still hung in the airless room.

'I can't,' she said. 'There's no time. I have to find a stretcher for this man. Pack his bags. Get him ready.'

'There are stretchers at the schoolhouse,' Molly said quickly. 'I've seen them.'

'Of course. But they have no vehicles, no transport.'

'Why not?'

'McFaul took it.'

Molly stared at her.

'How do you know?'

Christianne turned away, refusing to answer. Molly caught her up in the garden. She was standing beside a dying rosebush, emptying Llewelyn's bowl.

'What happened?' she asked. 'Why did he go?'

Christianne shook the last drips from the bowl, then began to scour it with a handful of grass. In the sun, it was already hot.

'You must know,' Molly repeated. 'You must know why he went.'

Christianne said nothing. When the bowl was clean she threw the grass away and wiped her hands on her jeans.

'I think it was Domingos,' she said at last. 'He loved that man, the family, everything. He told me so.'

'But Domingos is dead.'

'Exactly.'

'So why should he go away? Why should he – ' Molly broke off, remembering something that Bennie had said the previous evening. It seemed that McFaul had got hold of a weapon, a rifle of some kind.

'Did he have a gun? Yesterday?'

Christianne seemed not to be listening. She began to walk back towards the house, stepping into the cool of the kitchen. Molly looked at her watch. It was nearly eight. The time for arguments had gone.

'We've got an hour and a half,' she said briskly. 'I'll get the stretcher. Bennie can help me. You get packed and ready.'

Christianne was standing beside the sink now. The taps were beginning to rust.

'I'm not going,' she said quietly. 'I'm staying here.'

Molly smiled, sympathetic, understanding. She admired courage. She applauded independence. But seven days in Muengo had taught her a great deal about Africa. Staying behind, the one white woman left in town, was madness.

'Where?' she said. 'Where will you go? Who'll look after you? How will you cope when the rebels come?'

Christianne was halfway up the hall. Back in the bedroom, Molly watched her easing the dollar bills from Llewelyn's grasp. She put the question again, already looking for Christianne's cases. She remembered seeing them before. She thought they might be beside the wardrobe in the corner.

Christianne was shaking a thermometer. When the mercury had returned to normal, she slid it into Llewelyn's mouth.

'He'll need a hospital bed,' she said. 'You should get someone to talk to Luanda before you arrive.'

After the soldiers had searched McFaul, finding the little videocassette he'd buttoned into the pocket of his shirt, they pushed him back across the river. A line of waiting troops on the river bank watched curiously as McFaul splashed through the shallows towards them. The men behind him included the soldier with the broken teeth and McFaul had spent long enough in uniform to know what would happen next. With luck, they'd simply shoot him. The alternative could take far longer.

Out of the water, down by the camp, they marched him along the bank. Someone had thrown blankets over the bodies beside the torn remains of the dinghy. McFaul tried not to look at the carnage but when he paused for breath, trying to ease a searing pain in his leg, the soldiers kicked him onwards. Finally, beside an anthill, they pulled him to a halt. The men circled round, eyeing him the way you'd look at a good meal. The soldier with the broken teeth had taken his shirt off. Round his neck he wore a gold crucifix and McFaul fixed his eyes on it, knowing that was one of the ways you were supposed to cope. Shut your mind off, they always said. Concentrate on something real, something you can see. Prise away your mind from your body. Tell yourself it isn't hurting.

The first blows took him by surprise. They came from nowhere, a savage explosion of pain in his kidneys. McFaul gasped, his elbows still tied behind his back, and he began to fall forward, his legs giving way. The soldier with the broken teeth took a tiny step backwards, measuring his distance, and a second before the darkness came McFaul saw the boot rising to meet him, still dimpled with water from the river.

*

The unmarked Hercules made two low passes over Muengo before banking steeply beyond the river and side-slipping into the tiny strip. Molly watched it from the front of the Terra Sancta Land Rover, Bennie wedged in beside her. The pilot touched down, throwing the props into reverse, and the big plane shuddered to a halt in a cloud of dust.

Before it began to move again, taxiing back towards them, Peterson was out of the Land Rover, striding towards the semi-circle of army trucks. There were knots of UNITA troops waiting beside the trucks, and as the plane approached they turned their backs, covering their ears against the high-pitched whine of the turbo-props. The plane came to a stop for a second time, the pilot cutting the engines, and the UNITA soldiers signalled impatiently at the cockpit, wanting the landing ramp at the rear to be lowered. Katilo's price for the evacuation was a full consignment of supplies – food, fuel, alcohol, drugs – and Molly watched as the ramp finally came down and the soldiers clambered eagerly into the belly of the plane.

The men reappeared in seconds, bent double under huge sacks of rice. The army trucks bumped towards them across the grass, ribboned in black exhaust smoke. Bennie watched the men on the backs of the trucks sweating under the first sacks.

'Thieving bastards,' he muttered cheerfully.

Molly said nothing. She'd spent the last half-hour telling Peterson about Christianne. They had to go back and find her. There was no alternative. Alone in Muengo, she simply wouldn't survive. Peterson had agreed, cursing the girl's selfishness, and Molly had sensed that he somehow took her decision personally. He'd pledged to get Muengo's aid community safely back to Luanda. His commitment to the evacuation was total. Christianne's determination to stay was the purest folly. By choosing to remain behind, she'd wrecked his plans.

Robbie Cunningham had joined Peterson now. Together, they were talking to one of the aircrew. The man was looking at his watch and Molly saw Robbie shrugging. Work at the back of the plane had slowed. A couple of the soldiers were levering the tops from a line of wooden boxes, and others were on their hands and knees beside the truck, investigating the contents of the boxes. Robbie went over to them, trying to start a conversation, but the soldiers ignored him and after a while he gave up. These were the guys in charge. Arguments could end with a bullet.

Bennie was rolling a cigarette. Before he'd left he'd given Christianne the key to the schoolhouse. She was to help herself to anything she wanted. The stuff was hers for the asking. Molly had thought of asking him what a twenty-nine-year-old French nurse would do with several tons of de-mining equipment but in the end she hadn't bothered. Bennie's world had narrowed to the prospect of a pint or two in his Aldershot local. What happened to anyone else no longer mattered.

Molly shuddered, thinking of McFaul again, where he might have got to, what could possibly have happened. He was a strange man, stranger than anyone else she'd ever met. There was a silence about him, a deadness, that unnerved her. Yet listening to Bennie's stories, trying to imagine the life he'd led, she could understand only too well the scars he must be carrying. Not simply flesh and blood – his face, his legs – but inside, too.

Bennie began to laugh. A woman from the city was running across the airstrip. She had a child under each arm. They were stick-thin, their spindly legs trailing behind them. The aircrew were still deep in conversation with Peterson. The men turned to stare at her.

'What's she doing?'

'She wants them to take the kids to Luanda. Fuck knows how she got past the road-block.'

Molly nodded. A line of rebel soldiers guarded the road to the airstrip. When the convoy had passed through, there were already dozens of women at the roadside, squatting in the dirt, surrounded by children. At the time Molly had wondered what they were after. Now she knew. Any escape route. Anything to spare the kids the days and nights to come.

'What happens to them in Luanda?'

'They beg. Like every other fucker.'

'No parents? No relations?'

'Bugger all. Literally. Poor little sods.'

Molly nodded again, pursuing the conversation no further. Talking to Bennie was one of the most depressing experiences she'd ever had, a glimpse of what happened if you always assumed the worst. Inside, where it mattered, the man had caved in. She thought of McFaul again, and Christianne, and she smiled. Strength, she thought. And guts. And a refusal to go along with the rest of the world. Maybe the girl had been right to stay. Maybe Muengo was where anyone half-decent belonged. No matter what the cost. No matter what the consequences.

Peterson was signalling to one of the rebel soldiers. The woman and her kids were disappearing into the belly of the plane. The soldier nodded and sauntered after them. Seconds later, he was driving them back down the ramp, the woman flailing at him with her fists. Molly could hear her screaming, rage not pain, and she got out of the Land Rover, determined to do something about it.

Peterson met her halfway.

'They've been talking to the MSF people,' he said at once. 'On the radio.'

'Who have?'

'The aircrew. It seems Christianne has resigned.'

Molly stared at him. The woman with the two children was being marched back to the road-block at gunpoint. The soldiers involved were laughing.

'Resigned? When?'

'Yesterday. Through the Red Cross circuit.' He paused, frowning. 'Extraordinary no one mentioned it. I might have been able to change her mind.'

Molly was still watching the woman with the two kids. One of the soldiers was prodding her with his rifle, making her run. The kids were crying.

'I doubt it,' she said quietly.

McFaul was barely conscious when he heard the Hercules. Sprawled in the dirt, he tried to look up, shielding his eyes from the sun, waiting for the pain to resolve itself. For the moment, everything hurt. His hands began to explore his face, his fingers swollen and bruised where he'd tried to protect himself. The blood on his face had scabbed in the hot sun and when he tried to swallow, his tongue snagged jagged fragments of teeth, debris from the beating. The plane was louder now, almost overhead, and he lifted a limp arm, not knowing quite why. For a split-second, he felt a shadow pass then the whine of the turbo-props began to recede, and he lay still again, resigned to the heat and the pain. Ants, he thought vaguely. Everywhere.

BOOK THREE

Durability

Durability in a mine, comprising longevity and toughness, is a vital design objective. The mine must, above all, be waterproof to repel ground moisture, rain, dew, and snow. In alternative, extreme climes it may have to withstand great heat, or icy cold too. Whatever may be envisaged, the mine must not disintegrate or collapse and has to remain intact to function at the right moment.

LT.-COL. C. E. E. SLOAN
Mine Warfare on Land

CHAPTER TEN

Molly Jordan sat at a table outside the Café Arcadia, waiting for Robbie Cunningham. It was dark now, nearly eight o'clock, and across the water she could see the lights of the *Ilha*, the spit of land that enfolded Luanda's lagoon. The *Ilha* was the playground for the city's rich and poor, good pickings for the legions of homeless kids, smart beachside cafés for the journalists, and mercenaries, and *empresarios* who fed off Angola's war. Molly had spent most of the afternoon there, listening to Larry Giddings's dry analysis of exactly where the country had gone wrong. The foreigners are the real problem, he'd told her. Charter a couple of 747s, ship them all out, and the *povo*, the people, could start to organise themselves a few surprises. Like peace. And clean water. And an inflation rate a little lower than 2,500 per cent a year.

Molly reached for her coffee. She'd been back in Luanda for a couple of days now, fending off enquiries from the embassy. She'd been met at the airport as the ambassador had promised, a friendly young second secretary in a rumpled white suit, and when she'd politely turned down the offer of a lift back to town he'd taken her to one side and given her the TAP ticket and explained that the flight would be leaving at noon next day. TAP, he said, had a reputation for punctuality. It would be as well to check in early.

Molly had slipped the ticket into her bag, thanking him for the trouble he'd taken, telling him that she'd decided to stay a little longer. There were matters she'd yet to attend to, loose ends she needed to tie up. When he pressed her for details, she'd declined to elaborate. She was, she pointed out, an independent woman. She had no deadlines to meet, no responsibilities to consider. Terra Sancta had guaranteed her board and lodging and what little money she had would doubtless see her through. The way she'd put it – firm, courteous, self-confident – had surprised her and when the young diplomat finally beat a retreat to the embassy Frontera parked in the sunshine outside, she'd felt an extraordinary sense of release. My life. My decisions. My future.

A waiter appeared and chased away the kids beside the pavement table. Robbie had warned her about the kids. Eating in the open air was a great idea but they'd be pestering you all night, offering to wash your car, or guard your moped, or help you finish the finger-shaped bread rolls that came with the steaming bowls of garlic-scented fish soup. Molly had been amused by the warning. Seven days in Muengo had revised her ideas about more or less everything, charity included, and she'd already distributed the scoops of rice abandoned on an adjoining table. Now, the waiter back inside the café, the kids were circling again. None of them looked older than nine. One had a paper plate balanced on his head. Another wore a long, heavy over-coat, several sizes too big. The rest were barefoot in ragged shorts and dirty T-shirts. One of the T-shirts sported a line of penguins, a motif Molly recognised from an old Mothercare catalogue, and through the tear beneath one armpit, Molly could count the child's ribs.

Robbie arrived minutes later, sinking wearily into the empty chair beside her and ordering a beer. Since their return from Muengo, he'd been working non-stop, trying to dam a flood of telexes chattering out of Terra Sancta headquarters in Win-chester. Evidently the charity faced a crisis of its own in Angola. Their response to the country's obvious needs had been judged inadequate. There was gossip amongst sister charities about poorly thought-out aid plans and lousy fieldwork, and employees spending half their days on the beach. The Angola operation was a fiasco and signing up to Todd Llewelyn's little project hadn't helped. Why on earth was a Third World charity funding television documentaries? Why was Terra Sancta more interested in screen time than fresh water and decent sanitation?

Robbie had done his best to shore up the charity's local defences but he was beginning to lose faith in the organisation's leadership, sensing that events in the UK were out of control. What made the situation especially awkward was the news that another British television crew were in town, a freelance unit headed by a woman called Alma Bradley. According to the Director fretting daily on the telex from Winchester, Ms Bradley might be contemplating a hatchet job on Terra Sancta. Robbie thought this unlikely but had spent most of the last twenty-four hours trying to find out. He knew Alma Bradley well, and he trusted her.

The waiter arrived with the beer. Molly settled for another coffee. Robbie lifted his glass and swallowed half the chilled Sagres in a single gulp. Then he reached inside his jacket and produced a thick fold of telex paper. He passed it across to Molly.

'This is for you. I just picked it up from the Press Centre. God knows why it went there.'

Molly flattened the telex on the table, alarmed already. Telexes meant bad news. They'd found Giles. They'd stored him in some mortuary or other. They wanted her to fly back and identify his body. She peered at the lines of smudgy text, recognising the name at the bottom of the message. The telex had came from Patrick Brogan, her solicitor back home, and as her eye returned to the head of the page, trying to make sense of the message, she found herself thinking back to the last time they'd met. Counting the days, it had only been a couple of weeks but the cluttered first-floor office on Frinton's main street already seemed a world away, part of some other life.

Molly looked up. Robbie was reading the front page of the *Jornal de Angola*.

'Good news?' he asked, not looking up.

Molly glanced at the telex again.

'Who's Vere Hallam?'

'Tory MP. One of the Thames Valley constituencies. Can't remember which.' Robbie folded the paper and pushed it away. 'Why?'

'It seems he's part of my husband's syndicate. At Lloyd's. Him and a couple of other MPs.'

'Oh?' Robbie was interested now, his hand outstretched for the telex. 'May I?'

Molly hesitated. Before they'd left the UK, she'd confided a little about Giles's problems at Lloyd's. At the time, she'd felt relieved to share the news and Robbie had been immediately sympathetic, explaining how the Lloyd's arrangements worked when syndicates went bust. The outlook, he'd said, wasn't quite as bleak as it might have seemed. They'd have the house to live in plus the right to hang on to a fair whack of whatever Giles might be able to earn. Now, though, it seemed the situation had changed.

Molly passed across the telex. Robbie read it, shaking his head in disbelief.

'Amazing,' he said at last.

'What is?'

'This.' He tapped the telex. 'Extraordinary.'

'Why?'

'That New Jersey firm you were telling me about. The arms lot. Some witnesses have come forward, ex-employees. They're suing the company for negligence. Some of them have developed tumours. The Lloyd's people think there may be grounds to contest liability on the pollution claim. So they've decided to fight.'

Molly retrieved the telex. The company in New Jersey was called Rossiter.

'So?' She looked up. 'What will that mean?'

'You're off the hook. For now, at least. No big claim. No immediate liability. No bankruptcy.' He grinned, recharging his glass with beer. 'And no need for three by-elections, either.'

'Why's that?'

'Your three MPs. If they're declared bankrupt, they have to resign their seats. Bit sticky at the moment. Given the state of the polls.'

Molly looked at him for a moment, uncertain. Patrick, in the telex, was talking about the prospect of lengthy litigation. At the end, he seemed as cheerful as Robbie. 'So it's good news at last,' he'd written. 'Fingers crossed for Giles.'

'Do we get to keep . . .' Molly hesitated, 'everything?'

'For now,' Robbie nodded, 'absolutely.'

'And later?'

'Depends on what happens in the US courts. I imagine it could get worse, legal costs, all that. But your people might win and then you wouldn't lose a bean. Who knows?'

Molly looked away. The kids were still there, faces in the darkness peering into the pool of light. The one with the over-coat had acquired half a loaf of bread and he was tearing it to pieces, passing bits round. Molly watched him a moment, remembering the mothers with their children the morning they'd left Muengo. Some of these kids would be refugees from the country, orphaned by the war. They'd have arrived at the airport aboard some returning aid flight and they'd have been left to fend for themselves. No parents. No possessions. Nowhere to lie their heads except the street. Molly watched them a moment longer, then folded the telex and slipped it into her bag, ashamed.

'Did you find your journalist friend?' she asked, changing the subject.

Robbie sipped at the beer.

'Yes. She was at the Press Centre. That's why I went.'

'And is she really a problem? Is she . . .' Molly shrugged, 'hostile?'

'Not so far. She wants to do a film about the diamonds.

She's trying to get to the north, to the mines, like everybody else.'

Robbie broke off, asking the waiter for a menu, then leaned forward across the table, picking up the story. Angola, he explained, was potentially rich. In the north, she had oil and diamonds. The oil paid for the government's share of the war, plus the fleets of new Mercedes that cruised between Luanda's ministries, while the diamonds funded Savimbi's UNITA army.

'They own the diamonds? UNITA?'

'They control the area where they're mined. Place called Cafunfo, up in Lunda Norte. Most of the gems go across the border into Zaire. The blokes earn a fortune.'

'Which blokes?'

'Miners. Smugglers. UNITA. The industry's controlled by De Beers. They pay the earth to keep the diamonds off the open market.'

Molly was looking at the kids again. One of them was on his hands and knees, picking up the bigger crumbs.

'How much?'

'Alma says five hundred million pounds. And that's just last year's figure.' Robbie laughed. 'It's a wonderful story if you can get at it.'

'So what's stopping her? Why's she still here? In Luanda?'

'She's waiting for a permit. The government control every-thing. An individual journalist might be able to sneak himself up north but she's got a proper camera crew, couple of blokes, lots of equipment. You know . . .' he grinned again, 'the real thing. Not Mickey Mouse. Like our absent friend.'

Molly nodded, knowing exactly what he meant. The last time she'd seen Todd Llewelyn was at the airport the day they'd flown in from Muengo. He'd been stretchered off the Hercules and driven into Luanda on the back of a flat-bed truck. As far as Molly knew, he'd be spending the week at the Americo Boavida hospital, but when Robbie had mentioned her TAP reservation, wondering whether Llewelyn might take her place on the Lisbon flight, she'd volunteered the ticket at once. Llewelyn's need, she'd insisted, was greater than hers. He belonged back in England, between crisp white sheets. They could make a fuss of him there. He'd be better in no time. It had fallen to Robbie to make the arrangements, and Llewelyn had left at noon next day aboard the big TAP jumbo. According to Robbie, he'd been less than grateful, insisting that his camcorder and his video rushes fly with him. Robbie hadn't a clue where to find either and had told him so, and before he'd left the plane at Luanda airport, he'd at last had an opportunity to settle one or two personal scores. The Portuguese steward in charge of the flight had accompanied him to the head of the aircraft steps.

'Senhor Llewelyn says he's a big television star.' The steward had looked quizzical. 'No?'

Robbie had smiled, stepping off the plane, shaking his head.

'Delirium,' he'd explained. 'He told me yesterday he was a brain surgeon.'

Now, Robbie was ordering a meal. Molly asked for fish. He chose a steak. The waiter chased off the kids again and then retired to the restaurant. Robbie leaned back, savouring the last of the beer, musing aloud about what might await Alma Bradley if she ever made it to the diamond mines. Apparently the place was completely lawless, a time warp, a glimpse of the way it must have been in the gold-rush days. Living conditions were primitive. Everyone carried a gun. Men died in arguments over cans of beer. Yet the lure of a fortune was always there, a handful of gems that could feed a man's family for the rest of his life. Robbie shook his head, musing aloud about the kind of film Alma wanted to put together. She was a class operator. She knew exactly what she wanted and she had an enormous talent for getting through doors that no one else could unlock.

'You think she'll talk them into it?'

'She might. She wants it badly enough.'

'How long has she been trying?'

'Here? In Luanda?' Robbie frowned. 'Too long. That's the

309

problem. You arrive with a crew and then you sit and wait for the ministry to make up its mind. Without a permit, you're stuffed. And every day's costing you money.'

'So what happens if they say no?'

'She'll look for another film. She'll have to. She has no option. And then . . .' Robbie ran his finger around the top of the open bottle, 'God only knows.'

'You think she might . . .' Molly shrugged, 'try your lot?'

'Sure,' he nodded, 'it's possible.' He paused. 'Or she could bid for a big political interview. Dos Santos, the president, even Savimbi if she could get hold of him, but it's not really her style. She likes getting in amongst the small print. That's what she's good at and that's what people like.' He sighed. 'We talked about Terra Sancta tonight. She'd heard the rumours. I told her it was bullshit.'

'Did she believe you?'

'No, but that doesn't matter. She doesn't believe anyone.'

'Does she know about Llewelyn? What we've been up to?'

'No. She'd heard some rumour about Llewelyn flying out to Africa but that's as far as it got. She said she didn't believe it. She said he'd never be able to cope.'

'She's right. He couldn't.'

Robbie nodded, visibly brightening, and picked up the empty bottle in a silent toast. Far away, Molly could hear the whump-whump of one of the big army helicopters, and the noise grew and grew until the machine appeared overhead, a fat black shadow hanging in the night sky. Searchlights on the nose criss-crossed on the water and the helicopter dipped low over the lagoon before turning away towards the distant glow of the docks. Robbie was watching it, his head tipped back, his body slumped in the chair, the smile gone.

The waiter appeared with the food. Molly reached for her knife and fork. Robbie hadn't moved.

'What's the matter?' she asked.

Robbie didn't reply for a moment. He looked suddenly exhausted.

'Muengo fell this afternoon,' he muttered. 'I meant to tell you.'

It was past midnight when the soldier came to look at McFaul. He was sitting on a dirty square of straw matting at the back of Katilo's cave, using his fingers to scrape the last of the corned beef from the open tin. The guns had been silent now since noon and in the darkness outside, the camp seemed empty. Even the generator had stopped.

The soldier stepped towards him. The beam of his torch lingered briefly on McFaul's face then circled slowly round the rough sandstone walls. Katilo was sprawled in an ancient arm-chair beside a makeshift table, light from a candle shadowing his face. He was watching the soldier carefully, and when the beam of the torch swung towards him he signalled the soldier to switch it off. The soldier muttered something McFaul didn't catch. Katilo dismissed him with a brusque nod, reaching out for the torch and then returning to the sheaf of maps on his lap. Without the generator, Katilo was unable to use the little CD player propped on a corner of the table. Neither could he amuse himself with the pile of videos at his elbow. For the latter, McFaul was profoundly grateful. While the video-player had been working, he'd been obliged to watch Domingos's agony again and again, an experience that was worse, in many respects, than the beating he'd taken at the hands of the soldiers.

Katilo was making notes on a map with the stub of a blue chinagraph. After a while, he looked up. Llewelyn's video was at the top of the pile of cassettes. He picked it up, weighing it in his hand. When he moved his head, the diamond in his ear twinkled in the candle-light. He gestured at the torch the soldier had used.

'He says you were the one.'

'The one what?'

'The one behind the camera. He says he saw you. He says you made the film.'

For a moment, McFaul was lost. For two days, obsessed by what he'd seen on Llewelyn's cassette, Katilo had wanted to know who'd been responsible for the pictures. He'd run them again and again, pausing to savour this detail or that. The moment when Domingos had stepped on the mine had especially fascinated him: the tiny, rich blossom of flame, the soil and the dirt blasting skywards, the torn fragments of clothing fluttering slowly back to earth. He'd run the sequence backwards and forwards on the video-player, watching the little Angolan disintegrate and then become whole again. At first, McFaul had put this down to sadism. Katilo was a psychopath. He enjoyed playing God, he revelled in dispensing disfigurement and sudden death, and the glories of Japanese technology gave him the chance to savour his handiwork.

After a while, though, it began to occur to McFaul that there might be some other explanation. Katilo, after all, was no fool. Much of his interest seemed genuinely technical. He wanted to know more about the way the material had been organised, why some sequences were in close-up, why certain actions had been shot again and again from different angles, what the final film might look like. Faced with these questions, McFaul had denied all responsibility. The pictures had been shot by someone else. His own job began and ended in the mine-fields. Katilo had ignored his denials, telling him there was no shame in pointing a camera at scenes like these, and now he looked immensely pleased with himself, satisfied that at last he had proof of McFaul's complicity.

'He saw you,' he repeated. 'He was on the front line. You were there on the road, with another man. He was talking to the camera. You made the pictures. He recognised your face.'

Katilo's hand had strayed to his chin and he tapped it a couple of times, making the point. Scars, he was saying. The scars prove it. You were the cameraman. You made the film.

McFaul had caught up now, finally understanding what he meant. Early on, back in Muengo, he'd driven Llewelyn out of town. The TV man had wanted to describe the way James Jordan had blown himself up. Llewelyn had posed against a likely stretch of bush and McFaul had been behind the camera, pressing the right buttons, making sure it looked OK. Llewelyn's version of what had happened had been a joke, wildly out of order, and McFaul had never touched the camera again. But Katilo didn't know that. As far as he was concerned, his soldiers behind the sandbags down the road, glued to their binoculars had identified McFaul as the cameraman. And that, it seemed, changed everything.

Katilo stirred.

'You told me you used to be a soldier.'

'It's true.'

'I know.' He tapped the cassette approvingly. 'Only a soldier could make these pictures. You have to be strong, a strong man. *Machismo*, no?'

McFaul was thinking of Llewelyn again. Only a soldier, he thought. Or some burned-out journalist, prepared to trade another man's life for a day or two back in the limelight.

Katilo was on his feet. In a recess beside the entrance to the cave, a blanket hid a portable fridge. With the gennie turned off, the ice in the freezer was fast melting but the fridge was still stacked with beer. Katilo pulled out two cans, tossing one across the cave towards McFaul. It bounced a couple of times on the hard rock floor and when McFaul tugged on the ring-pull he covered himself with foam. Katilo watched him, roaring with laughter, then selected another can, opening it himself and passing it across.

The beer was colder than McFaul expected. He took a mouthful, letting his head sink back against the damp sandstone, allowing the beer to trickle slowly down his throat. The worst of the pain from the beating had gone now, dulled by sleep, and for the first time he found himself contemplating the possibility of survival. Not by doing anything heroic but simply by going along with whatever fantasy role Katilo was planning to offer him.

313

The rebel commander was back in the armchair now, sitting sideways, his legs hanging over one arm. Half-warrior, half-child, he picked up the cassette again.

'Where's the camera?' he asked suddenly.

'I don't know.' McFaul shrugged. 'Back in Muengo.'

'We'll find it. Tomorrow.'

McFaul looked at him a moment, understanding now why the camp felt so deserted. Muengo had fallen. The trucks had left for the city. The gennie, too. McFaul took another mouthful of beer.

'OK,' he said.

'You've got more of these?' Katilo tapped the cassette. 'We can shoot some more pictures?'

'Sure.'

'In Muengo?'

'Wherever you like.'

Katilo fell silent, brooding, and McFaul looked at his plastic leg, propped against the table next to Katilo's armchair. The soldiers had unstrapped it after they'd dragged him back from the anthill. Evidently it saved them the chore of having to rope him up. Not that McFaul had been in any state to contemplate a bid for freedom.

Katilo was looking at the maps, still deep in thought.

'This film,' he said at last, 'you take it back to England?'

'Of course.'

'Where? Who wants it?'

'BBC.' McFaul shrugged, warming to his new role. 'ITV. Everyone.'

'They'll show it?'

'Yes.'

'You know that?'

'Yes.'

'How? How do you know it?'

McFaul thought about the question, trying to anticipate where the conversation might lead. Katilo held the rank of

314

Colonel. UNITA discipline was strict but rivalries between senior officers were intense. Taking Muengo would have done him no harm. Maybe he wanted to cash in. Maybe he wanted to become a major player. Maybe he even fancied stardom.

'Western television likes pictures like those,' McFaul said carefully. 'They're worth a lot of money.'

'You sell them?' Katilo was looking at the cassette. 'You can sell this?'

'Of course.'

'How much? How much money?'

'Thousands of dollars.'

'And they show it? On television?'

'Yes.'

Katilo nodded, impressed, and McFaul remembered a story he'd picked up in Luanda from an American diplomat. The man had been working in Liberia, a couple of thousand miles north, until the country had erupted in civil war. Rival armies had descended on the capital, capturing the president. Within hours they'd tortured him to death, cutting off his ears, hacking him to pieces, and a video of the proceedings had become Africa's hottest-selling item. At the time, new to the continent, McFaul had found the story hard to believe but now he knew it was probably true. Like Bosnia, and parts of the old Russian empire, Africa seemed to glory in slaughter. It was everywhere, utterly commonplace. It was the currency brokered by rival warlords. It went with the heat and the harsh, pitiless midday light. Blood, for so many, was how you measured respect.

Katilo stood up, returning to the fridge. Bottles of Glenfiddich lay side by side in a tray at the bottom. Katilo took one out, breaking the seal, and in that single action McFaul recognised the shape of the deal he was offering. First they'd talk about making a film. Then they'd get drunk. And by tomorrow, if he played his cards right, they'd be back in Muengo looking for Llewelyn's precious camcorder. The camcorder was the key to McFaul's survival. The pictures he'd shoot might even take him back to the UK. Katilo wanted to be famous and McFaul was the man he'd chosen to make it happen.

McFaul looked up. Katilo was standing over him, the bottle in one hand, a glass in the other. McFaul blinked. The big gold Rolex was inches from his face.

'You like Scotch?'

McFaul watched the pale single malt slipping into the glass. The decision was made already, negotiations over, the deal concluded.

'Sure,' McFaul muttered, 'why not?'

Robbie Cunningham stood at the open door of Molly's bedroom. Slanting bars of sunlight striped the wooden floor and the growl of Luanda's morning rush hour drifted in through the half-open shutters.

Molly peered up, rubbing the sleep from her eyes, surprised to find a cup and saucer on the chair beside her bed. Morning tea was a luxury in the Terra Sancta house.

Robbie was settling himself in the bedroom's only chair. He looked, if anything, shamefaced.

'I've got to meet a friend,' he murmured. 'Wondered if you might come along.'

They drove the half mile to the Meridian Hotel. The lobby was full of money-changers, energetic young men with bulging briefcases and battery-powered ultraviolet machines for checking foreign currency. Molly settled herself on a low sofa, watching the men parcelling out huge wads of red kwanza notes.

'Room 1440,' Robbie said, returning from the reception desk. 'She's invited us up.'

They took the lift to the fourteenth floor. The door was opened by a young Angolan, a man in his early twenties. The dressing gown was several sizes too small for him and there was a wisp of cotton wool on his chin where he'd nicked himself shaving.

Alma Bradley was sitting at a table by the window. She was

wearing jeans and a baggy white shirt and her shoulder-length hair was gathered at the back by a twist of scarlet ribbon. Hunched over a small portable typewriter, she barely looked up as Molly and Robbie stepped into the room.

'Manoel.' She gestured vaguely towards the Angolan. 'He's from the Press Centre.'

Manoel produced bottles of Coke from the mini-bar. Molly stood by the window looking out at the view. Across the city, on the hill behind the fort, she recognised the pale sandstone of the embassy building where she'd met the ambassador. At the foot of the hill, on the causeway that connected the *Ilha* to the city, she could see a knot of men in blue manning a road-block. Larry Giddings had pointed them out to her yesterday. They wore Ray-Bans and chunky bullet-proof waistcoats and seemed to be a law unto themselves. The locals called them Ninjas.

Robbie was sitting on the unmade bed, describing their week in Muengo. Alma Bradley was still typing, a cigarette burning in the ashtray beside her elbow. From time to time she'd raise an eyebrow, or mutter a question. Finally, she pulled the sheet of paper from the machine and handed it to the young Angolan. He took it into the bathroom and shut the door.

Molly was still standing by the window. Alma glanced up at her.

'Sorry about your son,' she said briskly, 'must have been awful.'

'It was.'

She nodded, turning to Robbie again. On the pillow by his knee was an open packet of dates.

'Help yourself. You say there are pictures?'

'Llewelyn shot pictures, certainly. Sony Hi-8.'

'Of what? Exactly?'

'I don't know. I never saw them.'

'Great. Nice pitch. Really whets a girl's appetite.'

Alma ground the unsmoked half of the cigarette into the ash-tray and stood up. She had a lovely figure, Molly thought. Willowy yet firm. She checked her watch then shouted something in French at the bathroom door. The door opened. Manoel was washing his hair. Robbie started to laugh and Alma rounded on him.

'What's the secret?' she demanded. 'How the fuck do you get anything done round here?'

Molly was still thinking about the tape. She knew exactly what was on it. Bennie had told her. Shot by shot. Twice.

'It's about James,' she murmured, 'and the minefields.'

Alma broke off.

'What is?'

'That videotape.'

Molly described the shots on Llewelyn's cassette. He'd gone back over the accident, telling the story as best he could. He'd shot on the street in Luanda. He'd taken pictures the day they'd landed at Muengo. He'd done stuff in the schoolhouse where the mine people lived. Then he'd taken Bennie and Domingos to one of the minefields. Something out of the window had caught Alma's attention and she was half-turned in her chair, staring down at the city below.

'Then Domingos got blown up,' Molly said quietly.

'Where was Llewelyn?'

'Filming it.'

'What?' Alma looked round. 'What did you say?'

'He was filming it. There. While it happened. It's all on the video.'

'Are you serious? Guy gets blown up? On camera?'

'Yes.'

'And you've seen it?'

'No,' Molly shook her head, 'but I know it's there.'

Alma nodded, one hand reaching for the pack of Marlboro beside her typewriter. She hadn't taken her eyes off Molly.

'What else is on this tape?'

Molly told her about the scenes at the hospital, the shots that had so disturbed McFaul, Domingos lying on the bloodstained table, a surgeon hacking off his leg. At McFaul's insistence, Bennie had seen it all and Molly repeated his description, word for word.

The cigarette hung between Alma's lips, unlit.

'Where is this cassette? Does Llewelyn have it?'

Robbie stirred.

'No, definitely not. He was raising hell about it before he left.'

'So where is it?'

Robbie and Molly exchanged glances. Then Robbie shrugged.

'To be honest, he and I didn't get on.'

'Who? You and who didn't get on?'

'Me and Llewelyn. There were a million better things to do in Muengo. As you might imagine.'

Alma smiled for the first time.

'Is this another pitch? You doing your Terra Sancta number? Only from what I'm hearing . . .' she shook her head, 'we have to find the cassette.'

She finally got round to lighting the cigarette, inhaling deeply. Molly was trying to remember her movements, those last couple of days in Muengo, when Christianne had been nursing Llewelyn at the MSF house. The night he'd come over from the UN bunker was the night McFaul had found the telex about Giles. The telex had been in Llewelyn's jacket. Llewelyn had been in bed, delirious with fever. McFaul had been across the other side of the bedroom, reviewing the video through the camcorder.

'He took it away,' she said at last. 'I'm sure he did.'

'Who took it?' Alma's voice was low now, intense.

'McFaul. He was very angry. He put the cassette in his pocket and I never saw it again.'

'So where did he go? This guy McFaul? Where is he now?'

Molly looked at Robbie. Robbie shrugged, reaching for another date.

'No one knows,' he said. 'He just disappeared.'

*

McFaul rode into Muengo on the back of a UNITA truck. Katilo loomed over him, his huge hands on the grab rail that ran above the back of the driver's cab, his feet braced against the constant jolting as the truck bounced and swayed along the rutted dirt road. On the outskirts of the city, UNITA troops were already dismantling their road-blocks, and the soldiers straightened and saluted as the truck ground past them. Katilo returned the salutes with the merest nod. From somewhere he'd found an old paratroop beret, and he wore it pulled low above his eyes. When he turned his head, inspecting shell damage by the roadside, McFaul could see the faint shape of the outspread wings where someone had unpicked the cap badge. The sight of the red beret made him think of Bennie, and as they swung into the road that led to the schoolhouse, he wondered what had happened to him. Days and nights in the cave had blurred the passage of time. He might be home by now, back in Aldershot, settling into the life he always said he missed so much. Trips to Tesco with the missus. Couple of pints with his mates in the evening. Treats for the kids at weekends. McFaul eyed what was left of the city – the fallen power cables snaking through the dust, the burned-out carcass of a bus, piles of rotting garbage at the roadside – and for the first time he understood a little of the appeal of Bennie's suburban idyll. Compared to this, Aldershot would be wonderful.

The truck bumped to a halt beside the schoolhouse. Katilo travelled everywhere with a posse of bodyguards, four uniformed soldiers with a taste for Ray-Bans and yellow silk cravats. They vaulted over the tailgate and jogged towards the low brick building, peering in through the open windows, testing the locked doors.

Katilo watched them, deep in thought. So far, driving into town, there'd been no evidence of government troops or even local inhabitants. The streets had been empty, no sign of movement except for the rags of smoke still drifting across the city from fires caused by the recent bombardment. Earlier, before they'd left the camp by the river, Katilo had emphasised the importance of finding McFaul's camcorder. They'd be driving around the city for an hour or so. There'd be huge crowds, lots of cheering, maybe even rebel flags. He wanted the moment immortalised on video, a permanent record, evidence that UNITA had ended Muengo's long nightmare. The city was free. The communists had surrendered. At last the people could get on with their lives.

Listening to Katilo, McFaul had wondered exactly how much of this drivel he'd really believed. Both sides in the war were in the business of self-deception, proclaiming their patriotism and their popularity, but anyone working amongst the Angolans knew the truth: that the *povo*, the people, were sick of the bloodshed and the endless battles for local advantage. The war had long ago ceased to be about a cause or a creed. This wasn't communism against the free market, or East against West. It was a handful of warlords, men like Katilo, determined to bend whole cities to their will and grab what they could in the process.

Gangsters in uniform, thought McFaul, watching Katilo adjusting his new beret before joining the bodyguards. One of them had shot out the lock on the front door of the schoolhouse. Now, Katilo reached up from the roadside, helping McFaul climb down from the truck, gesturing impatiently towards the splintered woodwork. He was to go inside the schoolhouse. He was to find the camera.

McFaul limped across the beaten patch of red earth, still patterned with the tread marks of the Global Land Rover. Inside, the schoolhouse smelled foul. There were fresh animal droppings on the floor and someone – presumably Bennie – had scrawled a cheerful adieu across the blackboard. 'WELCOME TO MINESVILLE,' the message read, 'BEST FOOT FORWARD.'

McFaul went through to the dormitory. His own possessions were still in the kitbag at the foot of the bed but of the camcorder there was no sign. He'd left it on top of the kitbag. He was sure he had. He frowned, bending to retrieve a small black hair clasp from a fold of blanket beside the pillow. He turned it over in his hand. The clasp belonged to the Englishwoman, Molly Jordan. She'd been wearing it the morning she'd come across to the schoolhouse, the morning Bennie had obliged her with the news of what had really happened to her son. He'd seen it when she'd been sitting at the table. McFaul looked across the room at Bennie's bed a moment, wondering what had happened. The wall above the bed was still studded with tiny pellets of Blu-Tack but the photos of his wife and kids had gone.

McFaul shrugged. In the schoolroom next door he found Katilo studying a hand-drawn map of one of Muengo's minefields, still pinned to the big easel Bennie and McFaul had used for training sessions. The shape of the minefield was outlined in green Pentel and small red crosses indicated the location of each lifted mine.

Katilo was counting the crosses on the top map. There were seventeen. He saw McFaul in the open doorway.

'We blew them up,' McFaul said drily. 'In case you were thinking of using them again.'

Katilo reached out for the easel. Under the top map there were half a dozen others. Some of the minefields were fully cleared. The rest had yet to be declared safe. He studied the bottom map for a moment or two then let the rest flick slowly through his fingers. The man's got a problem, thought McFaul. He's been chucking mines around for so long he can't remember which bits of his nice new city are OK, and which bits are lethal. As long as he was outside Muengo, tightening the noose, none of that mattered. Now, though, it was different. If he was to keep the people alive, he needed access to the fields and the river but access to both was barred by mines. Katilo's perfect soldiers had changed sides. Soon, poor fool, he'd want them disarmed and back in their boxes.

Katilo glanced over his shoulder.

'Where's the camera?'

'I don't know.'

'You said it would be here.'

'It's gone.' McFaul shrugged. 'We could try somewhere else.'

They drove to the MSF house. A shell had fallen forty metres up the street, stripping one side of a tree of its branches. The blast had also shattered the windows of the house. When McFaul got no reply at the front door he began to knock the remaining shards from the nearest window frame. He was about to try and climb in, using his good leg to lever his body into the room, when Katilo pulled him out of the way. He'd been watching from the truck. He studied the front door, stepped back, then planted a heavy kick at the panel beside the lock. The wood gave way at once and he felt inside, releasing the lock.

McFaul went straight to Christianne's bedroom. The last time he'd seen Todd Llewelyn, the TV man had been prostrate here, flattened by malaria. In all likelihood, they'd flown him out on the Hercules but there was a chance, McFaul thought, that they might have reclaimed the camera from the school-house, and then left it behind in this room of Christianne's. McFaul began to search. To his surprise, Christianne's clothes were still hanging in the tiny wardrobe. He went to the bed, pulling back the single blanket. The sheet beneath was cold to the touch. McFaul frowned, picking up the pillow. Beneath, double-wrapped in polythene, he recognised the shape of the video-cassettes that fitted Llewelyn's camcorder. With the cassettes were a handful of spare batteries and a couple of leads. Katilo was looking at them too. For the first time, he was smiling.

McFaul gestured at the cassettes.

'Still no camera,' he said.

Katilo's smile faded. He went to the window and shouted orders at the men in the truck. They ran down the path to the front door and McFaul heard the splintering of wood and smashing of glass as they began to move from room to room, tearing the house to pieces. After half an hour, they hadn't found the camera. Katilo was standing in the wreckage of the kitchen, examining a pile of underwear in the sink. He picked up a pair of briefs, black lace, holding them between his finger and his thumb. His men watched him, following every movement.

'No camera?' he said softly.

McFaul shook his head, remembering the party Christianne had thrown, this same kitchen alive with the sound of laughter, and music, and the clink of glasses. Christianne had told him then that she wouldn't be joining the evacuation flight. At the time he hadn't believed her, blaming the booze, but a week later she'd evidently been as good as her word. Everywhere, amongst the debris, was the evidence that she hadn't left with the rest of the aid community: more clothing, books, shoes, make-up, even an envelope of photographs. The photos had been strewn across the greasy kitchen table and Katilo had already been through them, recognising Christianne at once from the afternoon she'd spent with McFaul at rebel head-quarters. Many of the photos had been taken on weekend expeditions upriver, and a couple featured Christianne standing topless in the muddy brown water. She had a beautiful body, big breasts, nice shoulders, her skin lightly tanned, her head slightly tilted and her face framed by falling ringlets of auburn hair. Katilo had lingered on the shot for a long time, Christianne's smile telling him everything he needed to know. He'd thrust the photo at McFaul.

'She had a boyfriend?'

'Yes.'

'English? Like you?'

'Yes.'

'But younger,' he'd laughed, showing the pose to his men, 'eh?' McFaul had nodded.

'And dead,' he'd said, turning away in disgust.

Now, they left the house. The bodyguards had looted as

much as they could carry, armfuls of trophies, and they tossed the booty into the back of the truck, awaiting Katilo's next orders. Katilo was looking at his watch. It was late morning, normally the busiest time of the day in Muengo, but still the streets were empty.

Katilo looked down at McFaul. Both men were sweating now, the sun hot.

'You think it went on the plane? The camera?'

McFaul looked away, back towards the house. Christianne would return here, and when that happened the soldiers would find her. Their blood was up. He'd seen it in their faces, looking at the photos on the table, pulling open drawers, sorting through her clothes, sniffing the tiny phials of perfume she kept in a carved wooden box on the dressing table. In the hands of these men, Christianne would be helpless. Afterwards, if she was lucky, they might kill her. Otherwise, they'd just do it again, or sluice her down and pass her round the rest of the army. Little something to amuse the troops. Little present from a grateful commander.

Katilo was still waiting for an answer. McFaul told him there was one other place they should look.

'Where?'

'I'll show you.'

The drive across the city took them past the ruins of the cathedral. One end of the roof had taken a direct hit and the road beneath was littered with broken terracotta tiles. The walls were pock-marked with shrapnel damage and a plaster saint in an alcove overlooking the plaza was newly headless.

The soldier behind the wheel was driving fast, enjoying himself, weaving the truck from kerb to kerb, avoiding the bigger chunks of masonry. On the other side of the city were the streets of tiny bungalows built by the Portuguese decades ago for the clerks and engineers they'd shipped in from the coast. Domingos had lived there and so, still, did his brother, Elias. McFaul had been to Elias's place a couple of times with

Domingos, and now he took the driver around the grid of streets, looking for landmarks he might recognise. Towards the end of the second circuit, the driver was getting visibly anxious. Katilo gave orders only once. Unless you obeyed, unless you did his bidding, the consequences could be painful. So where did this friend of McFaul's live?

McFaul shrugged. An old man had appeared in the road up ahead. He was standing beside the remains of a tree. The driver slowed the truck, then stopped.

'Elias.' McFaul said. 'Ask him for Elias.'

The driver spoke to the old man in Ovimbundu. The old man lifted a wizened finger, indicating a turning fifty metres away. The driver gunned the engine, and the old man disappeared in a cloud of dust. The turning took them into another road. The driver began to count the bungalows. At the fifth, he stopped. A dog lay sprawled in the road, its torn throat black with flies, and McFaul took a deep breath, knowing that time was running out. The driver was right. Katilo had no patience. If Christianne wasn't there, they'd both be in deep trouble. The only card he had to play was the camcorder. Without the means to put Katilo onto videotape, McFaul was worthless. Even his de-mining skills Katilo would probably discard.

He got out of the truck, crossing the road. He recognised the bungalow now, the stand of orchids beside the gate, the peeling blue paint on the shuttered windows. McFaul paused in the shade of the veranda. A lizard watched him for a moment then darted into cover. McFaul knocked twice on the front door, waiting for a response. Nothing happened. He heard the tailgate of the truck clatter down, then the stamp of boots in the dust. It was suddenly very hot. He knocked again. This time he thought he heard movement inside the house, and a child's voice, quickly silenced. He knocked a third time, calling Christianne's name. The bodyguards were at the gate, watching him. At last there were footsteps inside. The door opened an inch. McFaul recognised Elias. Like Domingos, he had far too many teeth.

'Christianne?' McFaul said.

The Angolan had seen the soldiers at the gate. He looked terrified. He shook his head.

'No.' He shook his head. 'Go away.'

'Please . . . is she here?'

'No.' Elias began to shut the door but McFaul put his foot against the jamb. He'd seen movement in the gloom beyond Elias. He'd seen a face. The face was white.

'Christianne?'

He pushed inside, not waiting for an answer, pulling the door shut behind him. There was a strong smell of blocked sewers, laced with disinfectant. At the end of the tiny hall, Christianne was nursing a baby. She stared at McFaul, at last recognising the face, and McFaul realised that he hadn't been near a mirror for days, not since the beating. He must look awful, the bruises beginning to yellow, his face still swollen beneath the heavy stubble. Christianne was whispering to somebody in another room. Celestina appeared, taking the baby, her face averted. She stepped aside and Christianne's arms were suddenly round McFaul, hugging him. Elias was at the window now, peering through the shutters. The soldiers were coming. Two of them. Three of them. Four.

Christianne led McFaul into another room. It was even darker in here and McFaul felt his legs giving way beneath him. He reached out, his hand finding the edge of a table, and for a moment he caught his balance. Then it went again and he crashed to the floor, his head snapping back against the cold tiles. Conscious again, seconds later, he could hear the soldiers beating at the door. Somewhere close, a child was crying. McFaul struggled upright. Christianne appeared from another room. She had something in her hand.

'What are you doing?'

She paused a moment.

'I'll stop them,' she said. 'I'll give them this. Then they'll go away. Leave us alone.' She made a quick, impatient gesture with her hand.

'What is it?'

'A movie camera. I found it at the schoolhouse. Bennie gave me the key.'

McFaul stared at her then lay back, helpless with laughter. He heard Christianne at the front door, shouting at the soldiers in French. He got to his feet, one hand nursing the back of his head. He could feel the swelling already and when he took his hand away, his fingers were sticky with blood. Katilo parted the knot of soldiers at the front door. They were already admiring the camcorder, passing it round. Katilo retrieved it and gave it to McFaul. Time was short. He needed shots of himself entering Muengo. They were to return to the airstrip, organise a column of vehicles, tour the city all over again. He wanted shots from the side of the road, shots from on board, shots of his face. He'd seen what McFaul had done with Domingos in the minefields, the care he'd taken, all the pictures he'd recorded before the little man had triggered the mine. He wanted the same attention, the same treatment, nothing less.

McFaul nodded, reaching for Christianne's hand.

'She comes too.'

Katilo hesitated a moment. Christianne was wearing a tight Terra Sancta T-shirt and his men couldn't take their eyes off it. Finally, Katilo shrugged.

'OK,' he grunted, eyeing Christianne's hand, scarlet now with McFaul's blood.

Molly Jordan had never been to Larry Giddings's apartment. The suggestion had been his. Since her return to Luanda from Muengo they'd met twice, once for an afternoon on the *Ilha* and once for a brief drink at a café on the Avenida Marginale, across from the pink stucco of the Banco Naçional. On both occasions, for reasons she didn't fully understand, Molly had felt completely at ease in the American's company. She liked the softness of his voice and the way he never pushed himself at her. She liked the gentle amusement he seemed to derive from life and the way he refused to take either Angola or himself too seriously. And she liked, especially, the knack he had of making her feel wanted, someone worth listening to, someone whose experience, so different to his own, was of genuine interest. All too often, back home, she felt caged by her sex, and her appearance, and by the fact that she was so obviously middle class. Out here, with Giddings, none of that seemed to matter.

The apartment was on the third floor of a modern block off the Rua Abdul Nasser near the UN office. There were guards on the door at street level and both the lifts were broken. Giddings shepherded her up six flights of stairs, pausing on the landing outside his door to find his key. For a big man, in late middle age, he was remarkably fit.

The door finally opened and Giddings stepped aside, inviting Molly in. The apartment was tiny, a sitting room with a small balcony, a galley kitchen, a narrow bedroom, and a curtained cubby-hole at the end of the hall that contained a shower, a hand-basin, and a toilet. Giddings completed the tour and they returned to the sitting room. One wall was dominated by a poster for an Edward Hopper exhibition at the Guggenheim in New York, and on the sideboard below was a neat semi-circle of portrait photos, identically framed. There were four of them, kids no older than seven or eight. They were all black and Molly found herself gazing at them, surprised. Giddings looked too old to have children so young.

Giddings smiled at her, anticipating the question.

'Adopted them all,' he said. 'Took them all home with me, coupla years back. Surprised the hell out of Rose.'

Molly found herself grinning. Rose was Giddings's wife. He had photos of her, too. He carried them in his wallet, an ample, handsome woman with a face like an opera singer. His evident infatuation with her was one of the reasons she felt so much at ease.

'Your kids came from here? They're Angolan?'

'Sure. One's from Luanda. City kid. The rest come from up-country.'

'And you just met them?' Molly shrugged. 'Made friends?'

'No better way. The kids here are knock-out. It's one of the reasons you know things will get better. There's begging, sure. Kids got no choice. But you ever see the way they share stuff out? Can you imagine that? Back where I come from? The land of plenty?'

He beamed at the row of little faces on the sideboard and Molly thought of the meal she'd shared with Robbie at the Arcadia, the eyes in the darkness beyond the light. At the end of the meal, while Robbie was paying the bill, she'd emptied her purse of small change and given it to the oldest and she could still see him solemnly dividing the money between them. Giddings was right. White kids weren't like that at all. Too much money. Too much to lose. Funny, she thought, how wealth breeds selfishness.

Giddings was making coffee. Molly sat at the small circular table, inspecting his collection of CDs. They occupied a shelf beside her head, a long list of jazz titles, names she'd never heard of.

'You like the saxophone?'

He was back already, balancing a tray and closing the door to the kitchen with his foot. There was a bottle of Jack Daniel's on the tray and he splashed generous measures into two glasses without checking whether she liked bourbon. The smell of fresh coffee from the cafetière filled the room.

Giddings leaned over, selecting a CD, slipping the disc into the player on the shelf below. Molly recognised the soft, rich wail of a saxophone. The theme was vaguely familiar and she thought at once of James. He'd gone through a phase when he'd listen to nothing but jazz, haunting a club in Colchester, returning at three in the morning with plans to buy his own instrument. She wasn't sure but she thought the saxophone was what he had in mind, and she told Giddings how he'd saved up for months, finally blowing the money on a very old motor bike.

Giddings smiled, his feet tapping to a burst of wild drumming. Then he raised his glass.

'To James,' he murmured. 'Safe journey.'

They talked all afternoon. By nightfall most of the bourbon had gone. Molly sat in a low chair, out on the balcony, watching the sky crimson in the west. The sun was low now, fattening by the minute, flooding the ocean with colour, and the air was still warm, tainted by the smell of prawn heads and cheap petrol.

Giddings had changed into a T-shirt and a pair of baggy jeans. He sat on the concrete floor of the balcony with his back against the French windows, nursing the last of the bourbon. Molly had finished telling him about Giles. The news from Lloyd's about their financial affairs, she said, didn't matter one way or another. Given the choice, she'd gladly trade solvency for her husband's safe return.

Giddings held up his glass, squinting at the sunset through the pale liquid.

'You wanna talk to this guy?'

'Who?'

'This Patrick guy? The one you mentioned? The attorney? Only there ain't a problem. You got the number there?'

Giddings disappeared into the sitting room and returned with a telephone. Molly looked at it. She'd been trying to phone England since her return from Muengo but she'd never got past the operator. International lines were always busy. Even Alma Bradley, it turned out, did everything by telex.

Giddings was offering her the phone.

'Go ahead,' he said. 'Just do it.' Molly began to explain about her earlier attempts but he waved her protests aside. 'Just do it,' he said. 'It's a satellite phone. No big deal. Just go right ahead. Trust me. You got the country prefix? Know the number?'

Molly nodded, fingering the touch pad. She'd no idea why a satellite telephone should be so special but if the call got through she didn't much care. Faintly, she heard a series of clicks. Then the number began to ring. She blinked, sitting upright in the chair, suddenly aware of how much she'd drunk. Patrick, she thought. Probably minutes away from leaving the office. And now me to cope with.

The number answered and Molly recognised the plummy tones of the receptionist. The woman was explaining why Patrick was busy. Molly cut in.

'It's Mrs Jordan,' she said. 'Just put me through.'

The line went dead for a full minute and Molly was about to hang up when she heard Patrick's voice, a gentle enquiry, no surprise, no drama, utterly characteristic.

'Molly? Is that you?'

Molly blinked again, Luanda a blur. She looked around, wiping her eyes with the back of her hand. Giddings had disappeared.

'Me,' she agreed, sniffing. 'Sorry about this.'

'Sorry about what?'

'Nothing.'

She closed her eyes a moment and counted to five, determined to get things in the right order. Patrick was telling her how anxious everyone had been. Angola sounded a million miles away. Most people he talked to hadn't a clue where it was.

'It's nice,' Molly heard herself saying. 'A nice place.'

'Good, good. So how are you?'

The conversation went on, Molly marvelling at how easy it was to slip into small talk. Her son was dead. Her husband was missing. And here she was, asking Patrick about Alice. Was she well? Was she still playing golf?

'It's nearly Christmas,' Patrick was roaring with laughter, 'bit chilly for golf.'

The laughter subsided. There was a silence. Molly focused on a crack in the concrete, summoning the courage to ask about

Giles. Was there any news? Had the search been called off? Might there be . . .?

Patrick cut in.

'The search was called off four days ago,' he said gently, 'and I'm afraid the signs aren't good.'

'Why? What's happened?'

Molly felt the chair moving beneath her, then realised it was her body swaying back and forth. Patrick's tone of voice. Bad news. Definitely.

'Tell me, Patrick,' she said. 'Just tell me.'

'Fishermen have turned up some bits and pieces. French chaps, day before yesterday.' He paused. 'They took them into Boulogne.'

'What? Took what?'

'Some rigging. Some bits and pieces of hull.'

'*Molly? Molly Jay?*'

'I'm afraid so, yes.' He paused again. 'These are trawlermen, Molly. They were dragging the bottom. I'm very sorry.'

Molly nodded, gazing out at the ocean. The sun had nearly disappeared.

'So it's definite? She sank?'

'I'm afraid so.'

'And Giles? Did he . . .? Did the fishermen . . .?'

'No trace, I'm afraid. But . . . it's November, Molly. I've talked to the air/sea rescue people. They're saying an hour, maximum.'

'An hour what?'

'An hour in the water. After that . . . it's just too cold.'

'But he had one of those suits, those special things. I know, I saw it on board, before I came out here. It's orange. It made him look like the Michelin man. It was hanging in the—' She broke off, hearing Patrick's voice again, coaxing her towards the truth.

'An hour,' he was saying, 'even with a survival suit.'

Molly nodded, knowing he was right. This wasn't the tropics, the sea warmed to blood-heat, the kids skinny-dipping all day. This was the English Channel in the depths of winter, slate-grey, hostile, ice-cold. She shuddered, reaching for Giddings's glass, trying to remember the chart she'd seen in the cabin the afternoon she'd driven over to the marina. Giles had plotted a course south. It would have taken him through the Straits of Dover. Night, she thought. He must have been off-watch. He must have been hit by something. Something big. Something that had chopped his little boat in half and left him thrashing in the darkness, watching the lights recede, knowing that the game was up. Maybe he hadn't been wearing the suit at all. Maybe it had all been too sudden for that. She tried to swallow the bourbon but couldn't, letting it trickle back into the glass. Patrick was saying something about life insurance. Giles had been fully covered. The assessors had already been in touch. The absence of a body was a problem but he was doing his best to sort everything out.

Molly opened her mouth, trying to speak, but nothing happened. She half-turned, seeing a movement behind her in the sitting room, then Giddings was stepping onto the balcony. He was carrying a towel. He knelt beside her, mopping the tears. She clutched at the towel, burying her face in it, the phone abandoned. Giddings picked it up, muttering an explanation, promising to call back. Then Molly felt his hands pulling her gently up, and she let him take her inside, away from lengthening shadows on the balcony.

The bedroom was cool after the warmth of the sunset and Molly turned on her side, hearing the door close. She put the knuckle of her forefinger in her mouth and sucked it, something she hadn't done since childhood. The curtains were drawn over the window above her head. Grief and bourbon thickened the darkness and by the time Giddings returned, minutes later, she was asleep.

She woke up to a raging thirst. She tried to look at her watch. It was past midnight. She got out of bed, wondering where the cellular blanket had come from. Very gently, she opened the door to the sitting room. Giddings was curled on the sofa, his head pillowed on his arms. The light on the CD player was winking in the darkness and the doors to the balcony were still open, the night wind stirring the long net curtains. She retreated to the bedroom again, not wanting to wake him, and she'd resigned herself to the thirst when she saw the tumbler of water on the chair beside her bed. Propped against it was a packet of tablets and a scribbled note. 'Take two,' the note read. 'God bless.'

Molly reached for the water, ashamed already of the scene on the balcony. It was her responsibility to cope. That's what she'd been doing so well. That's what she'd have to do for the rest of her life. Breaking down like that was unforgivable. She didn't want sympathy. She didn't want people feeling sorry for her. She just wanted something strong, something positive, to come out of this whole ghastly experience. She swallowed a mouthful of the water, then another, then the rest of the glass. Stepping back towards the bed, she paused, hearing a noise in the street below. It sounded familiar but for a moment she couldn't quite place it.

She went to the open window, pulling back the curtain, leaning out. A young man was hurrying away up the hill, his shoulders hunched over the wooden crutches, the stump of his left leg hanging from his shorts. The sound of the crutches echoed up from the surrounding buildings and Molly could still hear him as she slipped between the sheets. Tap-tap, the young man went, tap-tap.

CHAPTER ELEVEN

The rains returned past midnight, curtaining the schoolhouse from the dim silhouettes of the nearby buildings. McFaul lay beneath a blanket on his camp-bed, savouring the smells of the newly dampened earth, listening to the drumbeat of the rain on the metal body of the army truck parked outside. The cordon of armed sentries around the schoolhouse had been Katilo's idea, a public confirmation of McFaul's importance. There were half a dozen soldiers in all and McFaul pictured them now, huddled beneath the dripping eaves, looking for protection from the downpour.

Across the room, Christianne lay asleep in Bennie's bed. McFaul could see the shape of her body beneath the single sheet. Her face was turned towards the wall, her knees drawn up to her chest, and from time to time she gave a tiny cry, almost a gasp, as if someone had touched her.

Katilo had kept his promise, allowing her to come along on the filming, and she'd helped McFaul as best she could but by the end of the day she'd been exhausted. Katilo's agreement that they both return to the schoolhouse, safe behind a ring of armed troops, had been a godsend. He'd given them a boxful of army rations, supplies delivered by the incoming Hercules, and after plates of tinned sardines and rice they'd retired to bed.

McFaul smiled in the darkness. While Christianne slept, he'd reviewed his afternoon's work, replaying the video footage through the camcorder. For an amateur, he thought, he hadn't done badly. A device inside the camera kept everything in focus and some of the angles he'd used did ample justice to the image he knew Katilo wanted to portray. Katilo's soldiers had driven some of the locals out of their homes and the modest cavalcade had paraded around and around a grid of shell-pocked streets while Katilo formally took possession of the conquered city. The locals, under orders to cheer, had answered his regal wave with a display of wary enthusiasm and McFaul had done his best with the faces at the roadside. Some of them he even recognised, women and children who'd attended his lectures about the minefields, and he'd wondered quite what they made of his role in this strange masquerade. Did they think he'd been working for UNITA all along? Or would they simply shrug and turn away, blaming the insane logic of war? In his heart, McFaul knew it didn't matter. These people had far more important things to think about than the loyalties of a one-legged white man.

Across the room, Christianne had begun to stir. The rain, if anything, was heavier, sluicing noisily off the roof, puddling the earth beneath. Somewhere in the room McFaul could hear a steady drip-drip, then another, and he got up on one elbow, trying to locate the leaks. Several shells had landed nearby during the bombardment. He'd seen the craters only this afternoon and he knew the blast must have loosened the tiles on the roof. Christianne was awake now, sitting upright, holding the sheet to her chest. As she did so, the sound of the dripping quickened and she swore softly in French, her feet finding the wooden floor.

'You OK?'

'Wet,' she said. '*Merde*.'

She got out of bed, peering up at the ceiling. In the darkness she could see very little. McFaul watched her for a moment then got out of bed himself, pulling back the blanket.

'Here,' he said. 'I'll sleep on the floor.'

Christianne was already pushing the camp-bed towards the

middle of the room, trying to avoid another leak. The driest spot was a foot away from McFaul's pitch. She told him to get back into bed. Everything would be fine.

McFaul sank back and reached for the blanket, quietly relieved not to be spending another night trying to will himself to sleep. The damp from the cave seemed to have seeped into his bones. There wasn't anywhere in his body that didn't ache.

Christianne was back in bed now, her face close to McFaul's. She reached out, touching him, and McFaul felt himself tensing, immediately unnerved. The beating at the hands of Katilo's soldiers had affected him more than he cared to admit. Not the pain necessarily but his helplessness at the hands of others. There'd been nothing he could do, no way of fighting back. His sole option had been to submit and under the circumstances he suspected he'd been lucky to have lost consciousness so quickly. That way, at least, he was spared a little of the pain.

Christianne was whispering now, asking him how he felt. So far, he'd told her nothing about the last couple of days, checking only that she'd delivered the money to Celestina.

'Fine,' he said, 'I feel fine.'

'Your head?' Her fingers found the back of his scalp where he'd fallen at Elias's house. 'Still bruised?'

'It's nothing. It's OK.'

'And everywhere else? Tell me, I can help.'

Her fingers trailed briefly across McFaul's face, over his mouth and chin, then slipped down towards his chest and McFaul caught her hand, feeling hopelessly exposed. His body was a wreck, he knew it. Christianne was like a surprise visitor turning up at the front door when he hadn't cleaned or tidied for weeks. He was pleased to see her. He wanted to let her in. But he was ashamed of what she'd find, the state of the place, the extra bruises she might inflict by beating an embarrassed retreat. Some women were like that. They always expected everything to be perfect.

'Listen . . .' he began.

He could see her smiling at him in the darkness. The sleep must have done her good. She looked far from exhausted.

'You hated him, didn't you?' she said suddenly.

'Who?'

'James. He said you hated him.'

'He's wrong. I don't hate anyone. It's a waste of time, hating.'

She looked at him a moment, thoughtful, then she rolled sideways in the bed, propping her head on one elbow. She wore a crucifix around her neck and the thin gold chain looped down over the neck of her T-shirt.

'Katilo?' she said at last. 'Don't you hate Katilo?'

'He's different. I hate what he's done, what he's doing, but whether I hate him personally . . .?' McFaul thought about the question, not knowing the answer.

'You should. You should hate him. He's evil.'

'You think so?'

'I know it. I was there this afternoon. Remember?' She withdrew her hand, scratching her nose, then reached out again, the softest touch. 'I think James was jealous really. He admired what you did. He thought you were brave. I know he did. He told me so.'

'Then he should have listened,' McFaul said drily.

'I know. That's what I told him. But he wasn't like that. He didn't listen to anyone.' She paused. 'Do you listen to anyone?'

McFaul laughed, taken aback.

'What sort of question's that? Of course I listen.'

'Did you listen to your wife?'

'My wife?'

'Yes, did you listen to her? Were you close?'

McFaul stared at her. She'd never been less than candid. It was one of the reasons he'd always liked her, always enjoyed her company.

'I've had two wives,' he muttered, 'and I think I listened to both.'

'But were you close? Really close?'

'Obviously not.'

'No?'

'No.' He shook his head. 'At the beginning maybe but . . .' he shrugged, 'you grow apart.'

'Always?'

'For me?' He nodded. 'Yes.'

'Why? Why did you grow apart?'

McFaul lay back, turning his head away. He'd wrestled with this question for most of the last five years. He had a thousand answers, a thousand explanations, but none of them really hit the mark. He'd married his first wife far too early. He'd been too young, too trusting, too callow. That he knew for sure. But the rest of it?

He shook his head.

'Dunno,' he said. 'Can't say.'

'You have children?'

'No.'

'You wanted children?'

'Yes,' he nodded, 'definitely.'

'And your wife? Your first wife? She wanted children?'

'Sure. And we tried, believe me.'

'And your second wife?'

'She couldn't. She had . . .' he frowned, 'a problem.'

Christianne nodded, saying nothing, and McFaul peered up at the ceiling, remembering the letter Gill had shown him, that last week in the Falklands, before he'd finally left. As an eighteen-year-old, a decade earlier, she'd had a fall from a horse. Her broken pelvis had been set a week later in a Buenos Aires hospital. The letter from the Argentinian surgeon confirmed that her chances of successfully conceiving were probably slim. Not that she'd ever bothered to share the news.

McFaul closed his eyes. Another betrayal, he thought. Another home defeat.

'Marriage can be tricky,' he said at last. 'It's not as simple as it seems.'

'Did you ever think it would be?'

'Yes, once I did. But not now.'

'So who is it?'

'Who's what?'

'Who is it in your life? Who matters? Who do you write to? Who do you miss?'

'No one.'

'*No one?*'

'No, there's no one. I've got friends, sure, people I see from time to time, people I'm fond of. But not, you know ...' McFaul frowned, unable to find the right word. He looked across at Christianne. It was hard to be certain in the darkness but he thought he recognised the expression on her face. 'Don't pity me,' he said. 'I don't need that.'

Christianne shook her head at once.

'I don't pity you. It's not pity.'

'What then?'

She gazed at him for a long time before beckoning him closer. McFaul hesitated, uncertain, then he eased his body towards her. Her face was very close now, her lips slightly parted.

'You know how it is,' she whispered, 'with some men?'

McFaul shook his head.

'No.'

'They don't see in front of their noses. They don't see the obvious, what's really there. James didn't. You don't. And you know why? Because you don't look.'

She knelt upright on the camp-bed and pulled off her T-shirt. Then she leaned towards McFaul, reaching out, easing him gently towards her. McFaul found his face buried between her breasts. He moistened his lips, dancing his tongue across the sweet, firm flesh, finding the nipple. He sucked it gently, feeling it grow in his mouth, hearing her beginning to groan,

341

and he rolled across the intervening space, sliding off her knick-ers, fitting himself to her body, not caring any more about the scars he carried. She began to move beneath him, her hands on his buttocks, pulling him down. Then she stopped, her eyes half-closed, her hair splayed across the pillow.

'Don't be frightened,' she whispered.

'What does that mean?'

'Don't be frightened. I won't hurt you.'

McFaul began to protest but she kissed the tip of her finger and then sealed his lips. McFaul felt her legs parting beneath him, and a pressure on his shoulders as she guided him gently down her body until his tongue found the tight curls of pubic hair, already moist. She arched her back, bringing herself to meet him, and he lapped and lapped, tasting layer after layer of sweetness, hearing her tiny gasps, that noise again. She was open now, and swollen, and when she began to moan he levered himself upwards, entering her, moving very slowly. After a while, he felt the pressure again, her hands pressing him deeper, and he began to quicken, pumping harder, his eyes closed, the pain and the rage forgotten. She was crying out now, half French, half English, calling James's name, and then she bucked wildly, rigid with orgasm, and McFaul heard his own wild shout, glee-ful, abandoned, before he scalded her with a final thrust and collapsed face-down on her glistening body.

There was silence for a moment between them. Then the drumming of the rain returned, and the soft sound of laughter, outside in the wet darkness.

Molly Jordan sat in the window of Alma Bradley's hotel room, the interview finally over. Alma's cameraman, a taciturn young Scot called Keith, was checking the tapes on a small colour monitor, propped against one leg of the bed. Alma stood beside him, her eyes on the screen.

'There,' she said.

Keith stopped rewinding the tape. They'd just begun the interview again after a break. Molly was talking about Muengo, the impact the place had made on her after the madness of Luanda. The word she was using was 'shock'. She was shocked by the poverty. Shocked by what the war had done. Shocked, even, by the way the people managed to cope. Life in the UK would never be the same again, she said. Cancelled trains or the odd spot of vandalism didn't matter. Muengo did.

Alma was nodding. She rarely smiled.

'You were good,' she said. 'Bloody good.'

'So were you.'

'Yeah?'

Alma shrugged the compliment aside, her attention caught by the next passage in the interview, and Molly leaned back, gladdened by her own performance. With Alma Bradley it had been easy, a genuine conversation, woman to woman. Alma didn't lard her questions with Todd Llewelyn's brand of false sincerity. She didn't pretend to be personally involved. She wasn't after tears or confessions. On the contrary, she was simply curious to know the way it had been. Just tell me the story, she'd said at the start, and we'll take it from there. Molly had done just that, explaining about James's determination to work in Africa, about getting the news of his death, about deciding to fly over, and whenever she got to a bump in the road, a potentially sensitive detail, Alma had simply nodded, helping her over it, keen that the account shouldn't be disfigured by what she termed 'swampy moments'. The facts, she'd said at the end, always speak for themselves.

Now, Alma was deep in conversation with Robbie and Molly watched her, fascinated by how brisk she was, and how business-like. She never pretended emotion she didn't feel. She didn't play the games Llewelyn played. Robbie was explaining again how hard it would be to get into Muengo. The place was in UNITA hands. The government people in Luanda were hardly going to sanction an official visit.

'Then what do we do?'

'I don't know.'

'How did you get in?'

'Through a private deal. South African guy Llewelyn found. Big dollars. Do anything.'

'Where is this guy?'

'Don't know,' Robbie said again, 'but I'll find out.'

Alma nodded. They both knew how important it was to get back to Muengo. The film Robbie had proposed centred on Llewelyn's cassette. If the thing still existed then McFaul was the key to finding it. And the first place to start looking for McFaul was Muengo.

'What's he like? This McFaul?' Alma asked.

Robbie shrugged, looking across at Molly. His own dealings with McFaul had been minimal. Molly was still sitting by the window. This new film, as she understood it, was to concentrate on the minefields around Muengo. Amongst the many lives the minefields had taken were those of Domingos and James. Domingos was an Angolan, James was an outsider, but they'd both been trying to help. By telling their separate stories in graphic detail, Alma's film might just prick the conscience of the West. That's where most of the mines came from. That's where the real money was made. It was this angle that had persuaded Molly to go along with Robbie's proposal. A film like that, she thought, would be infinitely more worthwhile than Llewelyn's original idea. She was no longer interested in baring her soul. Her private grief would never again be public property.

Alma was still looking at her, still waiting for an answer to her question.

'McFaul knows it all,' Molly said quietly. 'He's the one you should really be talking to.'

'Great.' Alma looked exasperated. 'So where in God's name is this man?'

*

McFaul limped towards the cathedral, trying to keep up with Katilo. The idea for the sequence had been the rebel commander's. He'd arrived at the schoolhouse at daybreak. McFaul had been asleep beside Christianne, barely registering the stamp of boots across the wooden floor next door. Katilo had burst in, two bodyguards in tow, rousing McFaul with brisk prods from the swagger stick he'd taken to carrying. He'd been delighted with the shots McFaul had taped the previous day. He knew already that the film would be wonderful. Now it was time to try something a little more ambitious.

The square in front of the cathedral was filling up with people. Most of them were women and children, herded into the city centre by Katilo's soldiers. They jumped from the backs of army trucks, laden down with rolls of rush matting and the tiny handful of personal possessions they still had left to sell. Katilo moved amongst them, telling them where to lay their mats, explaining the way he wanted the place to look. It was market day. The city was enjoying a precarious peace. The people were buying and selling. For the moment, the war was over.

The people did his bidding, avoiding the cold eyes of the watching soldiers. When the last mat was unrolled, there were more than thirty pitches around the dusty square and on a further command from Katilo, one of the trucks began to rumble from pitch to pitch, the soldiers on the back heaving sacks of UN maize and rice to the waiting traders. McFaul watched the women opening the sacks, wide-eyed, scarcely believing their luck. Extras, he thought. Movie props for Katilo's march to stardom.

Katilo came striding back across the square. His shirt was tighter than usual, emphasising the massive shoulders and the heavy belly, and he waved an arm, telling McFaul to get pictures of the traders. There'd be more local people arriving any minute, lots of them. He wanted shots of buying and selling, of haggling, the market in full swing, the clearest evidence to any watching audience that life under UNITA was nothing to be afraid of.

McFaul nodded.

'And then?'

'And then, my friend, you film me.'

'Doing what?'

'Talking.'

Katilo grinned, offering no further explanation, stepping aside to cuff a soldier who'd dropped a sack of rice, spilling the white grains everywhere. McFaul did what he was told, waiting for the next trucks to arrive then moving slowly around the square picking up the kind of shots he thought Katilo could use. The women largely ignored him, squatting amongst the piles of UN supplies, bartering eagerly with the growing crowd of townspeople, and for the first time McFaul realised that the distribution of food was for real. The soldiers wouldn't be demanding this stuff back. On the contrary, the food would find its way into every corner of Muengo, and by this single act Katilo might well bump start the city's fragile economy.

The taping over, McFaul returned to Katilo. He was standing in the middle of the square, surrounded by his bodyguards, beaming at the crowds that had gathered. Head and shoulders above the swirl of bodies, he looked like a circus ringmaster, pleased with the day's attendance, eager now to get on with the show.

He took McFaul's arm, hauling him across the square. On the far side, away from the cathedral, he stopped. McFaul was to have the camera ready. When the time was right, he would walk through the crowd, across the square, and into the cathedral. There, he'd pray before the altar, giving thanks for the great miracle of his victory. For Catholic audiences all over the world, these would be fine pictures.

McFaul looked across towards the cathedral, wondering what he'd find inside. Shell damage had destroyed part of the roof and there'd be no problem with light but the aisle might be blocked with fallen debris. He began to suggest a recce, a preliminary look, but Katilo dismissed the idea. These things, like everything else in life, were best done at once. If God so willed it, it would happen. McFaul shrugged, unconvinced. The least he expected was someone to guide him backwards, carving a path through the crowd, and Katilo nodded at one of the bodyguards, issuing the appropriate order.

McFaul checked the cassette. There was still twenty minutes of tape left, ample time for the sequence. He put the camcorder to his eye, securing the strap around his hand, adjusting the framing to accommodate Katilo's upper body. In a normal film, McFaul suspected that this sort of material would be recorded within a formal interview, Katilo talking to someone off-camera, but the rebel commander had no time for the polite conventions of Western broadcasting. He knew exactly what he wanted to say and he wanted nobody between himself and the camera. The message, McFaul suspected, would be brutally direct.

McFaul glanced behind him, indicating that the waiting bodyguard should tug a corner of his shirt, physically guiding him backwards. Then he returned to Katilo, pressing the 'Record' button and waiting for the red light to appear in the viewfinder before raising his thumb.

Katilo frowned a moment, looking at someone in the crowd, then he looked down at the camera, beginning to move, describing his days and nights in the bush, waiting for the moment he could deliver Muengo from the godless hands of government troops. He had a strong, deep voice and he used it well, the way McFaul had read about in tabloid features on £100–a-day media training courses. Address the camera as if you were talking to a specific individual, someone you know, someone you want to stay friends with. Don't treat it like a public meeting. Don't shout. Don't go in for grand phrases. Keep it simple. Keep it intimate. Share a confidence or two. And look as if you mean it.

They were approaching the cathedral now, Katilo's huge hand flat against his chest. The night of the final bombardment had been a torment for him. So much violence. So much bloodshed. And all of it because the troops in the city refused to surrender. No commander enjoys slaughter, he confided. But no commander willingly wastes the lives of his own men. And so the big guns had spoken. And the walls of Muengo had finally tumbled down.

McFaul felt flagstones beneath his feet. The sunshine had disappeared. It was abruptly cooler. Katilo had stopped. He was looking up. The camcorder followed his tilted head, fighting to compensate for the sudden change in light. Dimly, in the background, a skein of rafters appeared. McFaul felt a tug on his shirt. Katilo was on the move again, the big eyes back on the lens of the camcorder. He'd come, at last, to make his own peace. Not the peace of the battlefield. Not the peace of the negotiating table. Not the peace that might one day be signed in Lusaka. But the other peace, the peace between himself and the Lord. Katilo paused again, grave. The Lord had spoken. And Muengo had returned to God's children.

Katilo nodded, then stepped past McFaul. McFaul panned round, keeping the huge body in shot, hearing the bodyguard behind him struggling to get out of the way. With the camcorder pointing towards the altar, McFaul watched – fascinated – as Katilo bowed before the altar, then crossed himself and knelt in prayer. The image was extraordinary. Katilo's passage down the aisle had raised clouds of dust from the piles of fallen masonry and now the dust was lanced by shafts of sunshine, spearing through the gaping holes in the roof.

McFaul let the camera run and run, using his other hand to steady the shot. Eventually, Katilo stood up. He lumbered back down the aisle, tramping through the debris. When he got to McFaul, he reached out, wanting the camera. The dust had flecked his hair, greying it, and for a moment McFaul could see what he'd look like if he ever achieved old age. He offered Katilo the camera. Katilo had learned how to rewind the tape and now he put his eye to the viewfinder, watching the end of the sequence. The sight of the interior of the cathedral brought a smile to his face and he nodded, returning the camera.

'God's will,' he boomed, stepping towards the door.

*

Piet Rademeyer was nursing a glass of mango juice when Molly Jordan finally spotted him. He was sitting at a table in the corner of the Bar Alberto, a big blue canvas bag at his feet. Since the flight down to Muengo, he'd acquired a deep cut over his left eye and when he looked up Molly could see the neat line of stitches, and the livid purple swelling beneath.

Rademeyer ordered drinks at the bar. When he sat down again, Molly apologised for hounding him. She'd been phoning the Luanda number on the card he'd given her for two days now, leaving endless messages on his answerphone until finally they'd made contact. Meeting at the Bar Alberto was Rademeyer's idea. Evenings were boisterous – the diplomatic crowd, the UN people, diamond dealers down from Zaire – but in the afternoons you often had the place to yourself.

Molly was still looking at the bruising around his eyes.

'What happened?'

Rademeyer shrugged.

'Bump in the car,' he said briskly. 'Not my fault.'

He changed the subject quickly, asking her about Muengo. Molly spared him most of the details. The place had been chaotic. She'd little idea what went on behind the scenes but she felt very sorry for the people who had to live there. Getting the aid workers out made a great deal of sense. Unfortunately, a couple had been left behind.

Rademeyer nodded. He seemed to be barely listening, his eyes on the door beyond the bar that led to the street. The bar was decorated with bits of bicycle and old car, refashioned into pastiche masks and spears, and a crop-haired young barman lurked in the shadows behind the espresso machine. The way he kept smiling at Rademeyer told Molly the two were probably close.

'These people in Muengo,' Molly said. 'One of them's a friend of mine.'

'Oh?' Rademeyer had moved the bag to one side, making it easier for him to get out.

'She's a French girl, a nurse. Her name is Christianne . . .'

Molly paused, slightly irritated by the young pilot's evident lack of interest, '. . . and the other one's older, English. He works in the minefields.'

Mention of the minefields brought Rademeyer's eyes briefly back to Molly.

'UNITA are into Muengo,' he pointed out.

'Quite.'

'So what are these people doing there? Why didn't they come out with the others?'

'I don't know.'

'I thought she was your friend, this French girl.'

'She is but . . .' Molly shrugged, colouring slightly. She'd got the pilot wrong. Rademeyer had been listening to every word. He was looking across at the bar now. The barman was crouched in one corner, whispering urgently into a phone.

Molly leaned forward, sensing that her time with Rademeyer was probably limited. It had taken her two days to get this far. Pinning him down again wouldn't be easy.

'I want to get them out,' she said. 'As soon as possible.'

The barman had left the bar. He was signalling to Rademeyer and the pilot got to his feet at once, stooping to retrieve the canvas bag. Molly felt his hand on her arm.

'Come with me,' he said.

Molly got up and followed him across the floor. They left the bar through a fire exit at the back. Outside, it was pouring with rain. A big Mercedes four-wheel was waiting amongst the piles of rubbish in the alley. Nearby, Molly heard a squealing of tyres and then a wild shouting, two or three men at least. Rademeyer pushed her into the Mercedes and for the first time it occurred to Molly to resist. This was the way you got kidnapped. Larry Giddings had warned her about it. She should have listened harder.

The Mercedes was on the move now, accelerating down the alley, splashing through the puddles of muddy brown water. Molly was in the back, wedged between Rademeyer's bag and the door. The driver was Angolan, a squat youth with an ear-ring and a nervous laugh. Rademeyer was giving him instructions in Portuguese. At the main road, the driver hauled the four-wheel across two lines of oncoming traffic, and began to thread his way out of town, the fat tyres hissing on the wet tarmac.

Molly recognised one or two landmarks. They were heading for the airport.

'What's going on?'

Rademeyer had relaxed now, his body slumped against the canvas bag, his eyes on the rear-view mirror.

'They'd have picked you up,' he said briefly. 'It's best you came with me.'

'Who? Who'd have picked me up?'

'Our Ninja friends. The goons in blue.'

'You mean – ?' Molly gestured back, remembering the commotion they'd left behind them.

Rademeyer nodded.

'They get a bit excited sometimes. You can try reasoning with them but they're not really interested in conversation. Just being with me would be enough to get you arrested.'

'Are you serious?'

'Very.'

'They'd arrest me?'

'Yes.'

'What for?'

'Conspiracy. Crimes against the state. I know we had an election but . . .' he shrugged, gazing out at the rain, 'democracy's not that easy. Especially for beginners.'

Molly stared at him, wondering again about the line of stitches above his eye. A car crash was beginning to sound less than likely. No wonder he'd been so jumpy. The Mercedes had slowed down, merging into the line of vehicles grinding towards the airport. Rademeyer was looking thoughtful.

'These friends of yours . . .' he began, 'in Muengo.'

It was Molly's turn to look at the rear-view mirror. Rademeyer's remarks about getting arrested had frightened her. An hour or two with Larry Giddings left you with no illusions about Angola's system of justice. Once they had you behind bars, anything could happen.

'That answerphone of yours . . .'

'Yes?'

'I left my name. And the Terra Sancta phone number.'

'That's right.'

'Was that wise?' She glanced across at Rademeyer. 'Be honest.'

Rademeyer was playing with the zip on the canvas bag, sliding it back and forth.

'It depends,' he said. 'Sometimes they're not that organised. You might be lucky. Other times . . .' he pulled a face, 'you never really know.'

'So what have you done? To cause all this . . .' she frowned, 'fuss?'

Rademeyer smiled at Molly's choice of phrase. Then he reached forward and tapped the young black on the shoulder, muttering something in Portuguese. The youth nodded, easing the Mercedes into the nearside lane. Ahead, Molly could see an untidy line of vehicles pulled off the road. The youth nosed the four-wheel between a sleek BMW with tinted windows and a Russian-made truck piled high with treadless rubber tyres. Beyond the truck, two women were bent over a fire. When the youth opened the door, Molly could smell sardines.

Rademeyer stretched, yawning. For a man on the run, he seemed to have very low blood pressure.

'You haven't answered my question,' Molly pointed out. 'I asked you what you've been up to.'

'Nothing. Making a living. That's all.'

'Is that enough? To upset them?'

'That's plenty.'

'Why?'

Rademeyer shook his head again, refusing to elaborate. The

driver was coming back, hunched against the rain. He was carrying a pile of steaming baps, wafered between sheets of soggy newsprint. He held the back door open with his knee, offering one to Molly. She took it, still waiting for Rademeyer. Rademeyer was inspecting the inside of his bap. Satisfied, he buried his teeth in it. Molly could smell something spicy now, tomatoes and peppers and thin green chillis.

Rademeyer wiped his mouth with the back of his hand.

'I'm flying up to Muengo this afternoon,' he said. 'You're welcome to come with me.'

'I thought they were looking for you?'

'They are. Some of them.'

'Then why aren't they at the airport? Waiting?'

Rademeyer looked amused again.

'Money,' he said briefly. 'Spend it wisely, spread it around, they leave you alone. The guys at the airport, anyway. Our Ninja friends?' His fingers strayed to the wound above his eye. 'They're off the payroll.'

Molly watched him for a moment. Christianne, she thought. And McFaul. Two more reasons for getting out of Luanda.

'Are you really going to Muengo?'

'Yes.'

'Why?'

'Federal Express.' Rademeyer patted the bag.

'But the city's fallen. You told me yourself.'

'Sure.'

'You know these people? The UNITA people?'

'I do business with them.'

'And that's why . . .? Back in the bar . . .?'

Rademeyer put a hand on her arm, silencing her. Then he passed her a wad of Kleenex, nodding at the bap.

'Eat,' he said.

Molly took a mouthful of bap. The sardines were delicious. She patted her mouth with the Kleenex, staring out at the rain. She was due to meet Giddings this evening. He was leaving

Luanda for a week or so. Then there was Robbie. And Alma. So far she hadn't told them about Rademeyer. That was to be her surprise, her initiative.

'How much?' she asked through a mouthful of bap. 'To get me to Muengo?'

'Nothing. I'm going anyway.'

'What about getting back? Flying the others out?'

'We'll talk about that.'

'But you're coming back?'

'From Muengo?' Rademeyer pulled a face. 'Too right I'm coming back.'

He swallowed the rest of his bap and began to lick his fingers one by one. Then he unzipped the canvas bag and pulled out a two-way radio. Inside the bag, Molly could see blocks of something black, wrapped in polythene. Rademeyer switched on the radio. It was already tuned to Channel Two.

'Here,' he said. 'Be my guest.'

Molly hesitated a moment. She had no money. No toothbrush. No change of clothes. Nothing.

'Maybe I should come next time,' she said uncertainly.

Rademeyer shook his head, looking at his watch, telling the youth behind the wheel it was time to go.

'There won't be a next time,' he said. 'Not from here, anyway.'

McFaul was back at the schoolhouse by early afternoon, stepping in from the sunshine, aware at once that something was wrong. The place had been wrecked, everything wooden stripped from the schoolroom. The door jambs had gone, the window frames, even some of the floorboards. Gone, too, were the desks and chairs where the students had once sat. In their place, strewn everywhere, were items from the crates of equipment Bennie had readied for the evacuation flight. In the event, Katilo had refused permission for the equipment to leave Muengo, and now McFaul understood why.

He knelt amongst the debris, trying to make a mental inventory, trying to remember exactly what Bennie had packed. The Ebingers had gone for sure, the $2,000 state-of-the-art detectors that would signal even the tiniest trace of metal, buried in the earth. Then there were the survey toolkits, and prismatic compasses, and the big HF radio that had been so temperamental. Both GPS locators had gone too, the priceless navigational kit that used satellites to give you a spot-on terrestrial fix. The stuff that was left was largely domestic – blankets, cooking gear, a couple of tropical tents – and McFaul began to rummage amongst it, struck by another thought.

Christianne had appeared from the dormitory. She stood in the open doorway, framed by the bare brickwork. The soldiers, she told him, had arrived at noon. They'd come on Katilo's orders. They'd only been interested in the de-mining equipment, plus anything wooden they could lay their hands on. Next door, where she and McFaul slept, they hadn't touched a thing.

McFaul was still on his hands and knees amongst the litter of pots and pans. Eventually, he looked up.

'The laptops?' he enquired. 'The disks?'

Christianne nodded.

'Those, too.'

'They took them both? The disks as well?'

'Yes.'

McFaul slumped back against the wall. The little laptop computers contained all the data they'd amassed over the last five months. Every waking hour of the Muengo operation, every mine, every cleared metre of earth, was recorded in the laptops and on the disks. Bennie should at least have sorted out the disks. Even after Katilo prohibited the shipping of equipment, he should have taken them. He could have slipped them into a pocket. He could have given them to one of the aircrew. But he hadn't. He'd just left them, along with everything else. McFaul knew that. He'd checked, only yesterday, spotting them through the slats in one of the crates, wrapped in polythene and taped to one of the laptops. The data was also stored in the laptops' memory but that made no difference because now the laptops had disappeared as well.

Unforgivable, he thought. Absolutely one hundred per cent fucking unforgivable.

Christianne knelt beside him. All McFaul could do was shake his head. Five months. Three hundred and seventy-four lifted mines. Acres of ground made safe for crop raising, for kids, for animals, each square metre carefully logged. But now the records had disappeared, and with it had gone that total certainty that had become the trademark of Global operations. One hundred per cent clearance, McFaul thought grimly. That was the way we always worked. That was our promise. And now it meant fuck all.

Christianne was talking about the soldiers. She said she'd done her best to stop them but they'd ignored her. McFaul wasn't listening.

'What happened to the easel?'

'They took that too. They said they wanted firewood.'

'What about the maps?'

'I don't know about the maps. I didn't see.'

'Why not, for God's sake?'

'I . . .' Christianne was staring at him.

McFaul struggled to his feet, pushing her aside, searching through the piles of discarded equipment again. The maps, he thought. They'd never take the maps. Not lines of red dots and bits and pieces of fancy cross-hatching. That would mean bugger-all. That would mean nothing. Just bits of paper. He tossed the blankets aside. He kicked the saucepans into the corner. The maps had gone.

'Who were these guys? Where did they go?'

'I don't know.'

'Did you get their names? Could you recognise them?'

'Maybe.' She nodded, wary now.

McFaul hesitated by the doorway. Katilo had moved into the MSF house. He'd taken the camera back there. He was already talking of more filming, extra shots around Muengo, then a whole new sequence, somewhere else, somewhere completely different.

Christianne was standing by the window, examining a splinter in her hand. When McFaul turned to leave, she called him back.

'Where are you going?'

'To find Katilo.'

'You want me to come?'

McFaul shrugged, too angry to care.

'Suit yourself,' he said, limping away into the sunshine.

Katilo was addressing a circle of soldiers in the kitchen of the MSF house. One of the bodyguards in the garden outside, recognising McFaul, had accompanied him down the hall. Now, McFaul stood in the open doorway, waiting for Katilo to finish. He was talking in Ovimbundu, a long monologue, punctuated by flourishes with a length of bamboo he carried in his right hand. Beside him stood the easel.

McFaul was already looking round for the maps. Except for rubbish abandoned before the evacuation, the kitchen was empty. McFaul waited a minute or so longer then began to go through the rest of the house. Christianne's bedroom had been taken over by Katilo. A generator was already purring in the front garden and a length of cable through the window powered the television and video-recorder. On the screen was a picture of Katilo, a single frame from his march across the cathedral square. He was looking up, distracted by a flock of birds, and the lowness of the angle magnified his bulk. He looked almost biblical, the prophet come to free his people, and McFaul knew at once that he must have chosen this image himself. He can't leave it alone, he thought. He's been spooling and respooling the footage, infatuated with the role he's assigned himself. Redeemer. King. Messiah.

McFaul heard footsteps behind him, turning in time to see

Katilo's huge frame pause by the door. He'd been on his way out. Now he joined McFaul, his eyes at once going to the television.

'Good, eh?'

McFaul nodded, asking at once about the equipment from the schoolhouse. Katilo's men had taken computers, small ones. Where were they? Katilo picked up the remote control for the video-player. The image flickered briefly on the screen and then began to move. Katilo was heading for the cathedral. Again.

'Gone,' he muttered. 'They've gone.'

'Gone where?'

'Huambo.' He nodded. 'They belong to UNITA now.'

'When? When did they go?'

Katilo was grinning, watching himself pausing beside the big wooden door, delivering his lines about peace. The angle of the sun through the bedroom window flooded the screen with light, and Katilo knelt beside the television a moment, turning it carefully away from the glare, an object of reverence.

McFaul was losing his temper. This clown was responsible for laying the fucking mines. McFaul and his team had risked their lives trying to lift them. Without the maps, or the computer records, they were as good as laid again.

'Maps,' he said slowly. 'There were maps on the easel, pinned to the easel, when it left the schoolhouse. Where are they now? Where have they gone?'

Katilo ignored the question, transfixed by the video. He was kneeling before the altar, caged by the shafts of dusty sunlight, and McFaul watched him crossing himself again as he saw the sequence anew. McFaul stepped in front of the screen, blocking Katilo's view.

'Maps,' he said thickly.

Katilo looked up, surprised, as if he'd just heard the question for the first time. He frowned a moment, then went to the window and bellowed to one of the bodyguards. The soldier came running, the same man who'd let McFaul into the house. Katilo muttered something McFaul didn't understand, his eyes returning to the TV set. Behind the set, for the first time, McFaul recognised the bottles of Glenfiddich he'd last seen in Katilo's fridge. Katilo was bending down, feeling blindly. His fingers tightened around a bottle and he picked it up, passing it to McFaul without a word.

'Go with the soldier,' he muttered. 'He knows about your maps.'

McFaul felt a tug on his arm. The soldier was taking him away, taking him to where the maps were. They stepped outside, into the sunshine, McFaul still holding the bottle. The house next door had belonged to a sister charity, Oxfam. A handful of soldiers were squatting around a fire in the corner of the garden, surrounded by a small mountain of hacked-up wood. McFaul paused, recognising the desks from the schoolhouse. The soldiers looked up, curious. One of them was stirring a pot of *funje*. McFaul peered at the fire. A corner of charred plywood looked familiar. He reached forward with his foot, turning it over. On the other side, clearly visible, were the letters G-L-O-B-, part of Bennie's carefully stencilled label for the onward shippers at Luanda airport. Bennie had used black paint. McFaul had watched him do it.

The soldiers were still looking at McFaul. He tried to ask them about the maps, using sign language. At first they didn't understand. Then the bodyguard got the drift, explaining what McFaul wanted. There'd been paper on the easel. Sheets of paper with marks on them. Where were they now? One of the soldiers pointed at the fire, miming a box of matches. Paper lights fires, he was explaining. Fires cook food. Food fills empty bellies. The other soldiers watched him, laughing, and McFaul turned away, limping back through the knee-high grass, his face betraying nothing.

Piet Rademeyer's little blue Dove landed at dusk. With a hiss of pneumatic brakes, he brought it to a halt at the end of the tiny strip. One of Katilo's trucks came bumping across to meet the plane and the soldiers gaped as Rademeyer helped Molly down from the rear door. The aircraft secured for the night, the truck rolled away towards Muengo, Rademeyer and Molly in the back. On the outskirts of the city, dark now, they took the road to the schoolhouse. When the truck stopped, Molly could see a flicker of candle-light in the room the men had used as a dormitory. Rademeyer lowered the tailgate and jumped down from the truck. So far, he hadn't let go of the blue canvas bag. The truck roared away.

Molly and Rademeyer exchanged glances, then Molly led the way into the schoolhouse. The door to the classroom was missing. She stepped inside, tripping at once. Rademeyer helped her to her feet. Uncertain now, she picked her way slowly across to the other side of the room. The door to the dormitory was missing too. She could see the candle-light playing on the bare walls. She paused in the doorway, peering in. Across the room, beside the candle, two camp-beds had been pushed together. There were bodies on the camp-beds, unmoving. Molly thought she recognised the French nurse but she couldn't be sure. She called her name, very softly.

'Christianne?'

Nothing happened. Molly looked at Rademeyer, fearing the worst. Rademeyer unzipped the canvas bag and produced a gun. Molly stared at it. It was an automatic, a big thing, steady in his hand. He moved carefully across the room, the gun trained on the bodies. For the first time, Molly saw the bottle. Rademeyer was beside the nearest camp-bed now. He reached out, peeling back the single sheet. Then he let it fall.

'Long guy?' he queried softly. 'Thin? Scars on his face?'

Molly nodded.

'McFaul,' she confirmed.

Rademeyer began to laugh, chuckling in the semi-darkness. 'Rat-arsed,' he said. 'The girl, too.'

*

It was nearly midnight before Katilo came to the schoolhouse. Molly woke up to the cough of an engine. She heard voices outside. In the darkness, she could see nothing. Then the beam of a torch appeared at the window, sweeping around the dormitory, settling on the camp-beds by the wall. Molly kept very still. Already, she felt like a prisoner, unwashed, frightened, her life in the hands of total strangers.

'Molly?' she recognised Rademeyer's voice behind the torch. 'Over here.'

The torch swung towards her. She shielded her eyes. There was movement across the room. She heard a low curse. McFaul, she thought. She got up and stepped across to the beds. The torch tracked with her. McFaul was sitting upright, rubbing his eyes.

'What's going on?'

'It's me. Molly.'

'Who?'

'Molly. Molly Jordan.' She paused. 'James's mother.'

Christianne began to stir, pushing the sheet back, then Molly heard another voice at the window, deeper, an African speaking English with an American drawl. He was saying something about a party.

'Party?'

Christianne sounded bewildered, reaching for McFaul, and Molly heard the African chuckling as the torch left her face and drifted down to find the empty bottle of Glenfiddich beside the bed.

They drove away from the schoolhouse in the MSF Landcruiser, Katilo at the wheel. He'd evidently commandeered the vehicle for his personal use and kept trying to start a conversation with Christianne, telling her how responsive it was. Christianne sat between Molly and McFaul in the back, her head in her hands, trying to fight the movement of the vehicle. McFaul sat beside her, stiff, unbending. After recognising Katilo at the window of the dormitory, he hadn't said a word.

Molly spotted the MSF house from the end of the street. In the garden next door a huge bonfire was alight, flames licking upwards, showering the sky with sparks. There were soldiers everywhere, swaying to music, milling around the garden, spilling on to the street, and they parted with a slow, smiling insolence the moment they recognised Katilo at the wheel of the Landcruiser. There were trucks parked at the side of the road, more soldiers, and when Katilo stopped and opened the door to get out, Molly could hear the music more clearly. It was loud, exultant, something Latin-American, and it ran like a pulse through the mill of dancing soldiers around the fire.

Katilo opened the rear door, looming over the Landcruiser, motioning McFaul out on to the street. Just the sight of him frightened Molly. The man was so obviously powerful, so obviously in charge. Whatever he wanted, he could have. He was still looking at McFaul. She'd never seen a smile so empty of warmth.

'The camera, my friend. Pictures. I want more pictures.'

McFaul was still looking at the bonfire. Beyond the dancers, tethered to the stump of a tree, was an animal, something big. Molly saw it, too.

'What's that?'

McFaul had his arm round Christianne.

'A cow,' he said quietly. 'Tonight's cabaret.'

'What's it doing there?'

McFaul glanced up at her, a look at once pitying and contemptuous. Rademeyer leaned into the car, indicating Katilo with a jerk of his head.

'He means it. He wants you out. Something to do with a movie.' He sounded anxious.

McFaul laughed.

'Tell him the camera's bust. Tell him the batteries need charging. Any fucking thing.'

Rademeyer looked back at Katilo. The UNITA commander had heard every word. He reached in, across McFaul, his huge hand cupping Christianne's chin, turning her head towards him.

'There's dancing,' he murmured. 'Afterwards.'

'After what?'

'Good question.'

He let the phrase linger on, then withdrew his hand. Rademeyer was back again, his voice urgent.

'He's not joking, man,' he said. 'I know this guy.'

'Yeah?'

McFaul eyed him without enthusiasm, then shrugged, getting out of the Landcruiser. He pushed past Katilo without a word and disappeared inside the MSF house. Within a minute he was back. Molly recognised Llewelyn's camcorder in his hand. Katilo had joined a group of soldiers beside the bonfire. He was beckoning McFaul across. McFaul told Rademeyer to bring Christianne. Molly, too.

Molly caught up with McFaul, oblivious to the leering soldiers on either side.

'What happened to Llewelyn's cassette?' she whispered. 'The one he shot here? The one with Domingos?'

'It's in there.' McFaul indicated the MSF house.

'Is it OK? Safe?'

'Yeah. He loves it.'

He paused at the kerbside, looking at Katilo, and Molly stopped beside him. Even here, twenty metres from the bonfire, she could feel its heat. There was a strange smell, too, pungent, bitter-sweet, and she began to turn her head, looking for its source.

Beside her, McFaul lifted the camcorder to his eye, panning slowly across the circle of faces around the bonfire. The soldiers were laughing and joking. Some had cans of beer. McFaul ignored Katilo's beckoning finger, stepping sideways, moving closer and closer to the fire. Rademeyer stopped him.

'He wants you.'

'Fuck him.'

'Do it, buddy.'

Katilo was sauntering across now. He bent to Rademeyer's ear and whispered something. The pilot nodded, disappearing into the shadows, and Molly watched him talking urgently to a soldier. The soldier, unlike the others, had a gun, an AK-47. He stooped to pick up something at his feet and Molly recognised Rademeyer's canvas bag. Rademeyer was coming back. He had a small package in his hand, wrapped in polythene. He tried to give it to Katilo but the rebel commander shook his head, gesturing towards McFaul. Rademeyer stepped across, still holding the package. Molly stared at it.

'What is it?'

McFaul didn't take his eye from the viewfinder.

'Ganja,' he said. 'It's party time. These guys are out of their heads.' He lowered the camera. 'Can't you smell it?'

Someone turned up the music. Katilo told McFaul to follow him. He had his arm round Christianne now, and he loomed over her, the kindly uncle. They circled the fire. On the other side, still tethered to the tree stump, was the cow. It was trying to move from foot to foot, disturbed by the noise and the activity, but other lines snared both legs and a noose around its neck restrained the big head. Molly looked at it a moment, seeing the flames dancing in its huge black eyes.

A group of soldiers detached themselves from the bonfire, seeing Katilo. Their shirts were open to the waist and their bodies glistened with sweat. One of them was smoking. The others began to dance around the cow, clapping their hands, stamping their boots in time to the music. They knew the lyrics of the song by heart and every time they got to the end of a line the soldier with the cigarette weaved towards the cow, stopping inches from its face, blowing smoke up its nostrils. The animal, terrified, tried to back away, but each time it moved the lines tightened, restraining it.

Katilo watched the soldiers for a minute or two, his body

swaying to the music, his arm still encircling Christianne. Finally he released her and she nearly fell, reaching out to McFaul to keep her balance. McFaul's hand found hers. Rademeyer was talking to Katilo.

'He wants you to film the next bit,' he said to McFaul. 'He says it's very important.'

'I bet.'

McFaul muttered something to Christianne and Molly saw her tucking the T-shirt into her jeans. Katilo clapped his hands. Slowly, the dancing soldiers came to a halt. Katilo made a short speech. Afterwards, there was cheering. Then he gestured impatiently to the soldier with the AK-47. The man produced a long machete. Katilo took it, cutting the air a couple of times, short, vicious sweeps, the men quiet now, watching him. He stepped across to the cow. The animal saw him coming, rearing desperately backwards, but the lines held it fast, and Katilo paused for barely a second before bringing the machete up, a single movement, the blade tearing through the exposed wind-pipe. The cow opened its mouth, gasping, and Molly heard the hiss of escaping air as its legs began to buckle. Katilo slashed again, deeper this time, and blood fountained over the watching soldiers as the animal collapsed.

Molly turned away, sickened, hearing the men beginning to cheer, and then the music pulsed again, even louder, and she looked round to see McFaul, inches from the dying animal, following Katilo's every movement as he sliced open the hanging bulge of stomach, spilling loops of hot viscera into the dusty grass. His work done, he tossed the dripping machete to a soldier and gestured for him to butcher the animal. Then he began to clear a circle in the grass, tossing fragments of broken school-desk into the flames. The soldiers helped him, building the bonfire even higher, and when the circle was wide enough, Katilo looked round, calling for Christianne.

Soldiers found her in the road, bent double, vomiting. They brought her back, presenting her to Katilo, and Katilo dismissed them with a wave, taking her hand, spinning her round, a grotesque jive, Christianne already dizzied and reeling. Katilo caught her before she fell, holding her upright, acknowledging the roars of his men, and then he made her dance, the puppeteer with the rag doll, her body pressed to him. McFaul taped everything, barely feet away, ignoring Katilo's jibes, oblivious to the yelling soldiers, the stamp of a hundred boots, and when Katilo finally released her, he tracked her falling body, tightening the shot as she lay sprawled at the African's feet.

Katilo stood over her, gazing down. Then he barked an order and abruptly the music stopped. The men stopped, too. No more yelling. No more dancing. Katilo began to unbutton his shirt. Naked above the waist, he looked round, finding McFaul, making sure he was still taping. Then he began to address the soldiers again.

Rademeyer knew a little Ovimbundu. Molly was standing beside him. She was beyond fear now. The waiting was over. Whatever they did to Christianne, they'd do to her. James, after all, had got off rather lightly.

She glanced at Rademeyer, seeing the surprise in his face. Katilo's speech was over. He was standing above Christianne, gazing down at her fallen body. She lay quite still, her knees drawn up to her chin, her eyes closed. Katilo looked at her a moment longer then spread his shirt wide, stooping and draping it over her. The soldiers stared at him. Then, disappointed, they began to drift back towards the fire. Molly watched them, flooded with relief. McFaul was looking at Rademeyer.

'What did he say?'

Rademeyer was watching the soldiers at work on the cow, hacking at the warm flesh.

'He said we're leaving tomorrow.' He shrugged. 'Something to do with Zaire.'

CHAPTER TWELVE

They left Muengo an hour after dawn. Soldiers in a truck called at the schoolhouse and took them to the airfield. In the cool morning light, the city seemed almost normal, women and children making their way to the market, old men sifting through piles of rubbish, even the occasional dog chasing the fat black crows that stalked through the pale grass at the roadside.

Katilo was already at the airfield, prowling around the Dove, peering into the recesses of the engines while Rademeyer completed his checks. From somewhere, he'd produced a new set of camouflage fatigues and he had an enormous automatic strapped to one thigh. He was eating a banana and when McFaul lowered himself from the back of the truck he unbuttoned the breast pocket of his shirt and handed him a slim cassette. The camcorder, he said, was already on board the plane. He wanted pictures when they took off, pictures in the air. They'd be calling at Huambo first, UNITA's city to the north, and he wanted McFaul to be taping there too. Colonel Katilo was embarking on his travels. And he needed the evidence to show the world.

McFaul took the cassette without a word. Christianne was already inside the aircraft, occupying a seat on the left, immediately behind the bulkhead that separated the cockpit from the cabin. McFaul joined her, sitting across the aisle. Christianne barely acknowledged his presence, her hands tightening on the lap-strap, her knuckles white. She'd spent the night in a corner of the schoolhouse, silent, brooding, too shocked by what had happened to sleep or even talk. The realities of the war had broken her. Her commitment to Muengo was at an end.

They took off to the east, Katilo in the co-pilot's seat, McFaul trying to steady himself in the open cockpit doorway. Using the camcorder in so confined a space wasn't easy and in the end he simply held the thing at arm's length, pointing it sideways at Katilo, hoping the shot would work. The Dove climbed steadily in the still morning air and at Katilo's insistence Rademeyer hauled the aircraft into a long, shallow turn, circling the city before setting course for Huambo. In the cabin, Molly gazed down. From two thousand feet, Muengo seemed barely touched by the war, a sprawl of toy-like houses enfolded by the river, the long shadow of the cathedral clearly visible. Only as the Dove began to level out, still climbing, did she recognise the track that led out of town, following it until she found the tiny clump of mango trees dotting the hillock below which James lay buried.

Molly pressed her face to the cold Perspex, keeping the trees in view as the aircraft droned north. Unlike Christianne, she'd managed a couple of hours' sleep and now the events of the previous evening seemed curiously remote, something she might have seen in a film, or read about in a certain kind of novel. It wasn't that she didn't believe it had happened. On the contrary, her head still thumped from the cans of Castle lager that Katilo had forced on them all. But there was something else about the scenes around the bonfire that seemed to sum up the last two weeks. From the moment she'd stepped off the jumbo at Luanda airport, Molly's life had changed. Not simply the smells, and the heat, and the colour. Not simply the poverty and the lengths to which you were forced to simply survive in the place. But something infinitely more personal. She'd come here to find out the truth about James and she'd discovered, instead, the depth of her own ignorance. Life was at once simpler and more complex than she'd ever imagined. Things that had once seemed to matter – money, possessions, status – were in fact worthless.

Things she'd maybe overlooked – curiosity about others, compassion for their needs – were literally beyond price. Life, in the end, was about other people. Turn your back on your neighbour, and you were nothing.

McFaul stepped back from the cockpit, pulling the door shut behind him. He glanced down at Christianne then sank into the seat across the aisle from Molly, pulling a cassette from his pocket and showing it to her.

'Is this what you wanted?'

Molly looked at the cassette, recognising Todd Llewelyn's scrawl on the sticky label. 'Muengo,' he'd written. 'Minefields.'

'Is this the one with Domingos?'

'Yes.'

'From Katilo?'

'Yes.'

'He just gave it to you?'

'He has to. He wants to be part of a film I'm supposed to be making. He's seen it dozens of times. He's no fool. He knows what it's worth.' He paused. 'Back home.'

'And *you're* making this film?'

'Yes.' McFaul nodded. 'Court photographer. By royal appointment.'

'And he believes you?'

'Of course. And so he should.'

'You mean it's true? You're really doing it?'

'Absolutely.' McFaul gestured at the camcorder. 'I've used one of these before. In Afghanistan. You just point and shoot. Amazing piece of kit.'

'But what happens afterwards? In the UK? What will you do then?'

'I'll put it together.'

'By yourself?'

'If I have to, yes.'

Molly thought of Alma Bradley. Wasn't film-making complex? Difficult? Didn't you need years of experience? McFaul had pocketed the little cassette again and now he was examining the camcorder.

'There's a woman in Luanda . . .' Molly began, 'a professional TV producer. She's English. From London.'

'Oh?'

'Yes. She's very interested in,' her eyes went to the pocket of McFaul's shirt, 'all the stuff Llewelyn shot.'

McFaul nodded, saying nothing. Behind the usual mask, there was something new in his face. The eyes, Molly thought, something kindled, something burning, the surly indifference he'd shown the previous evening quite gone. Molly leaned across the aisle, raising her voice against the drone of the engines.

'Her name's Alma . . .' she said, 'Alma Bradley.'

'Who?'

'The TV producer. The one in Luanda. She's very well connected. She seemed . . .' Molly shrugged, 'very nice. Not at all like Llewelyn.'

McFaul raised an eyebrow at the mention of Llewelyn's name then the plane hit an air pocket, dropping like a stone and McFaul managed to catch the camcorder before it tumbled from his lap. He nursed it, protective, leaning back in the seat, gazing out of the window, and Molly watched him for a moment or two, wondering whether to try again. If Alma made the film about the minefields, it would get Robbie off the hook. No threat of a Terra Sancta exposé. No awkward explanations back in Winchester. She felt McFaul's hand on her arm. He was nodding at the cockpit door.

'He hasn't even bothered to bring a bodyguard,' he said. 'Doesn't that tell you something?'

Molly frowned, confused.

'About what?'

'Katilo and me,' he patted the camcorder, 'and this.'

*

370

The Dove landed at Huambo forty minutes later, spiralling down in a tight corkscrew from ten thousand feet. Piet Rademeyer taxied back to the apron of oily tarmac, closing down the engines. A single aircraft was parked in front of the blackened concrete of the terminal building, the dented nose propped on a pile of shredded lorry tyres. Katilo appeared from the cockpit of the Dove, his massive frame filling the narrow aisle, and he paused beside Christianne, motioning her out. She got to her feet, unsteady, avoiding McFaul's eyes.

Molly gazed up at her.

'What's happening?'

'I'm getting off.' She shrugged. 'It's all arranged.'

She reached out, the touch of her hand cold and lifeless, and Molly sensed at once that she didn't want to prolong the conversation. Then Katilo stirred, nudging her down the aisle, and Molly felt the heat bubbling in as the door opened at the rear of the cabin. A truck had appeared on the tarmac outside and Molly heard the boom of Katilo's voice, turning to the window in time to see him organising a gaggle of soldiers. The truck backed up to the Dove and Rademeyer body-checked down the aisle, yelling in Portuguese. The de-mining equipment from the schoolhouse was secured in the cargo space at the rear of the fuselage and the aircraft rocked as the soldiers began to unload. Another vehicle was weaving between the line of parked aircraft, a dirty Peugeot estate car with a torn Red Cross flag tied to the bodywork. It pulled up alongside the truck. A man and woman got out, both young. The woman ran to Christianne, hugging her.

'MSF.'

Molly looked up. McFaul was standing over her, bent to the window. Dropping Christianne off had evidently been his idea, part of the deal he'd struck with Katilo. Huambo was currently in UNITA hands, the rebels' prize after months of siege. The city was home to tens of thousands of refugees and Médecins Sans Frontières had stayed on, protected by guarantees from UNITA's high command. Aid flights still operated from here to Luanda, and within a day or so Christianne would be on a 747 back to Europe.

Molly watched her getting into the Peugeot, settling herself in the back. An ancient fuel bowser had turned up now and Rademeyer was dragging a frayed length of hose across to the wing tanks on the Dove. Christianne was pointing at him, talking to the woman beside her, and as the Peugeot began to move she caught Molly's eye. Molly lifted a hand, responding to Christianne's tired wave, looking up at McFaul as she did so but McFaul had already turned away, no longer interested.

They left Huambo half an hour later, climbing into a clear blue sky. Katilo had reappeared with a handful of fresh fruit and he sat in the cabin, sawing into an overripe pineapple with McFaul's bayonet. Back on the ground at Huambo, McFaul had gone forward into the cockpit and found the map Rademeyer was using. The pilot had already chinagraphed the route north from Huambo, and the thick blue line dog-legged to Kinshasa via a tiny dot marked Cafunfo.

Kinshasa was the capital of Zaire, an hour's flying time north of the Angolan border. Here, according to McFaul, Katilo planned to conduct a little business. He'd be meeting a couple of key contacts in the war against the socialists, men without whom UNITA's army simply couldn't function. They were comrades-in-arms, fellow-travellers on the road to a free Angola, and it was important for the film that Katilo should be pictured in their company. Quite what these meetings would entail, McFaul didn't know, but more pressing was the detour en route. Cafunfo was in Lunda Norte, a remote northern province, the home of Angola's diamond mines. McFaul had never been there but the area was infamous. It produced millions of pounds' worth of gemstones, enough to fund the UNITA war machine. Cafunfo, McFaul suspected, was where the rebels kept their piggy-bank.

Molly listened to McFaul's musings, remembering hearing something similar from Robbie back in Luanda. He'd been talking about the same place, she was sure of it. Alma was hoping to make a film there, though she couldn't lay hands on the right government official to fix a permit. That's why Robbie had got her so interested in a different film. And that's why Molly had found herself back in Muengo, looking for Llewelyn's wretched cassette.

Molly adjusted the seat, making herself comfortable. The sun was hot now through the Perspex beside her face and after the traumas of the last twenty-four hours she felt an extra-ordinary sense of peace. Something in McFaul had definitely revived. There was a sense of confidence, of purpose about the man, and when he told her not to worry about the next few days, she was glad to believe him. She was to treat it like a holiday. They'd pause for an hour or so at Cafunfo. Then they'd fly on to Kinshasa. They'd doubtless spend the night there. They might even book into a hotel. Hot water. Soap. A chance to wash her hair, wallow in the bath, climb into fresh clothes, borrowed or bought. The thought brought a smile to her face and she gazed down at the land below, the pale green flanks of Africa, an animal sprawled in the heat. Her eyes began to close and she drifted away, lulled by the drone of the engines, waking with a start minutes later. Katilo's huge bulk occupied the seat in front of her. His face was pressed to the window, childlike, the eyes dreamy, transfixed by the view. At length he became aware of Molly watching him and he half-turned in the seat. His voice was soft for once, barely audible over the noise of the engines.

'You know what Angola means? In Kikongo?'

'No.'

'Iron.' Katilo smiled. 'You understand?'

Molly gazed down at the view again. She could see the gleam of a river, and mountains beyond.

'Land of iron?' she queried. 'Like the diamonds?'

'No,' Katilo's smile had broadened, 'iron land. Like the people.'

The Dove began to descend an hour or so later. Katilo was still in the seat in front of Molly and he reached back to McFaul, shaking him awake, telling him to get the camcorder ready. The plane was losing height quickly now, Rademeyer throttling the engines back, and Molly watched through the window as they banked steeply, chasing their own shadow across the flat expanse of bush. A river came into view below the wing. The water was muddy brown, flecked white where rocks feathered the current, and on either side the river banks were pocked with huge pits. There were men in the pits, tiny black dots, and Molly could see them looking up as the aircraft roared overhead, screening their eyes against the sun.

Katilo was talking now, playing the tour guide. The men below were *kamanguistas*, illegal miners, poor Angolans who risked everything in their fevered hunt for diamonds. Tens of thousands of them trekked here from all over Angola, driven by stories of fabulous wealth. Angola's gems were amongst the world's finest. Most of them were mined from the bed of the river, or from the banks either side. Elsewhere, the state company, Endiama, diverted the river, using bulldozers to excavate the gravel bottom, but here the *kamanguistas* did everything by hand, preferring to take their chances on their own. Every week, said Katilo, a dozen or so bodies were recovered from the river, miners who'd drowned trying to make their fortune. But every week as well, other *kamanguistas* would emerge from the turbid water with a tiny handful of gems, enough to feed their families for the rest of their lives.

The plane began to bank again and the river disappeared. Molly heard the rumble of the undercarriage and then the engine note changed and the nose dipped and the smudgy browns and greens of the bush came up to meet them. The landing was hard, the Dove jolting to a halt in a cloud of dust. Katilo was on his feet already, eyeing the rear door. His hand had closed on the butt of the big automatic and Molly noticed that the strap securing the gun was hanging loose. The engines raced briefly as the plane taxied back down the strip. Through the window, Molly could see a big American four-wheel, a Chevrolet, keeping pace with the Dove. There were two men in the front. The one behind the wheel was grinning.

The aircraft finally stopped, Rademeyer killing the engines. Katilo was already out of the rear door, striding towards the four-wheel, one hand buttoning the holster. Molly smelled the hot breath of the bush, wriggling out of her seat and following McFaul into the sunshine.

Katilo was embracing the man behind the wheel. He was small and lean with quick brown eyes and a pink shell-suit. Katilo introduced him as Dominique. The other man rounded the four-wheel. He carried a small, black sub-machine-gun and he shook Katilo's outstretched hand, exchanging greetings in French.

They got into the four-wheel, leaving the man with the sub-machine-gun to guard the Dove. At Katilo's insistence, McFaul was taping again, the camcorder glued to his eye as the four-wheel bounced along the rough dirt road. Soon they were back beside the river. At ground level, the pits were even bigger than they'd looked from the air, and Molly gazed into them as the Chevrolet roared past. At the bottom of each there were men on their hands and knees, tearing at the glistening mud, pausing from time to time to reach for a pick or a shovel. Iron, Molly thought. Iron, and diamonds, and twelve funerals a week.

They drove into Cafunfo twenty minutes later. The small bush town was falling apart: rutted dirt roads, shacks thrown together from scrap ends of timber and rusting sheets of corrugated iron, scenes that would have disgraced peacetime Muengo. Yet everywhere in this slum was the evidence of the wealth the diamonds must have brought. Two kids playing football with $100 Reebok trainers. A young Angolan with Ray-Bans and a fancy leather jacket stooping to unlock the door of his newly dented BMW. Two women hauling a Zanussi fridge across the street.

Molly gazed out, half-listening to Rademeyer. Evidently he knew the place well. The leather jackets, he was telling McFaul, came in by the container load. You paid a couple of thousand dollars for a jacket but there was no choice of style or cut because all the garments were the same. Ditto the trainers, and the fridges, and the Japanese-made hi-fi stacks that were, in Cafunfo, de rigueur. To live here, you needed serious money. For a beer, you'd part with ten dollars while filling your BMW might – on a bad day – leave you with no change from five hundred.

The Chevrolet slewed to the left and came to a halt before a line of armed soldiers. Katilo fingered the control on the electric window and one of the soldiers saluted, recognising him at once. He stepped aside, waving the others away, and the four-wheel nosed into the compound.

A line of washing hung between two spindly trees at the end. Beneath one of the trees, a goat was tethered to the wing mirror of a sleek Mercedes saloon. The far side of the compound was occupied by a mud-walled shack. Either side of the splintered wooden door were two guards, both armed.

Katilo got out of the Chevrolet, telling McFaul to follow him. Rademeyer got out too, holding the door open for Molly. The soldiers stood aside, respectful, answering Katilo's grin with shy smiles. Inside the shack, metal shelving was piled high with Western goods. There were bottles of Budweiser. Piles of ovenware. Racks of CDs. Molly recognised the tin of Bath Olivers at the end. The last time she'd seen them had been in Harrods.

Katilo was already deep in conversation with a thickset Angolan sitting behind a big wooden desk. Insects and damp had eaten away at one of the legs of the desk and it was supported by a pile of magazines. Molly stared at them, wondering who in Cafunfo would possibly subscribe to *Vogue*. Katilo was laughing now, leaning across the desk, pumping the Angolan's hand, introducing him to McFaul's camcorder. His name was Ivan. He was a good friend of Katilo's. He ran Cafunfo. Nothing happened here without his permission.

The Angolan nodded, eyeing the camcorder without enthusiasm, unmoved by Katilo's flattery. His fingers were laden with heavy gold rings. A thick wad of $100 notes bulged from the pocket of his shirt. He reached for a pair of scales on the side of the desk and opened a drawer beside him, pulling out a handful of polythene bags. At the bottom of each bag was a tiny pile of uncut diamonds and he began to shake them onto the scales, a hard, flinty noise that Molly knew she'd never forget. Ivan had a calculator out now, and after the fourth bag he punched in a row of figures, turning the calculator towards Katilo. Katilo reached for it, playful, shielding the lens of the camcorder as he checked the sum for himself, then grunted something in French. Dominique, the Angolan in the shell-suit, produced a pen and scribbled a signature on a sheet of paper. He showed the paper to Katilo then pushed it across to Ivan. Ivan was re-bagging the diamonds, pouring them in from the scoop. Katilo tied knots in the tops of all four bags, holding them up for McFaul's benefit, the way an angler might display a handful of prize fish. Then, abruptly, they were back outside, the guards as respectful as ever, Ivan standing in the open doorway, sharing a joke with Dominique.

Molly understood a little French. Best to get to Kinshasa before nightfall, Ivan was saying. Shame to share the diamonds with the scum at the airport.

Back at the airstrip, after Rademeyer had refuelled from the 40-gallon drum stored in the rear of the fuselage, one engine on the Dove began to give trouble. They'd taxied downwind to the edge of the treeline and Rademeyer was readying the aircraft for take-off, but when he ran the engines up there was an audible banging and popping from the cowling on the starboard wing. Rademeyer tried to clear it with another burst of throttle but when it happened again, louder this time, he shut down both engines and appeared in the cabin with a handful of tools and a plastic shopping bag marked 'Jan Smuts International Airport'.

'Mag drop,' he announced briskly. 'Got to change the plugs.'

Molly watched him for a while, the sun hot through the aircraft window, and when she woke up two hours later he was still bent over the exposed engine, his head and neck now protected by a wide-brimmed straw hat. By the time he'd finished, it was late afternoon, the shadows beginning to lengthen across the narrow airstrip. Back in the cockpit, the rear door secured, Rademeyer ran the engines up again, holding the throttles fully open until he was sure the problem had gone away. Minutes later, they were airborne, climbing over the broad strip of the Cuango river, setting course for Zaire.

Kinshasa is 500 miles north-west of Cafunfo, and it was dark by the time Rademeyer hooked open the cockpit door and announced preparations for landing. Molly leaned across the aisle, waking McFaul, then tightened her seat-belt. Below, through the window, she could see a distant gauzy sprawl of lights, tiny twinkling diamonds in the darkness. They were losing height now and the city began to widen and take on shape before one wing dropped and the darkness returned. Minutes later, Rademeyer eased the Dove on to the tarmac at Kinshasa's international airport and Molly watched the runway lights slowing as he applied the brakes. In the distance she could see the fat-bellied jumbos parked in front of the terminal building, and she stared at them for a moment, amazed. Then she smiled to herself, undoing her lap-strap. These planes had come from Europe. Ten hours ago they'd been in Paris, or Brussels, or Lisbon, names that belonged to another life. It was like coming back from outer space.

She glanced up. McFaul was standing over her, stooped in the narrow cabin. He was loading a new cassette into the camcorder, steadying himself against the seat back as the aircraft bumped along the taxiway. When they finally came to a halt, he went forward to the cockpit, asking Katilo what he wanted to do, and Molly watched as the UNITA commander squeezed through the doorway and stepped into the cabin. There was transport arranged. He was expecting to be met.

A white BMW was waiting beside the Dove. Rademeyer locked the aircraft and joined them in the car. They drove to the terminal building. The place was in almost total darkness. Officials were everywhere, hurrying from counter to counter. They carried their own lamps and calculators, and wherever they stopped they plugged in their equipment, examining tickets, checking travel documents, tiny pools of light in the teeming chaos. Molly had already told Rademeyer that she had no passport but the young pilot had dismissed the problem with a sardonic grin. Katilo, he muttered, had semi-diplomatic status. No one argued with him. The normal regulations simply didn't apply.

Molly followed the big Angolan across the crowded concourse. Underfoot, the floor was littered with rubbish and broken glass, and whenever they stopped, strangers would appear, offering porterage, or help with customs, or thick wads of local currency. The more persistent ones surrounded Molly, cutting her off from the others until McFaul fought his way back, taking her by the hand and carving a path towards the door marked '*Sortie*'.

Outside, amongst the taxis, they found the BMW. The back door was open and Katilo stood beside it. He nodded at McFaul's camcorder.

'You OK with that?'

McFaul paused at the kerbside, helping Molly into the car.

'What do you want?'

'Just be ready.'

'What for?'

Molly heard Katilo's cackle of laughter. Then he was getting into the front beside the driver. Rademeyer seemed to have disappeared. Evidently there were arrangements to be made about the aircraft. He wanted it guarded, at least two armed men. He'd be making his own way into the city.

Katilo was speaking to the driver in French. The man nodded, turning up the air-conditioning, easing the BMW into a line of taxis queuing for the airport's exit road. Out on the main highway, the traffic was light and Molly looked out, wondering what she'd find in Kinshasa.

She'd asked Rademeyer about the city back in Cafunfo. Rademeyer flew here regularly, always with Katilo. Katilo, he said, adored the place. If you had money, and no scruples, you could live like a king. President Mobutu did just that. In thirty years of absolute power, he'd robbed the place blind, tucking away a personal fortune of more than six billion dollars. The country itself – potentially one of the richest in Africa – was now bankrupt, crippled by foreign debt and 2,000 per cent inflation. As a result, Mobutu was hated and days of rioting had recently torn Kinshasa apart. The city had become the most dangerous in Africa, a vicious, lawless place peopled by gangsters and pimps and muggers, eager for easy pickings. Zaire, said Rademeyer, was a glimpse of life at its most corrupt and Kinshasa never ceased to amaze him. With the right government contacts, you could buy a licence to fly a 747 for just sixteen dollars.

They were entering the outskirts of the city now, the traffic heavier. At first Molly found it hard to associate the soaring apartment blocks and the elegant tree-lined boulevards with Rademeyer's apocalyptic vision but when she looked a little closer she began to see what he'd meant. Many of the shop fronts were boarded up. Others were fire-blackened and ransacked, the glass on the windows gone, the interiors looted and empty. Rademeyer had called it *le pillage*. In four brief days, rioting troops had apparently stripped the city of everything that could be hand-carried and sold. Much of the rest they'd either torched or demolished.

The crowds began to thin and the BMW purred across an intersection into another quarter of the city. There were more trees here, a park of some kind, and ample villas half-hidden behind tall, white walls. Katilo was talking on a mobile phone, using French again, roaring with laughter at some joke or other. Up ahead was a roundabout. A car on the roundabout, a beaten-up Datsun saloon, appeared to have stalled. The BMW began to slow. Molly looked sideways at McFaul. McFaul had seen the car as well. He was reaching for the camcorder.

The BMW came to a halt. Molly saw movement inside the car, someone behind the wheel, backing the Datsun towards them, cutting them off. Then she became aware of a face at the window, inches from her own. The man was wrenching at the door handle, trying to get in. Molly screamed, and the man stepped forward, pulling open Katilo's door. Katilo was still on the phone. The man had a knife. He was young, a teenager. He was screaming at Katilo, the knife at his throat, his other hand reaching across, trying to get at the controls on the central console to unlock Molly's door. He pressed the wrong button and Molly heard the window purr down. She shrank away from it, terrified, feeling McFaul's arm close around her, pulling her away from the window. The youth was withdrawing from the front now, his right hand already stretching back along the car. Katilo's first bullet caught him in the throat, spinning him around, and the second lifted him bodily into the air before he collapsed on the rubber-stained tarmac, blood pumping from his torn gullet.

Molly stared at him, dry-mouthed. Then she looked at McFaul, seeking comfort, explanation, anything to soften the implications of this terrible spasm of violence, but McFaul had the camcorder to his eye, his body bent forward in the seat, keeping track of Katilo. Katilo was out of the BMW already, making for the stalled car on the roundabout. Molly could see the driver behind the wheel, desperately trying to turn the engine, and when he tried to abandon the car Molly knew he'd left it far too late. Katilo hauled him out one-handed, the huge automatic jammed against his temple, and when he pulled the trigger Molly saw his head erupt in a fine mist of bone fragments and brain tissue. Katilo checked the interior of the empty car, still holding the sagging body, then let it fall to the ground. He turned it over with his foot, glancing in McFaul's direction, then emptied the rest of the magazine into the man's belly. The corpse jerked with the impact of the bullets and Katilo delivered a final kick before returning to the BMW. Under the dashboard there was a box of tissues and as the car began to move again Katilo wiped his hands for a moment or two before resuming his conversation on the mobile phone.

Molly had her eyes closed now. Her hands found the open window and she leaned out, vomiting quietly into the slipstream. She could hear Katilo again. The conversation on the phone was over. He wanted to check on the pictures. The pictures were fine, McFaul was saying. Just fine.

Katilo had rooms booked at the Intercontinental Hotel. Molly walked through the huge lobby, still numbed, still trying to orientate herself. There were signs for a travel agency, tennis courts, a swimming pool, a sauna. There were shops, still open. There was a pharmacy, shelves of beauty products, a display of perfumes. Everywhere she looked, she was back in Europe. Diorella. Johnny Walker. Benetton. Names she recognised. Names that signposted the journey home. Where did Katilo's brand of casual slaughter belong in all this? When would the horror end?

By the bank of lifts, Molly leaned briefly on McFaul. Katilo had disappeared.

'Help me,' she pleaded. 'Please.'

The lift doors opened and she felt McFaul's hand supporting her. It was suddenly very hot and she wondered vaguely whether she might faint. The lift hissed upwards, and the door opened, and suddenly they were in a corridor, walking again. Pictures, she thought, everywhere. Lush studies of the rain forest. Endearing photos of gorillas. An Africa softened and gentled for the hotel's clientele.

McFaul was bending to a lock. The door swung open. The room was enormous, the king-sized bed softly lit by hidden spots. The windows were floor to ceiling, and beyond the crescent of lights below Molly could see the darkness of the river. She leaned against the door, watching McFaul pull the curtains. Even now, even here, he still carried the camcorder.

He was crossing the room, asking her whether she'd be OK. She felt herself shaking her head. She wanted to be put to bed. She wanted to go home. Like Christianne, she'd had enough.

McFaul said nothing, scribbling something on a piece of paper. He offered it to her. She took it.

'What's this?'

'My room number.' He nodded at the telephone. 'Ring if there's a problem.'

'There's a problem.'

'No,' McFaul softened a little, 'you're upset, that's all. That's not a problem. Not compared to what you've coped with so far. Last night was a problem. Muengo was a problem. That's as bad as it gets. Believe me.'

Molly went to the bathroom and sluiced out her mouth with water. Then she sat on the side of the bed and took her shoes off. She could still taste the vomit.

'Muengo was paradise compared to this. I hate this place. I hate what he did. Can't you understand that?'

'Yes. Of course I can.' He paused. 'You should sleep. Try and forget it.'

'I wish I could.'

'Then try.'

Molly stared up at him, wondering what she had to do to get through to this strange man. The last twenty-four hours had robbed her of her bearings. She no longer knew where she was. She felt lost and very afraid. She wanted reassurance. She wanted to know she could go home.

McFaul bent to Molly and put his hand briefly on her shoulder. She reached up, squeezing it, then let him go. She heard his footsteps across the carpet. When she'd finished throwing up again, she rinsed her mouth and slumped against the side of the bath, her mind quite blank.

After a while, she crawled back into the bedroom. Beside the dressing table was a mini-bar. She opened it, selecting three miniatures of vodka and a carton of mango juice. She lined them up beside the bed and pulled back the covers, not bothering to undress. She began to shake again, deep tremors, wholly beyond her control. She closed her eyes, trying to find a point of reference, something to seize on, a lifebelt in the swirling tide. All too briefly, she saw her husband. Giles was standing in the well of the *Molly Jay.* It was summer. He was wearing an old pair of blue shorts. He was very brown. He was waving. Molly called his name, trying to attract his attention but he was looking the other way, upriver, grinning.

Molly felt tears, hot, on her face. They trickled down her cheeks, dampening the pillow. Giles wouldn't have left her like this. Giles would have stayed. He'd have comforted her. He'd have held her tight. He'd have been there in the smallest hours, when it mattered most. He'd have agreed with her about Katilo. The man was a monster. Life meant nothing to him.

Molly's hand reached up to the bedside cabinet, finding one of the miniatures of vodka. She unscrewed the top, holding the tiny bottle under her nose. She hated spirits, never drank them, never bothered with them. The vodka smelled of nothing. She closed her eyes again, wondering whether she should phone home. Getting calls out of Kinshasa might be easier than the endless tussle with the Luanda international operator. She could ring up Patrick, find out the latest on Giles, find out whether – by some miracle – he'd turned up. She tried to imagine the conversation, Patrick probably preparing for bed, pausing in the hall, lifting the phone, courteous and patient as ever. She'd be in tears within seconds, she knew she would, and at some point Patrick would have to confirm yet again what she already knew. That Giles was dead.

She shook her head, told herself to get a grip, tried to picture situations she knew she'd handled alone. Running, she thought. The path that led up the lane, beyond the kissing gate. The sounds she made in autumn, dancing through the fallen leaves, the first bright kiss of winter on her lips. By now, the fieldside puddles would be crusted with early morning ice. She tasted the air in her mouth, heard the mew of the seagulls, blown inland by the gales out at sea. She tried to linger on the images, proof that she could cope on her own, but then there was Giles again, back from the ocean, *Molly Jay* intact, the kettle on, the copy of the *Daily Telegraph* open on the kitchen table, already sticky with marmalade. He'd be looking up as she fell in through the door, exhausted, triumphant, the backs of her calves coated in drying mud. His long legs would reach beneath the table, pushing a chair towards her. His hand would close on the teapot. He'd offer her a slice of toast. He'd tell her she was mad, and she'd grin back, still breathless, agreeing.

Molly groaned, turning over, burying her head in the pillow, the miniature of vodka abandoned.

The phone woke McFaul at dawn. He rolled over in the huge bed and it was several seconds before he recognised the voice at the other end.

'Ken?'

'Yeah.'

'You got the telex?'

'Yeah.'

McFaul struggled upright in the bed. He'd sent the telex last night, handing it to the clerk behind the reception desk and insisting he dispatch it at once. Ken Middleton was normally at his desk in Devizes early. Global ran operations in umpteen time zones and he always claimed it gave him a head start on the rest of the headquarters team.

Ken was already talking about the tickets, checking the times and flight numbers.

'The twelfth is tomorrow.'

'That's right.'

'Why Paris?'

'It's closest. There are no direct flights.'

'Are you sure?'

'Yeah. I checked last night. Air France leave at midday. That should do us nicely.' McFaul paused. He'd asked Middleton for two prepaid tickets to be delivered to the Intercontinental. The way he'd put it in the telex hadn't left much room for argument. Muengo had been a disaster. He and Bennie had been lucky to get out in one piece.

Middleton was going through the arrangements again. Once you'd worked in the minefields, thoroughness became a state of mind.

'Who's this Jordan bloke?' he said finally.

'Friend of mine.'

'And why am I paying for him?'

'Her.'

'*Her*?'

'Yeah. Remember James Jordan? Kid who got himself killed? That report I sent you? She's his mother.'

'But why the ticket?'

'Dunno really.' McFaul smothered a yawn. 'I'd call it an investment if I were you.'

McFaul called Molly an hour later. She answered the phone at once, a small, cautious voice that suggested she'd been awake most of the night. McFaul explained the travel arrangements. They wouldn't be returning to Angola, they'd be flying straight back to Europe. The tickets would be prepaid. Katilo would be settling the room bill. Which only left one problem.

'What's that?'

'Your passport. You said it's still in Luanda. You'll have to go to the embassy here. They'll issue you with a temporary replacement. Tell them it got stolen or something. It happens all the time.'

Molly began to protest, something about not being the embassy's favourite person, but McFaul cut her short.

'Rademeyer's around somewhere,' he said briskly. 'I'll get him to take you. Best you stay together. Otherwise it might get tricky.'

'Tricky?'

McFaul heard the anxiety in her voice and told her not to worry. Given a fair wind, she'd be back in the UK by the weekend. Plenty of time to get herself together.

'What for? As a matter of interest?'

McFaul was sitting at the bureau by the window. Over the broad expanse of river he could see Kinshasa's sister city of Brazzaville, a friezc of white buildings against the enveloping green of the mountains beyond. Molly was repeating the question, angry now, and McFaul smiled, glad she'd survived the night.

'Christmas,' he said lightly. 'Only ten shopping days to go.'

Katilo was still in bed when McFaul knocked on his door. He let McFaul in and padded across to the bathroom. Beneath the unbelted silk dressing gown, he was naked. McFaul settled into an armchair, helping himself to a pile of cashews from the mini-bar. The summons from Katilo had come half an hour earlier.

'Lunch-time OK?'

Katilo had appeared at the bathroom door. He'd abandoned the dressing gown for a towel around his waist and McFaul could hear the splash of water filling the bath behind him.

McFaul nodded.

'I'll be here,' he said. 'Twelve o'clock.'

'You've got more tapes? These guys talk a lot.'

'No problem.'

Katilo looked at him a moment then backed into the bathroom. On the phone, he'd already established the importance of the midday rendezvous. The people he'd be meeting were key players, men who understood the situation in Angola, men who were determined to see the war settled in UNITA's favour. They were realists, businessmen, guys with no time for the socialists in Luanda. They had access to arms, anything you cared to name, and the purpose of the encounter was to agree a shopping list.

The way Katilo had put it on the phone made the arrangement sound almost benign, an act of charity, but McFaul had already guessed the way it would really be. In exchange for diamonds, Katilo would buy himself a planeload of weaponry. That's the way it worked. That was the reason for the detour to Cafunfo. Ivan, the man who ran Cafunfo, doubtless operated under UNITA's wing. In return for protection – the guards on the door, the line of soldiers fencing the compound from the street – he'd be expected to contribute a hefty percentage of his gems to the cause. The cause arrived regularly in the shape of men like Katilo, highly placed field commanders with the authority to conduct arms negotiations. Ever since he'd arrived in Angola, McFaul had heard about the rivalries between such men, each one jostling for advantage. The tightness of UNITA's discipline had helped suppress these rivalries but if Sarimbi ever won the war, peace would bring a scramble for the biggest prizes. A seat at the cabinet table. A posting abroad. Untold wealth. Untold opportunities. No wonder Katilo wanted to spread the word. In Africa, like everywhere else in the world, a video of your own was the shortest cut to sainthood.

Katilo was in the bath now. He called McFaul in. McFaul went to the door, peering through a curtain of steam. Katilo was playing with a plastic soap dish, pushing it to and fro. The water was inches from the top of the tub, displaced by his massive body. McFaul looked down at him. Naked, sprawled in the bath, he was defenceless. Killing a man would never have been easier yet Katilo seemed oblivious to the possibility.

'There's a big party,' he said. 'You should be there. With your camera.'

'When?'

'Soon. Maybe tomorrow. Maybe the next day.'

McFaul sank onto the toilet. He'd already established the importance of leaving on the Air France flight but he went through it all again. Television pictures were perishable. Getting Katilo's war on screen meant working fast. Hanging around in Kinshasa would be a waste of precious editing time. Katilo listened, poking at the soap dish, nodding at the logic behind each phrase. When McFaul had finished, he looked up.

'You think it'll work? The video?'

'Yes.'

'But for me, as well?'

McFaul stared at him a moment. Underestimating Katilo was a very dangerous game. Dozens of men must have done it and most of them were probably dead.

'Tell me what you will put in it,' Katilo was saying. 'Tell me the way it will be.'

McFaul shrugged. Getting the right words in the right order had never been so important.

'It'll be very violent,' he said carefully. 'Very bloody.'

'With the minefield?'

'Yes.'

'And your friend? Domingos?'

'Yes.'

'And me?'

'Of course.'

'Why? Why of course?'

'Because you put the mines there in the first place.'

There was a long silence. McFaul felt the sweat beading on his face.

'You think I killed Domingos?' Katilo said at last.

'I know you killed Domingos.'

Katilo looked at him for a moment. Then he nodded.

'You're right,' he said softly, 'but I also won.'

The British Embassy in Kinshasa lies close to the Zaire river. Piet Rademeyer had acquired a brand new Mercedes with tinted windows, and he pulled into a parking bay beside the embassy compound. The air-conditioning in the Mercedes didn't work properly, blowing hot air instead of cold, but he'd refused to lower the windows because he swore it ruined the look of the car. Image in Kinshasa was everything.

Molly got out of the Mercedes and approached the Gurkha on the embassy gate. She'd bought a dress from a boutique at the hotel, borrowing money from McFaul, but it was already damp with sweat, clinging uncomfortably to her. Trying on the dress had been a revelation. In the last two weeks, she must have lost nearly a stone.

The Gurkha directed her to a small office inside the gate. She'd already phoned from the hotel, explaining the passport problem, and the woman who'd taken the call had given her a reference number. Molly quoted it now, waiting for a minute or so while the official behind the thick plate-glass consulted a list. Finally, he looked up.

'Mrs Jordan?'

'Yes?'

'The Chargé would like a word. Someone will be over to collect you.'

Molly thanked him, stepping outside again. Clouds were towering over the river, heavy with rain, and gusts of wind were stirring the trees along the Avenue des Trois. Molly bent to the Mercedes, telling Rademeyer that he might have to wait a while. The despair she'd felt overnight had gone. With the promise of a ticket home had come an extraordinary calmness. She'd been tested and she'd survived. She owed apologies to no one.

A young man from the embassy appeared in the road, inviting her into the compound. The embassy was surrounded by tall walls topped with razor wire. Inside, there were a handful of Barratt-style houses and a swimming pool. Range Rovers occupied the parking spaces, and there were a couple of Zodiac inflatables strapped to launch trailers. Molly looked at the scene as they made for the main door, amused. Forget the flame trees and the trellis of bougainvillaea and she might have been back on some estate in the Home Counties, turning up for midday drinks.

The Chargé d'Affaires turned out to be a woman in her forties, severely dressed in a neat two-piece suit. Her hair was drawn back from her face in a tight bun and she wore a look of almost permanent impatience. When Molly sat down in front of the desk, she didn't bother with small talk. She had a telex in front of her, key phrases ringed in red.

'I've been in touch with Luanda,' she said at once. 'They're not best pleased.'

'I'm sure.' Molly smiled. 'Have I broken any laws?'

'That's hardly the point. As I understand it, they advised you not to go inland. Advice you chose to ignore.'

'Yes.'

'Not once but twice.'

'Yes.'

'And on both occasions you went to . . .' She frowned, her eyes returning to the telex.

'Muengo,' Molly said. 'My son's buried there.'

The woman nodded, wrong-footed for a moment, and Molly found herself studying a small, framed photo on the desk. It showed the Chargé perched on a five-bar gate. She was wearing a green anorak and a stout pair of boots. Beside her, bent against the wind, was a fit-looking man in his sixties.

'You take risks,' Molly pointed out, 'when you lose someone close, someone you love.'

'That's hardly the issue, Mrs Jordan. This isn't Stow-on-the-Wold.'

'Does that make a difference?'

'Yes, I'm afraid it does.' She leaned back in the chair, softening a little. 'I'm sorry about your son. We all are. But life can be dangerous out here. Angola's in a state of war. People die.' She shrugged. 'It happens all the time. We do what we can, of course, but it's never easy.'

'What isn't?'

'Getting it through to people like yourself.'

'You think I should have stayed at home?'

'I think you should have stayed in Luanda, like we suggested. Flying out in the first place was obviously your decision. It's a free world. But after that . . .' she sighed, 'it might have paid you to listen.'

Molly leaned forward adjusting the hem of her dress. She couldn't remember when she'd last felt so angry. What could this woman possibly know about James? How dare she condense the last two weeks into a lecture about travel arrangements?

'I went to Muengo to find out about my son,' she said softly. 'I wanted to know how he died.'

'I understood your son stepped on a mine.'

'He did.'

'Then perhaps he should have listened, too. Most aid workers are more careful. We get very few casualties.'

'That's not the point.'

'It isn't?'

'No.' Molly shook her head, colouring now. 'My son didn't simply die. He was killed. Someone killed him. That's why I came to Africa. That's the question I wanted answered.'

'It was a mine,' the Chargé said again, 'he stepped on a mine.'

'Of course he did. But mines are put there. They're not part of the landscape. They don't grow. They're made by somebody. Sold by somebody. Bought by somebody. Two weeks ago, I didn't know that. Now I do.'

'And does it help? Knowing that?'

'Yes, it does.'

'Why?'

'Because . . .' Molly stopped, looking at the photograph on the desk again. 'It's important, that's all.'

'Important for who? You?'

'Others. Other mothers. Other sons.' She nodded at the photo. 'Even husbands.'

The Chargé looked at her a moment, as cold as ever.

'That's my father,' she said at last, 'in case you were wondering.'

'OK,' Molly shrugged, 'your father, then. It makes no difference. Somebody close to you dies, you want to know why. It's not an act of God. It's not an earthquake or a hurricane or something. It's man-made. Literally. Someone dies. Someone gets killed. There has to be blame. Does that make sense? Or am I being silly?'

'Foolish. You're being foolish.'

'*Foolish*? To care about what happened? *Foolish*?' Molly paused, remembering the morning in the schoolhouse, Bennie's voice drifting in through the open window, telling her exactly the way it had been with James. 'My son was blown up by a big mine. It tore him nearly in half. They brought his body back to Muengo. There was nowhere to keep it. He had a girlfriend. She wanted to—'

'Please, Mrs Jordan . . .'

The Chargé was frowning now, embarrassed, wanting the conversation over, but Molly shook her head, refusing to let her off the hook. She'd started this conversation, for God's sake. And now she had to listen.

'My son did nothing wrong. In fact he was trying to find a child when it happened. He might have been headstrong but his heart was in the right place. He was trying to help. Can you understand that?'

'Perfectly.'

'And you'd understand how a mother would feel? Back in the UK? Getting a phone call explaining that her son was dead?'

'It must have been awful.'

'It was. But there are things you can do. Weeping's not enough. You have to find out.'

'Find out what, Mrs Jordan?'

'Find out what happened. Find out who killed him.'

'And you've got an answer? To that last question? A name?'

Molly paused, taking a deep breath, letting some of the anger subside. Then she shook her head.

'I'd love one,' she said quietly, 'but it isn't that simple, is it?'

McFaul arrived late for the midday meeting. It was ten past twelve before he made it back to Room 631. Two large Africans stood outside the door, both wearing black jump-suits. McFaul showed them his hotel registration card and asked for Katilo. When Katilo opened the door, McFaul could smell the rich, heavy scent of cigar smoke.

He stepped inside, retrieving his bag from the guard who'd been searching it. Two men were sitting on the long crescent of sofa. One was enormous, a middle-aged man spilling out of a rumpled linen suit. He had a dark, almost Mediterranean complexion and the cigar between his pudgy fingers left circles of blue smoke as he talked animatedly to the man beside him. The latter looked a little older, a well-dressed black in his late fifties. He had a wild head of hair, beginning to grey at the edges, and when he saw McFaul he smiled.

Katilo did the introductions. The fat man's name was Sarkis. He was a trader. He had a fine house in the mountains behind

Beirut. Another in Antwerp. He came to Zaire often. He knew lots about diamonds. The other man's name was Mr Lawrence. He was an American, a good friend of Katilo's, a firm ally of Angola's, a man UNITA could trust.

McFaul was already unpacking his bag, getting the camcorder ready, wondering whether Katilo had bothered to warn these two men that their conversation would be taped. The American had already got up and drawn Katilo aside, and the pair were deep in conversation on the other side of the room. It was raining hard now, the city a blur beyond the big picture windows, and McFaul saw Katilo frowning and shaking his head, emphatic denials, listening to the American. Mr Lawrence was wearing a dark three-piece suit, exquisitely cut, and he had an almost courtly manner, using his hands a lot when he talked, sealing each point with yet another smile.

At length the two men returned, the American guiding Katilo by the elbow, the gentlest touch. Katilo looked a little crestfallen, gesturing at the low glass table in front of the sofa. For the first time, McFaul saw the diamonds. They were laid out on a square of black velvet behind the tray of coffee. Sarkis reached forward, poking the diamonds with his forefinger, selecting one of the smaller gemstones. He produced a magnifying lens and pouched it in one eye, inspecting the diamond in the light from the window.

McFaul glanced at Katilo, asking him whether he wanted him to tape. Katilo looked at the American.

'Mr Lawrence . . .' he began.

Lawrence put his hand on Katilo's arm, taking over. He spoke in a slow southern drawl, a deep voice, beautifully modulated.

'The colonel has told me about your film,' he said at once. 'It sounds an exciting project. I'd love to help you all I can but we have ourselves a problem here. You'll appreciate these conversations . . .' He gestured loosely towards the pile of diamonds. 'It could be sensitive.'

McFaul said he'd do what everyone wanted. Katilo came up with an idea. Before the real business began McFaul would shoot the three of them just talking. That way, the audience would get to see the other side of Katilo's work without having to share any secrets. The American was smiling again.

'Sure,' he said, 'go ahead. Only leave me out.'

'You mean that?'

'I'm afraid I do.'

Katilo looked briefly annoyed, then shrugged. Sarkis had finished with the diamonds. He, too, was less than interested in appearing in Katilo's video, not bothering to hide his irritation.

'Why didn't you mention this already?'

'I thought it was no problem.'

'No problem?' Sarkis squinted up at him. 'You kidding?'

The American sat down again, reaching for his coffee. Katilo, robbed of his video sequence, was eyeing them both, visibly frustrated. Watching him, McFaul began to sense the limits of his authority. In the bush, Katilo could play the emperor. Here, it wasn't quite so clear-cut.

Finally, Katilo walked across to the wardrobe, telling McFaul to have the camcorder ready. McFaul did what he was told, pressing the record button as Katilo stooped to pull out a big cardboard box. He beckoned McFaul closer, opening the flaps on top of the box. Inside, nestling amongst little shells of polystyrene packing, were dozens of anti-personnel mines. Katilo selected one, weighing it in his hand for a moment or two, musing aloud about the shape of the deal. He'd come to Kinshasa for resupplies. There were friends here who would give him anything he needed. Samples were delivered to his hotel room. The rest would go straight to the airport for onward shipment.

Katilo looked up. His eyes narrowed.

'Right, Sarkis?'

McFaul put the camcorder down, glancing round towards

the sofa. Sarkis was shovelling the diamonds into a small leather bag, ignoring the question. Lawrence, the American, was staring out of the window. Katilo shrugged again, then tossed the mine to McFaul. McFaul caught it in his left hand, hearing Katilo's low chuckle.

'For you, my friend,' he murmured, 'souvenir from Kinshasa.'

McFaul took the mine back to his hotel room. It was one of the PMNs, circular, the size of an ashtray, and McFaul could tell at once from the weight that it was a dud, a demo that salesmen used to secure a contract. Soviet-made, the real thing had claimed more victims than any other mine in the world.

McFaul went to the window, gazing out. The rain had stopped again and one of the Brazzaville ferries was nosing out into the river. It lay low in the water, slightly lopsided, the decks crowded with passengers. There were more of them on the roof, a riot of colour, and gouts of greasy brown smoke from the funnel drifted away on the wind as the ferry set course for the distant smudge of Brazzaville.

McFaul looked at the mine again, fingering the ring pull on the side that armed it. He'd lifted hundreds of these in Afghanistan. There were factories all over the world turning out copies, and you could buy them by the dozen in Pakistan. He'd seen a boxful himself in the market in Miranshah. Six dollars each. No questions asked.

He went back to the bed, swamped by the memories. In Afghanistan, he'd often found the PMNs semi-exposed, protected by a summer's growth of scrub and grass. In that situation, you were bloody careful, working slowly round the thing, using garden secateurs, snipping away the vegetation before lifting the mine out by its sides, like a surgeon removing a cyst. McFaul closed his eyes, back amongst the rocky hillsides. That's where he'd found Mohammed, the little Afghan goat herd, the body curled amongst the rocks. That's where his anger and his rage had first taken root.

McFaul's hand closed around the mine. At this very moment, Katilo was probably buying thousands of the things, plus laying orders for any other mine that took his fancy. The diamonds on the table in the room downstairs would give him the pick of the stuff on the market. Type 72s. Valselas. SB-33s, Claymores. Anything he could load into Rademeyer's Dove and fly south. More work for the surgeons. More limbless kids begging in the streets of Luanda.

McFaul sank onto the bed. He and Bennie had returned Mohammed's body to his home village, the scruffy cluster of packed-earth dwellings on the road to Jeji. They'd wrapped the boy in a blanket and carried him down the hillside, trying to keep their footing in the loose scree. The kid was days dead, his body stiffened, the flesh eaten away where the wild dogs had been at him, and the journey had seemed endless. Afterwards in the village there were the parents to cope with. Oddly, their grief had been muted. Mines had narrowed the land, hemming them in, and they seemed to have done something similar to the people's feelings. They were resigned. They were stoical. Their children were dying all the time. It was something you had to live with, like the implacable weather, and crop failure, and the fat Soviet helicopters that came chattering down the valley, scattering yet more mines.

McFaul rolled over, letting the PMN fall to the floor. They'd stayed the night in the village, sleeping in the Land Rover. Next morning, he'd shaken Mohammed's father by the hand, not knowing quite what to say, the gruffest farewell. Driving back to Kabul, he'd told Bennie that simply clearing up wasn't enough. Ridding Afghanistan of mines might take a hundred years. There had to be another way. Bennie had laughed, like he always did. The money was good. They were saving lives. What else could you do?

McFaul thought about the question now. The spilling of

blood carried certain responsibilities. That's what he'd wanted to say to Mohammed's father. That's what he'd tried to say to Celestina. An eye for an eye. A leg for a leg. A life for a life. He got to his feet again, looking at his watch, brooding.

CHAPTER THIRTEEN

The sauna of the Intercontinental Hotel is on the ground floor, tucked between the changing rooms for the outdoor swimming pool and the line of squash courts that flank the building to the east. Molly left her clothes in a locker in the changing room, wrapping a towel round herself. The attendant beside the plunge pool assured her that the sauna was nearly empty. One or two guests at the most. No hassle. No sweat. Molly thanked him, smiling dutifully at the joke, pulling open the heavy pine door. A fat bubble of hot air enveloped her at once, and she lifted her face, savouring the smell of resin, knowing that this decision of hers had been right. Something to take her mind off Kinshasa. Something to stop her thinking about Katilo, and the Chargé at the embassy, and the prospect of another night in this appalling city.

'Hi . . .'

Molly looked round. The sauna was empty except for a man on the corner bench nearest the door. He had a yellow towel round his waist and one leg was missing below the knee, the stump dangling down over the edge of the wooden slats.

Molly reached at once for the door. McFaul looked amused.

'Too hot for you?'

'Not at all.'

'Then stay.' McFaul nodded at the empty benches. 'No need to worry about me.'

'It's not that . . .'

400

'No?'

'No.' Molly shook her head, still hesitating by the door. She eyed him a moment, then forced another smile, settling herself carefully on the adjacent bench. She liked McFaul but she didn't understand him. The life he led seemed indescribably dangerous and the scars he carried slightly frightened her. McFaul was what happened when you got used to these awful mines. For him, they'd become a way of life.

McFaul reached for the scoop, splashing more water on the hot coals, and Molly felt the temperature rise at once, a thick woolly blanket of air, tightening around her. She was sweating already, leaning forward, her elbows on her knees, avoiding contact with the wall. McFaul had settled again. His forearms were dark from exposure to the sun but the pale white skin of the rest of his body was yellowed with bruising. The bruises were everywhere, down his ribcage, across the small of his back, and there were graze marks too, as if he'd been dragged across rough ground.

McFaul was cleaning the dirt from his fingernails. The silence between them unnerved Molly.

'Those cassettes you've got,' she said lightly. 'What happens to them now?'

'We take them back to the UK.'

'We?'

'Me,' he glanced up, wiping his face with the back of his hand, 'and you. If you're interested.'

'I'm not with you.'

'There's a programme to make. You could be part of all that.'

'You mean Alma?'

McFaul shrugged.

'Sure. Or whoever else.'

Molly looked at him a moment, uncertain. The film had begun with Todd Llewelyn. At Robbie's invitation, Alma Bradley had stepped in. Now, McFaul was evidently thinking of a third party.

'Who do you mean?'

'I don't know. I'm not an expert. Television? You tell me.'

'But you want to see it through? This film? Whatever it is?'

'Absolutely. No question.'

'And Alma? The woman I told you about? In Luanda?'

'She's welcome. More than welcome. As long as – ' He broke off, frowning, studying his hands again.

'As long as what?'

'As long as she sees it the way we saw it, the way it happened. No more bullshit. No more dressing up. Katilo thinks we're making some kind of PR film. Llewelyn wanted his name in fairy lights. And maybe your Alma friend's got some angle too. I don't want that, don't need it. The stuff's there, you've seen it, most of it, first-hand. Why don't we just cut it all together? Tell it the way it was? Eh? I'm no film director but I don't think we're short of material, do you?' He looked up, staring at her, the sweat pouring from his hairline, the veins in his temples raised and throbbing, and for the first time she realised that McFaul was no more immune to what had happened than she'd been. The last two weeks must have touched him, she thought. Deeply.

'Not at all. I think you've been extraordinary. Doing what you've done.'

'Yeah?'

'Yes.' Molly nodded. 'That night in Muengo when we went to the bonfire. The night they slaughtered the cow. I don't know how you did it, watched it. I just . . .' She shook her head, one hand tightening the knot that secured the towel at the top of her breasts.

McFaul reached for the scoop again. The water hissed on the coals, evaporating immediately.

'You have to,' he said savagely, 'there's no choice. It got us out of Muengo. That's one thing. But I'd have done it anyway if I'd thought hard enough. People don't know. They don't have a clue. They think Africa's one big basket case. They think they can solve it with raffles and rock concerts and appeals on telly. It never occurs to anyone there might be a reason these people are starving. You know about Angola? How rich it could be?' He paused. 'And you know where most of the money goes? Anyone ever tell you?'

Molly nodded. Rademeyer had told her on the plane, that first flight down to Muengo.

'Arms?' she suggested.

'Yeah.' McFaul was staring at her. 'Guns, shells, mines, you name it. Both sides. Katilo's lot. The government. They're both at it. You know how much those clowns in Luanda spent last year? Buying stuff in?' Molly frowned, trying to remember the figure. McFaul beat her to it. 'Two billion dollars. Two *billion*. That's money spent by a government that can't feed its own people. A government that chops its kids off at the knees.'

Molly reached out for him, hearing the rage in his voice. His head was down again, his hands tightly knotted together, the bands of muscle in his forearms standing out. She'd rarely seen anyone so tense. No wonder he'd come for a sauna. A question had been nagging at her for days. She'd tried to think of ways of softening it but she knew now that there was no point.

'Your own injuries,' she said quietly. 'What happened to your leg and your face. Is that why you're so angry?'

McFaul's head came up. He looked at her for a moment or two, a speculative expression on his face, as if he'd never considered the question before.

'No,' he shook his head, 'not at all.'

'Your friend told me about it. Bennie.'

'Did he? Kuwait? All that?'

'Yes. It must have been dreadful, ghastly.'

McFaul shrugged.

'We were well paid. We knew the odds. It wasn't the same at all. It wasn't like this.'

'Like what?'

403

'Like here. Angola. Muengo . . .' He paused. 'Innocent people, decent people. Blokes like Domingos.'

'Or James?'

'Yeah,' he nodded, 'or James.'

Molly said nothing. It was the first time McFaul had betrayed the slightest sympathy for her dead son and she risked a smile, a small expression of gratitude. McFaul ducked his head, embarrassed. After a while, he looked up again. His voice was lower, contemplative, much of the anger gone. He sounded, if anything, resigned.

'Do it commercially,' he said, 'and you lose your judgement. It's like any other deal. Contracts. Deadlines. Penalty payments. You're so keen on the money, you stop thinking. That's why . . .' He gestured at the remains of his leg, not bothering to finish the sentence.

Molly wanted to ask another question. There were parts of McFaul it was possible to touch. Just.

'Does that make it easier?'

'What?'

'Knowing it was your fault? Or partly your fault?'

'Sure,' he nodded, 'it was a mistake. And you only make it once. Either it kills you, or you end up like me.' He looked down at his leg again. The stump was puckered, like the top of a peeled orange.

There was a long silence.

'Bennie told me you were covering for someone else. He said it was his fault. Not yours.'

'Makes no difference. With most blokes, it's greed. That's a weakness. I was just soft in the head. I should have shopped the guy, turned him in. That's a weakness, too.'

'Compassion?'

'Bad judgement. The guy was a dickhead.' He eyed her a moment. 'I'm hopeless with people. Always get it wrong. Always have. Always will. Bennie tell you that, too?'

'Yes,' Molly smiled, 'he did.'

'Well, then . . .' He ducked his head again, desperate to change the subject. There were firms working in Africa, he said, who were clearing minefields commercially. Same deal as Kuwait.

'You mean in Angola?'

'Not so far. Mozambique mainly.'

'But isn't that OK? Aren't they the experts? The ones who'd know best?'

'Oh sure, sure. But there's a twist. Some of these firms are in the mines business already. They deal at both ends. They make the stuff, flog it, and then pop back a couple of years later and clean it all up. Isn't that neat? Getting paid twice? Once for killing people? Maiming them? And then again when they've had enough?' He shook his head, picking at a shred of loose skin on one of his fingers. 'This game stinks, stinks. That's why I'm keen on doing some kind of film. People should see for themselves. People should know.'

'Will they ever show it?'

'God knows. I hope so.'

'And is that enough? Will people take any notice?'

McFaul was staring at her again, anger and surprise.

'You think they won't?'

'I'm just asking the question.' Molly frowned. 'People get to see a lot nowadays.'

'But you think it needs something else?'

'I don't know.' Molly was looking at his leg again. 'What else can you do?'

After the sauna, McFaul slept. When he awoke, it was nearly dark, the last of the sunset mirrored on the broad sweep of the Zaire river below the hotel window. He dressed slowly, pensive. When he descended in the lift to the hotel lobby, a note awaited him from Katilo. He was to take the camcorder up to his room. He was to leave it there with a note explaining how to make the thing work. The colonel's plans for the evening had changed. He'd be back in the hotel by nine.

McFaul collected the camcorder and found his way to Katilo's room. The room had been cleaned since the midday meeting. There was fresh fruit in a bowl on the coffee table, and a vase of flowers in an alcove above the long crescent of sofa. The curtains had been drawn over the tall picture windows and the top cover on the bed had been folded carefully down. Three champagne glasses stood on a silver tray beside the bed, and McFaul looked at them a moment. A note on the tray directed Katilo to the mini-bar, and McFaul opened it, finding three bottles of Krug nestling in buckets of ice-cubes. He closed the door, looking at the bed again. Three glasses. A bottle each.

The phone began to ring, trilling softly beside the bed. McFaul ignored it, positioning the camcorder on the edge of the dressing-table. Katilo hadn't specified why he wanted the camcorder but McFaul could guess at the kind of sequence he had in mind. The major international hotels were served by Kinshasa's top call girls. For visiting businessmen crazy enough to risk AIDS, a couple of hundred dollars would buy an hour or two of à la carte sex. For Katilo, given his military status, the full menu was probably on the house. McFaul bent to the camcorder. Through the tiny viewfinder, he could see at least three-quarters of the bed. He moved it a little, first left, then right, wondering quite where Katilo preferred to perform. At length he settled on a shot that included the pillow and the waiting triangle of crisp white sheet.

The phone was still ringing. McFaul picked it up. It was Rademeyer.

'Katilo there?'

'No.'

'*No?*'

McFaul explained about Katilo and his request for the camcorder. Rademeyer confirmed his suspicions.

'Man's insatiable.' He laughed. 'He keeps a scrapbook of photos. He's talked me through them a couple of times.' He asked McFaul if he could see a package Katilo had wanted delivered. Brown Jiffybag. Size of a paperback book. McFaul scanned the room.

'No,' he said, 'can't see it.'

'Cupboards? Wardrobes? Tried them?'

McFaul began to search. Except for a Bible, the chest of drawers beside the mini-bar was empty. Across the room, behind the louvred doors, was a walk-in closet. McFaul limped towards it, skirting the huge bed. He was still looking for Rademeyer's Jiffybag, when he spotted the trip-wire. He froze, motionless beside the bed. The trip-wire was at ankle-height, barely inches away, and his eyes followed it to the wall. The mine was a Claymore, a container the size of a kid's paintbox, taped above the skirting-board. On the outside, a line of raised letters read FRONT TOWARDS ENEMY. McFaul stepped slowly backwards. The other end of the trip-wire ran to a fixing point by the hinge of the door that led out to the balcony. Beyond the trip-wire, lay the closet.

McFaul circled carefully round the bed. Then he bent to the Claymore, making sure there were no funnies. It was easy to booby-trap a mine like this. Get it wrong, make a single mistake, and the seven hundred steel balls inside would tear him apart. Claymores were the mines you used to protect whole sections of men in the field. Anyone closer than a hundred metres was history.

Finding no booby-traps, McFaul knew he had to make the mine safe. In a leather pouch on his belt he carried a fold-up multi-tool. The multi-tool included a pair of wire cutters and he crouched beside the Claymore, holding the firing pin steady with one hand, cutting the trip-wire with the other. Then he got to his feet, unsteady for a second, suddenly aware of the sweat darkening the thin cotton shirt. Only Katilo would have been crazy enough to risk triggering a Claymore within the confines of a hotel bedroom. God knows what would have happened had the thing gone off.

Remembering Rademeyer, McFaul returned to the phone.

When he told Rademeyer he couldn't find the Jiffybag the South African cursed. He'd been planning to go out. Now he'd have to wait until Katilo returned. He gave McFaul his room number in case Katilo turned up, then rang off. McFaul was still looking at the closet. The door was half-open. Inside, there were clothes hanging on a rail and below the clothes was the cardboard box he'd seen earlier. McFaul replaced the phone and crossed the room again, examining the closet doors for more booby-traps. Finding nothing, he knelt beside the box. Inside, plainly visible, were the land mines. McFaul frowned. There were maybe a dozen mines piled on top of each other, different types, none of them live. He could see the carrying caps, the small plastic screw-in blanks you removed before inserting the detonator. In all, the mines were worth no more than a couple of hundred dollars. Why go to the trouble of booby-trapping a dozen unfused mines? Why post a sentry as lethal as a Claymore?

McFaul's own room was two floors away. Tucked into a pocket of his holdall was a slim MagLite torch. He returned to Katilo's room, locking the door behind him, squatting awkwardly beside the box in the confined space of the closet. Katilo's camouflage smock, hanging on the rail above his head, smelled of cigar smoke. McFaul switched on the torch, the pencil beam probing the recesses of the box. At the bottom, beside a nine-inch anti-tank mine, he saw something sparkling. He moved the torch a little, peering in, trying to make sense of the dancing lights. He put the torch in his mouth, knowing already what it was he'd probably find. The Claymore, after all, hadn't been such a bad idea.

McFaul reached in, extracting the mines one by one, laying them carefully beside the box. At the bottom of the box was a small polythene bag. Inside the bag were diamonds. McFaul held up the bag, the torch still in his mouth, trying to count the tiny uncut gems. At fifteen he gave up. There were thirty, forty, maybe more. Back in Europe, they'd be worth a fortune. Out here, in Kinshasa, Katilo could exchange them for hundreds of thousands of mines. By taking the diamonds, by putting them to better use, McFaul might spare Angola a little of the agony to come. Fewer shredded limbs. Fewer broken lives. The proposition brought a grim smile to his face and he eased himself out of the closet, leaning back against the bed. Minutes earlier, finding the mines, he'd wondered about setting his own booby-trap. One of the little Chinese Type 72As, for instance, armed and waiting beneath Katilo's pillow. The notion was beautifully simple, a certain death sentence, years of suffering – his own and others' – repaid in a millisecond of splintered bone and pulped brain tissue. But a moment's thought told him the plan was far from foolproof. What if he was right about the call girls? What if someone else's head hit the pillow first?

McFaul hesitated a moment then pocketed the diamonds. According to the clock beside the bed, it was nearly eight. He began to repack the mines, lowering them carefully into the box, then realised there was no point. The first thing Katilo would check on his return was the Claymore. Finding the wire cut would take him to the closet and once he knew the diamonds had gone, the first name on his lips would be McFaul's. Who else had the key to the room? Who else knew how to disarm a Claymore?

The phone began to ring again. McFaul looked at it, uncertain. It was already ten past eight. Maybe Katilo had come back early. Maybe he was after his key. McFaul glanced at the camcorder, wondering whether to take it, then dismissed the thought. What mattered now was getting away from the hotel. The less he carried, the better. He turned for the door, then paused. At some point or other, knowing Katilo, he'd proceed with the evening's entertainment. Diamonds or no diamonds, he'd owe himself a party.

In a folder on the desk, McFaul found a sheet of hotel notepaper. The Biro didn't work properly and his hand was shaking more than he cared to admit but the scrawled instructions were still legible. 'Once you've found the Power and Self-

View buttons,' he wrote, 'everything takes care of itself.' He smiled, folding the instructions and leaving them beside the camcorder. Nice adieu, he thought, checking his pocket for the diamonds.

Rademeyer was watching television when McFaul tapped on his door. McFaul stepped inside without an invitation. Across the room, on a big twenty-three-inch set, Kevin Costner was doing battle with the Sheriff of Nottingham.

'You find the package?'

Rademeyer was sprawled in the armchair, his hand outstretched, his eyes still fixed on the screen. McFaul shook his head.

'No,' he said briefly. 'Turn that thing off.'

Rademeyer glanced round, one eyebrow raised.

'Why?'

'Just turn it off.'

'Tell me why.'

McFaul lowered himself onto the sofa and emptied Katilo's polythene bag onto the low glass-topped table.

'Where did you get these?'

'Katilo's room.'

'You're crazy, man. He'll kill you.'

McFaul shrugged. He wanted to know about the diamonds. Were they the ones from Cafunfo? The ones he'd collected from Ivan, the dealer?

'Yeah, probably.'

'And does he always help himself?'

'Sure.' Rademeyer was inspecting them, turning each one over, holding it up to the light. 'I ship them over to a dealer in the city. Guy pays top dollar. Straight into an account in Zurich.'

'Was that why you wanted the package? The Jiffybag?'

'Of course. I'm cheaper than Federal Express.'

'So what happens to the rest?'

'They pay for the shopping.'

'You mean arms?'

'Sure. Whatever's on the market. Katilo's very fashion conscious. Likes the best.'

McFaul nodded, remembering his first encounter with Katilo in the cave by the river. He'd been showing off his latest acquisitions. The SB-33, the little Italian mine they called the 'Gucci', had been his favourite. Rademeyer was still looking at the diamonds.

'You really steal these?' he said at last. 'Lift them from his room?'

McFaul ignored the question.

'Katilo's due back at nine,' he said. 'I need to be out of here.'

'Very wise.'

'And you need to take me.' McFaul frowned. 'Me and Mrs Jordan.' Rademeyer was on his feet, hands raised, fending off the suggestion.

'Shit, man . . .'

'I'm serious.'

'You be as serious as you like. The answer's no. I know nothing about it. Not this. Not you. Not any fucking thing. You want to end up in the river, that's your business. But don't involve me, eh?'

McFaul was dividing the diamonds into two piles. The biggest pile he pushed towards Rademeyer.

'Yours,' he said briefly. 'Mrs Jordan's downstairs in the lobby. You've got a car. You've got a plane. We need to be away before the shit hits the fan.' He paused a moment, thinking of Katilo again. Had he tucked a 72A under his pillow, it would have been a wonderfully apt phrase.

Rademeyer was back beside the diamonds. A little of the fear had drained from his face. He picked up the diamonds, weighing them in his hand.

'You really think I can fly out of here? Just like that?'

'Yes.'

'And you really think this is all it takes?'

McFaul ignored the question, reaching forward and scooping the smaller pile of diamonds into the polythene bag.

'Half down. The rest on completion.' He smiled. 'Deal?'

Rademeyer's eyes had returned to the empty TV screen. He reached for the remote control. He was frowning.

'I need to make a call.' He nodded towards the door. 'Give me five minutes.'

McFaul rejoined Molly in the lobby. So far he'd told her nothing. Simply that the schedule had changed. They had to go to the airport. They were leaving Zaire a little earlier than planned. Now, she sat beside the new Adidas holdall she'd bought from one of the hotel boutiques. The expression on her face told McFaul everything he needed to know.

'Pleased to be off?'

'Delighted.'

McFaul sank into the chair beside her. A delegation of some kind had just arrived, a dozen or so black businessmen in identical purple blazers. They were clustered round the reception desk, arguing about room allocations. Molly asked again exactly where they were going and McFaul heard himself talking about Angola, his eyes never leaving the big revolving door that led to the street outside.

'Angola? You mean Luanda?'

'Yes.'

'I thought—'

'We're going with Rademeyer. The Dove's a bit short on range for anything more ambitious.' He glanced at her a moment. 'It makes no difference. There are flights back to Europe from Luanda. You'll be home in a couple of days.'

'But what about the tickets? Air France? I thought—'

'Doesn't matter. We go tonight.'

Something in his voice brought her questions to a halt and he saw the first doubts ghost across her face. Something had happened. Something awful. And now they had to go. McFaul felt a hand on his knee. She was leaning forward, one arm outstretched.

'What's he done now?' she asked. 'Tell me.'

'Who?'

'Katilo.'

McFaul tried to look unconcerned.

'Nothing,' he ran a tired hand over his face, 'yet.'

Rademeyer arrived minutes later. McFaul spotted him by the lifts, recognising the blue canvas bag. The last time he'd seen it was under armed guard at the barbecue in Muengo. He got to his feet, shepherding Molly towards the door. Rademeyer joined them outside. It was raining again, fat drops falling from an inky sky. Rademeyer left the bag beneath the hotel awning, telling them to wait. The Mercedes was in a nearby parking lot. He'd bring it round. McFaul began to protest but Rademeyer was already halfway across the road, his jacket pulled up over his head, running towards the fenced compound reserved for hotel cars.

The rain got heavier and a wind began to stir the line of trees along the Avenue Batetela. The wind brought with it the smells of the river, the hot, swampy breath of Central Africa, and McFaul felt the touch of Molly's hand again, slipped through his arm. He looked down at her. She was staring out, beyond the road, beyond the river bank, her face quite emotionless, and McFaul sensed at once how frightened she was.

Beyond the gatehouse that guarded the approaches to the hotel, he could see the headlights of an approaching car. It turned in from the road, a long stretch limousine, tyres hissing on the wet tarmac. Beneath the hotel awning, it stopped. The windows were of smoked glass, the occupants invisible. The front passenger door opened and a tall man in a black jumpsuit got out. McFaul recognised him at once, one of the guards he'd met outside Katilo's room. The guard was bending to the limousine, opening the rear door, and McFaul watched Katilo appear, first his legs, then his arms, then the rest of him. He stood unsteadily on the pavement. He was very drunk. He saw McFaul and waved imperiously at the car.

'You want it, my friend? Tonight? You and your lady? Please . . .' He offered Molly an extravagant bow.

Molly turned away. McFaul couldn't take his eyes off the car. The rear door was still open, and the guard was looking in, saying something in French. At length, a woman got out. She was in her twenties. She was wearing an Air France uniform, pleated blue skirt, white blouse. She had fine auburn hair, carefully plaited and secured at the back with a butterfly clip. She was beautiful.

Katilo was beaming at her, introducing McFaul.

'*Mon metteur en scène,*' he said. 'He makes my films.'

He looked round at McFaul, wanting confirmation, and McFaul nodded, still looking at the girl. A flurry of rain caught her in the face and McFaul heard a soft curse as one hand went to her head and she ducked for cover, letting Katilo encircle her with his arm, capturing her, protecting her, pulling her inwards. She looked up at him and for a moment McFaul thought he detected real warmth in her smile. Then Katilo had turned on his heel, sweeping her into the revolving door, dismissing the car and the guard with a regal wave.

Rademeyer was at the kerbside, sitting behind the wheel of the Mercedes. The front window was down and he was watching Katilo and the air hostess making their way across the hotel lobby. The receptionist already had the key, her arm outstretched, and Katilo took it with another stage bow, playing to the audience of impressed African businessmen. Then he began to carve a path across the crowded lobby, heading for the lift, and as the purple blazers closed ranks behind him, McFaul heard Rademeyer calling impatiently from the kerbside.

They drove out of the hotel, the rain sheeting down in the glare of the headlights. Ahead lay the Avenue des Nations Unis, the boulevard which ran beside the river. To get to the airport, you turned right. Rademeyer was indicating left. McFaul leaned forward, one hand reaching for his shoulder.

'Where are you going?'

Rademeyer smiled.

'Detour,' he said briefly. 'Trust me.'

McFaul hesitated a moment, uncertain, then sat back against the dimpled leather. Whatever happened now, they were in Rademeyer's hands. He was the one who'd get them to the airport. He was the one who'd fly the plane. McFaul's hand went to the breast pocket of his shirt. The last couple of days, he'd been carrying the little Hi-8 video-cassettes everywhere. There were three of them in all and he knew he owed them his life. They'd been his passport out of Muengo. They'd taken him here, to Kinshasa. And now, with luck, they'd see him safely back to the UK. He smiled to himself, reaching for Molly's hand, feeling her answering squeeze. Never again would he slag the likes of Todd Llewelyn. The media might still be a sick excuse for real life but just sometimes it had its uses.

Rademeyer was looking in the mirror again, beginning to slow. Set back from the boulevard, McFaul could see the looming bulk of a large building. It looked like an apartment block, or perhaps a hotel. It was shrouded in darkness, no lights anywhere. Rademeyer turned in off the road, slowing to avoid pot-holes. They were in some kind of parking lot and as Rademeyer pulled the Mercedes into a wide turn, the headlights drifted over the bodies of abandoned cars. Some had burned out. Others had wheels missing. One or two were without doors. The Mercedes was still moving, Rademeyer peering into the darkness. At length he grunted, spotting something, flashing his headlights, letting the car coast to a halt.

With the engine off, McFaul could hear nothing, just the incessant drumbeat of the rain on the roof. Rademeyer's window purred down. The noise of the rain got louder. Molly stirred, moving closer to McFaul.

'What's happening?'

'I don't know.'

Rademeyer slid the wrapper off a stick of chewing gum. The clock on the dashboard read 21.31. McFaul leaned forward.

'When does the airport close for the night?'

'It doesn't.'

'You can fly out any time?'

'Weather permitting,' Rademeyer nodded, 'sure.'

'Will this stop you? Rain?'

Rademeyer didn't answer. He was looking out of the window, staring intently into the darkness. The building towered above them, ten storeys at least. From somewhere close came the stench of raw sewage. Rademeyer had relaxed again, working the chewing gum back and forth in his mouth.

'This used to be the best hotel in town,' he murmured at last. 'Can you believe that?'

'Yeah?' McFaul had seen a shadow across the car park. Someone moving. Maybe two people.

'Yeah, Hotel Okapi. Great music. Great food. Great views.'

'What happened?'

'They burned it during the riots. Coupla years back. No one's got round to fixing it yet. Not that there's very much left.'

The shadows had disappeared inside the building. Rademeyer had seen them, too. He was bending forward now, fumbling in the parcel shelf under the dashboard. Eventually, he found what he was looking for, turning on the interior light and then opening the door and stepping out into the rain. Molly was watching him and McFaul felt her body tense as Rademeyer opened the door beside her. His voice was light, almost apologetic. The big automatic was inches from Molly's temple.

'The rest of the diamonds. Just put them in her lap.'

McFaul looked at Molly. Her face was chalk white. She was taking deep breaths, fighting for control. The diamonds were in McFaul's breast pocket, nestling behind one of the little cassettes. He pulled out the polythene bag and laid it carefully in Molly's lap. She was trembling now. He could feel it.

'Give them to me.' Molly reached for the bag, passing it out of the car. 'Now get out. Both of you.'

Molly glanced at McFaul. McFaul nodded.

'Do it,' he muttered.

Molly got out of the car. McFaul joined her. Within seconds he was soaking wet, the rain rolling down inside his collar, warm on his skin. They began to walk towards the hotel, Rademeyer behind them. Lightning flickered on the horizon, the sound of thunder rumbling across the river seconds later. The steps up to the hotel were slippery with rain. At the top, the entrance to the lobby lay open to the weather, the big doors ripped from their hinges, electric cables hanging down from the ceiling. Rademeyer had produced a torch. McFaul watched his own shadow advancing across the wreckage of the lobby. Even now, years later, the sour smell of a major fire hung in the air.

'Hold it there.'

McFaul stopped. Another voice, a deep American accent, somewhere to the left. He reached for Molly, finding her beside him. The voice sounded familiar. Noon, he thought. The get-together in Katilo's room. The wild-haired American with the courtly manners.

'Turn the torch off.'

Rademeyer did what he was told. The lobby plunged into darkness for a moment then another torch found Molly's face. McFaul looked down at her. She was frowning.

'Larry?' she said softly. 'Is that you?'

McFaul heard a chuckle in the darkness behind the torch. He was still looking at Molly. She was shaking her head, relief and bemusement. She glanced up at McFaul.

'I know this man. His name's Larry. Larry Giddings. I met him in Luanda. He works for a charity called Aurora.'

The torch began to move. McFaul heard footsteps. He held up his hand shielding his eyes.

'Lawrence,' he said, 'his name's Lawrence.'

The torch stopped, barely a yard away, touching distance.

McFaul saw a hand extended, long elegant fingers, a single signet ring. Molly didn't move.

'Piet here tells me you have a problem.'

McFaul glanced over his shoulder. Rademeyer was standing behind him. The automatic was hanging by his side.

'He's right.' McFaul nodded. 'What else did he tell you?'

'He said you wanted out.'

'Yes.'

'Tonight.'

'Right again.'

'Hey.' The American touched Molly briefly on the arm. 'We're friends here. Don't fret. You wanna take a look at the place? Before we go? Says a lot. Believe me.'

The torch swung round, illuminating the bare, rain-streaked walls, the holes where the air-conditioning units had been ripped out, the fire-blackened sweep of the reception desk, the dark fingers of vegetation creeping in through the gaping windows. In an alcove beside the darkness where the front doors had once been, the torch came to rest on an office safe. It was lying on its back, the door hanging open, the interior full of crumpled beer cans.

The American chuckled again. Then McFaul heard the hiss of tyres and a big four-wheel came to a halt outside. Abruptly, from the darkness behind them, two men appeared. They were both young, white. One had a crew cut and a tight-fitting T-shirt and McFaul recognised the small, neat profile of an Uzi sub-machine-gun cradled in his right arm. The other one was whispering to Rademeyer. Like Giddings, he had an American accent.

Giddings led the way to the entrance. Outside, the rain had eased. At the top of the steps, Rademeyer paused beside McFaul.

'You're with Larry now,' he said. 'It's simpler, believe me.'

'For who?'

'You,' he smiled, 'and me.'

He nodded at Molly wishing her luck, then he was away down the steps, skirting the corpse of a dead cat. Molly watched as he headed for the Mercedes.

'My bag,' she said helplessly.

'It's OK, ma'am. Taken care of.'

The American with the T-shirt was at Molly's elbow. He was nodding at the four-wheel at the bottom of the steps as another flash of lightning revealed the shape of a Nissan Patrol. The rear door was already open, the other young man scanning the shadows in the parking lot. McFaul shook his head, marvelling at the precision with which these men moved. This was a military operation. Semi-official. No question.

Giddings touched him lightly on the arm, and he followed Molly down the steps. The back of the Patrol felt enormous. The American with the Uzi sat on a jump seat, facing McFaul. The heavy clunk as the door closed suggested armour plate but the American had the Uzi raised, the safety catch off, his legs braced against the thick pile carpet as the four-wheel swung out of the parking lot. Back on the Avenue des Nations Unis, McFaul saw Rademeyer's Mercedes peeling off to the right, back towards the Intercontinental, and he realised for the first time exactly how cleverly the young South African had played it. Whatever had happened in Katilo's room would be nothing to do with him. The English guy had disappeared, the Englishwoman too, but his own hands were clean and when the time was right he could quietly exchange the uncut diamonds for a great deal of hard currency.

Molly was talking to Giddings now. The American occupied the other jump seat, his elbows on his knees, his body swaying from side to side as the Patrol growled along the waterfront. Soon, McFaul recognised landmarks they'd passed on the way in from the airport. In the middle of the city they turned left into a business area. McFaul began to relax, warmed by the familiar names. Hertz. Barclays. Sabena. At a corner, beside a big shopping centre, the Patrol slowed. A narrow street led towards the river. Halfway down was a compound protected by a high wall. The Patrol slowed again, the driver flashing his headlights, and a heavy steel gate opened inwards. Uniformed men emerged from the shadows, checking the underside of the vehicle with mirrors and McFaul heard the whirr of a motor as the gate closed again, sealing them off from the city.

The Patrol came to a halt. The back door opened and McFaul found himself in a paved courtyard. The rain had stopped now and the night air was heavy with the scent of frangipani. A three-storey house stood before them. Inside it was cool, the floors tiled, the walls hung with tasteful water-colours. Giddings paused beneath a partly furled flag. Glancing up it, McFaul recognised the Stars and Stripes. Giddings was beaming at Molly. He seemed very much at home.

'You folks eaten?'

McFaul declined the offer of a meal. Molly said she'd like a drink.

'You bet.'

They walked along a corridor and Giddings led the way into a small bar. The room was empty. Giddings helped himself to a bottle of Jack Daniel's, pouring half a tumbler and offering it to Molly.

'Ice,' he said, 'as I remember.'

Molly nodded, gazing up at the framed Inauguration photo of President Clinton that hung above the bar. Giddings poured two more drinks, joining them at a table at the back of the room. He settled into the leather armchair, undoing the button on his jacket. The suit McFaul had admired in Katilo's room was still uncreased. Even the dark splashes of rain had gone.

Giddings raised his glass.

'Piet explained about the Air France deal,' he said. 'Tonight you stay here. Tomorrow we ship you out to the airport. No problem.'

'We?' It was Molly who asked the question.

Giddings nodded, as affable as ever.

'Sure.' He made circling motions with his hands. 'Me and a couple of buddies. Nice people. People you'd like.'

'But who? Exactly?'

'Can't say,' he smiled, 'exactly.'

McFaul eased his long frame in the armchair. The bourbon was working already, stealing round his body, turning off the alarms. The pattern was obvious. He'd seen it everywhere in the Third World, Americans in nice suits, spending their dollars on this side or that, backing rebels, defending governments, offering what insiders in Washington termed 'covert assistance in support of democracy'. In Angola that would mean UNITA, or – more precisely – Katilo. Thus the meeting in Room 631. Thus the link with Rademeyer.

McFaul took another long pull at the bourbon. Giddings was smiling at Molly.

'That little get-together this morning.' McFaul frowned. 'My apologies.'

'No problem.'

'I embarrassed you.'

'No,' Giddings shook his head, 'not me, buddy. Our Lebanese friend maybe, but not me. You've got some kind of alternative? For this film of yours?'

'No, but that doesn't matter either. Katilo's got the camcorder. As far as I'm concerned, the film's dead and buried. As long as we get out tomorrow.'

'Yeah?' Giddings was looking at him carefully. 'You mean that?'

'Sure.'

'But I thought . . . our UNITA friend told me . . .'

'It's bullshit. I work in the minefields. I'm an ex-sapper. I don't know one end of a camera from the other.'

'You kidding?'

'No. Katilo thought different. I didn't bother him with the truth. I was happy to go along with it. That's why I'm here. That's why we're still in one piece—' He broke off, emptying the tumbler, accepting a refill, aware of Molly watching him. The bewilderment was back in her face, her eyes returning again and again to Giddings. She must have known this man well, McFaul thought. Well enough to trust him.

Giddings got up and disappeared into the corridor, apologising for the delay in Molly's food. He'd ordered soup and crackers and a light salad. He'd find out what had happened. Molly waited for a moment or two, watching the door.

'Who is he?'

McFaul shrugged.

'CIA. Or something bloody close.' He looked at her. 'Who did you think he was?'

'I told you. I thought he worked for the charity people, Aurora. In fact I thought he ran it.'

'He probably does.' McFaul paused a moment. 'You know about the CIA? Zealots in nice suits? All that stuff?'

'Yes, more or less, but how does that . . .' Molly gestured helplessly with her glass, 'square with the rest of it? Aurora is religious. He told me about it. He lives in Florida. He's an evangelist. He's worked in Angola for years. He wasn't lying, I know he wasn't. In fact, I—' She broke off, looking across at McFaul, wanting him to solve the riddle, to plot a way back from the impasse.

McFaul reached down, pulling up the leg of his jeans and loosening the straps on his leg.

'Two hats,' he said, 'at least. It happens all the time. Cambodia. Afghanistan. Middle East. Man says he does one thing, it's probably true. What he doesn't tell you about is the rest.'

'And you think Larry's like that?'

'Yes.'

'So what does that make him?'

'A patriot. These guys wave a flag for it. Freedom. Democracy. God, even. They have convictions, real beliefs. Belief justifies pretty much anything.'

'What do you mean?'

'With Giddings?' McFaul waved his glass towards the corridor. 'He'll be in town to keep an eye on Katilo. UNITA was a client. Washington backed them all the way. Probably still does.'

'How?'

'How do you think?'

'I don't know. Tell me.'

Molly was leaning forward now, half-fascinated, half-repelled. There was still no sign of Giddings or the food.

'How?' she said again.

McFaul looked at her a moment.

'Fact or speculation?'

'Fact.'

'OK,' McFaul began to tally the points on the fingers of one hand, 'Mobutu runs Zaire. He got there with CIA help. Through Mobutu, Washington has been supplying arms. To people like Katilo.'

'You mean Larry? Larry supplied arms?'

'He'd have been part of it, certainly. He'd have been fronting for various organisations. There are cut-outs, fuses that blow along the way. Nothing's ever traced directly to Washington but that's where it would have come from. In the end.'

'These arms,' Molly was staring at him now, 'they include mines?'

'Of course.'

'American mines?'

'All sorts. Whatever's available.'

'And they went down to Angola?'

'Yes. Amongst other places.'

'But how? How did they get there?'

'By plane mostly. You've seen the state of the roads. They're impassable, most of them.'

'So who's been flying them? These mines?'

'Who do you think?'

Molly looked away, saying nothing and then she thought of Rademeyer, back in his room at the Intercontinental, counting the diamonds. In all, he'd be looking at a small fortune. Enough to retire. Enough to make room for someone else to risk their life shipping munitions south. UNITA paid top dollar. And Central Africa was probably full of eager young men like Piet Rademeyer. Molly cleared her throat. Her face was flushed. Anger and bourbon.

'So you're telling me that Giddings gets the arms for Katilo?'

'Got, certainly. He'd have been part of all that.'

'So . . .' she gestured helplessly towards the door, 'the mine that killed James might have come from here? Through him?'

'Yes.'

'And Piet might have flown it?'

'Possibly. Unless it came up through South Africa . . . and even then he might have got the contract.' He paused. 'Rademeyer's different. He does it for the money. Pure and simple. If that's a phrase you can live with.'

'And Giddings?' She bit her lip. 'Larry?'

'He believes it.'

'Does that make any difference?'

'Sure,' McFaul smiled, at last hearing Giddings's footsteps in the corridor outside, 'that makes him more dangerous.'

Giddings appeared at the door. He was carrying a silver tray, playing the butler. McFaul got to his feet. He needed to use the toilet. Giddings gave him directions and he limped out of the bar, leaving his empty glass beside the bottle of Jack Daniel's.

Giddings offered the tray to Molly. She looked up at him, shaking her head.

'No, thank you.'

'I thought you were hungry?'

'I was.'

'Something the matter here? Something happened?'

'Yes.' Molly nodded.

He looked down at her a moment, concerned, then put the tray on the bar top.

'Tell me about it.' He pulled his armchair a little closer.

'I did. In Luanda.'

'Your husband?'

'James. My son.'

'Hey . . .' Giddings frowned, 'I don't get it.'

He leaned back in the chair, watching her. After a while, he reached for his glass, nursing it, his eyes still on her face.

'Why didn't you tell me?' she said at last.

'Tell you what?'

'About all this,' she gestured round, 'this other life of yours. Whatever it is you do. Meeting these people. UNITA. Katilo. Giving them things. Weapons.' She paused. 'Land mines.'

'Land mines?'

'Yes.'

'Is that what you think? You think I give these clowns land mines?'

'Yes.'

'Not true.' He shook his head. 'I meet them, sure. I get to be around them a good deal. You might even say I keep them on track. But land mines?' He shook his head again, doubly emphatic. 'No way.'

'But you know he's buying them?'

'Sure.'

'And you know where they're going?'

'Yep.'

'Then it's the same thing,' she sat back in the chair, 'isn't it?' Giddings shook his head, saying nothing, wary now. Molly looked at him for a long time, wanting him to defend himself, wanting him to explain. Finally she leaned forward again.

'You never told me,' she said, 'about any of this.'

'You never asked.'

'But I never knew. I never knew anything. There I was, trusting you, telling you everything, wanting you to be my friend, wanting you to—'

Giddings broke in. He sounded injured.

'And wasn't I? Wasn't I your friend?'

'Yes, that's the whole point. You were. And I believed you. You helped me. You truly did. And now this.'

'Now what?'

'This. You here. Helping sell stuff, helping give stuff away, helping keep them on track, whatever it is people like you get up to. Don't ask me what you do. I don't know. I don't even want to know. I just want my son back. Does that sound pathetic enough? Mr Preacherman?'

Giddings reached out for her hand, trying to calm her, console her, but she pushed him away, swallowing hard, fighting to choke back the tears.

'I thought you were a friend,' she said simply, 'and you betrayed me. All the time you betrayed me.'

'How come?'

'By knowing what you'd done. What you'd helped do. By . . .' she shook her head, maddened by the complexity of it all, 'being part of what happened. James. Domingos. Those poor bloody people in Muengo. You'll tell me it's war. You'll tell me it's too bad. You'll say I don't understand. That's what you'll say. You'll pat me on the head and say I don't understand. You'll say it's very complicated and very important and then you'll tell me we can still be friends. No?'

Giddings nodded.

'Yes,' he said quietly, 'friends. Friendship. There's still room for that. Whatever you think.'

'You're wrong.'

'I hope not.'

'You are. And you're evil, too. You're evil because you know what you're doing. You know where it leads. You know what happens at the end of it. People like you kill kids like mine. Dear God . . .' She turned away, aware for the first time of McFaul standing by the door. He was looking at her. And he was nodding.

426

McFaul awoke in the middle of the night. Giddings had given him a room on the first floor. It was small and bare, a single bed, a metal washstand, and tall wooden shutters hooked back against the wall beside the window. The door lay diagonally across from the bed and before he'd gone to sleep, McFaul had rolled a sock in a ball and left it behind the door. Now, the sock was a yard into the room. He could see it quite plainly in the light through the open window.

McFaul got out of bed. He'd folded his clothes on top of his holdall. Both had gone. He stood in the half-darkness for a full minute, knowing he'd been right. People like Giddings weren't stupid. Amateur or otherwise, McFaul had been using a camera and in the ceaseless propaganda war, pictures were what hurt you most. Yesterday, in Katilo's hotel room, McFaul had in fact shot nothing but Giddings wasn't in the business of taking risks. He'd want to know. He'd want to check. He'd want to be sure.

McFaul smiled to himself, limping across to the washstand and splashing his face with water. This was the first time he'd ever slept in a bed without removing his false leg and sleep had been a long time coming. But given the contents of the leg, the little cassettes he'd wedged inside, it had been worth it. He studied his face in the mirror, fingering the little ridges of scar tissue, the smile wider now, knowing the way it would go. Tomorrow, Giddings would be as good as his word. He'd take them to the airport. He'd see them through the formalities. And as fast as he could, he'd get them out of Africa.

CHAPTER FOURTEEN

Molly was half-asleep when she heard the knock on the front door. She pulled back the duvet and crept across the bedroom to the window. For some reason the central heating hadn't come on and she began to shiver, peering through the slit in the curtains. Patrick's Volvo stood outside in the lane. Alice was sitting in the front. She was looking up at the bedroom window. She was waving.

Molly found Giles's dressing gown on the back of the door, and she tightened the belt round her waist as she made her way downstairs. The dressing gown enveloped her with Giles's smell, a sweet mustiness that made her catch her breath. The clock in the hall said ten past three. She'd been home less than an hour.

Patrick was waiting on the front doorstep. Alice was halfway up the garden path. Almost shyly, Patrick offered her an enormous bunch of flowers.

'From your trusty family solicitor.' He beamed at her. 'Lovely to have you back.'

Molly made them a pot of tea, clearing the pile of unopened mail off the kitchen table and apologising about the state of the place. She'd left in a hurry. She'd asked the daily help to look in from time to time, and the poor woman had obviously done her best, but nothing emptied a house of warmth quicker than prolonged absence.

'Of course, dear,' Alice murmured, 'of course.'

Alice was a plump, pampered woman several years older

than Patrick. She'd never had any children of her own but she somehow affected a knowledge of more or less everything. Including bereavement.

Molly had found some wholemeal digestives and a slice or two of banana cake.

'It's a question of adapting,' Alice was saying. 'It'll be hard, believe me, but in the end you'll get there.'

'Get where?' Molly surprised herself with the depth of feeling behind the question. She'd spent the journey back from Heathrow staring out of the train window. Never had England depressed her so much. The cold, grey skies. The endless suburbs. The slack-faced executives queue-jumping for taxis at Liverpool Street station. Giles had been lucky, she'd thought. Kissing goodbye to all this.

Alice and Patrick were exchanging covert glances and Molly wondered for a moment what they'd been expecting. Her duty, plainly, was to be brave.

She picked up the teapot, offering Patrick a refill.

'Tell me about Giles,' she said. 'Tell me they've found him.'

Patrick looked startled.

'I'm afraid I can't.'

'Not even a body?'

'Not even that. One day maybe but . . .' he reached for the sugar tongs, trying to mask his embarrassment, 'not quite yet.'

'Might he turn up, then?'

'Yes . . .' Patrick glanced at Alice again, 'but it could be months, even longer than that. Evidently these things are hard to predict.'

Molly nodded, saying nothing, warming her hands on the teapot. She'd bought a copy of the *Daily Telegraph* at the station and the colour supplement lay on the floor at her feet. Pages and pages of Christmas offers plus a special feature on the New Year's best ski destinations. None of it mattered. None of it made the slightest particle of sense.

Patrick was leaning forward on the table, intimate, sympathetic, the pose he often favoured in the office. Alice had beaten a tactful retreat to the sink, rolling up her sleeves and pulling on a pair of rubber gloves. Molly wondered how long it would take her to wash up two cups and a plate.

'I've been talking to the life insurance people,' Patrick was saying, 'on your behalf.'

'Oh?'

'I think I may have mentioned it on the phone. When you called. Last week . . .' He paused a moment, then continued, 'Giles had been extremely prudent. In fact, if anything, he was over-insured.'

Molly nodded, her eyes still on Alice. She was soaping the cups for the second time.

'He always believed in insurance,' she said vaguely, 'but then I suppose he would, wouldn't he?'

'Of course,' Patrick chuckled, 'and a good thing too. I know it must feel pretty meaningless just now but in the end you'll be due a sizeable settlement. Once they've found a body.'

Molly offered him a weak smile. She meant it as gratitude but she could tell at once that he was disappointed. She reached for his hand, giving it a squeeze.

'Thanks,' she said, 'it's sweet of you to take so much trouble.'

'It's nothing, my dear.'

'I mean it.'

'I know you do,' he put his other hand on hers, 'but that's not the best of it.'

'It's not?'

'No. Lloyd's have confirmed they're disputing the New Jersey claim through the courts.' He nodded. 'That's extremely good news. The best, in fact.' He released her hand, gesturing round. 'The pressure's off. No bailiffs. No need to skimp and save. Should do wonders for your peace of mind. Yours and one or two others.'

He smiled at her, fatherly, leaning back in the chair and

making room for Alice as she bustled round the table, wiping it with a wet cloth. Molly watched her, suddenly exhausted, wanting them both gone. With luck, in minutes, she'd be back in bed, the room curtained against the last of the daylight, willing herself into unconsciousness.

Alice was talking about Christmas. Did Molly have plans? Was she going away? Molly shook her head, smothering a yawn.

'I hadn't thought about it, to be honest. It hadn't crossed my mind.'

'Then you must come to us, you absolutely must. Mustn't she, Paddy?'

Patrick nodded. He had his pipe out now and Molly's heart sank, watching him fill it, tamping down the tobacco with his big, square-ended fingers. Christmas in Frinton would be endless, three days of rich food and bad television and quiet chats around the fire. These people were kind and well-intentioned but they'd suffocate her with their sympathy. She thought for a moment about Angola, the scenes she'd left behind, the people she'd met, and she realised with a shock that she missed it.

'We have the meal early,' Alice was saying. 'Normally around half-past one. That gives us a little break before the Queen.'

Patrick nodded, sucking at the pipe.

'Nice stiff walk in the morning. Church at eleven.'

'And sherry afterwards at the rectory. Just a few of us. The vicar's little treat for the regulars.'

Molly nodded.

'Sounds wonderful.'

Alice was back at the sink. She began to hum 'Hark the Herald Angels Sing', wringing the cloth dry and draping it over the taps. Patrick had found the pile of unopened mail. He leaned forward, picking up an envelope on top.

'Seen this?'

He handed an envelope to Molly. It was cream-coloured. In green, on the back, was the shape of a portcullis and the words 'House of Commons'. Molly picked it up and opened it. The letter was typewritten and brief. It offered Molly regrets and consolations for Giles's death. It said he'd been a good friend. The word 'tragic' was used twice. Molly looked at the signature at the bottom. The name sounded familiar though she couldn't quite remember why.

'Vere Hallam?'

Patrick nodded.

'MP for Aylesbury. Not really a chum of Giles's, more of a business associate.' He paused. 'Nice enough man though, from what I hear.'

Molly read the letter again. Vere Hallam had been devastated to learn about Giles's death and in the final paragraph he pressed her to get in touch if there was anything she needed.

'Business associate?' she queried.

'On the syndicate. Giles roped in a couple of MPs. With his track record, they were queuing up.' He smiled, reaching for his matchbox, nodding at the letter. 'I imagine Mr Hallam's pretty relieved. Bankruptcy's bad enough. If the syndicate had gone down, he'd have been out of a job, too.'

'Really?'

'Oh, yes. Bankrupt MPs are automatically suspended from the House. Might have been nasty for HMG. Given the current situation.'

Molly folded the letter, remembering now where she'd last heard Hallam's name. Robbie Cunningham had mentioned him, back in Luanda, the evening they'd met at the Café Acardia for a meal. Robbie had been amused at the coincidence, Giles's syndicate top-heavy with Tory MPs, pulled back from the brink of disaster, leaving the government's fragile majority intact.

Molly returned the letter to the pile on the sideboard. Alice had run out of domestic chores. She was standing beside Patrick's chair, her hand resting lightly on his shoulder. Patrick reached up, touching it a moment, then smiled again.

'Glad to be home?'

Molly looked at them both, the fond tableau, the proof that one couple at least could weather life's storms.

'No,' she said truthfully, 'I don't think I am.'

'No?' Patrick expelled a fat plume of blue smoke, then waved it away.

'No.' Molly shook her head. 'It doesn't feel like home at all. It feels different. Like nowhere I've ever been. And nowhere I ever want to be.' She shivered, pulling Giles's dressing gown more tightly around her.

Alice had stolen a look at her watch.

'Of course, dear,' she said soothingly, 'it's bound to feel a little bit that way. Just for a day or two. Before you get used to it all. Believe me. Take a tip from someone who knows.'

Molly nodded, trying to look grateful. Alice, to her certain knowledge, had led a seamless, trouble-free existence, undisturbed by any of life's nastier surprises. Her idea of a crisis, as Patrick had put it in one of his occasional quiet asides, was early closing day.

'I'm sure you're right,' Molly said. 'I'm just tired, that's all.'

'Of course you are, dear.'

'And a bit grouchy, I expect.'

'Not at all, not at all. Golly, if you can't be honest with us . . .' She reached for her coat, leaving the sentence unfinished.

With obvious reluctance, Patrick got to his feet while his wife explained about the family dog. They were due at the kennels to pick him up after a minor operation. With Labradors like Sammy you had to be so careful. Molly nodded, accompanying them into the hall, overwhelmed again by the gulf between the world she'd left behind, and the cosy certainties of life in middle-class England. In Muengo, Sammy would have lasted five minutes. Skinned and spit-roasted, he'd have kept an entire family alive for a week.

Patrick had paused by the door. He buttoned his coat, waiting while Alice returned to the kitchen to pick up her handbag. Out of earshot, he bent to Molly and kissed her lightly on the forehead. Molly froze, feeling his hand find hers.

'Any time, my dear,' he murmured, 'just phone.'

It was dark by the time McFaul got to Devizes. On Ken Middleton's instructions, he'd picked up a hire car at Heathrow, driving first to Southsea to dump his kit. He had a tiny terrace house a stone's throw from the sea, an inheritance from his mother, and he'd cat-napped for several hours on the sofa before coaxing a dribble of hot water from the shower and getting on the road again. His own car, a neat Escort automatic, was garaged in a lock-up round the corner. He'd spent most of his brief summer leave trying to sort out a problem with the automatic choke, but he had no appetite now for rejoining the battle. His priorities, after all, were clear. Get down to Devizes. Show Ken the precious footage. Make him commit to a full-blown film.

Ken Middleton was on the phone when McFaul arrived. Global Clearance occupied a brand-new unit on an industrial estate on the northern edges of the town, and Ken had commandeered the big room upstairs as his personal office. The last time McFaul had seen it was three months back. Then it had been an empty shell, still smelling of fresh paint and newly sawn timber. Now it looked like a military command post. Two of the walls were covered in maps, and there were three separate workstations, each with its own computer screen, each dedicated to regions where Global had a special involvement.

Ken Middleton was sitting at the desk marked 'South-east Asia', talking to someone at the other end about a shipment of detectors. He was a small, round-faced man with a fuzz of thinning blond hair and a little too much weight around the waist. The latter was a consequence of the hours he kept. Like McFaul, Middleton was a divorcee. He rarely left the office earlier than nine and existed almost entirely on take-away meals. McFaul could see the remains of the last one in the bin by the window, a crumpled pizza box crusted with congealed tomato paste.

Middleton ended the conversation with a snort. On the phone from Heathrow, McFaul had given him the details of Llewelyn's camcorder. Now, Middleton was nodding at a pile of big cardboard boxes on the desk he reserved for what he called 'General Admin'. All three boxes carried the Sony trademark.

McFaul looked at them.

'What are they?'

'You asked for editing facilities.'

'I said we had to sort the pictures out.'

'Same thing, isn't it?'

Middleton got up. He reached for a bayonet from a shelf overhead and began to saw his way into one of the boxes. His obsession with technical equipment was legendary. Within a year, he was planning to interlink all Global's field operations via satellite to a central computer, giving himself hourly updates on de-mining progress across the planet. There was, in this, a hint of megalomania but McFaul had yet to meet anyone in the de-mining business who didn't regard Ken Middleton with enormous respect. If he wanted to play the puppeteer, pulling strings across the world, then so be it. The man's determination to lead a personal crusade had already put the mines issue squarely on the public agenda. Mines were evil. Kids were dying. Eyes should be opened. End of message.

Middleton was examining the contents of the biggest box. According to the label on the front, it was an Edit Controller. Middleton obviously hadn't a clue how it worked. McFaul smiled, watching him racing through the instruction manual. As ever, he read it backwards, starting from the end.

'Where did this lot come from?'

'Place in Bristol. Bloke drove it down this afternoon.'

'How much? As a matter of interest?'

Middleton ignored the question, his finger anchored halfway

down a page. Years of fund-raising had given him a profound reluctance to discuss money but he had a real talent for chiselling big sums from sources across Europe. The EEC Commission in Brussels had, to McFaul's certain knowledge, contributed millions and there was a rich shipping magnate in Oslo who was happy to sponsor individual initiatives. The editing equipment, in Middleton's eyes, would have been small change.

'What's happened to Bennie? You heard from him at all?' Middleton's eyes didn't leave the page.

'Top drawer,' he said, 'Africa desk.'

McFaul limped across to the workstation by the door. A big Michelin map of Africa was pinned to the wall above the computer screen. The map had been laminated in clear plastic and white chinagraph ringed areas where Global was involved. McFaul paused, looking at Angola, hunting for Muengo. The town had earned itself a red pin, Middleton's private code for operational disaster. Red pins meant withdrawal under fire, the job incomplete, the worst possible outcome after months of patient fieldwork.

'Top drawer,' Middleton said again, 'and good luck with the writing.'

Bennie's letter lay beneath a sheaf of telexes from the British embassy in Luanda. It ran to five pages in all, a long, rambling account of what had happened in Muengo. According to Bennie, everything had gone wrong. The organisation had been shit, the support non-existent, standing rules violated, operational procedures ignored. Terra Sancta had arrived out of nowhere, uninvited, and the result had been a shambles. Was Global there to clear mines? Or play at showbiz? Wasn't Angola dodgy enough already without people like Todd Llewelyn around?

McFaul folded the letter and returned it to the drawer. Middleton was unpacking the other boxes. McFaul watched him a moment then nodded at the drawer.

'You see him at all? Bennie?'

'Yeah. He was down here yesterday. Looking for back pay.'

'What did he say?'

'Say?' Middleton glanced up for the first time. 'He said you'd gone ape. Walked out on him. Got hold of a gun from somewhere.'

McFaul looked at him a moment. If he said yes, if he admitted it, Middleton would sack him. Carrying a weapon in the field was a capital offence, stripping Global of its neutral role. Middleton was still watching him, still waiting for an answer.

McFaul shook his head.

'It's bollocks,' he said briefly.

He reached for the cassettes he'd brought down from Southsea and laid them on the desk beside the edit controller. Middleton peered at them then picked one up, weighing it in his hand, the issue of the weapon dismissed.

'Is this the stuff you talked about?'

'It's a couple of hours' worth. You wouldn't want to watch much more.'

'And you shot these?'

'I shot two of them. The other one belonged to Llewelyn. The bloke Bennie talks about in the letter.'

'So what do we do with that?'

'Use it.'

'Does he know? Is he the legal owner?'

'Fuck knows. Does it matter?'

Middleton frowned, looking at the cassette again. One of the reasons for Global's success had been his passion for detail, for the smallest print of each successive transaction. From the outset, Middleton had realised that wars are won inch by inch, skirmish by skirmish. Take on the heavies, confront the arms industry and the Establishment, and you can't afford a single mistake. Get it wrong, leave a single loophole unguarded, and they'll hang you out to dry.

'If it's his property we'll need his permission. You have to find him.'

McFaul shrugged. It seemed logical enough.

'OK.'

'You know where he is?'

'No. Last time I saw him he was half-dead.'

'How come?'

'Cerebral malaria. They must have flown him out of Muengo. Back here, I imagine.'

'Yeah, they did.'

Middleton abandoned the box. In the drawer in the Africa desk he began to rummage through the sheaf of telexes. Finally he found the message he was after.

'Last week,' he said. 'They flew him home on that woman's ticket. Pissed off the embassy people no end.'

'Why's that?'

'They were trying to get rid of her.' Middleton stuffed the telex back in the drawer. 'Talk to the Hospital for Tropical Diseases. He's probably still there.'

'Or dead.'

'Yeah,' Middleton was already eyeing the editing equipment again, 'or dead.'

Towards the end of the evening, past ten, they drove to a pub on the main road called The Fox. McFaul sank into a chair by the fire, exhausted, while Middleton ordered the drinks. It had taken him a while to get the editing gear working. The edit controller came with two video-players and two monitor screens. You loaded the rushes into one player and compiled the pictures you wanted onto the other. Middleton had experimented with a sequence or two, trying to crack this new technical challenge, but he'd quickly realised his own limitations. Editing was clearly an art. They needed someone who knew what they were doing.

Middleton came back from the bar carrying McFaul's Guinness.

'There's a bloke I know down near Salisbury,' he said briskly. 'Wrote to me last year.'

'Oh?'

McFaul grinned, reaching for the Guinness. Middleton had just sat through sequence after sequence of appalling pictures. A man blown up, his leg in shreds. More bodies at the hospital. An amputation without anaesthetic. A cow butchered in close-up. And finally Katilo's little prank in down-town Kinshasa, a teenage mugger and his accomplice blown apart yards from the watching lens. Yet not once had he registered the slightest emotion, simply an acknowledgement that time was short and the material deserved professional attention. As far as Middleton was concerned, McFaul's pictures were bullets for Global's gun. The quicker it was loaded, the better.

'He's a pro editor,' Middleton was saying, 'name of Geoff. Wanted to tell me some idea or other.'

'Is he good?'

'Yeah. He sent me some stuff he'd done. Sailing films. I know fuck all about boats but it seemed pretty good to me.'

'So what do we do?'

'I'll phone him. Get him over. You go and find Llewelyn. If we have to, we'll buy his fucking pictures.' He paused, struck by another thought. 'The black guy, your pal, the big bugger.'

'Katilo?'

'Yeah, him. That stuff at the end. In Kinshasa. Where he blows those kids away. Is that actionable? Are we talking murder charges? Or what?'

McFaul thought about the question a moment. Nothing he'd seen in Kinshasa indicated much concern for law and order. McFaul reached for his Guinness again, lifting the glass in a silent toast.

'No problem,' he said.

'Sure?'

'Absolutely certain.'

'OK.'

Middleton hunched over his orange juice, telling McFaul what he planned to do with the film once it was ready. As ever, his mind was outrunning the technical problems, leap-frogging ahead, looking for ways of maximising the impact. There'd be massive publicity, for sure. And that might sit nicely with another little plan he'd hatched.

'What's that?'

'EDM. Early Day Motion. We have to take this whole thing to the politicians. Make them see the logic of the case. Make them understand.'

'Good fucking luck.' McFaul pulled a face, swallowing another mouthful of the Guinness. Middleton had been knocking on politicians' doors for years now, lobbying MPs, organising fringe meetings at the party conferences, enlisting support wherever he could. Each new contact was another entry for his Filofax but the biggest windfall by far had been an eight-minute sequence in a television documentary about Cambodia. Middleton had directed the producer's attention to a Global operation in Battambang, a province near the Thai border, and the TV crew had returned with heart-breaking pictures of crippled kids. Middleton had appeared in the programme himself, a terse, angry condemnation of First World complacency, and letters of support had poured in for weeks afterwards. Ever since then, Middleton had done his best to acquire more screen time but the more programmes he did, the more he realised just how chancy television had become. In the hands of a dud producer, or an overbearing senior executive, items could actually backfire. What Global needed was total control, a property so hot that no one else would interfere. And now, thanks to McFaul, they'd got one.

'An EDM,' he was saying again. 'Parliament's the key. We link the EDM to the film. Get those bastard politicians onside. Shame them into it.'

'Into what?'

'Into legislation. I think they'll sign up to the protocol but that's not enough. Not any more. We want a total ban. Manufacture. Sale. Transfer. Stockpiling. The lot. Anything that qualifies for the word mine.'

'You kidding?'

'No.' Middleton looked at his watch, the orange juice gone. 'You hungry?'

They went to an Indian restaurant in the town centre. Middleton handed the menu to McFaul and told him to choose. The waiter knew his own order by heart. McFaul ordered chicken vindaloo and a couple of side dishes, listening to Middleton fine-tuning his assault on the politicians. A protocol agreement already existed that voluntarily bound signatory nations to a ban on the export of land mines. The USA had signed up and so had France and a number of other major players. To date, the UK had said no, determined not to tie the hands of British arms manufacturers. Britain, as the Foreign Office never failed to point out, owed a hefty slice of its export earnings to arms sales. Agreeing to a ban was tantamount to economic suicide.

McFaul returned the menu to the waiter, adding another Guinness to his order. Thanks to Middleton, he'd left the last one at the pub.

'You're telling me they'll sign the protocol?'

'Yeah. Bound to in the end if only to keep themselves in the game. Just like they handle the EEC. You know the way it works. Get in there and wreck it. Stop the buggers doing anything daft.'

'You mean extending the ban?'

'Of course.'

McFaul nodded. The British were no longer interested in simple land mines, the kind of stuff that littered the Third World. The crude anti-personnel mines, like the Type 72s, often came from factories in China and Pakistan at a couple of dollars a throw. That kind of money wouldn't feed workers in Leeds or Birmingham. What they needed was something far more sophisticated, something that would command a decent price tag. One answer was a mine that would self-destruct after a certain period. Another was a device that would make mines switch themselves on and off. In both cases, the technology didn't come cheap. But the smarter the mine, the bigger the profit.

Middleton was scribbling now. He carried a little notebook everywhere and he had it open at his elbow. Finally, he ripped off the top sheet and handed it to McFaul.

'Contact at the Hospital for Tropical Diseases,' he muttered. 'I had to send a bloke there last year. Where was I?'

'The protocol.'

'Oh, yeah. The Brits want to defend their position. You know that. Hi-tech mines. Freedom to manufacture. Freedom to export. All that. We have to stop them. Blow the argument apart. The only ban that works is a total ban. Dumb mines. Smart mines. The whole fucking lot. Otherwise we're pissing in the wind. You agree?'

Without waiting for an answer, Middleton got up and disappeared into the lavatory. When he came back, he was wiping his hands on his trousers. McFaul leaned forward, tapping the plastic tablecloth with the end of his fork. A couple of hours with Middleton and you were in danger of losing the thread.

'The woman I came back with,' he said. 'The one you paid for.'

'Jordan? Mrs Jordan?'

'Yeah. She lost her son.'

'I remember,' Middleton nodded, 'you sent a report.'

'Well . . . she's seen it all. She's been there. And she might have one or two things to say.' McFaul shrugged. 'That's all.'

'And she'd do it? She'd play ball?'

McFaul hesitated. The last time he'd seen Molly had been at the airport. They'd said goodbye beside the escalator that descended to the tube. He'd asked her whether it felt good to be back and she'd nodded a couple of times but he could tell from the coldness in her eyes that she was far from convinced.

'Yes,' he said at last, 'I think she might.'

*

442

Molly spent the next week sorting out the cottage. Two sets of clothes. Two sets of books. Endless records, tapes, mementoes, postcards, every last trace of the two men she'd shared her life with. Downstairs, in the dining room they'd so rarely used, she made space on the carpet for two piles. By far the biggest contained the things she'd get rid of. The other pile, tiny by comparison, was reserved for the items she knew she'd keep for ever, photographs, letters, James's school reports, odd certificates that Giles had picked up. The task was enormous, occupying infinitely more time than she'd ever anticipated, and after nearly breaking down on the first morning she began to play a game, telling herself she was a stranger to the cottage, a visitor, a nice, well-intentioned middle-class lady in from the village helping out at a difficult moment in someone else's life. The subterfuge worked for a while. She even slept well. Then halfway through the third day, she found an old attaché case full of letters at the bottom of Giles's wardrobe, and abruptly the charade was over.

She fingered the letters, then picked them up in thick bundles and lifted them to her nose. They smelled, unaccountably, of lavender and when she delved into the case again she found a couple of the little hand-sewn muslin sacs she'd made those first years they'd been married. She'd used them to sweeten drawers of clothes, the way her mother had taught her, and the thought of Giles doing the same with these letters of his made her gulp. For a minute or so, she fought the urge to cry. Then she bent double, hiding her face from an empty house, howling. Her hands were hot with tears. Her whole body shook. Grief, she thought dimly, smells of lavender. Finally, when she thought she could cry no more, she sat back against the sideboard, blowing her nose, letting the room slip back into focus.

The letters were on her lap and she picked one up, then another, reading them. Most were in her own hand, wild outpourings after she and Giles had first met, first been to bed with each other, but the rest, a tiny handful, had been written by James to his father. She went through them one by one, eavesdropping on a correspondence she'd never been properly aware of, numbed by how distant, how faint, the voices already seemed. However much she resented it, her days in Angola had thrown a wall across her life, cutting her off from her past, turning her in another direction. For this, she knew she ought to be grateful. Nothing could be worse than being trapped here, a sitting target for endless phone calls, endless commiserations. Word had gone round the village that she was back and the invitations were flooding in. Could she possibly make up a bridge four? Might she lend a bit of tone to an otherwise dull dinner party? Was there a chance of playing a walk-on role in the village panto? She fielded each request with a weary gratitude, wondering how best to say no without causing offence. These were nice people, kind people, true friends. They meant no harm. On the contrary, they were offering support, company, even hope. But none of them knew what she really needed. A little peace. And a little quiet.

In the end, under control again, she took the phone off the hook, burying it under a mountain of Giles's coats, and when people began to venture up the lane and knock on the front door, she hid from them behind the curtains.

By the weekend, she'd finished sorting everything out. Pleased with herself for surviving, she got up early, pulling on her shorts, lacing up her Reeboks, curious to find out whether her body could cope with a gentle lap or two of the circuit she'd made her own. She ran very slowly at first, sucking in deep lungfuls of air. It was a glorious morning, icy blue, a light wind blowing across the saltmarsh from the north. The wind, cold, brought with it the rich, muddy smells from the tidal creek at the foot of the fields, and when she paused for a moment or two at the kissing gate she could see the big blue shadows of the container ships berthed at the ferryport at Felixstowe. The air was crystal clear and the sunlight glittered on the water and when she thought of Giles she knew it was important to remember days like this. Alive, he'd be down at the marina already, pottering about, inventing jobs for himself, a man cocooned by his own happiness. All his life, he'd wanted nothing more complex than this: the chilly kiss of the sunshine, the gurgle of the ebbing tide across the mudflats, the pipe of the oyster-catchers strutting amongst the reed-beds. She smiled, thinking about him, knowing how lucky they'd been. Then she eased her body through the kissing gate and began to run again, picking up speed this time, newly strong.

Back in the lane, forty minutes later, Molly saw Patrick's Volvo parked outside the cottage. Patrick was sitting behind the wheel, the big square silhouette unmistakable. Of Alice, there was no trace. For a moment, Molly thought about returning the way she'd come, doing another lap of the circuit, maybe even finding a path across the fields, entering the cottage from the back, but she saw Patrick's hand go up to the rear-view mirror, adjusting it, and she knew then that he'd seen her. His door opened. He was standing in the lane, his arms outstretched, beaming.

'Molly! What a sight!'

Molly began to walk again. She was still breathless from the run and she knew she looked a mess. Hair plastered to her forehead. Bare legs covered in mud. Giles's old rugby shirt blotched dark with sweat. She paused by the car, letting Patrick embrace her. He smelled of tobacco and aftershave and she wondered for a moment whether Alice knew what he was up to. Saturday mornings they normally reserved for shopping. It was Patrick's job to push the trolley.

'Not at Safeways?' she asked.

Patrick pulled a face.

'Excused duty,' he said. 'Old man's perks.'

They stood together in the road, slightly awkward, until Patrick nodded at the cottage. He'd obviously tried knocking on the door already. She could see where he'd picked up the milk bottles, ready to present them to her, then put them down again on the other side when she hadn't appeared.

'Not going to invite me in?' he said cheerily. 'Nice cup of tea?'

'Of course.'

Molly led the way round the cottage to the back door. For some reason she felt uncomfortable, letting him see where she'd hidden the key. She unlocked the kitchen door, inviting him in, switching on the electric kettle. He had his coat off in seconds, warming his backside on the rail on the front of the Aga. Giles used to do that, Molly thought, resenting the intrusion even more.

Patrick was talking about Alice. She was in bed with a headache. It seemed she often got headaches.

'She ought to be out and doing,' he said, 'like you.' He began to recall his own days on the running track. Evidently he'd once competed for the county, an event called the 440. He'd won medals. He'd been good. 'That's yards, not metres,' he said. 'Four hundred and forty.'

'Once round the track?'

'Exactly.' He beamed at her. 'Trust you to know that.'

'Giles told me. He ran that event, too.'

'What kind of time? Any idea?'

Molly looked at him a moment, trying to remember. Giles's certificate was next door. She'd put it to one side only yesterday.

'Fifty-two point three,' she said. 'Does that sound about right?'

Patrick went quiet for a moment then nodded.

'Terrific,' he said gamely. 'Excellent time. Puts me to shame.'

Molly masked a smile, wondering already how to get rid of him. She'd decided on a pressing engagement in the village – a coffee morning, say, or a chat to the vicar about Giles's memorial service – when she felt Patrick behind her. She was standing at the sink now, her back to the kitchen. He was pressing against her. She could feel his erection against the waistband of her shorts. She froze, aware of his hands encircling her, cupping her breasts. Then he was kissing the nape of her neck, murmuring her name, telling her how much he loved her. He'd loved her for years. It was never something he'd ever been able to confess. He'd told no one. He thought he'd never be able to say it to her face.

Molly turned round, easing his body away from her, much the way you might gentle a frightened horse. Patrick was flushed, his eyes glittering behind the thick glasses, the mildness she'd always known quite gone.

'No one will know,' he was saying, 'I promise you.'

'Know what, Patrick?'

'About us. You and me.' He shut his eyes a moment, swallowing hard. 'We could use the spare room. I quite understand, believe me.' Molly stared at him and then began to laugh. He opened his eyes, frowning. 'What's the matter?'

'You, my love.' Molly leaned forward, pecking him on the end of his nose, then rubbing off the kiss with her finger. 'You're a very dear friend. And so is Alice.'

'She doesn't understand me.'

'That's what all the boys say, Patrick.'

'It's true. She doesn't understand anything. She . . .' He shook his head, not trusting himself any further. He couldn't take his eyes off Molly's breasts. At length, he began to pull himself together. 'Giles was no angel, Molly. You know that, don't you?'

The kettle began to bubble then turned itself off. Molly felt the sweat chilling on her face.

'How do you mean? Exactly?'

'I mean that . . . all men have . . .' he gestured loosely at the gap between them, 'weaknesses.'

'Oh? And Giles?'

'He was no exception, that's all. It's not a criticism. Don't misunderstand me. It's just human nature.'

'What are you telling me, Patrick?'

'Nothing,' he looked suddenly shamefaced, 'nothing at all.'

Molly reached out, uncertain, then withdrew her hand when he tried to kiss it. She knew she ought to throw him out, bring this pathetic scene to an end, but somehow she couldn't. She wanted a name. She wanted evidence.

'Who was it, Patrick?' she said quietly.

He looked at her a moment, sobered.

'A woman called Carolyne,' he muttered.

'How do you know?'

'He told me.'

'He told you what?'

'He told me how much he cared for her.'

'When? When did this happen? Recently? Years ago?'

'October.'

'October? This year?'

'Yes.'

Molly stared at him. Autumn. The time when she'd first noticed the change in Giles, the long periods of silence, the sleepless nights, the regular bottles of Glenmorangie he'd bring in from the off-licence in the village, refilling the empty decanter. She ought to have known. She ought to have guessed.

Patrick was back behind his usual mask. Sincerity and concern in equal measures.

'He loved you, Molly. Never doubt that. He really did.'

'Thank you, Patrick.'

'I mean it. He wouldn't see you hurt. And neither would I. That's why . . .' he risked a smile, 'I came this morning.'

'To tell me about Carolyne?'

'To tell you . . .' he blinked, colouring slightly, 'I loved you.' He frowned. 'Love you. I bought you a present, too. A little keepsake. Just between the two of us. I . . .' He fumbled in his jacket pocket and for a moment Molly thought he'd bought her a ring. Then a photograph appeared. He offered it to her, shyly, like a child. 'I've got a nice frame,' he said, 'if you'd like it.'

Molly looked at the photo. Patrick was standing on a golf course, his club held high, grinning at the camera.

'Who took this?'

'Alice. It's her favourite shot.'

'And you've given it to me?'

'I've got a couple of spares. She thinks it does me justice. I thought you might like it. That's all.'

Molly studied the photo a little longer then tucked it into the top pocket of Patrick's jacket. Nothing could disguise the expression on his face. He looked crestfallen, robbed of something he believed to be rightfully his.

Molly began to shepherd him towards the door. She picked up his coat from the chair. She didn't want him back. Ever.

In the hall, Patrick made a brief stand.

'You wouldn't . . .?' His eyes were on the stairs.

'No thank you, Patrick.'

'Only I thought—'

'Your coat.'

Molly gave him the heavy tweed, folding it over his arm and reaching for the door. Outside, the wind was chill, making her shiver. Patrick stood on the path. Alice wasn't to know. She thought he'd gone to the golf club. She'd be heartbroken if she ever found out. Molly shook her head, looking at him, then closed the door, hearing him shuffling towards the gate. He beeped the horn once, driving away, and then – at last – there was silence.

McFaul got to the private hospital at noon. Saturday visiting hours were virtually unlimited, according to the woman he'd talked to on the phone. Todd Llewelyn had been transferred here only a day after his admission to the Hospital for Tropical Diseases. His private insurance entitled him to a room on the fourth floor. His visitors, so far, had been sparse.

McFaul crossed the road, turning up his collar against a light shower. The Marlborough was on a quiet corner in the heart of Mayfair. Smoked-glass windows and a revolving door at the front gave it the air of a discreet hotel. Rooms on the fourth floor were supervised from a nursing station midway along the central corridor. McFaul paused by the desk, giving his name, asking for Todd Llewelyn.

The nurse was Welsh, a dark-haired, pretty woman in her mid-twenties.

'Are you a relative?'

'No.'

'Friend, then?'

'Colleague.'

'From the television?' The woman was smiling.

McFaul shook his head.

'Real life.'

The woman capped a pen, ignoring the dig. She selected a clipboard from a row of hooks beneath the counter and consulted it briefly. Then she looked up.

'You know he's had a stroke, I assume?'

McFaul stared at her. The last he'd heard of Todd Llewelyn, the man was half-dead from malaria. No one had mentioned a stroke.

'No,' he said, 'I didn't know.'

The nurse nodded, looking grave. Llewelyn had collapsed en route from Heathrow to the Hospital for Tropical Diseases. A day later, he'd been moved to the Marlborough. He'd survived malaria, only to succumb to a blood clot on the brain.

'How bad?'

'Pretty serious, I'm afraid. Both arms. Both legs. And his speech has gone, too.'

McFaul shook his head, wondering just how much was left. The nurse was leading him along the corridor now. Llewelyn's room was near the end. Outside the door, she stopped. Through the small square of window, McFaul could see the bottom half of Llewelyn's bed. Beside it, her back to the door, sat another woman.

The nurse beckoned McFaul closer.

'His brain's fine,' she whispered. 'He hears and he understands. But that's about all.'

'Who's in there with him?'

'A helper. We have a couple of them. She's there to change
the TV channels.' She glanced in. 'We have satellite here, of
course. It gives him a bit of choice. It's the least we can do,
under the circumstances.'

'And will she stay? While we talk?'

'No,' the nurse shook her head, 'that's why it's important
you know the code.'

'Code?'

'The way we get through to Mr Llewelyn.' She was looking
at him fondly now. 'One blink means yes. Two mean no. If he
wants the channels changing he blinks three times.' She smiled.
'It's all he's got left, poor love.'

'What's that?'

'Television.'

She reached forward, opening the door, touching the
woman on the chair lightly on the shoulder. She got up at once,
standing aside, making room for McFaul. McFaul was looking
at Llewelyn. He was sitting up in bed, his body propped on a
bank of pillows. He was wearing green paisley pyjamas and his
arms were carefully arranged on the counterpane. His hair was
newly parted, and around his neck he wore a plastic bib, a larger
version of the kind mothers attach to babies.

McFaul sat down, hearing the door close behind him. The
only thing that moved in Llewelyn's face were his eyes and
McFaul saw the gleam of recognition.

'It's me,' he said lamely, 'Andy.'

Llewelyn's head was pointing at the television. A panel of
housewives were answering questions about their favourite fantasies. One woman said she went to bed every night wanting to
make love to Lawrence Harvey. When the presenter pointed
out that he was dead, she said it didn't matter. Dead or otherwise, she'd give him the night of his life. The audience roared

their applause and Llewelyn's eyes found McFaul. He blinked three times, then did it again. McFaul was nonplussed for a moment before he remembered the code. The remote controller lay on the carpet beside the chair. He pressed the channel changer, going forward. A single blink from Llewelyn. He paused. Three more blinks. He changed channels again, then again. Images came and went, far too quickly to make any sense, then Llewelyn stopped blinking altogether and McFaul looked up at the screen in time to see a lion mauling an antelope. The sequence belonged to some kind of wildlife documentary, and Llewelyn stared at it as the huge jaws tore at the animal's throat. There was a tree nearby, a big old baobab, and fat black birds sat on the lower branches, indifferent to the carnage below.

McFaul watched a moment longer, then turned the television off.

'I've come about Muengo,' he said gruffly. 'I'm sorry you're so . . .' he frowned, unable to find the right word.

Llewelyn's eyes hadn't left the television. The skin on his face seemed paper-thin. Since Angola, he'd aged a hundred years.

McFaul went on, regardless, telling Llewelyn about the film that had emerged from the pictures he'd shot. The last three days he'd spent in a bungalow in a village outside Salisbury. Middleton's contact had invited him down for the duration of the edit, and he'd arrived with the new Sony equipment and the field tapes. Geoff, the editor, had devoted half a day to reviewing the material and had then put together what he termed a 'rough-cut'. From somewhere, he'd found some blues music, very simple, minor key, saxophone and occasional double bass. The musicians had improvised around a single theme and the music came and went, blowing through the film like smoke, pulling the material together, creating tensions, resolving them, sculpting the darkness at the heart of the film. The film itself was relentless, pulling you in from the start, an opening montage of the worst images underscored with the urgent wail of the saxophone, and McFaul described it now, shot for shot, determined that Llewelyn should understand.

Domingos dead, the action moved to Katilo, accompanying his triumphal entry into Muengo, the camera always on the move, the shots raw but effective, the rebel commander never off the screen. Next came the scene outside the cathedral, Katilo carving a path through the crowd, his earnest monologue intercut with more images from the hospital. McFaul went on, describing the night at the barbecue, the slaughter of the cow, Katilo's taunting dance with Christianne. Then they were airborne, climbing out of Muengo, dropping down into the diamond mines, the saxophone bubbling away as the pits by the river flashed by. After Cafunfo, Zaire. McFaul pulled his chair closer to the bed, going into detail, telling Llewelyn exactly the way it had been in Kinshasa, two men dead, their heads blown apart. The film had ended here, more slaughter, the images come full circle, fresh blood spilling across the darkened road.

McFaul paused, looking at Llewelyn. His chin was on his chest now but his eyes were still bright.

'What do you think? Good, eh?'

Llewelyn blinked once, an affirmative, the signal for yes, his eyes moistening, and McFaul watched a single tear roll down his cheek. He reached for the dead hand on the counterpane, squeezing it, hearing the door open behind him. Then the Welsh nurse was bending over Llewelyn, drying his eyes, scolding McFaul for upsetting him.

'Upsetting him?' McFaul was on his feet. 'You kidding? He loved it.'

McFaul phoned Devizes from a pay-box on Waterloo station. He'd promised Middleton the latest on Todd Llewelyn.

'He's paralysed,' he said. 'Can't speak. Can't write. There's no way he can object to what we've done.'

'You're sure?'

'Positive. I stayed most of the afternoon. Poor bastard, I almost felt sorry for him . . .'

McFaul could hear the football results in the background now. A passion for Swindon Town was Middleton's one concession to a life outside his work. After a pause, and a groan, he was back on the phone.

'What about the woman? Your friend? Mrs Jordan?'

'I've been phoning. She's always engaged. Can't get through.'

'Keep trying.' He paused again. 'Geoff brought the film over this afternoon. Let me have a dekko.'

'What do you think?'

'I think it's fucking incredible. Spot on.' He favoured McFaul with a brief, mirthless laugh. 'Even a politician might get the point.'

Molly was back from the pub by half-past nine. She'd driven out on the Harwich road, trying to find somewhere small and anonymous, a chair in a quiet corner where she could curl up with her paper and her Campari and soda, safe from interruptions. Staying in the cottage after dark had begun to unsettle her and the knowledge that it was Saturday night somehow made the feeling worse. She wanted the assurance of other people around her. She wanted to hear laughter and conversation without having to contribute anything of her own. After a couple of drinks, she'd thought, the cottage wouldn't seem so daunting. Alcohol would cushion her fear of the silence. With luck, she might even sleep.

The pub, though, had been a disaster. She'd found a place called The Wheatsheaf, miles from anywhere. In the darkness it had looked inviting, half-curtained windows, wooden tables, a hint of candle-light. Inside, she'd found a small, cluttered room hung with sepia prints of the old Thames barges that used to work the estuary. There'd even been a dog, an ancient cocker spaniel, blind in one eye. She'd bought her Campari and her bag of peanuts, and settled in a corner, waiting for the pub to fill up. But nothing had happened. Just a handful of glum regulars who'd tottered in from God knows where and leant heavily on the bar, staring at her.

She'd somehow imagined a darts tournament, cheerful, thirsty young men, high-spirited, loud, boisterous, a thick blanket of noise she could pull around herself, keeping out the cold. Instead, she'd felt progressively more exposed, all too aware of the long silences, the muttered conversations, the sense that she'd intruded into this gloomy weekend ritual. She'd hung on as long as she could, her spirits raised by each approaching car, but when nothing happened, and the grandfather clock by the door struck nine, she gave up. Even the cottage, she'd thought, would be better than this.

Back home, she emptied the last of the single malt from Giles's bottle of Glenmorangie and sat at the kitchen table, her coat still on. She'd spent most of the day trying to forget what Patrick had told her but try as she might she couldn't erase the woman's name. It was like a persistent leak in the top of her head, dripping and dripping. Carolyne. Carolyne. Carolyne. She tried to visualise the woman, put a face and a body to the name. She tried to rationalise it, tell herself it was nothing serious, just a middle-aged man getting himself in a bit of a muddle. God knows, the poor lamb was probably bored out of his head. After twenty-seven years of marriage, who wouldn't be? She pushed the thought as far as she dared, imagining them meeting, probably in London, probably at lunch-times, probably in some wine bar or other, snatched moments together, a little private oasis in their respective lives. Was she married? Divorced? Single? Did she have a place of her own? Did they ever go there? Or had it been some cheap hotel? Scrawled entries in the visitors' book and a couple of desperate hours between nylon sheets? She confronted the questions one by one, hauling them up from her subconscious until the kitchen began to blur around her and the glass at her elbow was empty.

The phone made her jump. She must have put the receiver back on the hook before she'd left for the pub. She looked at it for a full minute. Then she got up from the table and walked unsteadily towards the dresser. The phone was still ringing. She peered at it a moment. She'd connected the answering machine as well, and there was a message waiting for her.

She picked the phone up. It was Robbie Cunningham. She recognised the voice at once and it brought a smile to her face. Someone young. Someone decent. Someone who wouldn't damage her. She began to talk, curious at the way her words ran into each other, little dodgem cars, colliding and colliding. She began to laugh, hearing the concern in Robbie's voice. He'd been trying to get through for days. The phone was always engaged. Was she OK? Was she coping? Was there anything he could do?

Molly told him everything was fine. Twice. Then she began to cry. Robbie did his best to comfort her and she reached for a dishcloth, drying her eyes, feeling foolish. She told him she was drunk. Best to go to bed. Best to sleep it off. Was it urgent? This call of his? Or could it wait until the morning?

Robbie hesitated.

'It's not me, exactly,' he said, 'it's Alma. Alma Bradley. You remember her?'

Molly nodded. Luanda, she thought. The big room in the posh hotel overlooking the city. She'd been interviewed there. Alma's had been the face beyond the lights.

'I remember,' she said thickly. 'Nice woman.'

'She wants to talk to you. She wants to meet.'

'Oh?'

Molly frowned, wondering how practical it would be to return to Angola. The prospect of Africa was becoming daily more attractive. Even Kinshasa, she thought, might be preferable to this. Molly bent to the phone, telling Robbie she was happy to fly out. Maybe he could come too. Just like old times.

'Africa?' Robbie sounded bewildered.

'Luanda. Angola. Wherever she is.'

'She's back here. She lives in Chiswick.'

'Oh . . .' Molly nodded, staring blankly at the wall, 'Chiswick.'

Robbie was giving her a phone number. She looked for a pen but couldn't find one.

'Got that?'

'Sort of.'

'I know it's late but I know she'd appreciate—'

'Of course.'

Molly shut her eyes, squeezing them hard, suddenly wanting the conversation over. She wasn't up to this. Not real life. Not any more. Robbie was back where he'd started, asking her whether she was OK. Molly said she was fine, making an effort to bring the exchange to a sensible end. She tried to remember the name of Robbie's partner. He'd talked about her a lot in Angola, telling Molly about their plans together.

'How's that lovely girlfriend of yours?'

'She's pregnant.'

'She's what?'

'Pregnant. We're going to have a baby. Mid-June. Best news ever.' He paused. 'All I need now is a proper job. Terra Sancta's on the rocks. I've got to find something else. Fast.'

Molly heard herself congratulating him, telling him what wonderful news it was, then the thought of a child overwhelmed her and she put the phone down, no longer able to cope with the conversation. She and Giles had felt exactly that way, exactly that excitement, years back, when her own pregnancy had been confirmed. They'd been living in Chelmsford. She'd taken a train to London and met Giles outside Lloyd's, dragging him across the road to a pub and giving him the news. Even then, with six months to go, they'd been convinced it would be a boy.

She stood by the dresser, looking at the empty glass on the kitchen table, wondering whether to start on one of the bottles of Rioja Giles had been saving for Christmas. Then she remembered the message waiting for her on the answerphone. She pressed the play button, steadying herself on the back of a chair. There was a click and a brief burst of static, then she heard a voice. It was a woman's voice, warm, steady, beautifully controlled. She'd been phoning and phoning. She wanted to arrange a meeting. She wanted to talk. She lived in London but she was happy to travel down. Her time was no problem. She'd fit in with whatever suited Molly best. She gave a telephone number, repeating it twice, and Molly found a stub of pencil, scribbling it down, staring at it. It was an 01296 number. Alma Bradley's had been 0181. She was sure of it. Absolutely certain. The woman was coming to the end of her message. She'd be in all day Sunday. Perhaps Molly could phone.

She paused, then laughed.

'By the way,' she said lightly, 'the name's Carolyne.'

CHAPTER FIFTEEN

Two days later, a week before Christmas, McFaul and Ken Middleton met outside Green Park tube station. They walked along Piccadilly, picking their way through the mill of Christmas shoppers, and then crossed the road. Halfway up Shaftesbury Avenue they turned left, into Wardour Street. The address Alma Bradley had given McFaul on the phone was at the far end. McFaul pressed the top button on the speakerphone, giving his name.

Alma Bradley was waiting for them at the top of the stairs. She had a scarlet AIDS ribbon pinned to the shoulder of her black trouser suit and she was smoking a small cheroot. She offered them both a brief handshake and led them to a room at the end of the corridor. The room was long and narrow. Shelves of film cans lined one wall and a sagging venetian blind hid the single window. Beneath the window, on a table, McFaul recognised the editing gear Geoff had been using to cut the pictures he'd brought back from Africa. It was the same model. Exactly.

Ken Middleton had Geoff's tape in the pocket of his anorak. Since the rough-cut, Geoff had condensed one or two sequences, excising what he called 'flab', but the piece had lost none of its rawness. On the contrary, it delivered hammer blow after hammer blow, a remorseless assault on whatever preconceptions one might have about life in the Third World. Hunting for a title, Middleton had finally settled on a suggestion of

Geoff's. Listening to Ken talking about the minefields, he'd picked up the phrase 'The Perfect Soldier'. Sappers and salesmen used the phrase alike. It referred to the anti-personnel mine, ever alert, ever lethal, never off-guard. Applied to Katilo, it was equally ironic. Here was the battlefield commander who would use all that high explosive, littering it around Angola with the guileless abandon of a child tossing away sweet papers. Katilo was the reality behind all the silky phrases in the sales brochures. Katilo was what the men in suits really meant when they talked about 'interdiction' and 'terrain denial'. Put Katilo and land mines together and you ended up with a film like this.

There were three chairs arranged in a semi-circle around the screen. Alma settled herself in the middle chair while Middleton loaded the cassette. In a week and a half, he'd mastered the first page of the instruction manual.

'How long?' Alma was looking at McFaul.

'I'm sorry?'

'How long is the film?'

'Oh . . .' McFaul frowned, 'about twenty-five minutes. Maybe a bit less.'

Alma nodded, saying nothing, and for the first time McFaul noticed the Harrods shopping bag hanging from a hook on the wall. Priorities, he thought grimly. Twenty-five minutes in the minefields, then back to the serious stuff.

Middleton started the tape, taking a seat. McFaul had seen the film half a dozen times now and he let the tidal flood of images wash over him. During the darker sequences he watched Alma's reflection in the screen and he marvelled at her lack of reaction. When the Norwegian surgeon hacked through the last of Domingos's leg, wrapping it in newspaper, she reached down for her handbag and lit another cheroot. Apart from that, nothing.

At the end of the screening, she asked McFaul to turn on the lights. He did so, returning to his seat while Alma made a phone call, ordering a minicab. The initial request to see the film had come from her. She'd traced Global to Devizes a couple of days back and phoned Middleton, explaining her interest. She'd already done an interview with Molly Jordan. She was familiar with the story. She understood there might be field tapes. How could she help?

Now, she put the phone down. Middleton was waiting for a verdict. This woman said she had access to the networks. She was the shortest cut to a huge audience.

'It's horrible,' she said at last, 'revolting.'

'That's the point.'

'I'm sure, but it's untransmittable like that. No one'll touch it. And that's a guarantee.'

Middleton and McFaul exchanged glances. In the street outside, they'd both anticipated a strong reaction, maybe even tears. But not this cold rebuff. Alma was reaching for the eject button on the video-player. She took the cassette out, examining it.

'Who cut this?'

'Guy called Geoff. Geoff Hunt.'

Alma frowned a moment, then shook her head.

'Don't know him.' She glanced up. 'You have the rushes? The field tapes?'

'Yes.'

'Where?'

'Back home.' Middleton paused. 'Why?'

'I'll need them.'

'Why?'

'To put together something realistic, something transmittable.' She tapped ash into the bin. 'Something we can sell.'

'It's not your material,' Middleton pointed out, 'it's ours.'

'Of course,' she shrugged, 'if you really want to bury it, that's your decision. All I can give you is advice.' She nodded at the cassette. 'Take that to anyone on the networks and they'll show you the door.'

'Channel Four?'

'Even them.'

'So what . . .' Middleton picked up the cassette, 'would you do with it?'

'Me? I'd tear it apart and start again. The focus should be Molly Jordan. You've met her?' Middleton shook his head. 'Then you should. She's an impressive woman. An ideal witness. She lost her son in the minefields. You probably know that. She's been out to Angola, too. She knows what the country's like.'

McFaul stirred.

'She was there,' he said softly, nodding at the screen, 'she saw it all.'

'All what?'

'Everything on that film. Except Domingos.'

Alma half-turned on her chair. She looked astonished.

'You're telling me she went through all that? The stuff round the bonfire? The mugging sequence?'

'Yes.'

'And you didn't get her on tape?'

'No.'

'Why not?'

'It was irrelevant.'

'*Irrelevant?* A white woman amongst all that? *Irrelevant?* Do you know anything about television? What sells? What turns the punters on?'

'No,' McFaul picked up the cassette, pocketing it, 'but I know about Angola. And I know about mines.'

McFaul stood up. Middleton was looking uncomfortable. Alma began to backtrack.

'Listen . . .' she was saying, 'don't get me wrong. Those are extraordinary pictures. I've never seen anything like them in my life. Thank God. But we have to be realistic. The networks will never stand for material like that. Never. So why don't we just talk about this? Take a fresh look?'

McFaul was already heading for the door.

462

'It's the truth,' he murmured. 'That's not a bad place to start.'

Molly Jordan stood on Thorpe-le-Soken station waiting for the train from London. The woman called Carolyne had left another message. If Molly didn't phone to cancel, she'd be arriving at three minutes past twelve.

Molly shivered, knowing she should have worn a thicker top. The sun was out, and it was a glorious day, but the wind was off the sea again, cutting through her thin angora sweater. She began to walk up and down, keeping to the sunny side of the platform, wondering yet again quite how she'd handle the next hour or so. She'd booked a table at a pub in the village. At least they'd have something in common to talk about.

The train clattered into the station and a handful of passengers got out. Most of them were retired pensioners returning from shopping trips to Colchester. Molly scanned the faces, wondering whether Carolyne, after all, might have had second thoughts, surprised to feel the first stirrings of disappointment. She'd nerved herself for this moment all morning. The last thing she wanted was another let-down.

A porter had appeared. He was wheeling a collapsible ramp. He stopped beside the waiting train, unfolding the ramp and securing the top end inside the guard's van. A woman appeared, backing carefully down the ramp, steadying a wheelchair. In the wheelchair sat another woman, much younger. She was wearing a headscarf of the deepest blue, a beautiful colour, and as the wheelchair bumped down onto the platform the sunlight spilled across her face. She had a lovely face. It was oval-shaped, her skin slightly olive, her jet-black hair pulled back beneath the scarf. She was smiling at Molly. She was lifting a gloved hand.

Molly ran towards her, not quite believing it. The woman behind the wheelchair was adjusting a plaid blanket, tucking it in around the younger woman's knees. The noise of the depart-

ing train drowned her first words but Molly had no need for
introductions. This was the voice on the answerphone. Definitely. She bent to the wheelchair, offering her hand, but the
woman reached up, kissing her lightly on the cheek. She smelled
of something expensive, L'Air du Temps maybe. Molly was
grinning, ashamed of herself, giddy with relief.

'Carolyne?'

'Yes.'

'Lovely to meet you.'

Molly led the way out of the station. Only when she was
unlocking her car did it occur to her that getting her guests the
mile up the hill to the village might not be simple. She glanced
down at Carolyne. She had dark brown eyes and a warm smile.

'Leave it to Helen,' she said, 'she's marvellous.'

The woman behind the wheelchair asked Molly to open the
back door of the car. Then she lowered one arm of the wheelchair and retracted the footrests, positioning the chair alongside
the car. Standing in front of Carolyne, she folded the blanket,
handing it to Molly, then bent down again, tucking her hands
beneath Carolyne's thighs. Carolyne winked at Molly, putting
her hands round Helen's neck. Molly heard the older woman
counting quietly to three, then, in a single movement, Carolyne
was standing up, supported by Helen. She was wearing a blue
pleated skirt and expensive leather boots. Helen nudged her
body towards the car then lowered her gently into the back
seat, bending briefly to tuck her legs in.

Molly shook her head, impressed, trying to imagine Giles
mastering the manoeuvre. If this was what it took to get into
a car, how could this woman possibly cope with anything as
demanding as an affair? Molly opened the boot, ashamed of
herself for even listening to Patrick, standing back while Helen
collapsed the wheelchair and stowed it away. When she mentioned the pub, Helen said that wouldn't be a problem. She'd
been with Carolyne for years. There wasn't a pub that had
beaten them yet.

At The Bell, they had a big table near the window. Carolyne

stayed in the wheelchair, eating from a tray on her lap. She explained at once that time was short. She had to be back in London by half-past four. The train left at ten past two. Molly nodded, curious now about the reason for her visit. It had to have something to do with Giles but she couldn't think what.

'You knew my husband?'

'Yes,' Carolyne nodded, reaching out, touching Molly on the arm, 'and I'm sorry. Deeply sorry. He was a good man. You were very lucky.'

'I was. I know I was. I often . . . you know . . .'

Molly broke off, hiding her embarrassment behind a spoonful of soup, and Carolyne watched her for a moment, visibly anxious.

'You didn't mind me inviting myself out here? Phoning up like that?'

'Not at all.'

'Are you sure?'

'Absolutely.'

Carolyne nodded, cutting off a corner of pâté and balancing it on a triangle of brown toast. Her husband, she explained, had been a friend of Giles's. They had a relationship going back years, mainly business, spiced with the odd lunch. Occasionally, when he could afford the time, Giles would come across to the house. Which is where she'd first met him.

'At home?'

'No,' Carolyne smiled, 'the House of Commons.'

Molly gazed at her a moment, her napkin poised. The cream-coloured envelope, she thought. The one that had caught Patrick's attention.

'Your husband's an MP?'

'Yes.'

'Vere Hallam?'

'Yes.'

'He wrote to me. I'd no idea you were . . . you were . . . married.'

'My fault. I should have said on the phone. Funny the way

you always make assumptions.' She laughed. 'But I'm here now so it doesn't really matter, does it?'

She nibbled at her toast. She had long, slender fingers, perfect nails. She was extraordinarily beautiful.

'What happened?' Molly was looking at the wheelchair. 'Do you mind me asking?'

'Not at all. I had an accident.'

'When?'

'Years ago. In Florida.'

It was a story she must have told a thousand times. She'd been seventeen years old. She'd been mad about swimming. She'd dived into the ocean from a wooden pier and she'd got the depth of the water wrong. As simple as that.

'So what happened?'

'I broke my neck. They call it a C6 fracture. The sixth bone down from the top.' She reached for the butter. 'Nothing works below the waist.'

'Nothing at all?'

She looked up, her eyes steady, the merest hint of a smile.

'Nothing. Helen sorts me out most of the time. Vere and I manage the rest between us.'

'You knew him before the accident?'

'No.' She shook her head. 'He was doing the rounds at Stoke Mandeville. He'd just won his first by-election and the hospital's in his constituency.' She paused, reflective, looking at the toast. 'If you're thinking that makes him some kind of saint, you'd be right. I was pretty down in the dumps. Meeting him made up for everything.'

Molly nodded, impressed.

'Tell me about Giles,' she said.

'He was sweet. Vere joined his syndicate. You probably know that. He made us oodles of money and we needed it, believe me. There was a lousy insurance settlement after the injury and paralysis doesn't come cheap.'

Molly nodded, aware from her own voluntary work in the

466

village just how expensive full-time care could be. Helen alone would cost a fortune.

'So Giles helped . . .' she prompted, 'during the good years?'

'He certainly did. He made it easy for us, and that was important from Vere's point of view. He wanted to get ahead, naturally, and you know what politicians' hours are like. Late sittings at the House. Endless committees. Constituency business. It goes on and on.' She paused, licking the butter from her fingertips. 'With Helen around, there was never a problem. I could have a life, too. And that was important to both of us, believe me.'

Molly glanced at Helen. She was already looking at her watch. Molly leaned forward.

'Giles's syndicate went bust,' she said. 'At least, that's what we all thought.'

'Quite. And Vere was the first to know. Giles rang him from Lloyd's. He happened to be home that day.'

'When was that?'

'October. I'll never forget it. Giles was in a terrible state. Vere said we'd all meet in town.'

'And did you?'

'Yes. Giles looked ghastly. He kept trying to find out . . . you know . . . how much it cost for me. I think that's what upset him most. The thought that I might have to go into some kind of home.'

'And would you? Was he right?'

'Yes.' She nodded. 'We did the sums, Vere and I. According to Giles we were liable for three-quarters of a million. That would have wiped us out. Me in some Cheshire Home. Vere at the Job Centre.' She looked up. 'You know about MPs and bankruptcy? That upset Giles, too.'

Molly was thinking back to October. No wonder Giles had gone so quiet. No wonder he'd had trouble sleeping. Carolyne was exchanging glances with Helen. Helen produced an envelope and passed it across the table to Molly.

'Open it,' Carolyne said, 'please.'

Molly slid her nail under the gummed flap of the envelope. Inside was a typed cheque made out in her name. The figure in the box said £47,000.

'What's this?'

'It's yours. It belongs to you.'

'But what is it?'

'It's the insurance settlement on Giles's yacht. For some reason the policy was assigned to us.' She hesitated. 'He meant well. He was a sweet, sweet man.' She nodded at the cheque. 'My husband insists you have it.'

Molly put the cheque to one side. She didn't entirely understand the logic but just now it didn't seem to matter. Giles had never been less than responsible. It was a curse he'd taken to the grave. Carolyne was watching her carefully, the toast abandoned.

'My husband wants you to know how upset we are. About Giles. He'd be here today if it had been at all possible.'

'Yes . . .' Molly was looking at the cheque again, the old uncertainty creeping back. This woman was beautiful. Giles could be very silly, very soft. Especially when people were hurt, or needy. She looked up. 'May I ask you a question? Something personal?'

'Of course.'

'How well did you get to know Giles?'

'Well enough to miss him.'

'You met often? Talked a lot?'

'Yes,' she smiled, leaning forward, her hand closing on Molly's, 'mostly about you.'

'Me?' Molly looked blank.

'Yes, you. He worshipped you. He was lost without you. He couldn't talk for five minutes without your name coming up.' She hesitated a moment, brushing a crumb from her skirt. 'That's one of the reasons why I wanted to come out here today. Just to see for myself. And you know something?'

'What?'

'He was right.' She leaned forward, kissing Molly on the cheek. 'Your soup's getting cold. And we have to go.'

Molly had been back at the cottage less than a minute when the phone began to ring. She was standing in a pool of sunshine at the kitchen sink, filling the kettle. She felt radiant, almost light-headed, the darkness and the chill of the past week quite gone. She walked across to the phone, eyeing the pile of unopened Christmas mail on the table. Last year, they'd cut thick streamers from rolls of crêpe paper and hung them from the picture rail. She'd pinned cards to the streamers, columns and columns of them, and the effect had been immensely cheerful. This year, she thought suddenly, she might do something similar. James would have liked that. James would have approved.

She picked up the phone, recognising McFaul's voice. She knew at once that he was drunk, the way he used her Christian name, the way he plunged straight into the conversation. He'd been to see someone about the film. They wanted to recut it, alter it, turn it into something safe and tame and acceptable. They couldn't cope with the truth, couldn't hack it, didn't know the meaning of the word. He'd just spent an hour and a half arguing the toss with Ken Middleton. Even he, even Ken, was beginning to have his doubts. Had he been there? Had he seen it? Did he know what it was like to watch someone you loved sawn in half? Did he?

Molly at last got a word in.

'Who is this? Who saw the film?'

'Alma. Your pal. Alma Bradley.'

'What did she say?'

'What I just told you.' There was a pause while McFaul fed more coins into the pay-phone. 'She'll ring, I know she will. Or maybe Ken will. Someone will.'

'Why?'

'They'll want you to perform again. They'll want you on the film. Milk and water. No roughage. Nothing crude. Can you believe these people? Molly?'

Molly reached for a chair, pulling it towards her, loosening the scarf at her throat. Hearing McFaul like this, she felt an extraordinary sense of kinship. She'd been this way, exactly this way, only days ago. Maybe it was Africa, she thought. Maybe this is what it did to you.

'Where are you?' she said.

'London.'

'Do you want to come up here? Talk about it?'

'No.' He broke wind, apologising at once. 'Just tell me you won't do it, whatever they say.'

'I won't do it.' Molly smiled. 'Whatever they say.'

'That's a promise?'

'Yes. And I wouldn't do it anyway, not even for you.'

'Why not?' He sounded wounded now, an almost comical sense of hurt, 'Why not?'

She thought about the question a moment, softening her tone. In truth, McFaul was one of the few people she'd trust utterly. Not once had he let her down. Not once.

'OK,' she conceded, 'I'd do it for you. But only you. Television I can do without. Believe me.'

McFaul grunted something incoherent. Molly took it as an expression of approval. Then he was telling her about the film again, the way they'd cut the pictures together, the message it sent to whoever cared to listen. The thing was a kick in the belly, a really nasty piece of work. The last five years, he'd wanted to get the message across, and now he'd done it.

'But you're telling me they won't use it.' Molly frowned. 'So what's the point?'

'Exactly.'

'You're going to change it?'

'No way.'

'What, then?'

There was a long silence. Molly could hear an announcement in the background. The 15.32 to Guildford had been cancelled. McFaul came back on the phone.

'We hire some place,' he was saying. 'We invite the press. That Terra Sancta bloke.'

'Robbie?'

'He's in touch with these people, journalists. That's his job. He can help.' He paused. 'We need an MP, too. Someone to sponsor us. Ken's got some motion or other he wants to put through Parliament. Apparently it has to be a Tory. He says they're the only ones that count. Don't ask me why.'

'A Tory MP?' Molly was looking at the cheque on the table. Vere Hallam had a nice signature, elegant, almost legible. McFaul was off on a new tack now, telling her about another idea he'd had. He'd been to see Todd Llewelyn. The man was dead from the neck down but his telly had lots of channels. Stuff the networks. There had to be other ways of getting the thing on the air. Did Molly know anything about satellite television?

'A Tory MP,' Molly said gently. 'You mentioned a Tory MP.'

'Yeah.'

'Are you serious? Do you want a name?'

'Yeah.'

'OK, but I'll have to phone him first . . .' She paused. 'Do you want me to do that?'

There was a long silence and for a moment Molly thought he'd hung up. Then he was giving her a number where she could find him. She wrote the number down, listening to him talking about the film again. Then he broke off.

'You know something?' he said suddenly. 'You did fucking well in Africa.'

Molly tried to get through to Vere Hallam for most of the evening. When she phoned the number on the letter he'd written, she found herself talking to a secretary. The secretary recognised her name and gave her two other London numbers. One of them evidently belonged to a flat Hallam occasionally used. He was back at the flat by ten. He sounded extremely cheerful.

Molly apologised for phoning so late. She had a favour to beg. She hoped he didn't think her rude.

'I'm so sorry, who did you say you were?'

'Molly. Molly Jordan.'

There was a brief pause. Then Hallam was back again with apologies of his own. He was delighted to hear her. He was so glad she'd rung. He was desperately sorry about Giles. Of course he'd help in any way he could. Molly explained about the mines. She'd just come back from Africa. Mines were a terrible problem. She paused, hearing a woman's voice in the background. Carolyne, she thought. Spending the night in town.

'Africa?' Hallam was back on the phone.

'Yes. Angola.'

'And you say you've just been out there?'

'Yes.'

'God awful place to go, surely?'

Molly gazed at the telephone a moment, wondering just how much Hallam knew. Maybe Giles hadn't told him about James. Or maybe he'd been away somewhere.

'My son got killed out there,' she said hesitantly, 'I went to fetch him home.'

'Killed? James?'

'Yes,' Molly swallowed hard, 'he stepped on a mine.'

'My God, I'd no idea. You have been through it, haven't you? Hang on a moment.'

Molly heard a door closing. Then Hallam was back again. He was sorrier than he could say about James. After Giles, it must have been a terrible blow.

'It happened before Giles. Before Giles disappeared.'

'I see. I'm so sorry.'

'No,' Molly shook her head, 'it's OK.'

There was a long silence. Molly tightened her grip on the phone, determined not to break down again, listening to Hallam asking her whether she wanted to talk about it. Something in his voice, a warmth, a sincerity, made her think at once of Carolyne and a life confined to a wheelchair. This man understands loss, she thought. He's been there. He's seen it. He can cope. Hallam put the question again and she nodded, settling into a chair by the phone, telling him about Angola. She described Muengo, the conditions the people had to cope with, the things she'd seen, the lessons she'd learned. She'd gone out there to discover who'd killed her son. And she'd returned a different woman.

'How? How different?'

'I don't know.' Molly frowned, picking at a loose line of stitching in the hem of her dress. 'I thought these things were simple, black and white. They're not.'

'Grief? Isn't that simple?'

'Yes, and selfish too. It swallows you up. It cuts you off.'

'From what?'

'Pretty much everything. I wanted a name, someone I could blame for killing James. But when you get down to it, once you get out there, it's just not like that. The place is a mess, bits of it, maybe most of it. But the people are fine. They're wonderful. The women, especially.' Molly paused, remembering the little girl's mother she'd met in the ruins of the cinema in Muengo. Her name had been Chipenda. Chipenda had lost a child, too, and more or less everything else. Five minutes with Chipenda put one or two things in perspective. Like her own situation. McFaul had been right all along. James had died because he hadn't listened.

'James always knew best,' she heard herself saying, 'always.'

'That's what Giles said. Wouldn't be told.'

'Exactly.' Molly nodded. 'He was headstrong. He knew it all. That's what killed him. That's what took him off the road.'

'I'm sorry?'

'He was looking for a little girl called Maria. She'd wandered off into the bush. James went after her.'

'The bush was mined?'

'Yes.'

'But James thought it was safe?'

'I'm not sure.' She paused. 'Maybe he did. Maybe he was just brave.'

'Quite.'

'And foolish.'

'Of course. But brave, too. Hang on to that, Molly. Courage matters, believe me.'

Molly nodded, thinking of Carolyne again, listening to Hallam's voice on the telephone. He was asking her about Angola. Molly had flown out to bring back James's body. Had she succeeded?

'No. He's still there.'

She explained about the grave at Muengo. She'd arrived too late. Disinterment was unthinkable.

'Does that matter? Were you disappointed?'

Molly thought about the question for a moment or two, then shook her head. After Giles, her son had been the most important person in her life. She'd miss him until the day she died but she'd made a kind of peace with what had happened. James and Africa had been made for each other and it was right that he should be buried there. A spirit like his belonged in Muengo. Not in some sodden graveyard in deepest Essex. She heard Hallam's murmur of agreement and the feeling that he somehow understood made her smile. He had, after all, known Giles. Like father, she thought, like son.

She caught sight of Hallam's cheque again, lying on the kitchen table, and she thanked him for it, changing the subject. Then she brought the conversation back to Global Clearance. There was a man called McFaul. He made minefields safe. He and his boss wanted some kind of sponsor in Parliament. Maybe Hallam could help.

'Of course.' Hallam paused. 'This McFaul. Is he a friend of yours?' Molly hesitated a moment, giving the question some thought. Then she smiled.

'Yes,' she said at last, 'I think he is.'

The worst of the hangover had gone, next day, when McFaul's phone rang. McFaul was lying on the sofa, resting his leg, listening to Chris Rea. He'd spent the morning walking the length of Southsea beach, letting a keen westerly wind sluice over him, clearing his head. He tucked the phone into his shoulder, reaching for his third cup of tea, wondering how on earth anyone could be so cheerful.

Molly was talking about an MP associate of her husband's, someone called Vere Hallam. She'd been on to him this morning. She thought he sounded sympathetic.

'To what?'

'To all this mines business. He said he'd welcome a discussion. In fact he wants to buy us dinner.'

'Us?'

'You and me.' Molly paused. 'And Ken, of course. Can you make it up to London?' She gave him an address off the Strand. The Savoy Hotel was on the south side, down John Adam Street.

'He's suggesting tomorrow night,' she said. 'Apparently he's away after Christmas.'

McFaul scribbled the details on the morning paper, wondering about getting a call through to Devizes. Middleton had been threatening to fly out to Afghanistan. Some problem with a new clearance operation. Molly was talking about Alma Bradley. It seemed she'd been on the phone all morning, begging Molly to come up to London and discuss some more filming. McFaul broke in, still thinking about Ken Middleton, struck by another thought.

'This MP bloke,' he said, 'is he a Tory?'

He heard Molly laughing. Then she was back on the phone.

'Must be,' she said. 'Who else is silly enough to put their money into Lloyd's?'

Middleton, as it turned out, couldn't make it to the Savoy. By the time McFaul got through to Devizes, he was already on his way to Heathrow. McFaul phoned him on the mobile, explaining the situation, but the problem in Afghanistan was evidently pressing. Global's local agent had crossed swords with a village headman and officials had been called in from Kabul to adjudicate. The next direct flight was three days away and by that time the authorities might have closed down the operation entirely.

Middleton was somewhere on the M4, his voice coming and going as he threaded the Global Range Rover through heavy Christmas traffic.

'What's this guy's name again?'

'Hallam.' McFaul peered at the scribbled note on top of the *Guardian*. 'Vere Hallam. You know him at all?'

McFaul heard the wail of the two-tone horns Middleton had recently fitted to the Range Rover. Then he was back on the mobile again. Evidently, Vere Hallam was MP for Aylesbury. He was young and ambitious, one of the high-fliers who'd served their time on the back-benches and were now tipped for promotion. Middleton wasn't sure but he thought he'd recently been given a job in the Whip's office.

'Why him?' he sounded puzzled. 'He's way out on the right. Real ultra. Dry as a bone.'

'God knows.' McFaul shrugged. Politics, like the pace at which Middleton led his life, had always been a mystery. Middleton was still speculating, posing another question.

'Does he know what we're after? Support for an EDM?'

'He's been told about the mines. I think that's as far as it goes.'

'But he knows our position? Where we're coming from?'

'He might. I dunno.'

'You're going to tell him? Or you want to wait till I get back?'

McFaul explained that Hallam would be away after Christmas. The invitation to dinner sounded too good to refuse. Whatever Molly's relationship with the man, now was the time to turn it to Global's advantage.

'Whose relationship?'

'Molly. Molly Jordan's.'

'She knows this guy?'

'Seems to.'

McFaul heard Middleton grunting. It was the noise he made when things weren't going well. Ideally, McFaul knew, he'd like to be there. Taking the helm was Middleton's stock-in-trade.

'You'll need the text of the EDM,' he said reluctantly. 'Get the office to fax it down to you. And you'd better show him the film, as well. Geoff's knocked off a couple of VHSs.' He paused. 'On second thoughts, maybe you'd better eat first. Stuff like that might put him off his pudding.'

McFaul was scribbling again. EDM was Middleton's shorthand for Early Day Motion, a parliamentary manoeuvre that McFaul still didn't fully understand.

'So what's the bid?' he queried. 'What are we after?'

'Support. Show him the EDM. Get him to sign up. Tell him there's votes in it.'

'What about getting him out there? Somewhere active? Angola?'

The mobile faded for a moment, then came back again. Middleton was laughing.

'After that film?' he said. 'You've got to be joking.'

Next day it was late afternoon before Molly left for London. She took the train, settling herself in an empty first-class compartment, sitting back and watching the bare, flat fields speed by. She'd had another call from Vere Hallam since her conversation with McFaul. He'd phoned from his office, confirming the evening's arrangements. They'd meet in the American Bar at half-past seven. He had a table booked in the Grill Room at eight. Afterwards, if she and McFaul wanted to spend the night in town, he'd reserved rooms for them. The rooms, like the meal, were – of course – at his expense. Given the circumstances, and the season, it was the very least he could do.

She thought about the voice on the phone as the train clattered through Wivenhoe, the last of the daylight gleaming on the river. Vere Hallam had talked to her the way you'd talk to an old friend, real warmth, real affection, and afterwards Molly had found herself wondering whether this was simply a card every politician played or whether, for once, it was sincere. Listening to him on the phone, it was impossible to forget her first glimpse of his wife, the wheelchair edging slowly down the ramp onto Thorpe station, the square of plaid blanket tucked around her knees. Sustaining a marriage like that, coping with a lifetime of paralysis, took someone pretty special.

The train was late getting into Liverpool Street and McFaul had been waiting for nearly half an hour when the cab dropped Molly outside the Savoy. He was standing beneath the canopy, his tall frame hunched inside a thin, belted raincoat, and he lifted a hand as Molly turned from the cab. Molly hurried across the pavement, strangely pleased to see him. She reached up, kissing him on both cheeks then moistening her forefinger and rubbing off the lipstick.

'You look different,' she said. 'Haircut?'

McFaul nodded, visibly embarrassed, running a hand across his scalp. In Angola, he'd worn a bristly crew cut. Now, he was practically bald. She looked at him a moment, then put her arm through his, tugging him towards the big revolving door, telling him he should have waited inside, out of the cold. The door swallowed them both. A lavish Christmas tree dominated the lobby. McFaul looked round, watchful, awkward. Two women, shrouded in furs, were waiting impatiently for the lift. Molly was already at the entrance to the American Bar, peering in, wondering whether Vere Hallam had arrived. The bar was half-empty. A man in a dark suit rose from a table at the end. He was tall, the suit exquisitely cut. His blond hair was long, curling over his collar, and his smile revealed a row of perfect teeth. He came towards them, his hand outstretched. He moved like an athlete, on the balls of his feet. He looked extremely fit and his face had a glow that suggested a life outside London.

'Molly Jordan?'

Molly shook the proffered hand, introducing McFaul. McFaul managed a tense smile.

'Drink?'

Molly chose Campari. McFaul settled for a bottle of Guinness. They sat down, Hallam asking Molly about the journey up, her plans for Christmas, whether or not she'd finished her shopping, deftly getting the evening afloat on a raft of small talk. After the intimacy of their exchange the previous evening, it was strange putting a face to the voice on the phone. Early forties, Molly decided. Maybe a little older. Hard to tell when he was so obviously in such good physical condition.

A waiter arrived with a handful of menus and Hallam told him to put them on the table. Molly counted them. There were three.

'Isn't Carolyne coming?'

'I'm afraid she's had to stay at home. Touch of flu. She sends her regrets.' He paused. 'She was devastated to hear about James. She felt awful about not knowing.'

'It doesn't matter. That wasn't her fault.'

'And Giles, too. He was such a nice man. We miss him dreadfully.'

'So do I.'

'Of course you do.' He reached across, ever attentive, offering her a comforting pat on the arm, and Molly caught the faintest whiff of perfume, something light, the scent of lemons.

McFaul had produced a video-cassette from a plastic bag. He put it on the table beside Hallam's glass.

'Compliments of Global,' he muttered. 'My boss thought you might like to watch it some time.'

'Ah . . .' Hallam touched the cassette with his fingertips, still looking at Molly, 'is this the one you mentioned on the phone?'

'I haven't seen it,' Molly said. 'Not personally. But . . . you know . . . maybe tomorrow or something . . . when you have the time.'

'Of course.' Hallam picked up the cassette and put it carefully to one side. 'Pretty rugged stuff, I hear.'

'You do?'

'Yes.' He smiled at McFaul. 'Word gets around. London's a small place, smaller than you think. I understand you've been trying to get a TV sale. Is that right?'

'Not sale, exactly.' McFaul frowned. 'A showing. That's all we want.'

'To tell the world?'

'Yes. And the more people the better. Obviously.'

'Obviously.'

The waiter returned to take the order, hovering at Molly's elbow while she tried to decide. Hallam was recommending the traditional Christmas dinner. Year after year, it was always superb.

'You come here often?'

'I'm afraid I do.'

'It doesn't show.' Molly nodded at his waistband. 'You must have a wonderful metabolism. Lucky thing.'

Hallam accepted the compliment with a smile, asking the waiter for a bottle of Burgundy. McFaul had settled for steak and kidney pudding. The waiter disappeared and Hallam eased his long frame backwards in the chair, reaching for his Perrier.

'So tell me about these land mines of yours,' he said, looking at McFaul. 'Pretend I know nothing.'

The meal lasted most of the evening. Hallam had reserved a table in the far corner of the big dining room, beside one of the tall windows and Molly sat with her back to the wall, picking at her food while McFaul told Hallam about the minefields. He talked in a low monotone, favouring the MP with his usual candour. He described his early days in the Royal Engineers, learning the job, textbook clearance work, driving breaches across scrupulously laid minefields. He explained the way things were when you obeyed the rules, each minefield tagged and labelled, as neat and tidy as a flowerbed in a city-centre park. He drew diagrams on the tablecloth with the end of his fork, describing the standard patterns, diamond shapes, box shapes, the various ways you could guard the big anti-tank mines with a screen of A/Ps.

'A/Ps?'

Hallam paused, his fork spearing a fat Brussels sprout, wanting everything spelled out, no ambiguities, nothing lurking in the shadows of this strange conversation, and McFaul nodded, translating the term, turning the bare acronym into flesh and blood.

'Anti-personnel mines.' He nodded at a packet of cigarettes beside Hallam's plate. 'Pick that up. What does it weigh? A couple of ounces? An ounce? Less than that?' He paused. 'You know how much TNT you need to take a foot off? Three-quarters of an ounce.'

He bent to the table again, swallowing another mouthful of red wine, telling Hallam about his days in the Falklands. He'd fought there during the war in 1982. A couple of years later he was back again, part of the mine clearance operation, hunting for millions of Argentinian mines. In the war's final stages, the Argies had scattered them from helicopters, totally at random, no attempt to keep records or plant warning signs. As a result, the islanders were condemned to live with them for ever. There were beaches on East Falkland where human beings would never walk again. Ever. Miles and miles of sand, permanently off-limits. That's what mines did. Once they got into the wrong hands.

Molly was watching McFaul, spellbound. She'd never heard him talk this way, so coherent, so forceful, so effective.

'Terrible.' She shook her head. 'Ghastly.'

Hallam patted his mouth with his napkin.

'I agree. Appalling.'

McFaul glanced up, his concentration broken for a moment. He looked, if anything, faintly amused. Hallam gestured at the food cooling on his plate but he shook his head, returning to the minefields, explaining the way it worked in the Third World, peasant economies strangled, whole villages necklaced by the little tablets of high explosive. He described his days in Afghanistan, the people he'd met, the kids he'd seen buried. He talked about the markets in remote corners of Pakistan, places where the arms dealers dumped the stuff they didn't want any more. Chinese mines. Soviet mines. American mines. Hundreds of them. Thousands of them. Each one another coffin. Each one another cripple, begging in the streets.

The courses came and went, McFaul barely touching his food. In Angola, he said, there were now more land mines than people. In Cambodia, they were running out of crutches. There were people out there trying to help, sure, but each time you went back to these places the problem had got worse. Laying a mine took less than a minute. Finding them again, lifting them, returning the earth to the people, would be the work of many lifetimes.

A waiter appeared with a tray of crackers. A Japanese couple at the next table were wearing paper hats. The waiter offered the crackers to Molly.

'Take one, madam,' he said, 'there are ten-pound notes in some of them.'

Molly and McFaul exchanged glances. Hallam took three crackers, leaving them beside his plate.

'Tell me how I can help,' he said quietly.

McFaul produced a folded sheet of fax paper. He passed it across the table. Hallam read it, then looked up.

'I think you'll find we don't export mines like that.' He nodded at the cigarette packet. 'They're yesterday's technology. You should be talking to the Chinese, or the Pakistanis. They're turning out millions of the things.'

'I know. But we want a total ban. *Every* kind of mine.'

'That might not be wise. Or even necessary.'

'Why not?'

Hallam reached for the fax and flattened it against the table. Molly tried to make sense of the closely spaced lines of type. The fax contained the text of a formal motion to be presented to Parliament. Halfway down, it spoke of the need for the government to recognise the unacceptable nature of all anti-personnel mines and ban their manufacture, use, export, transfer and stockpiling. She read the sentence twice. It didn't seem to leave much room for ambiguities.

Molly looked up. McFaul was toying with a cracker while Hallam, quietly emphatic, made a series of points about the defence industry. Arms sales were a real success story. We'd managed to capture 20 per cent of the world market. Export earnings ran into billions. One job in ten depended on defence. When he'd finished, he spread his hands wide, a gesture Molly interpreted as helplessness.

McFaul hadn't taken his eyes off Hallam's face.

'Have you ever watched a kid bleeding to death?' he said. 'Or his mother trying to hoe a field on one leg?'

'That's hardly the point. You can't blame our mines for that.'

'A mine's a mine,' McFaul insisted, 'there's absolutely no difference.'

'You're wrong. You should listen to what the MOD people are saying. I popped over this afternoon. Took the precaution of getting myself briefed.'

'I know what they're saying,' McFaul said thickly, 'and it means fuck-all.'

The Japanese couple at the next table were looking apprehensive. Molly encouraged them with a smile. Hallam was leaning forward now, patient, sincere, eager to explain.

'On the contrary,' he was saying, 'I think the army boffins are talking a great deal of sense. The technology's there to be used. As I understand it, we're making mines safe. Doesn't that meet with your approval? Given your obvious . . . ah . . . interest?'

McFaul looked away a moment, lost for words, and Molly reached out, restraining him, anxious to avoid a scene. The fax was still lying on the table. She found a phrase that had earlier caught her eye.

'I'm a bit lost,' she said. 'What does "self-neutralising" mean?'

Hallam folded his napkin and put it carefully to one side.

'It's a gadget they put in mines these days. I gather they become harmless after a certain period of time. It's a new technology. We're up there with the world leaders.' He smiled. 'For once.'

Molly glanced at McFaul, wanting confirmation. McFaul was still looking Hallam in the eye. She'd never seen such naked contempt.

'This is a game the Brits play,' he said quietly. 'The guys who work in the field, the guys who know, want mines banned. All mines. We say they're no better than gas or germ warfare. We say they're weapons of mass destruction. And you know what? Some of the major players are beginning to agree with us. You take the States. Even France. They've introduced voluntary bans. No export. No sales abroad. But the Brits? They just move the goalposts, start hiding behind the technology. Your friend here's right. There are firms making mines that switch themselves off. There are smart mines, mines that talk to each other, mines that get up and boogie. The Brits think that's a wonderful combination. Nice clean conscience. Lots and lots of export orders. In fact they've even got a word for it. You'll find it in the sales brochures. They call it "value added".'

Hallam was looking pained, his fingers steepled together over his empty plate.

'That's hardly fair . . .' he murmured.

'You're right. And you know why? Because some of them don't work.'

'A tiny fraction.'

'So what? You sell these things by the tens of thousands. One dud in a hundred and you're back where you started. You know the failure rate in the Gulf War? These so-called "smart mines"? Twenty per cent. *Twenty per cent.* That's one mine in five. Still lying there. Still live.' McFaul touched his face for a moment, then leaned forward again. 'So tell your friends in the MOD they're wrong. There's no such thing as a smart mine. A smart mine is a fairy-tale. Mines are unsmart. Mines are evil. All mines.' He picked up the fax, letting it fall to the table. 'You should ban them tomorrow.'

Hallam studied McFaul a moment. Heads turned across the room as a chef entered with an enormous birthday cake. There was a ripple of applause, growing louder. The chef stopped at a table and a plump girl in red began to count the candles. She stopped at twenty-one.

'So what do we do about the bad guys?' Hallam enquired. 'Just leave the mines to them? Deny ourselves the option of having any?'

'Doesn't apply.'

'Why not?'

'We are the bad guys.'

'That's naive, with respect. We live in the real world. Imperfect though that world may be.'

The birthday party were on their feet now, toasting the chef. Molly was looking at the cigarette packet, half-open on the table. James, she thought. Lying in the freezer in the schoolhouse. His body torn to shreds.

'He's right,' she murmured, looking at Hallam, 'mines are evil. I've seen the results. I've been there. And he's right.'

Hallam offered her a look of mute sympathy.

'Of course,' he said, 'but I can only go on the briefings we get. I'm assured we're not breaking the rules. We don't touch the kind of kit that finds its way to Angola. We're just not players in that game. We insist on the responsible use of mines. Absolutely insist. Otherwise there's no sale.'

McFaul stirred again.

'Responsible what?'

'Use.'

'What does that mean?'

'It means what it says. There's a convention, a code, you know as well as I do. Minefields must be marked, mapped. Civilians must be protected.'

'But they're not.'

'I'm afraid I don't believe you. As far as we're concerned, they are.'

McFaul snorted, a short, mirthless bark of laughter.

'Have you ever been in a war?'

'No, but that doesn't invalidate my—'

'Do you know what war means? Tearing up the rules? Getting right down to it? Kill or be killed? Dark night? Pissing down with rain? Some guy trying to slot you?' He paused, nodding. 'You should try it some time. See how responsible you feel then. With your map and your torch and your handful of signs.'

Hallam was showing the first signs of irritation, tiny spots of colour, high on each cheekbone. His Christmas pudding lay untouched in a pool of brandy butter.

'Forgive me,' he said, 'I'm simply trying to explain the logic behind our position.'

'There isn't one. You're trying to square the circle. It won't work.'

'It has to work.'

'Why?'

'Because that's the way we've chosen to make our living. As a country. As a nation. That's how we pay our way in the world.'

'Who? Who's chosen?'

'Me. And you. And fifty million others. I'm afraid we live in a democracy, Mr McFaul. Much though you might regret it.'

'Fine,' McFaul picked up the fax again, 'then why don't you put this through the Commons? See who dares oppose it? See how many votes there are in maiming women and kids?'

Hallam shook his head, under control again, more sorrow than anger, and Molly was suddenly aware of a woman picking her way towards their table. She was young, in her early twenties, and she wore a striking trouser suit with a low, scooped neckline. She paused beside Hallam, touching him lightly on the shoulder. She had beautiful eyes, barely any make-up. She was smiling.

'Do you have the key?'

Hallam glanced up at her, feeling in his jacket pocket. He produced a room key and gave it to her. She bent to his ear, whispering something, and Molly caught the scent she'd noticed earlier. A hint of lemons, underscored with something muskier. The woman was already turning away. She had poise, and grace, and confidence, apologising for interrupting the conversation, glancing back over her shoulder, smiling at McFaul. McFaul watched her as she made her way back across the Grill Room. When she'd disappeared, he reached for one of the crackers, offering it to Hallam.

'Pull it,' he said drily, 'then you can get off to bed.'

Outside on the street, half an hour later, the rain had stopped. McFaul turned up his collar against the wind, bending to kiss Molly goodbye.

'You can still stay,' she said. 'There's a room booked.'

'After that?' He looked over her shoulder, back into the hotel. Diners were streaming out of the Grill Room. Somewhere deep in the building, a dance band was warming up. Molly told him not to be silly. Politicians were tough as old boots. They never took things personally.

'I know.' He looked down at her a moment, buttoning his coat. 'That's part of the problem.'

Molly returned to Thorpe the next day. She spent the morning shopping in Knightsbridge then caught an early afternoon train, sitting in an overheated carriage, thinking about Vere Hallam. She'd seen him again on the way into breakfast at the hotel. He was leaving for an early appointment in the City, as charming and attentive as ever. He hoped her friend had enjoyed the evening. It was a shame he hadn't been able to stay longer. He absolutely understood the case he'd been making and only regretted that it lacked a certain balance. Politics was the art of compromise. One way and another, he thought the government had got this particular issue about right.

He'd walked her into the restaurant, finding her a table near the window. Carolyne was planning a Boxing Day get-together at the family house out in the Chalfonts before they left for Val d'Isere. Perhaps Molly would like to pop over? Molly had been surprised. Not by the invitation but by the prospect of Val d'Isere.

'Carolyne can make it to France?' she'd said. 'She can cope with all that?'

'Oh, no, she and Helen hold the fort at home,' the MP had looked at her, amused, 'much like other wives I know.'

It was dark by the time Molly got back to the cottage. She toured the ground floor, putting on lights, pulling curtains, still angry with herself for not telling Hallam the way she really felt.

About the mines. And now, dear God, about his marriage. How could a man lead such a blatant double life? How could someone inflict such public humiliation? And what, exactly, had he meant by 'other wives'?

She began to make herself a pot of tea, still brooding. Half a lifetime tucked up with the middle classes seemed to have robbed her of the capacity for rage. It was like a missing nerve, a deadness. Put her in a half-decent frock, invite her to a nice hotel, make the right social noises, and she behaved just like the rest of them. No fuss. No embarrassments. No awkward scenes. Just a quiet determination to make the evening a success. Nice wine. Lovely food. Good company. Was that why she'd asked McFaul to London? Was that what a monster like Hallam deserved?

She shook her head in wonderment, asking herself again why she'd been so feeble. Was it breeding? Should she blame it on her own mother? Her constant talk of manners? Of the need to behave properly? Of the importance of thinking of other people? She gazed across the kitchen, watching the first curls of steam from the kettle. Other people were important. Of course they were. That's what had shaped her married life. And that's what, perhaps unsuccessfully, she'd tried to pass on to James. But where had all that left her last night? And again this morning? Why had she so patently failed to even raise her voice?

She thought again of McFaul, sitting in the Savoy Grill Room, his spare frame hunched over the table, his meal cooling on the plate while he talked so forcefully about the minefields. Socially, he was a disaster. He'd looked clumsy and ill at ease. His small talk was non-existent. But Hallam had never been in a moment's doubt about how he really felt, and when McFaul had pushed back his chair and left the room without a backward glance, Molly had been immensely proud of him. It was poor form not to say thank you, not to end the evening with at least a handshake, but McFaul had come from another world. Thank God.

She turned off the kettle, scalding the teapot with hot water. The recording machine attached to the telephone was on the dresser and she saw the winking red light for the first time. The light meant that a message was waiting. She put the teapot down, walking across to the answerphone. The read-out said there were five messages. She frowned, respooling the tape, still thinking about McFaul. Absently, she pressed the play button, hearing a brief burst of tone then silence as the caller hung up. The second burst of tone was followed by another silence. She hesitated, alert now, looking round, feeling the first chill stirrings of fear. She hurried into the hall, making sure she'd locked the front door. Back at the phone, she checked the last three messages. On each occasion, the caller had again hung up.

She reset the tape, glancing at her watch. Ten to six. Still early. She thought about going out, calling on friends in the village, confecting some excuse or other, knowing at once that it would solve nothing. No matter how long she stayed, however warm the welcome, at some stage she'd have to come back. The cottage was where she belonged. Being alone was now a fact of life.

She tried to settle down again, starting on a pile of Christmas cards she'd promised herself she'd write, but even this small effort of concentration was beyond her. Names meant nothing. Her head had emptied of memories. After the third card, she gave up, putting the kettle on for another pot of tea then abandoning it for the last of the gin.

The phone rang an hour later. She picked up the receiver, steadying herself on the side of the dresser. After Angola, she told herself, she could cope with anything.

'Hello?'

There was a silence at the other end. She could hear the sound of someone breathing. Then a voice came on, a man's voice. He was saying he'd missed her. He was saying it was going to be OK. He was asking her to get a pen. Molly stared at the single plate drying in the rack on the draining board. The plate drifted slowly out of focus. She tried to speak. She couldn't. The voice had stopped. She could hear a door opening, the sound of traffic, then the door closing again. The voice returned. The voice was still there. Calling her name.

Molly shut her eyes, bending to the phone, not beginning to understand.

'Giles,' she whispered, 'is that you?'

EPILOGUE

Molly left for France the next day. She took a train to London, another to Portsmouth. At the harbour station, before getting a cab to the ferryport, she phoned McFaul. As far as she could gather, he had a house a couple of miles away. Giles had sworn her to silence but she wanted to make the briefest contact.

'I'm going away for a bit,' she explained when he answered the phone, 'I just wanted to say Happy Christmas.'

McFaul sounded surprised.

'Happy Christmas to you, too.'

'I mean it.'

'Yeah?'

There was a long, awkward pause. Through the smeary glass of the call-box, Molly could see a warship ghosting past. It was misty, the air clammy and damp.

'What are you up to?' she asked at last.

'Decorating. The hall's a mess. Rising damp. I've even had to take the bloody carpet up.'

'Oh.'

Molly was about to mention Hallam but McFaul beat her to it.

'I phoned his office this morning,' he said. 'Told him the news.'

'What news?'

'About the film? Hasn't your mate from Terra Sancta been on?'

492

'No.'

Molly frowned, listening to McFaul explaining about Robbie Cunningham. He'd been offered a job by Oxfam. He was joining their press department. He'd told them about the film and apparently they wanted to make it the centrepiece of a hard-hitting campaign they were planning about the minefields. They already had a number of public figures lined up. Showbiz people. Sports stars. Even the odd MP. They were spending a lot of money. They were taking it very seriously.

'They say the film sounds perfect. Just as long as it's tough enough.'

Molly grinned. After last night it was good to hear McFaul laughing.

'I've got to go,' she said, 'the boat's waiting.'

'Off somewhere nice?'

'France.' She bit her lip. 'Caen.'

'From here, you mean? Pompey?'

'Yes.'

McFaul whistled, scolding her for not calling in. Then he wished her good luck.

'I'm the one on the beach,' he said drily, 'waving.'

The ferry left at three. Molly stood on the deck, watching the city's seafront slip by. Once she thought she spotted McFaul and she lifted an arm, waving, but the tall figure in the raincoat turned away, not seeing her. Probably someone else, she thought. Probably not McFaul at all.

The boat docked in darkness. Molly joined the handful of foot passengers by the stairwell. The boat was nearly empty. Outside, she could hear men shouting. There was a rumble and a bump as the crane hauled the big covered gangway into place, and then she felt cold air on her face as one of the seamen tugged open the big embarkation doors. She peered out into the darkness, wondering if she might spot

Giles. He'd said he'd be on the quayside. He'd said he couldn't wait.

The passengers began to file off the ferry. Molly joined them. She'd packed a single suitcase. Giles had said she'd be back after Christmas. She hadn't a clue why.

On the quayside, the passengers were shuffling towards the waiting bus. It felt even colder than Portsmouth. Molly pulled her coat around her, shielding her eyes against the glare of the big overhead lights. She was still searching for Giles when she felt the slight pressure on her arm. She turned round, lowering the case. His coat smelled of cigarettes. She buried her face in it. He must have been waiting in some bar, she thought. Probably for hours.

When she was back in control, she looked up at him. He was thinner than she remembered but he was whole, undamaged, the same little crease lines round his mouth and eyes, the same tuft of unshaved hair beneath his nose.

'I don't believe it,' she said softly. 'I thought it was some awful trick.'

He had a car. They drove west, along the flat Normandy coast, past shuttered houses and empty streets. To the right, dimly, she could see a faint white line where the surf broke. Giles was talking, telling her what had happened, where he'd been. The shipwreck had been his own work. He'd sacrificed the *Molly Jay* in order to begin a new life. Molly had been barely listening, happy just to hear the sound of his voice. Now, she began to realise what he was saying.

'You sank the yacht?'

'Yes. Me and a friend.'

'Then what?'

'We went to Poland. Gdańsk. On his yacht.' He paused. 'Desperate measures.'

Molly looked at him. In the light of the passing street-lamps he seemed strangely content, a man at peace with himself.

'Isn't that illegal?' Molly asked. 'Staging your own death?'

'Yes, I'm afraid it is.'

She nodded, saying nothing. Then she leaned across, slipping her arm round his shoulders, kissing him on the soft triangle of flesh below the ear. The car swerved to the left. Then back again. Giles was grinning. He looked, for a second, just like James.

'Forgive me?' he said.

'Always.'

'Truly?'

Molly nodded, her eyes back on the road, wondering how best to put it.

'I love you,' she said at last.

Giles had booked a double room at a hotel called Le Trou Normand. Molly was already registered under the name of Pearson. While the receptionist looked for the key in the back office, she murmured the name to herself, and for the first time she began to feel uneasy. Her name was Jordan. Pearson sounded wrong. Was she really ready to spend the rest of her life pretending to be someone else?

They had supper in the restaurant. The long terrace room stretched the width of the hotel. Beyond the sea wall, she could see the sweep of a distant lighthouse. Giles was talking about the syndicate going down. At first, he hadn't believed it. He'd been certain from the start that the New Jersey claim should have been contested but somehow the case had never got under way. Only when the call came from the Council at Lloyd's did he appreciate how serious the situation had become.

'So you phoned Vere Hallam?'

Giles looked surprised.

'Yes, amongst others.' He returned to a lobster claw, shredding the white flesh. 'How did you know?'

'His wife told me. Carolyne.' Molly reached over, restraining his fork a moment. 'If you told them, why didn't you tell me?'

Giles put his fork down. The smile had gone.

'I couldn't. I just couldn't. I tried, believe me. It was just . . .' he shrugged, 'impossible.'

'But you told her,' Molly said again, 'you told Carolyne.'

'I had to. You've met her?'

'Yes.'

'Then you know why. She'd have ended up in a home. I couldn't let that happen,' he looked at her, 'could I?'

Molly didn't answer, turning away, looking out of the window. So far, she'd said very little about Africa, where she'd been, the things she'd seen, the difference it had made to her.

'I thought you were dead,' she said softly. 'I believed them.'

'I know, I know.'

'You'd planned it? You knew what was going to happen?'

'Yes,' he nodded, 'obviously I had.' He reached for the second bottle of wine, offering to fill Molly's glass, but she put her hand over it, shaking her head. He hesitated for a moment, eyeing his own glass, then put the bottle down. 'I thought about telling Patrick,' he said, 'but in the end I didn't.'

'Just as well.'

He caught the inflection in her voice, raising an eyebrow, but she shook her head again, discouraging questions. The waitress was hovering, waiting to set the table for breakfast. It was late, nearly eleven. Giles glanced up at her, murmuring something in French. The girl blushed and nodded, returning to the door that led to the kitchen.

'What did you say?'

'I told her you were my wife. I said we hadn't been together for a while.' He smiled at her. 'Nothing wrong with the truth, is there?'

He got to his feet and unhooked his jacket from the back of the chair, extending a hand towards Molly. Molly hadn't moved.

'No,' she said quietly, 'and there never was.'

The bedroom was upstairs at the front of the hotel. Molly and Giles lay beneath the duvet, the curtains drawn back, the window open. The tide was full now, the waves lapping at the sand beneath the sea wall.

Molly had been talking about Muengo. She'd seen where they'd buried James. It was a quiet spot, peaceful, shadowed by trees. She'd met the girlfriend, too. Christianne.

'She was French?'

'Yes. Dotty about him.'

'Typical.'

'I'm afraid so.' She gazed at him in the darkness.

A little later, Giles talked about the future. He'd been looking for places for them both to live. He had a forged passport, credit cards, even a French bank account, but life in France was expensive. Even with the proceeds from the cottage, and the settlement from the life insurance, they might be wise to look elsewhere. Somewhere far away from England. Somewhere non-European.

'Any ideas? Mrs Pearson?'

Molly had been thinking about the question for hours, knowing it had to come up. Giles was a criminal. By forging his own death he'd effectively ruled out any return to England.

'What about you?' she said. 'What do you think?'

Giles didn't say anything for a moment. Molly saw a flash of white in the darkness beyond the window as a gull soared up from the beach.

'I've been making enquiries about South Africa,' Giles murmured. 'I've one or two contacts there, people I can trust.' He paused. 'There's no extradition treaty if things get sticky, not so far, and it's a lovely place to live.'

Molly nodded. The choice made perfect sense, the clearest possible guide to the shape Giles's life would take. In South Africa, he'd be looking for a cocoon, somewhere to mattress his enforced retirement. He'd find a spot by the sea. He'd buy a little boat. He'd make friends at the yacht club. It would be Thorpe-le-Soken all over again. She turned her head away, listening to him talking about the resorts around Durban, describing the dream home they'd live in, the trips they'd plan, the people he knew who'd already made the move. Property prices were falling. The smart money was moving in. He reached for her hand beneath the duvet and held it for a moment. Molly lay quite still, fighting the urge to roll over and end the conversation. She'd heard talk like this before, barely a day ago, at the Savoy. Smart money. Big pickings. Major opportunities. The language that had built the life they'd shared, paid for the comforts she'd always taken for granted. She closed her eyes, picturing Hallam across the table, and she shuddered. Given similar circumstances, he'd probably choose the same destination, accept the same challenge, end up in the same rich ghetto, protected, cut off. She didn't want that. She didn't trust it. It was fake. It led absolutely nowhere.

Giles's fingers had found her wedding ring. He was bending over her in the darkness, still telling her about South Africa. He wanted reassurance, an answer, some clue to her feelings.

'Well?' he said. 'Mrs Pearson?'

Molly hesitated. Then she reached up and kissed him lightly on the lips.

'It's made for you,' she whispered. 'It's perfect.'

Molly woke at dawn. A cold grey light spilled into the room, washing over the bed. She looked at Giles a moment. His face was half-buried in the pillow and his eyes were closed and she could tell from his breathing that he was still asleep. She slipped out of bed, pausing beneath the window to collect her clothes. At the end of the hall there was a utility room. She was dressed in minutes, returning to the bedroom to pick up her suitcase. She kept a notepad in the zip compartment inside. Back in the corridor, she knelt briefly, steadying the pad on her knee. She'd spent most of the night trying to find the right words but in her heart she knew that nothing would soften the blow. These things were best done quickly. After Muengo, there was no going back.

'I'm glad you're still alive,' she wrote, 'and I'm sorry it had to end this way. I meant it when I said I loved you. It's just the rest I can't face.'

She folded the message and put it briefly to her lips. Then she slid it beneath the bedroom door and made her way downstairs. Outside, the promenade was empty. She walked across the road, pausing by the sea wall, pulling her coat around her. The tide had receded again, the wet expanse of sand gleaming in the steely light. She shivered, glancing back towards the hotel. All the bedrooms on the upper floor were shuttered except the window at the end. She looked at it a moment, watching the corner of the curtain stirring in the wind, then she turned and began to walk away.

Molly was back at the ferryport before she realised it was Christmas Eve. From the terminal building, she could see the white bulk of the cross-Channel ferry. The last sailing was about to leave. She bought a ticket, hauling her suitcase up the stairs towards the waiting stewardess. The last place she wanted to spend Christmas was France. France was as unreal, as irrelevant, as South Africa. No, it had to be England. That's where she belonged. That's where, one day, she might find a happier end to this story. Not by hiding herself away behind chintz curtains and a fat insurance settlement but by facing up to the challenge of her son's death. James had died because of people like Hallam. People like Larry Giddings. Running away to South Africa wouldn't change any of that.

The ferry left minutes later. Molly stood on the deck, watching the coast recede until the cold drove her back inside. Hungry, she treated herself to a three-course lunch with a half-litre of decent claret. Afterwards, she bought a bottle of Armagnac from the duty-free and retreated to the lounge with a copy of *Elle*. By the time she woke up, the ferry was rounding the shoulder of the Isle of Wight, inward bound to Portsmouth.

At the harbour station, the platforms were deserted. She

went to the booking office and enquired about through connections to Essex. The next train to London left in fifty minutes. By midnight, with luck, she could be home at the cottage, safely tucked up. She hesitated a moment at the booking-office window. The clerk behind the glass was already back in his crossword. His red crêpe hat had a tear over one ear and the tinsel had come adrift from the ticket machine. When the clerk looked up again, Molly smiled.

'Happy Christmas,' she mouthed, making for the door.

McFaul's address was in the phone book. She got in the taxi and gave it to the driver. It was raining now, the tyres hissing on the road, the streets empty. McFaul lived on the eastern edge of the city. They drove along the seafront, Molly gazing out, wondering how he'd take it. Maybe he had guests. Maybe he had family. Maybe this wasn't such a great idea.

McFaul's house lay at the end of a terrace. Molly paid the driver, watching the lights of the taxi disappear. Then she turned to the front door. She could hear music inside, a man's voice, deep. She listened for a moment longer, wondering where she'd last heard the song, then she knocked softly on the front door. She was about to knock again when the music stopped. She heard a door open, then a tuneless whistle and the sound of McFaul's footsteps echoing down the hall. The sound of his footsteps was unmistakable. She remembered it from the school-house in Muengo. Tap-tap-tap, went his footfall on the bare boards, tap-tap-tap.

The door opened and McFaul was standing there. He had a small cigar in one hand and a paintbrush in the other. Molly produced the bottle of Armagnac, holding it out.

'Present,' she said simply.

For a moment, McFaul said nothing. Then he smiled, stepping aside, inviting her in.

Anti-personnel mines are designed for use against enemy forces in conflicts but their greatest impact is on the lives of civilians long after wars have ended. Over 100 million anti-personnel mines litter the globe causing havoc especially in farming communities in the Third World. Each year they kill or maim up to 26,000 people, mostly civilians. The mines lie in the ground for decades and are effectively 'the world's worst serial killer'.

Oxfam has witnessed the damaging effect of these indiscriminate weapons in many of the countries where it works. If you would like to know more about anti-personnel mines and how you can help to stop the slaughter and help those in need, contact:

Oxfam's Landmine Appeal
Tel: 01865 312456

or write to:
The Landmines Appeal
Oxfam UK/I
274 Banbury Road
Oxford OX2 7DZ
UK

the OXFAM CAMPAIGN

together **FOR**

RIGHTS

together **AGAINST**

together **POVERTY**

The right to protection from violence